To Him who is both the Giver and the Gift

What people are saying about …

RELENTLESS PURSUIT

"What if a handful of people in *your* town died from a blatant case of food and water poisoning? Mystery lovers won't rest until they race to the final page of Kathy Herman's latest yarn, *Relentless Pursuit*, which I know her fans will devour."

Creston Mapes, author of *Nobody*

"In a collision of heart and soul, *Relentless Pursuit* is a poignant portrayal of God's passionate pursuit of us. With its gut-wrenching rendering of complicated family dynamics, heart-stopping suspense, and plain beautiful Louisiana charm, *Relentless Pursuit* is captivating. Kathy Herman has another winner on her hands."

Ronie Kendig, author of the
Discarded Heroes series

"Kathy Herman's *Relentless Pursuit* is truly relentless. A seemingly random act of violence and murder against innocent people launches a roller coaster of suspense. Characters we've come to care about are put to the test and plunged into danger. They are also pushed to the limit, which God's love often requires. Don't miss the finale of a great series!"

Lyn Cote, author of *La Belle Christiane*

"Relentless pursuit is indeed the theme of this powerful story of love and betrayal, guilt and remorse … and murder. Murder all the more terrifying to this small Cajun town because *anyone*—man, woman, or child—may be the victim of this ruthless killer's pursuit of revenge. But there's an even stronger pursuit here in God's effort to bring even the most resistant and fallen of His beloved children to Him for eternity."

Lorena McCourtney, author of the Ivy Malone Mysteries and the Andi McConnell Mysteries

"*Relentless Pursuit* is the dramatic and magnificent conclusion to the Secrets of the Roux River Bayou series. Kathy Herman weaves a tale of surprises and suspense that stands well on its own but draws subtly on the previous books in the series for those who have read them. Grace shines from the pages as the characters wrestle with the raw reality of living their faith. A triumphant story!"

Janelle Clare Schneider, author and spiritual director

What people are saying about …

DANGEROUS MERCY

"Kathy Herman's latest, *Dangerous Mercy,* brings up a question many Christians face—how to help without taking unnecessary risks. More importantly to readers, it's a riveting suspense ride, set in the Louisiana bayou country. A can't-miss!"

Lyn Cote, author of *Her Abundant Joy*

"This book gripped my attention from the very first paragraph and never let go. Kathy Herman's writing shines in *Dangerous Mercy.* This is a powerful and thought-provoking story about loving the unlovely and following God, no matter what the cost."

Carol Cox, author of *Dog Days, Who's That Girl?,* and *Tea and Sympathy*

"A well-drawn mystery with characters who leap off the page and into your heart. It's a story of redemption and hope, forgiveness and unconditional love—and the reminder that we are *all* redeemable through Christ. If you're looking for a good book to snuggle with in front of the fire, this is it."

Lynette Eason, best-selling, award-winning author of the Women of Justice series

Praise for …

FALSE PRETENSES

"With its perfectly paced suspense, Cajun flair, and riveting look at the high price of deceit, Kathy Herman's *False Pretenses* is a true page-turner. Highly recommended!"

Marlo Schalesky, author of the Christy Award–winning novel *Beyond the Night*

"Kathy Herman has raised her own bar for an action-packed novel with rich conflict and realistic romance. *False Pretenses* is deep and soul-searching with nonstop excitement. It will lead to nonstop reading."

Hannah Alexander, author of *A Killing Frost* and the Hideaway series

"Mysteries abound in Kathy Herman's latest foray into suspense. Though we know some of the characters well, new ones will intrigue readers. The story entwines the secrets of the past with the secrets of today. You'll enjoy this trip to Cajun country. A solid read!"

Lyn Cote, author of *Her Abundant Joy*

"In *False Pretenses,* Kathy Herman has begun a wonderfully intriguing new series set in Louisiana's bayou country—Secrets of Roux River Bayou. *False Pretenses* gets the series off to a fast-paced start filled with suspense, tension, and mystery that will grip readers from the first page."

Marta Perry, author of *Murder in Plain Sight*

"Kathy Herman has written a powerful story of tension, mystery, and danger. Anonymous messages point to a secret from the past that can destroy the future. But there's also a tender love story to challenge that secret."

Lorena McCourtney, author of the Ivy Malone Mysteries and the Andi McConnell Mysteries

RELENTLESS PURSUIT

SECRETS OF ROUX RIVER BAYOU

BOOK 3

KATHY HERMAN

David C Cook
transforming lives together

RELENTLESS PURSUIT
Published by David C Cook
4050 Lee Vance View
Colorado Springs, CO 80918 U.S.A.

David C Cook Distribution Canada
55 Woodslee Avenue, Paris, Ontario, Canada N3L 3E5

David C Cook U.K., Kingsway Communications
Eastbourne, East Sussex BN23 6NT, England

The graphic circle C logo is a registered trademark of David C Cook.

LCCN 2012933224
ISBN 978-0-7814-0342-9
eISBN 978-1-4347-0528-0

Published in association with the literary agency of Alive Communications, Inc, 7680 Goddard St., Suite 200, Colorado Springs, CO 80920

The Team: Don Pape, Diane Noble, Amy Konyndyk, Caitlyn York, Karen Athen
Cover Design: DogEared Design, Kirk DouPonce

Printed in the United States of America
First Edition 2012

1 2 3 4 5 6 7 8 9 10

022712

ACKNOWLEDGMENTS

The amazing bayou country of south Louisiana provides the backdrop for this trilogy and many of the images I describe in the stories. But Saint Catherine Parish, the town of Les Barbes, and the Roux River Bayou exist only in my imagination.

During the writing of this third book, I drew from several resource people, each of whom shared generously from his or her storehouse of knowledge and experience. I did my best to integrate the facts as I understood them. If accuracy was compromised in any way, it was unintentional and strictly of my own doing. I also made good use of numerous Internet sites relating to idiosyncrasies and customs of the Cajun culture and language.

I owe a special word of thanks to the Heritage Foundation's James Jay Carafano, PhD, deputy director of the Kathryn and Shelby Cullom Davis Institute for International Studies and director of the Douglas and Sarah Allison Center for Foreign Policy Studies. His many areas of expertise, including defense and homeland security, provided invaluable information for this work. I am grateful for the time he took out of his busy schedule to explain domestic terrorist scenarios in which Homeland Security would get involved and those that would involve only the FBI and/or state agencies. I knew a lot less than I thought I did, Jim. Thanks for your help!

I'm grateful to Retired Commander Carl H. Deeley of the Los Angeles County Sheriff's Department for the wealth of information and personal experience he's shared over the past several books, enabling me to keep the fictional Saint Catherine Parish Sheriff's Department running efficiently; and to Retired Lieutenant Gil Carrillo, Los Angeles County Sheriff's Department Homicide Bureau, for filling me in on the complicated but important relationship between law enforcement and the media. Thanks, Carl and Gil, for your willingness to share what you know. You made my job so much easier.

I want to thank my friend Paul David Houston, a former assistant district attorney, for researching and advising me regarding the execution of wills in the state of Louisiana; for explaining the intricacies of search warrants; and for advising me as to how certain crimes would be charged. Paul, as always, I appreciate your swift and concise answers. You're a joy to work with!

Also, a special thank-you to my sister Caroline Berry for sharing her personal experience of releasing the cremated remains of a loved one. It's a sensitive subject that probably makes some people uncomfortable, and I so appreciated your candor.

I'm immensely grateful to my faithful prayer warriors: my sister Pat Phillips; my dear friends Mark and Donna Skorheim and Susan Mouser; my online prayer team—Chuck Allenbrand, Pearl and Don Anderson, Judith Depontes, Jackie Jeffries, Susie Killough, Joanne Lambert, Adrienne McCabe, Deidre Pool, Kim Prothro, Kelly Smith, Leslie Strader, Carolyn Walker, Sondra Watson, and Judi Wieghat;

my friends at LifeWay Christian Store in Tyler, Texas, and LifeWay Christian Resources in Nashville, Tennessee; and my church family at Bethel Bible Church. I cannot possibly express to you how much I value your prayers.

To the retailers and suppliers who sell my books, the church and public libraries that make them available, and the many readers who have encouraged me with personal testimonies about how God has used my words to challenge and inspire you: He uses you to fuel the passion that keeps me creative.

To my agent, Joel Kneedler at Alive Communications. You're such an encourager. Thanks for helping me move forward with the next two trilogies. I never have to wonder if you're watching out for my best interests. Thanks for all you do.

To Cris Doornbos, Dan Rich, Don Pape, and the amazing staff at David C Cook for allowing me to partner with you in "transforming lives together." I'm proud to be part of the Cook family and look forward to working with you in the years ahead.

To my editor, Diane Noble, for untold patience while waiting for this book to finally come together. We did it! Thanks for your amazing encouragement and for having the wisdom not to push me, but rather to hold me up. You're the best!

And to my husband, Paul, my partner and soul mate, for your patient adaptation to my extended writing schedule on this book. Thank you for all the times you tiptoed past my door and gave me space to create the story you never doubted would end just as He intended.

And to the Prince of Peace, who offers us wings in the midst of woes: it is a joy to write stories that glorify Your Name.

CAJUN FRENCH GLOSSARY

Andouille—	A coarse-grained smoked meat made using pork, pepper, onions, wine, and seasonings; spicy Cajun sausage.
Beignet—	A pastry made from deep-fried dough and sprinkled with powdered sugar—a kind of French doughnut.
Bon appetite!—	Enjoy!
Boudin—	Sausage made from a pork rice dressing (much like dirty rice), which is stuffed into pork casings.
Breaux's—	A Cajun restaurant on *rue Madeline* that features live music.
Ça viens?—	How's it coming?
Cher—	Dear.
Co faire—	Why?
Comment ça va	How are you? How are you doing?
Donc beaucoup!—	So very much!
Down the bayou—	Cajun way of saying south.
Étouffée—	A Cajun dish, similar to gumbo, that is typically served with shellfish or chicken over rice. It is most popular in New Orleans and in the bayou country of the southernmost half of Louisiana.
Fais do do—	Go to sleep. Also a Cajun dance party.
Fuh shore—	For sure.
Going to make a hundred—	Cajun way of saying "going to be a hundred."
Hot hot—	Very hot. This kind of double adjective is used for emphasis (e.g., "It was cold cold outside last night"). Some African cultures speak this way. It may have come from the slaves in the region.
J'ai gros coeur.—	Makes me want to cry.

Je t'aime, Zoe.—	I love you, Zoe.
Joyeux anniversaire, mon ami.—	Happy birthday, my friend.
Mais, jamais d'la vie!—	Well, never in my life!
Lâche pas la patate—	Don't let go of the potato, or don't give up.
Mal pris—	Stuck in a bad situation.
Mes amis—	My friends.
Moitié fou—	Half crazy.
My eye—	Cajun expression meaning "No way!"
Pain perdu—	French toast fried in butter and served with powdered sugar sprinkled on top.
Papère—	Grandfather.
Petite fille—	Little girl.
P'tit boug—	Little boy
***Rue Madeline*—**	Madeline Street.
Un jour à la fois—	One day at a time.
Up the bayou—	Cajun way of saying north.
Voilà—	"Here it is"; used when you want to show something to someone, especially as a surprise.

PROLOGUE

"Turn from evil and do good; seek peace and pursue it." Psalm 34:14

Sax Henry carefully removed the dog-eared photo from his wallet and took another drink of tonic water. Why did he hang on to this old snapshot? Twenty-eight years would probably have changed her beyond his recognition. All he could remember of her voice were her haunting cries for help. If only he'd stepped up and done something instead of turning up the music and pretending to be somewhere else. *Coward!*

His ex-wives had all told him that he should see a shrink—that his misplaced guilt made him a slave to the past and unable to enjoy the present. But they weren't the ones saddled with the nightmares. And the regret. And the emptiness.

Sax tipped his glass and drank the last of the tonic water. He crunched an ice cube, aware of the blue and gold lights flashing on his wall, reflected from the Burgess Hotel across the street. He glanced out the window at the blazing western sky, which almost seemed to bubble like hot lava as the sun dipped below the horizon in the Big Easy. His band was on at ten. He would have to leave for the club soon.

He set the photo on the coffee table, then got up and turned down the air conditioner another five degrees. He reached into the closet, took out the navy blazer he wore onstage, and spotted two bronze urns on the top shelf. Even now, his parents were a powerful presence. He couldn't decide whether to scatter their ashes in the Gulf—or dump them in the landfill. So there they sat in the dark. Seemed fitting.

He pushed the door shut with his foot and poured another tonic water. So what if the guys in the band razzed him about being a teetotaler? He'd seen firsthand what booze could turn a man into. He was a failure on many counts, but drinking wasn't one of them. Every time he had entertained the idea of taking a drink, his hand would shake and he could smell whiskey and vomit—and almost feel a fist slam against his cheek.

He set his glass on the coffee table and flopped onto the couch, then picked up the photo and held it gingerly with his thumb and forefinger. What had his sister done with her life? Had she ever married? Had kids? Or was she turned off by men? What did she see when she closed her eyes? Surely her nightmares were worse than his.

He lifted his gaze to the shiny sliver of moon held in the night sky by the arms of gravity. What kind of all-knowing, ever-compassionate Being could allow innocent children to be victims?

But that was a long time ago. He wasn't a victim anymore. And he didn't need God. If judgment day was real, he would surely go to hell. Fine with him, as long as he got the chance to tell almighty God what he thought of Him first. And ask why he'd been born. He really wanted to know.

He couldn't keep a wife. Couldn't father a child. Couldn't hold a real job. Didn't have any close friends. Most of his life, he'd survived in an aching vacuum with no reason to get out of bed in the morning except for his music. The saxophone had been his drug of choice for years. But even that wasn't enough anymore. He wanted peace—whatever it took to get it. However long it took to find it.

He had to find his sister and make things right. If she refused to see him, he would just keep coming back. Even if she hurled insults and pummeled him with raw anger. Or simply slammed the door in his face. He would deal with it. But unless he found her and accepted responsibility for leaving her to fend for herself, how could he hope to silence the guilt?

Sax carefully put the photograph back in his wallet and picked up the Post-it note with the name and address of a woman his sister had worked for. The gig at the club would be over in three more nights. Then he'd have two weeks off before they started a road tour. He would drive up to Les Barbes and find this woman. It might prove to be another dead end. But what if it didn't? It had taken him three years to get this far. What did he have to lose?

Sax rose and stood at the window. Even if his sister didn't want a relationship with him, she should be told that their parents had died and have a say in how the ashes were dispersed. He owed her that much. The cruel irony was almost laughable: their father had gotten drunk, staggered out in front of a delivery truck, and died without ever knowing what had hit him. Yet their mother, after enduring years of marital abuse, had suffered from lung cancer for six months and died a horrible death. God was just full of surprises.

All Sax had now was three ex-wives, the scars of childhood, a mountain of guilt, and two bronze urns in the closet. He had to find his sister.

CHAPTER 1

Zoe Broussard burst into the kitchen at Zoe B's Cajun Eatery and turned on the TV, motioning for her husband to come over.

"Pierce, you need to listen to this," she said. "Hurry!"

Pierce Broussard, clad in his chef's hat and apron and dusted with flour up to his elbows, grabbed a hand towel and walked over to stand beside her. "What's going on, babe?"

"Jude's on the courthouse steps with Police Chief Norman. He's going to talk to the media any second. Something big is happening." She turned up the volume.

"We're live on the steps of the Saint Catherine Parish Courthouse," said a male reporter's brisk voice. "Sheriff Jude Prejean and Police Chief Casey Norman have just come outside and are standing in front of the microphones. We're told Sheriff Prejean will be the official spokesperson. The sheriff's taking the mike now. Let's listen...."

"I'm going to comment on a developing situation," Jude said, "but neither I nor Chief Norman will be taking questions at this time. During the past ninety minutes, eight residents of Saint Catherine Parish have been admitted to the emergency room at Hargrave Medical Center with symptoms consistent with cyanide poisoning.

Seven of the victims were treated with a cyanide antidote kit and are expected to recover. I'm sorry to report that four-year-old Dominic Corbin, the son of Joshua and Margot Corbin of Les Barbes, failed to respond to the antidote treatment and died."

Zoe sucked in a breath and couldn't seem to exhale, her mind's eye clearly seeing the adorable dark-haired, blue-eyed playmate of her daughter, Grace.

Pierce put his arm around her and pulled her close.

"Local health officials are working to pinpoint the source of contamination." Jude shot a glance at a uniformed officer who said something to Chief Norman. "The one thing we know for certain is that all the victims had eaten at the food bar at Marcotte's Market—"

Police Chief Norman cupped his hands and whispered something in Jude's ear.

Jude paused, visibly shaken, and then continued. "We've just been informed that two more people have now been admitted to the emergency room at Hargrave after eating at the food bar at Marcotte's. Chief Norman and I want to emphasize that there is no reason to assume this was a criminal act. The food bar at Marcotte's Market has been closed, and health officials are working with us to determine which food item or items were contaminated. The most important thing each of you can do is to remain calm and wait for updates on the situation. That's all I have to say for now. Chief Norman and I will come back with new information as we have it."

Tears spilled down Zoe's cheeks, and she struggled to find her voice. "I … I can't believe Dominic is *dead*. Margot and Josh must be devastated. How are we going to explain to Grace that her playmate isn't coming back?"

Pierce exhaled. His silence spoke more loudly than any words he might have uttered.

"I sure hope *our* food hasn't been contaminated," Zoe said. "What if it has? We could be serving our customers poison."

Pierce held her face in his hands and wiped her tears with his thumb. "Don't assume this goes beyond the food bar at Marcotte's. Jude didn't give any indication that's the case."

"He may not know yet!"

"Zoe, calm down. The authorities will keep us informed."

"Sure, *after* the fact."

Pierce kissed her cheek. "I can't worry about what *might* happen. I've got a whole stack of orders to fill. We need to stay calm, stay informed, and keep this place running. We can't afford to take a financial hit in the middle of tourist season."

Zoe's heart sank. "Oh, no! I just remembered I've got a carton of fresh fruit I bought at Marcotte's. I don't want the kids eating it. Or any of the produce either. I'm going to run upstairs and tell Maddie."

"Babe, there's no need to panic. Calm down."

"How am I supposed to calm down after what happened to Dominic? I'd rather be safe than sorry."

Zoe pushed open the front door of her apartment and went into the kitchen. Her daughter, Grace, was seated at the table, and her son, Tucker, was in his high chair—both eating pieces of fresh fruit.

Zoe snatched the fruit from each child and tossed it into the garbage disposal, aware of the startled expression on the babysitter's face.

"Mrs. Broussard, what are you doing?" Maddie Lyons took a step back.

Zoe grabbed some wet wipes and handed them to Maddie. "Here, wipe Tucker's face and hands. Hurry!" She plucked several more and wiped Grace's face and hands herself.

Tucker started to cry.

Zoe went over to his high chair, picked him up, and rocked him from side to side. "Shhh. It's okay, sweet boy. Mommy didn't mean to raise her voice."

"What's going on?" Maddie said. "Why did you throw out the fruit? Did I do something wrong?"

"No, honey. Something awful's happened." Zoe paused and caught her breath, relieved to see that her children were all right. She lowered her voice and told Maddie everything she'd heard on the news.

"Dominic is dead?" Maddie whispered. "Just like that?" She dropped into a chair, the expression drained from her face. "How could this happen?"

"That's what the authorities are trying to figure out."

Grace Broussard looked from Maddie to Zoe, her innocent topaz eyes questioning, her eyebrows furrowed. "Why are you sad?"

Zoe wondered if she should wait to tell Grace about Dominic. Would there ever be a right time? What if she heard it from someone else? Or on the news?

"Sweetie, Mommy needs to tell you something, and you have to be very brave, okay?" How could Zoe expect a four-year-old to grasp what she was about to say? She handed her son to Maddie and went over to Grace, bending down next to her chair.

"Domi ate something that made him very sick. He died." Zoe heard herself say the words but felt as if someone else were talking. "He's in heaven with Jesus."

"When is he coming back?" Grace cocked her head.

Zoe swallowed the emotion that she refused to unleash in front of her children and stroked her daughter's long blonde curls. "He's *not* coming back, sweetie. Remember, we talked about this. People don't come back when they die. But someday we will go to heaven and see Jesus. And then we'll see Domi again."

Grace's face fell, her little mouth drooping. She slid out of her chair and went into the living room and came back with a drawing. "Domi made this for me."

"May I see it?" Zoe asked.

Grace handed the drawing to Zoe. "The boy and girl is Domi and me, and the big heart is because he loves me lots and lots."

Zoe blinked the stinging from her eyes. "What a beautiful reminder of him. I think we should put this in a frame and hang it in your room. Would you like that?"

Grace gave a firm nod.

"I can't believe any of this," Maddie said. "What are you going to do about the eatery?"

"Stay open." Zoe forced herself to sound positive. "The authorities haven't indicated the threat goes beyond Marcotte's food bar."

"Then why did you rush in here and throw out the fruit?" Maddie said.

"Because I bought it at Marcotte's, and I'm not taking any chances with my children. Until we know more, I want you to feed them packaged snacks and only canned fruit. I'm sure the milk and cheese are fine. They've already had some."

"I was just about to fix their lunch," Maddie said. "How about grilled cheese sandwiches, frozen lima beans, and the canned pears I saw in the pantry?"

"Perfect." Zoe patted Grace's knee, then got up and took Tucker from Maddie and put him back in his high chair, her heart lightened by the big grin on his face. She glanced over at Grace. "You and Tucker eat only what Maddie gives you—so you won't get sick like Domi."

"Why did the food make him sick?" Grace's eyes were wide and round—the picture of innocence.

"We don't know yet," Zoe said. "Something bad got in the food bar at Marcotte's Market. The sheriff and important people who understand poisons will tell us what happened. Until then, I don't want you to eat anything unless Maddie says it's okay."

Grace heaved a sigh. "I wish Domi didn't die."

"Me, too, sweetie. We need to pray for his mommy and daddy. They're very sad." Zoe walked over to the fridge and took out all the produce she had bought at Marcotte's and put it in a trash bag. "I'll drop this in the Dumpster out back. I guess I'd better get back to the dining room and keep things operating as normally as possible."

"I'll keep the kids safe," Maddie said. "I still can't believe what happened to Domi."

Zoe paused for a moment to let the severity of the situation sink in. She dreaded facing Margot and Josh. How would she have ever dealt with it, had Grace or Tucker been the victim?

CHAPTER 2

Emily Jessup sat at a corner table at Zoe B's Cajun Eatery, enjoying a refreshing orchard smoothie and admiring the array of oil paintings for sale by local artists. At a nearby table, a young couple and their four kids, each dressed in a green souvenir T-shirt from GatorWorld, sat drinking limeades. What a contrast they were against the open grand step-back cupboard where Zoe's prize collection of D'Arceau Limoges collector plates was displayed.

Emily turned her gaze to her handsome friend Chance Durand as he took another sip of chicory.

"I've never developed a taste for that," Emily said. "My college friends all like it. But no matter how I psyche myself up, it still tastes like warm mud to me."

"I can't ever remember not liking it. Even as a kid I chose chicory over sweet tea or soft drinks. My dad said it was a fitting drink for someone who's dumber than dirt." Chance smiled wryly, his dark eyes peering over the top of his square glasses.

"You're kidding, right? You're the only one *I* know going to Harvard Med on a full scholarship."

"Yes, but when I was in grade school, Dad thought I was

stupid—before I had my eyes examined and the ophthalmologist told him how poor my vision was." Chance raised an eyebrow, which disappeared under the sleek brown hair combed across his forehead. "After my folks got me glasses, my grades went from Ds and Fs to straight As. And my teacher told them I had the highest IQ in the class."

"I hope your dad apologized for saying something so awful."

"That's not his style. He can be a real jerk. But you should've seen the look on his face the first time I brought home all As. I honestly think he was mad at me for *not* being stupid." Chance smiled sheepishly. "Sorry, I didn't mean to go off on that. What I started to say is that Dad couldn't stand chicory either, but Mom loved it and let me have it as a kid. Can't hurt you. There's no caffeine."

"I love caffeine," Emily said. "I would never have made it through my first year at LSU without it."

Chance pushed his glasses up higher on his nose. "I've found a more effective way to stay alert and study longer—"

"Not me. I've been offered every kind of upper imaginable. But I made up my mind from the day I started college that I wasn't going to depend on anything other than hard work and determination—and maybe a lot of caffeine. Not because my mom's a cop, either. I just don't want to start down that path. I've got a long way to go before I get into medical school, and I sure don't want to break the law to get there. I don't want any skeletons in my closet."

Chance held up his palm, a broad smile exposing a row of perfect teeth. "Whoa, girl. Neither do I. The way I'm able to stay alert and study longer is by *running* five miles a day. I focus better. I sleep better. And I have more energy."

"Oh." Emily stirred the luscious blend of fresh fruit, cherry juice, and vanilla yogurt, hoping her face wasn't as pink as her smoothie. "No wonder you're so fit. I used to jog with my mom almost every morning, but I got out of the habit when I started college."

"It's never too late to start up again. Maybe we can run together sometime."

"I'd like that." Emily mused, "Do you realize it was three weeks ago today that we met? My first outing after I arrived in Les Barbes was to check out the library. I certainly never expected to make a friend."

Chance took his index finger and traced the rim of his cup. "I'm glad our paths crossed. It's great hanging out with a woman who understands what it takes to pursue a career in medicine. I look forward to spending more time together."

"Me, too."

"So are you enjoying your stay at Langley Manor?"

"Absolutely," Emily said. "I always do. My sister and brother-in-law have turned it into the most popular bed-and-breakfast in the area."

"Are you staying in one of the guest rooms?"

"Actually, I'm not. Those rooms are booked all the time. I'm staying downstairs in the living quarters with Vanessa and Ethan. They have an extra bedroom. There's plenty of room to hang out with them—and with my nephew, Carter. He's turning nine next month. You'll have to come out and let me show you around. The grounds are amazing. The caretaker is a descendant of a slave who helped the founding Langleys move runaway slaves up north on the Underground Railroad. *Southern Living* did a whole spread on it last summer."

Chance nodded. "I heard that."

"I enjoy staying out there, but I love coming into town. I'm a city girl. I like people watching, especially in places like Les Barbes that draw tourists from all cultures."

Emily glanced out the window at the row of quaint, old-world buildings along *rue Madeline*, each with a gallery or balcony decorated with flowerpots and greenery and extending out over the sidewalk.

"The first time I visited Les Barbes," she said, "Vanessa and Ethan were up to their ears in the renovation of Langley Manor and living in the apartment upstairs." She nodded toward the ceiling. "I used to stand out on the gallery in the evenings and wave to the tourists. This place rocks after dark. It's like a carnival."

Chance smiled. "I guess it does. I don't give it much thought, since I grew up here. But I always thought the Broussards lived upstairs."

"They do, but there used to be two apartments. After Vanessa and Ethan moved out, the Broussards knocked out the walls and made it into one large apartment. Vanessa is still best friends with Zoe. That's how I got a part-time job waiting tables here."

"So are you staying all summer?"

Emily dipped her spoon into the orchard smoothie and took out a chunk of fresh peach. "Until the eighteenth of August, and then I'll drive down to New Orleans. I signed a lease for an off-campus apartment near LSU. My roommate, Clarissa, will arrive the same day. It's furnished, so getting settled before classes start on the twenty-third should be easy. What about you?"

Chance wiped his mouth with a napkin. "My classes start on the twenty-fifth, and my flight leaves for Boston on the seventeenth. My scholarship includes a private room at Vanderbilt Hall. It's furnished. All I really have to do is unpack. I have several friends from last year who will be staying there too. So do you know Clarissa, or is she just someone you hooked up with to pay half the rent?"

"We were in the same biology class last year. She's hoping to get into medical school. She wants to be an ob-gyn too."

Chance flashed a wry smile. "Think I'll stick with being a neurosurgeon. At least my patients will show up by appointment—and not at all hours of the night."

"I've wanted to deliver babies since I was a kid. Vanessa let me come into the delivery room when Carter was born. I was only ten, but it was awesome. I think the nurses thought it would be too much for me, but I went to the classes with Vanessa and was well prepared. Actually, I cried. I could hardly believe that living, breathing little baby came out of my sister—and I was holding him just minutes after he was born. Why are you looking at me like that?"

"You're intriguing. Intelligent. And you're really pretty. But I guess you hear that a lot."

Emily did hear that a lot. But it was usually a line. Why was she so inexplicably drawn to this guy? "Thank my parents. I had absolutely nothing to do with it."

He laughed. "I suppose not. But you got the pretty genes."

Emily heard a commotion and saw a man in a chef's hat, his back to her, talking to some customers in close proximity. She realized it was Pierce Broussard. His voice was lowered, and she strained to listen.

"The food here is perfectly safe," Pierce said. "The incident at Marcotte's was isolated. There's no reason for concern. I make everything from scratch, and we get our ingredients from a New Orleans wholesaler. And our produce from the farmer's market."

"I wonder what's going on," Chance said. "Judging from the intense looks on the customers' faces, it can't be good."

Zoe Broussard seemed to come out of nowhere and stood next to Emily. "Have you two heard about what happened at Marcotte's Market?"

Emily shook her head. "No, but I overheard Pierce talking to those customers. What's going on? Why is he talking about food safety?"

Zoe's face was flushed and splotchy, her blue-gray eyes wide and red-rimmed. "People are pouring into the ER at Hargrave after eating at the food bar at Marcotte's. One little boy died. The doctors said the symptoms are consistent with cyanide poisoning."

"*Cyanide*?"

Zoe put her hand on Emily's shoulder. "The little boy that died was Dominic Corbin. He was Grace's best friend at preschool. I still can't believe it. Authorities are trying not to alarm us, but they still don't know the extent of the contamination."

Emily sat stunned, staring at Chance.

"Did they give the names of the people who were admitted to the hospital?" Chance asked.

Zoe dabbed her eyes. "Not yet."

"How could a food bar get contaminated with cyanide?" Chance said. "I promise you I wouldn't want to be in the shoes of whoever's responsible."

Pierce came over to the table, deep lines scrunching his forehead. He whispered something to Zoe and then left without greeting them.

All the color drained from her face. "Three more people have died. I hope it's no one we know. I just had to tell our four-year-old daughter that her best friend isn't coming back."

Emily blew the hair off her forehead and tried to take it all in. She wondered if Vanessa had heard the news.

Chance's cell phone rang, and he glanced at the screen. "The sheriff's department? How weird. I need to take this."

Emily listened as he put the phone to his ear.

"Hello … yes, this is Chance Durand … I just heard about it … *What*? Are you sure …? How serious is it …?" Chance glanced over at Emily. "Can't you just tell me if they're going to be all right …? Don't tell me to calm down. We're talking about my parents …! No, I'm with a friend … I … I can be there in fifteen minutes." Chance put his cell phone in his shirt pocket and grabbed his keys. "I've got to go."

"What happened?" Emily said.

Chance didn't answer her and seemed disoriented.

Emily grabbed his wrist. "Talk to me. What happened?"

"Uh"—Chance blinked and then lifted his gaze—"A 911 call came in from my parents' address. The person who placed the call was gasping, so the 911 operator dispatched an ambulance. The EMTs found my parents unconscious on the kitchen floor."

"I'm so sorry." Emily hated that the words sounded rote. "Do they know what happened?"

"They think it's cyanide poisoning. But the deputy wouldn't tell me their condition." Emotion welled up in Chance's eyes. "I need to get over to the emergency room at Hargrave. I have a really bad feeling about this."

Emily jumped to her feet. "*I'm* driving."

"That's not necessary. I'm fine."

"You're not fine. You're in shock." Emily went around the table and took his arm. "Come on. You don't need to be thinking about the road at a time like this."

"Emily's right," Zoe said. "There's no way you're thinking clearly. Let her help. I don't know what to say, except I'm so very sorry."

Emily saw the terrified look in Zoe's eyes and wondered if it mirrored her own. When she got up that morning, could she ever have imagined that people would be collapsing right and left from cyanide poisoning? Or, worse yet, that one of them would be Grace's playmate and two of them Chance's parents?

Emily shut the door of the private room just off the ER at Hargrave Medical Center, listening to the cadence of Father Gauvin's heels clicking on the tile floor as he walked away. Could this really be happening?

She whispered a quick prayer, then went over and sat next to Chance on the sofa, unable to form any words and wondering if it mattered. Were there any words appropriate for this moment?

"I … I can't believe they're both gone." Chance's voice was little more than an exhale.

"I can only imagine what you must be feeling," Emily managed to say. "Is there someone you want me to call?"

"Not yet. I need to pull myself together."

"Are your grandparents still alive?"

"No, but both my parents had siblings. I'll have to go home and look for the phone numbers." Chance sighed. "How could they have died of cyanide poisoning? They were nowhere near Marcotte's Market today."

Emily shuddered. "It's frightening that the authorities aren't sure where the cyanide is coming from. But maybe it was in the bottled water, since the EMTs found two open bottles of it on the table. The deputy said they took it into evidence and are having it tested. There was probably bottled water at the food bar, too."

Chance buried his face in his hands. "Mom and Dad were supposed to go on their first cruise in two weeks. To Alaska. Mom had been trying for years to get Dad interested. Finally he said yes. And now ..." Chance let out a sob, then seemed to swallow it.

Emily blinked the stinging from her eyes and gently rubbed Chance's back. She didn't say anything—not that she was even able.

Father Gauvin had prayed with them, then left the room to perform the last rites on Chance's parents. Emily didn't know much about the traditions of the Catholic Church. But she liked Father Gauvin and found his demeanor comforting. Too bad he wasn't the priest who would be saying the funeral Mass—assuming there was going to be a funeral Mass. Chance hadn't really said.

She pictured two caskets side by side and for a split second saw the faces of her own parents and wondered how she could ever survive such grief. "You just want to sit here for a while?"

Chance took her hand in his. "I dread going home. When I left there this morning, I never expected to return as an orphan."

CHAPTER 3

Sheriff Jude Prejean wiped his forehead with a handkerchief and looked out his office window at the media set up in front of the Saint Catherine Parish Courthouse across the street. Four dead and ten hospitalized. How bad was it going to get?

A knock at the door caused him to turn just as Deputy Chief Aimee Rivette came into his office, her tan uniform as crisp as her short, bleached hair.

Aimee held his gaze. "Sheriff, the ME's preliminary exam confirmed that the three DOAs died of potassium cyanide found in Gaudry bottled water. But this was no accidental contamination." Aimee handed him a photograph. "Notice the shiny spot on the bottom."

"What is it?"

"A strong, clear adhesive of some kind. And when you look at the bottom of the bottle from the inside"—she handed him another photo—"you can see where a tiny hole was *patched* with it."

"So someone could have made a hole in the bottom and injected cyanide into the water," Jude said. "Then resealed the bottom and put it back on the shelf."

"Exactly. Who thinks to inspect the bottom of a bottle—especially when the expiration date is stamped at the top? The ME noticed the victims emitted a faint smell of bitter almonds, which is a dead giveaway for cyanide. Toxicology will need to confirm it. The DOAs' faces were bluish in color, suggesting they were oxygen deprived, which is totally consistent with potassium cyanide poisoning. We have to assume that the bottled water was intentionally poisoned. Which throws up a red flag about the food bar, too."

"So this is even worse than we originally thought." Jude swore under his breath and felt his hands turn to fists. "We're sure the Gaudry water was purchased from Marcotte's Market?"

"Leo Marcotte confirmed that the stamp on the bottles was theirs. And that Gaudry water was on the list of groceries delivered yesterday to the DOAs."

"Are we questioning the delivery person?"

"Castille and Doucet are in the process of locating him. He's sixteen—and the owner's great-nephew."

Jude blew out a breath. "We're not waiting for health officials. We need to close down Marcotte's until we get to the bottom of this."

"Leo Marcotte already closed voluntarily. He assures us we have his full cooperation, including a list of every employee, past and present, from the last five years."

"Good. Call Chief Norman immediately, and have him meet me on the courthouse steps. The public needs to know that cyanide was also found in Gaudry bottled water—and that the bottles had been tampered with."

Aimee made the call and put her phone on her belt clip. "Done."

"All right, walk with me." Jude led the way across the detective bureau and down the hallway. "Let's work with local health officials and make sure all Gaudry bottled water is pulled off the shelves in Les Barbes. We need to make sure Gaudry's home office in New Orleans is informed of the problem. They'll probably want to contact state officials and issue a recall."

"All right."

"Let's concentrate our efforts on interviewing each employee of Marcotte's, and the people involved in warehousing or transporting the food items used on the food bar—and Gaudry bottled water. We might need to get the state police involved in that. And get security tapes of the food bar at Marcotte's, starting with last night's cleanup crew."

"I'm on it," Aimee said.

"Did Chief Norman request manpower from other police departments?"

Aimee nodded. "Absolutely. We've got whatever manpower we need at our disposal. We should be able to contain the panic, but I doubt we can prevent it once the public is informed that Gaudry bottled water was poisoned. They won't know what's safe to eat or drink."

"People are going to have to be proactive! *We* can't do everything!" Jude paused and softened his tone. "The minute we announce the problem is coming from Marcotte's, whoever's doing this could strike somewhere else. We can't assume we've contained the problem."

"What are you going to tell the media?"

"The truth. We're going to need every man, woman, and child to be vigilant if we're going to prevent more casualties. People need to inspect all bottles, cartons, and packaging carefully for any sign of tampering."

"I have to believe there will be panic."

"That's why we have to remain calm and reassuring."

Jude stopped at the elevator and pushed the down button. A second later the door opened, and Gil Marcel stepped out, his face grim.

"What is it?" Jude said.

"Another couple was found dead in their home after drinking Gaudry bottled water. That's six dead—five adults from bottled water and the little boy from the food bar."

Jude sighed, shaking his head. "This thing is escalating."

Jude followed Aimee into the elevator and pushed the G button. Was the person or persons behind this despicable act going to drill into plastic milk cartons? Or those little juice boxes kids love? Were more children going to die? He blinked away the terrible thought. He couldn't let that happen.

CHAPTER 4

The bells of Saint Catherine Catholic Church rang three times as Zoe looked across the dining room at Zoe B's, noting that the empty tables far outnumbered those occupied. Normally on Saturdays, this place bustled all day long, the waiting area filled with people eager to be seated. She wondered whether Margot and Josh had mustered the courage to tell their other children that Domi wasn't coming home. And whether Emily was able to comfort Chance after the tragic deaths of both his parents.

Zoe walked over to a bare wooden table and unfolded a navy and gold fleur-de-lis–print tablecloth that coordinated perfectly with the striped curtains on the window at the front of the eatery. She spread the tablecloth evenly across the table, smoothing out the wrinkles. Little had changed in the fifteen years since she had opened Zoe B's, other than the size of the dining room, the addition of laminated wood-plank flooring, and the always-for-sale oil paintings by local artists. The same French country furnishings gave it the cozy ambiance customers loved and she never grew tired of.

She heard familiar voices and glanced over at the table by the window where Hebert Lanoux, Father Sam Fournier, and Tex Campbell were engrossed in a game of checkers.

Zoe smiled despite her melancholy mood. Those three old guys were good for each other, perhaps because they were nothing alike and brought very different life experiences to the mix. Hebert had been a grocer. Father Sam, a priest. Tex, an oilman. Hebert generally saw things one way and didn't budge in his opinion. Father Sam tried to keep an open mind and looked for the best in people, trying not to judge their motives. And Tex was the objective voice, always able to see multiple sides of an issue and not afraid to call it as he saw it.

The aroma of Pierce's seafood gumbo made its way to her senses. She wondered whether he should have bothered making it.

"Boss, what are you doing?" Head waitress Savannah Surette pulled up next to Zoe, pushing a cart filled with salt and pepper shakers, silverware wrapped in cloth napkins, and clear bud vases, each holding a fresh yellow daisy. "Let me do that."

"It feels good to be busy. It's dead around here."

"Because everyone's scared to death," Savannah said. "Ever since the press conference, there's been a run on frozen, canned, and packaged foods—macaroni and cheese, spaghetti and pastas, and whatnot. I heard stores are rationing."

"They are," Zoe said sheepishly. "I went down to Rouses and bought all the boxed macaroni and cheese and snack crackers I was allowed for my kids. They were almost completely sold out of frozen foods. There was a vegan behind me in line who was pretty upset. She said the organic grocery store had sold out of everything she could eat."

Savannah set a vase in the middle of the table. "So what does a person do if she doesn't eat meat, eggs, or dairy, and fresh produce safety is questionable?"

"I told her Pierce could make up some vegetarian 'takeout' for her, that we aren't using a single item from Marcotte's Market, that we buy our food in bulk from wholesale suppliers." Zoe made a sweeping motion across the empty tables. "But people aren't exactly flocking in here."

Savannah tightened her ponytail, her blue eyes wide. "To be perfectly honest, *I* wouldn't eat out in Les Barbes right now."

"I'd eat *here*," Zoe said. "Lots of tourists have come a long way to enjoy their vacation. If we can reassure them that it's safe to eat at Zoe B's, it might keep them from leaving town."

"Who's going to come to Sunday brunch tomorrow, after someone put poison in Marcotte's food bar?" Savannah said. "The authorities are telling people to stay away from food bars and smorgasbords until they know more."

"So we'll skip brunch this week. But Pierce can prepare our usual breakfast entrees. I think I'll go make a sign and hang it on the front door so people know we're using ingredients from wholesale suppliers, not grocery stores."

"I hope it works." Savannah arched her eyebrows. "I heard that the CDC might be called in. And the FBI and Homeland Security. And that they might close down all the restaurants in Les Barbes."

"*What*?" Zoe lowered her voice. "Could they really do that? Closing us down in the peak season would ruin us. We do over fifty percent of our business between Memorial Day and Labor Day."

Savannah shrugged. "It was probably a rumor."

"Dey can do what dey want"— Hebert looked up from the checkerboard set between him and Father Sam—"if dey suspect terrorists."

"Terrorists?" Savannah slapped her hand over her mouth and glanced at three other customers who were staring at her. She walked over to the old men's table and spoke in just above a whisper. "No one said anything about terrorists."

Hebert glanced up at Savannah, his mousy gray curls unruly, his yellow cotton shirt in need of ironing. "Dey won't say it. But dat's what dey're tinking."

Zoe walked over to the table and stood next to Savannah. "They're paid to think the worst," she said softly, "but *we* don't have to. This is probably the work of some nutcase."

"*Mes amis*," Hebert said, "dey haven't ruled out terrorists. Dat's a fact."

Zoe's heart sank. She hadn't allowed her thoughts to consider that awful possibility. "I suppose it's terrorism, regardless of whether it's the vicious act of an individual or an organized group. But I don't see terrorists like al-Qaeda targeting a small community like this. They would likely do something in New Orleans or Baton Rouge where they could get the maximum amount of casualties."

Hebert pursed his lips, his faded gray eyes intense. "Guess we'll see."

"We're certainly an easy mark, y'all," Savannah said. "Maybe that's the whole point. They want us to know they can strike wherever they want, even in smaller towns."

"Aw, come on now." Tex's silver eyebrows came together. "What's the point o' gettin' our bellies in a wad with speculation? We just need to stay up on the news and do what the authorities tell us."

Hebert scratched the sandpaper on his chin. "I guess if dey close Zoe B's, I could eat SpaghettiOs and baked beans."

"There's been a run on all canned goods," Savannah said. "I doubt you could even find any."

"There's no way I'm letting that happen." Zoe moved her gaze around the table. "Even *if* we're forced to close—which I don't think is going to happen—I'll cook for you in my own kitchen. I'll make sure you fellas have nutritious take-out food you can microwave."

"Aw, you take such good care of us." Tex hooked his thumbs on his red suspenders and looked up at her, his smile as wide as the Rio Grande, his sunburned head reflecting the light from the window.

Father Sam linked his bony fingers together on the table, his relief magnified in his thick lenses. "Honestly, I don't know if I'd even *remember* to eat, if I didn't have all of you to share it with. I don't have much of an appetite, what with all the meds I'm on."

Zoe squeezed the priest's shoulder. "We're family. We're in this together—whatever happens."

Zoe felt fear tighten the muscles in her neck. How long would it take the authorities to arrest whoever was behind this? How much contaminated food was still out there, ready to claim more victims? She thought of Margot and Josh Corbin. It didn't really matter to them whether the food was poisoned by one cruel person or a group of misguided terrorists. Their son was dead.

CHAPTER 5

Zoe sat at Adele Woodmore's kitchen table, her hand wrapped around a cold glass of raspberry tea, her mind racing with the day's developments.

"I'm glad you came over, hon." Adele brushed a lock of Zoe's hair away from her damp eyes.

"Seems I always end up at your table when I'm upset," Zoe said. "The latest news about cyanide in bottled water put me over the top. And Dominic … how do we even begin to deal with that?"

"It's overwhelming. Domi was such a sweet little boy. I can still picture him kneeling at my coffee table with Grace, putting puzzles together. They were so cute and such special friends."

Zoe cried unashamedly in the comforting presence of this precious woman who was as much a mother figure to her as a friend.

"Margot and Josh both seemed dazed when I stopped by the house," Zoe said. "I'm surprised they could even carry on a conversation. But they were gracious as always. I guess they have to maintain their sanity for the other children. I feel bad for Chance Durand, too. I don't know him well, but Emily seems taken with him."

Adele looked into her eyes. "Was she with Chance when his parents died?"

"She drove him to the hospital, but his parents were dead before they got there. It's so terrifying."

Adele squeezed Zoe's hand. "We have to trust the Lord."

"I do. But we have to be smart. If whoever's doing this can poison a food bar and bottled water, how can we trust anything we buy locally? I've decided to start taking my family's perishable groceries out of what we have delivered to Zoe B's—eggs, fish, meat, poultry, dairy items. Our wholesale supplier comes three times a week from New Orleans. I won't be shopping for any of those items at local stores, that's for sure. I'll order enough for you, too."

"Isabel and I will be fine," Adele said. "You take care of your little ones."

Isabel Morand stood in the doorway, her arms crossed, her long dark hair draping over her shoulders. "I think we should take Zoe up on her offer, Adele. We have no idea what's safe and what isn't."

"I insist," Zoe said. "I can easily adjust my food orders to cover it."

"I suppose it couldn't hurt. I'll pay you, of course." Adele picked up a copy of *National Geographic* and began fanning herself. "Could you have imagined this in a million years?"

Zoe shook her head.

"Maybe not this," Isabel said. "But after the nightmare with Murray Hamelin, nothing should surprise us."

Zoe caught Adele's gaze. "Have you heard from him lately?"

"Just last week." The corners of Adele's mouth curled up. "Murray's doing as well as a young man can do in prison. He's in a Bible study with a dozen other inmates. He's accepted that he'll never be up for parole. He said in his letter that he wanted to work for God right where he is, that he wanted to lead other prisoners to Christ so they could experience the freedom he has, despite the bars. It's remarkable."

Zoe wrinkled her nose and was immediately sorry she had shown her disdain. "Sorry. I know I should be rejoicing that he's found a relationship with God. But after what he did to you … I'm just glad he's locked up."

Isabel pursed her lips. "I'll never forgive him for what he did."

"Then perhaps both of you should concentrate on what he *didn't* do," Adele said. "That should put you in an attitude of gratitude."

"You're right. I should focus on that instead." *But not today.* Zoe glanced at her watch. "I guess I'd better get back to Zoe B's. The place was all but dead earlier, though I'm hoping business will pick up this evening. I posted a notice on the door, letting people know we buy our ingredients in bulk from a wholesaler out of New Orleans, and that it's perfectly safe to eat there."

"That may not be enough reassurance right now," Isabel said. "I'm sure the people who ate at the food bar thought it was safe."

Adele sighed. "I do hope Domi didn't suffer."

"Cyanide works quickly," Zoe said. "I doubt he even had time to react. I suppose that's the only relief in all this."

"It's not just the children I'm worried about, Zoe." Adele took her hand. "*You* be careful."

"I will. I want you and Isabel to be careful too. Don't drink Gaudry bottled water. And examine everything. From what I saw on the news, there was a clear spot on the bottom of the poisoned bottled water where the plastic had been tampered with. But who turns the bottle upside down?"

Adele sighed. "I'll bet we will now."

Emily sat next to Chance on the white leather couch at his home, wondering what thoughts must be racing through his mind. The front porch had been roped off with yellow crime scene tape, and sheriff's deputies and police officers were still in the kitchen, gathering evidence.

Two deputies walked out of the kitchen and sat in navy leather Queen Anne chairs, facing Emily and Chance.

"Chance, I'm Deputy Stone Castille, and this is Mike Doucet. Sorry we've kept you waiting so long. It's been a crazy day."

"That's okay," Chance said. "I had a lot of phone calls to make."

Stone nodded. "I'm sure. Deputy Doucet and I read the statement you gave the detectives. We just have a few follow-up questions."

"Whatever you need. This is my friend Emily Jessup. She knows the situation. We can speak freely in front of her."

Castille glanced at Emily and then turned his attention to Chance. "We're talking to the family members of all the victims, just to see if any of you might know some detail that will help us—something that may not even seem important but could be key."

Chance seemed to stare at his hands. "I told the detectives everything I know. I'm blown away by this. I can't believe both my parents are dead. They've gotten their groceries from Marcotte's since I was a little boy. Who would do this?"

"What can you tell us about the delivery boy?"

"Adam Marcotte?" Chance shrugged. "Just what I told the detectives. He's a nice kid. He had just gotten his driver's license when I was home on Christmas break, and his great-uncle hired him to deliver groceries after school and on weekends. You don't think he had anything to do with this?"

"We're just gathering information," Castille said. "Right now, we can't rule out anyone."

Doucet wrote something on his tablet.

"Do you know if your parents always had their groceries delivered on Friday?" Castille said.

"I'm not sure." Chance leaned his head back on the couch. "I'm away at school most of the year. But since I've been home this summer, they have."

"Were you home yesterday when Adam brought the groceries?"

"Yes, sir. I was. It was around four thirty."

"Was there anything different in Adam's demeanor?"

"Not at all," Chance said. "He was personable as ever. Cheerful and polite."

"Who put the bottled water in the refrigerator?"

"I did."

"In hindsight, did anything about it seem odd? Had the plastic netting around it been cut and reattached?"

"My mom laid out all the groceries and handed them to me. I didn't pay attention." Chance's eyes welled with tears. "It never occurred to me someone could poison bottled water."

"Did your parents always buy Gaudry brand?"

Chance nodded. "It's the only kind my dad would drink. He said Looziana spring water was the best."

"Did either of your parents have a grievance with someone at Marcotte's?"

"I doubt it. They loved that place. Like I said, they'd been buying groceries there since I was a kid. Before they started having groceries delivered, they knew the checkers by name—and how their kids were doing."

Doucet scribbled something on his notes.

"Chance, do you think there's any possibility this attack was personal?" Castille said.

"It was to me." Chance put his fist to his mouth and swallowed hard. "But if you're asking whether I think someone deliberately targeted my parents, I doubt it. Everybody liked Mom and Dad."

"You're sure about that?"

"As sure as I *can* be."

"So you think they were just unfortunate victims of a random attack?"

"I don't know what else to think," Chance said. "I can't imagine anyone wanting to hurt them."

"So you never heard anyone threaten them—even in jest?"

"Never."

"No estranged friends? Neighbors? Relatives?"

Chance heaved a sigh. "No, sir. Not that I know of. They've had the same friends and neighbors for as long as I can remember. They played bridge with a lot of them or knew them from the country club."

Stone glanced at the report. "Okay, I see you've already given us their names and phone numbers. I think we're done for now. If something comes up that we have questions about, we'll be in touch.

We appreciate your talking to us. I know this has been a terrible ordeal."

"Deputy Castille, I have a question," Emily said. "How many people were poisoned?"

"Sixteen. Six died—one from Marcotte's food bar and five from Gaudry bottled water."

"Is that brand of water still on the grocery shelves?" Emily said.

"No, it's been voluntarily pulled from the shelves in Les Barbes. And there's also been a state recall on all bottles with that expiration date, originating from the Lafayette plant."

"I thought plastic bottles were tamperproof," Emily said.

"Tamper *resistant.*" Castille arched his eyebrows. "I doubt any containers are truly tamperproof. If a person is determined, he can get into almost anything. What else?"

"That's all. Thanks," Emily said.

The two deputies rose to their feet and shook hands with Chance.

"We're very sorry for your loss," Castille said.

Doucet nodded. "We'll do everything in our power to find out who did this."

"Thank you," Chance said. "I know you will."

Emily linked her arm in his as the deputies walked out to the kitchen. "Are you all right?"

"Would you be?"

Dumb question, Emily thought. "Whoever did this is not going to get away with it."

Chance exhaled. "I wish I were as confident as you are."

"It's serious enough that the authorities won't quit until they figure out who's responsible."

"I hope you're right." Chance got up and pulled Emily to her feet. "I've got to go to the mausoleum and make sure the prearrangements are in order. And then I need to meet with Monsignor Robidoux at Saint Catherine's. I'm not religious, but Mom and Dad would want a Catholic funeral."

"I'll drive you," Emily said.

"I thought you were working the dinner shift at Zoe B's."

"I was, but Zoe sent me a text and said not to come in—that business was almost dead at the moment. I'm here as long as you need me."

Jude hung up the phone and looked out his office window. Across the street, the stately Saint Catherine Parish Courthouse stood tall and proud, its white pillars taking on a soft yellow glow in the evening sun. A perfect picture if it weren't for the media mob out front.

Aimee walked into his office, her hairdo wilted but her demeanor cool and calm. "You wanted to see me, Sheriff?"

"Yes, you can leave the door open. Take a seat."

Aimee pulled up a chair next to his desk and sat.

"Officials from the Department of Health and Hospitals have arrived," Jude said. "I want you to fill them in and give them whatever they need."

Aimee's jaw tightened. "We can do this without DHH."

"Maybe," Jude said. "But sixteen people poisoned with cyanide—six of them fatally—was bound to turn a few heads in Baton Rouge. The governor wants to make sure this thing is contained before it becomes a statewide risk. We can use all the help we can get. Be gracious about it."

"You know I will. Anything else?"

"Have we finished interviewing the families of the victims?"

Aimee nodded. "Immediate family. We're getting their statements into the computer so you can review them."

"I want hard copies too. It's easier for me to compare them that way. So what's your assessment?"

Aimee pursed her lips. "Overall, they seem devastated."

"Any anger? Threats to sue?"

"Some. But I think it's just grief talking. Most are still stunned. I imagine the anger will come later. Leo Marcotte was so stressed he started hyperventilating. His son took him to the ER, and they sedated him. Poor guy. He started the Market from the ground up and has run it himself for over fifty years. He's horrified that something like this could originate from there."

"Have we checked to see if any family member of the victims works in an industry that has access to cyanide?"

"We're in the process. So far, that hasn't yielded anything."

"Well, lots of people had access to that food bar. What do we know about the great-nephew, Adam Marcotte? He certainly could have moved about freely in the store without drawing suspicion."

"The kid's only sixteen. He seemed pretty upset—and scared. He knows he's a person of interest. But truthfully, I think he's just a high school kid making deliveries. There's nothing in his background to suggest he's capable of this or had access to cyanide. His home life seems stable. Dad's an attorney. Mother's a stay-at-home mom. He's an honor student. On the swim team. And captain of the debate team."

"Did he deliver groceries to all the victims of Gaudry water?"

"Yes. Three homes. Five victims. The kid said he took the water off the shelf to fill the orders. According to the stockroom records, that water arrived by Loo-Z-ana Transit Thursday afternoon and was checked in just after midnight on Friday, then put out on the shelves or in the cooler after three p.m. More than a dozen employees on several shifts had access to the water, and we've questioned all of them. None of them look good for this."

"I want you to take a closer look at Adam Marcotte," Jude said. "See what he does in his spare time. Who his friends are. What contacts he has on social networking sites. The kid seems a little too perfect to me."

"We will. Is that everything?"

"Make sure you take the DHH officials down to Chief Norman's office and introduce them. He knows they're coming."

"Will do—and I'll be gracious." She flashed a manufactured grin.

Aimee got up and left Jude's office, and he sat quietly, listening to the bustle in the detective bureau.

No new poisoning cases had occurred since early afternoon when the food bar at Marcotte's was closed down and the public advised of the contaminated bottled water. Was the threat over? Or was the person or persons behind this evil action just regrouping, preparing to attack somewhere else? The public had been called to vigilance. But if the killer was determined to poison more food or water, could he really be stopped?

CHAPTER 6

Sax Henry drove his silver PT Cruiser down Cypress Way, eyeing the lovely mansions and massive live oaks draped with Spanish moss. From the moment he entered the city limits, he could see that Les Barbes was as charming as the travel brochures claimed. Why hadn't his jazz band ever done a gig here?

He spotted Magnolia Lane and turned left, stopping in front of the one-story frame house on the corner—white with green shutters and a dark slate-shingle roof. He checked the address he had written on a Post-it note. This was it. Nice place.

Why did he suddenly feel foolish? Even if this woman turned out to be the right Adele Woodmore, would she even know where his sister was? Every lead he'd followed in the past three years had led nowhere. If this turned out to be another dead end, did he have the strength to keep pursuing it? How could he not?

He thought of the two bronze urns in his closet. His sister deserved to know both parents were dead now. She was entitled to half of the estate, meager as it was. And she should have a say-so in how their mom and dad's ashes would be dispersed—though he wondered if her idea of how to do it would be even more irreverent than his.

His motivation to find Shelby went much deeper than resolving the present. How could he ever find peace until he admitted that he'd been a coward? That he'd left home so he wouldn't have to confront the unthinkable? Neither his sister nor his mother ever talked about it. It was as though not talking about it made it not so. Music and marijuana made his pretending much easier.

It was time to tell the truth. And it was long overdue.

Sax got out of the car and tucked in his plaid shirt, his no-wrinkle khaki pants not quite living up to their name. He rubbed the five o'clock shadow he rarely shaved off and patted his moussed hair. Did he look presentable enough that Mrs. Woodmore wouldn't close the door in his face before he had a chance to ask his questions?

He walked in front of the car and stepped up on the curb, passing between two flowering crape myrtle trees as he made his way toward the front of the house. According to the man who had provided this lead, Mrs. Woodmore was a nonjudgmental, levelheaded individual. And if anyone would know where his sister was, it was her.

Sax climbed the brick steps up to the small porch, his heart pounding and perspiration dripping down the small of his back. If this didn't pan out, he would be right back to square one.

He rang the doorbell, shifting his weight from one foot to the other, thinking he should have worn shoes instead of Birkenstocks, and wondering if he could even articulate his thoughts. All he could hope for was that Mrs. Woodmore would hear him out—and give him a truthful answer.

The door opened, and an attractive young woman with long dark curls and intriguing brown eyes met his gaze. "Yes?"

"My name's Sax Henry. I'm looking for Adele Woodmore."

"Is she expecting you?"

"No. I was referred here by Julien Menard, who used to be her chauffeur when she lived in Alexandria. Is Mrs. Woodmore home?"

"What shall I tell her is the nature of your business, Mr. Henry?"

So I've got the right Adele Woodmore! "It's personal. Tell her my sister, Shelby Sieger, used to work for her."

"Wait here ..."

The young woman closed the door and left him standing on the porch with his toxic insecurity and the oppressive June humidity. Sax put his hands deep in his pockets and rocked from heel to toe, rehearsing in his mind how he planned to broach the subject with Mrs. Woodmore. How hard could it be? She either knew where Shelby was or she didn't.

The door opened again, and an elderly white-haired woman, dressed in white slacks and a pink blouse, stood in the doorway.

"I'm Adele Woodmore, Mr. Henry. Isabel said you're looking for Shelby Sieger."

Sax nodded. "She's my sister. We've lost touch, and I very much want to reconnect."

"Define reconnect," Adele said.

"I want to see her. I have news about our parents and some personal business to discuss with her."

The elderly woman's eyebrows came together. "I see. And you're of the opinion that I can help you?"

"Yes, ma'am. I've been trying for three years to find her. I recently found your name and address in my mother's address book. She listed you as Shelby's employer. I went to your home in Alexandria, but I was told you had moved. The woman who lives there now gave me the phone number of Julien Menard."

"And Julien told you where I was?"

"He just said you had moved to Les Barbes. You're the only Adele Woodmore in the phonebook."

The woman's blue eyes turned to slits. "How long has it been since you've seen Shelby?"

"Quite a while."

"Be specific, Mr. Henry. I'm a straightforward woman."

"I haven't seen Shelby since she was thirteen. That was twenty-eight years ago."

"How do I even know you're her brother, since your last name isn't Sieger?"

"Actually, it is—was." He took out his old driver's license and handed it to Adele. "I changed my name from Michael Austin Sieger to Sax Michael Henry when I got interested in jazz and learned to play the saxophone."

Adele arched her eyebrows. "Oh my, like Kenny G?"

"Not exactly like Kenny G. He plays soprano sax."

She studied the picture on his driver's license and then handed it back to him. "The name Sax Sieger has a nice ring to it for a musician. Why did you go for Henry?"

Sax was at the same time amused and annoyed at the woman's asking personal questions. "It's a long story, Mrs. Woodmore. Do you know where I can find Shelby?"

Adele studied him. Was she going to tell him no—the one word he did not want to hear?

"Why don't you come inside where it's cool, Mr. Henry? Have a glass of raspberry tea, and let's talk some more."

Was the woman serious—or was she messing with him?

Adele opened the door wide. "Come on, come on," she prodded. "It must be close to a hundred out there."

"Thanks. It's downright oppressive. And please, call me Sax. Everyone does."

He stepped inside, the aroma of warm bread filling his senses. "I didn't mean to intrude on your dinner."

"Isabel and I have already eaten."

I wish I had. Sax's stomach rumbled, and he tried to muffle the sound.

"I suppose you heard about the cyanide poisonings?" Adele said.

"Uh, no. I haven't. I drove up from New Orleans and listened to CDs the whole way. I haven't heard any news today."

"I'm afraid Les Barbes isn't the ideal place to be right now. A number of people were taken ill after eating at the food bar at Marcotte's Market, and then several more from drinking Gaudry's bottled water. Sixteen people in all—six have died."

"Six people—today?" Sax said.

Adele nodded. "The authorities say it was cyanide poisoning, and it was definitely deliberate."

"I could believe that kind of thing in New Orleans," Sax said. "But here?"

"I assure you everyone in town is shaken to the core. Most of us knew someone who died today. Isabel is baking bread to take to friends of ours who lost their four-year-old son." Adele stopped at the kitchen door and spoke to the pretty young woman with dark curls who had answered the door. "Isabel, would you bring us some raspberry tea and some of your scrumptious butter cookies?"

"I'd be glad to," Isabel said, her voice dripping with curiosity.

"Let's sit out here in the sunroom." Adele led him into a room that was glass on three sides and offered a gorgeous view of her perfectly manicured lawn and a mosaic of colorful flowers all along the fence.

"Very nice," Sax said. "I imagine you get a lot of use out of this room."

"Indeed I do. I so enjoy being close to nature. I loved my country estate in Alexandria. The grounds were delightful, particularly my rose garden. But I have to admit, it's been a relief to scale back."

She sat at a glass table, and he sat across from her, intrigued for a moment at the hummingbirds hovering at a feeder attached to the window.

"I assume you know where Shelby is," he said, "or you wouldn't have invited me in."

Adele tented her fingers. "Your sister was a trusted member of my household staff. We were well acquainted. She left my employ about fifteen years ago."

"But you know how I can get in touch with her?"

Isabel breezed through the doorway, carrying a tray holding a glass pitcher of raspberry tea, two stemmed glasses filled with ice, two china plates and matching napkins, and a small platter of butter cookies. She arranged it neatly on the table and filled the glasses with tea, then stepped back. "Can I get you anything else?"

"This is lovely, hon," Adele said. "Thank you."

"These look good." Sax took a cookie off the plate and bit into it. "I was so eager to get here that I didn't bother stopping for dinner."

"Those butter cookies will melt in your mouth. Have as many as you like." Adele pursed her lips. "Before Isabel came in, you asked if I know how you can get in touch with Shelby."

"Do you?"

Adele wrapped her hands around the stem of her glass and held his gaze. "That's not how this is going to work. If I'm convinced your intentions are good, I'll consider contacting Shelby to see if she's interested in reconnecting with you. It should be up to her."

Sax sighed. "She might not agree to it unless she knows how important it is. We haven't seen each other since we were teenagers. And there're some issues we need to address."

"Yes, I know. Do you even know what she looks like now?"

Sax blinked away the regret stinging his eyes. He reached into his pocket and took out his wallet, then removed Shelby's school picture and handed it to Adele. "This is how she looked when I left home. She was in middle school. I try to put age on her and imagine what she looks like now."

Adele took the picture and studied it. "She doesn't look anything like this. She's prettier. A healthier weight. And her eyes aren't sad." Adele handed the picture back to him. "I doubt you would recognize her."

"She definitely won't recognize me," Sax said. "I was seventeen when I left home—hair down to my shoulders. A mustache and beard. I don't know how old she was the last time she actually saw my face."

Adele took a sip of tea, her eyes peering over the top of her glass. "Tell me about yourself, Sax. It would take more than what you've told me for me to contact Shelby. You have no idea how hard she's worked to reconcile her past. I realize you want to salve your conscience, but I'm not willing to help you do that at Shelby's expense."

"I never said anything about salving my conscience."

"No, you didn't." Adele's cheeks turned pink. "Let me rephrase. What good will come of her dredging up the abusive past she's worked so hard to put behind her? What do you hope to gain?"

Sax wiped his mouth with the napkin. Adele wasn't going to make it easy for him. "I hope to start fresh. I realize I'll have to earn her trust. She may not be open at first. Or maybe ever. But I have to try."

"Why? You've gone this long without any relationship."

Sax shifted his weight and avoided eye contact. "I'm not proud of that. I promise you, not a day went by that I didn't think about Shelby. I went back to Devon Springs several times after I left home. I met with my mother privately and begged her to leave my dad, to take Shelby and go to a women's shelter. She wouldn't. She said she loved my dad despite his drinking. I never could understand it. My old man was mean as a snake."

Adele's lips formed a straight line, her piercing gaze telling him she knew more than she was saying. "And yet you never took Shelby under your wing. You were of age. Had you let her live with you, would your mother really have objected?"

Sax felt his face turn hot. Did he really want—or need—to have this conversation? "With all due respect, Mrs. Woodmore, I think we're getting into private matters that really aren't your concern."

"If you're using me to get to Shelby, they most certainly are. Everything that affects her concerns me."

"Because you were her employer? I don't think so."

"No, because I'm her friend—and her daughter's godmother."

"Oh." Sax took another cookie, his pulse quickened. He hadn't seen that one coming. This was too good to be true. "So I guess you and Shelby are close?"

"Let's stay on the subject, young man. We can agree that it's none of my business why you left Shelby in an abusive environment. But I need to know more about you before I'm going to get involved in putting you two together."

"There's not all that much to tell. I have an apartment in New Orleans. I'm a professional musician in a jazz band called Smooth Blues. You can check out our website. We've been together almost ten years. I'm a responsible person. I pay my bills. I've never been in trouble. I'm divorced. No kids. Actually, I've been married three times. My ex-wives are still friends with me. But none of them could deal with my highs and lows over the unfinished business in my life."

"By unfinished business, I assume you're referring to your having left home, knowing full well how vulnerable Shelby was?"

Sax suddenly felt hot and dabbed the perspiration from his forehead. "You cut right to the chase, don't you?"

"I'm quite familiar with your upbringing, Sax. Shelby told me all about your father's drinking and his violent, loathsome behavior. He stole that child's innocence because he couldn't control his lust or his whiskey. And it happened repeatedly."

He was taken aback by Adele's bluntness. So it was true. He suddenly felt sick to his stomach. "If I … I'd known what to do for Shelby, I would have done it. I was a kid myself—and a coward. I was afraid of my dad."

Adele started to say something and then didn't. Finally she said, "Couldn't you have at least let the authorities know what was going on?"

Sax stared at his hands. "That was almost thirty years ago. No one talked openly about sexual abuse like they do now. Shelby never said a word about it, and neither did my mother. I wasn't even sure that's what was happening. I guess I didn't want to know. But every time Dad was arrested for drunken behavior, he came home madder and meaner. Mom did everything she could to cover for him. Any time the police got involved, she backed up his story. Shelby and I were stuck."

"Yes, when you were still a minor," Adele said. "What I struggle with is why you didn't ask Shelby to live with you when you were on your own."

"I was in a rock band. That's how I supported myself. Shelby didn't tell you?"

"She mentioned it. She didn't elaborate."

"I was on the road most of the time and lived in a bus with four other guys that drank and drugged and brought women in." Sax felt his cheeks warm. "It was no life for a young girl. Plus, I believed if I took Shelby out of the house, my dad would kill my mom and make it look like an accident."

"Were you into drugs and drinking?" Adele said.

Sax drew a line on the condensation on his glass. "Not exactly. I've never touched alcohol in my life. I saw what it did to my father, and I didn't want any part of it. I smoked plenty of pot, but I never did anything more serious than that."

Why was he letting Mrs. Woodmore give him the third degree?

What choice did he have? She was his only way back into Shelby's life. He might as well keep it honest with her.

"Music is my drug of choice these days," Sax said. "I gave up marijuana at the same time I quit smoking cigarettes ten years ago." He sighed. "Look. I really shouldn't have to tell you all this. I've had a tragic personal life. I married three really great women and couldn't make any of them happy. All this guilt I'm carrying has poisoned my relationships. I'm not the abusive loser my father was. But my life's a mess. I want to know Shelby. She's my sister. My own flesh and blood ..." He choked on the words and let a wave of emotion pass. "I don't have anyone else. Our parents are both gone now."

Adele exhaled. "I suppose Shelby should be told about that. It's going to bring up such painful memories."

"Surely she's wondered about them—about me?"

"I suppose she has," Adele said. "But she never talks about any of you anymore. And she made no effort to contact your parents when her children were born."

"So she has more than just the one daughter?"

A row of lines formed on Adele's forehead. "I'm not comfortable telling you anything else. I think that should be Shelby's choice."

"But she's happy now?"

"Yes." Adele seemed lost in thought for a moment. "I can't begin to tell you what a toll her upbringing took on her. But she's full of life now."

"That's what I want. I just don't know how to get there."

"How hard are you willing to work, Sax? I can assure you that Shelby can't give you a magic formula. She had to work through the pain."

"Well, I didn't give up on finding her, even after every lead turned out to be a dead end. I'm not afraid of working through the pain, Mrs. Woodmore. What I am afraid of is living with it for the rest of my life."

"I see." She linked her fingers together, her unwavering gaze seeming to bore a hole in his defenses. Was she enjoying making him squirm? Making him wonder if he had come all this way for nothing?

Sax leaned forward on his elbows. "You said you're a straightforward woman. So be straightforward. Are you going to tell Shelby I'm looking for her, or not?"

CHAPTER 7

The western sky was emblazoned with streaks of fiery pink and purple as Sax parked his PT Cruiser in the guest parking lot at Langley Manor. He sat for a moment, grateful that Adele Woodmore had made the suggestion that he try to find a room there. According to the proprietor, Vanessa Langley, it was highly unusual for there to be a vacancy this time of year. He'd just happened to call right after someone canceled. What were the odds of that happening? He had to wonder if the cyanide poisonings had something to do with it, but Vanessa hadn't alluded to it on the phone.

He got out of the car and stood for a moment, admiring the stately white plantation house, its four pillars taking on the sunset's rosy hue. The historic antebellum home was nestled between flowering shrubs and under the arms of a magnificent live oak. Stunning.

The room rate was a lot more than he had planned to pay, but he felt as if retreating from the city would do him good while Adele was making up her mind whether to contact Shelby. Adele promised to tell him within the next few days.

Sax grabbed his suitcase and walked up the front steps, the smell of old wood pervasive except for the glorious scent of mock orange blossoms somewhere nearby. He looked through the sheers on the glass panes in the door, then turned the shiny brass knob and went inside. A second later a young man with dark, curly hair and glasses walked up to him and shook his hand.

"Welcome to Langley Manor. I'm Ethan Langley. You must be Mr. Henry."

"Yes, call me Sax." He smiled. "It's a nickname. I'm a musician. I play the saxophone."

"Really? That's cool. Kenny G is my favorite. I must have every CD he's done. You like him?"

"Well, he single-handedly took traditional jazz and transformed it into pop with great success. It's hard to fault a guy that's sold a bazillion million CDs. I'm a traditionalist, myself." He didn't want to spend the next five minutes talking about Kenny G. "I'm really glad you can accommodate me, Ethan. I drove up today from New Orleans and didn't even think about making reservations ahead of time. I didn't realize Les Barbes is such a tourist town."

"Tourism is huge," Ethan said. "We stay busy year-round, but the town draws half its revenue during June, July, and August—and the week of Mardi Gras."

"Was the cancellation I benefitted from due to the cyanide situation?"

Ethan hesitated as if he were caught off guard. "It was. The couple with the reservation got caught up in the media hype and was afraid to come to town. Truthfully, there's nothing to fear here at Langley Manor. We've decided to get our groceries and our bottled water in Baton Rouge until the crisis is over."

"That's good."

"Keep in mind, though, the source of the problem seems to be Marcotte's Market, and it's been closed."

"I'll eat a big breakfast here. That usually holds me all day."

Ethan looked over the top of his glasses. "Vanessa makes the best crepes in the known world—except maybe for Zoe B's. The chef there taught her how. But we also serve scrambled eggs. Grits. Bacon, sausage, and boudin. Biscuits and beignets. Lots of fresh fruit. Vanessa even makes her own granola. She puts out quite a spread. Would you like me to show you the house, or would you like to go to your room now?"

"If you don't mind, I'd just as soon get settled in my room and tour the house and grounds some other time."

"That's fine. You're in room four upstairs." Ethan picked up Sax's suitcase and started up the white staircase.

Sax followed Ethan halfway down the hallway to a door with a brass numeral four on it.

Ethan opened the door wide, went inside, flipped the light switch, and set the suitcase on the floor. "Here you go."

Sax moved his gaze across the pale blue walls and white crown moldings and stopped on a walnut poster bed made up with a blue, yellow, and white comforter.

"I don't know anything about antiques," Sax admitted, "but I can appreciate the historic look of the room. Very inviting. This'll be great."

"I'm glad you like it. Too bad you won't need that fireplace." Ethan smiled. "The white marble does add to the ambiance, though."

Sax noticed a small plate of chocolate chip cookies on the secretary. "Those look good."

"Vanessa makes them from scratch. If you want something else to munch on, there are chips, pretzels, cheese and crackers, and other snacks in the dining room until ten. And cold drinks in the mini-fridge in the alcove. Just go back down the stairs, and the dining room is the first room on the right. The alcove is adjacent."

"Thanks."

"As you can see"—Ethan nodded toward the secretary—"there's a variety of books to read. And also a brochure there on the desk, if you want to know more about the history of the house and the furnishings."

"I heard this house was used as a station on the Underground Railroad."

Ethan nodded. "Noah Washington, who's the caretaker and like a part of our family, is a descendant of the slave Naomi, who helped my ancestors move the runaway slaves up north. Vanessa and I are very excited to have Noah partner with us to share what happened here. If you like, we'll even take you through the secret tunnels used by the slaves."

Sax put his hand on Ethan's shoulder and shook his hand. "Thanks. We'll see how I feel tomorrow. Tonight I just want to crash. It's been a long day."

"Are you here on business or pleasure?"

"I'm going to try to get in both," Sax said. "We'll see how it goes. But while I'm here, I plan to kick back and enjoy some alone time."

"You came to the right place. Breakfast is served in the dining room downstairs between eight and ten. Checkout is at eleven. Vanessa said you'll be staying a few nights with us."

"That's right. I'm not sure yet just how long. Is that all right?"

"Normally we're booked. But with this cyanide scare, we can be flexible. We *would* appreciate your letting us know before seven p.m. the night before you plan to check out."

"I will."

"Housekeeping comes every morning at eleven. Be sure to use your do-not-disturb sign if you plan to sleep in. Hope you have a restful night," Ethan said. "Call us if you need anything."

"Thanks. I will."

Ethan left and closed the door behind him.

Sax locked it out of habit, then admired the room. Cozy. He walked over to the poster bed, climbed the walnut step stool, and flopped onto the bed. He bounced to see how much support the mattress offered. Just right. Regardless of what Adele decided, his time here at Langley Manor should be pleasant—perhaps a reprieve from the turmoil.

Adele said that Shelby was happy. Had Shelby found the key to peace? How could he not be glad for her? But unless she agreed to let him into her life and work things out, he would never know peace.

Jude strolled with his wife down *rue Madeline,* enjoying a bag of caramel corn and an unexpected breeze that cooled the sultry summer evening to almost pleasant.

"I'm sorry this isn't exactly a date," Jude said.

Colette Prejean shot a playful glance his way. "Actually I'm happy to help. Everyone's scared to death. It's good that we're out here together, where people can see us."

"You enjoying that buttered pecan caramel corn?"

"Are you kidding?"

"You're not afraid it's poison?"

"If it is, at least I'll die happy." Colette smiled. "I really shouldn't joke about it. I'm as scared as the next person."

"I know." Jude looked around at the smaller-than-usual crowd. "I don't see that many locals out here tonight. But I'm glad to see that a respectable number of tourists decided not to leave. I can't imagine the economic impact the cyanide poisonings will have if the killer isn't found soon."

"Sheriff Prejean!"

Jude spun around and saw a reporter and a cameraman coming in his direction. The camera was rolling.

"What can I do for you?" Jude recognized the late-night anchor from Channel Five News: Louis Dupont.

"Sheriff, can you tell us if there've been any new developments in the cyanide poisonings?"

Jude pasted on the most positive look he could muster. "Lou, I briefed the press just two hours ago. If there were further developments, I would have come back to you with the information. We *want* the public fully informed so we can all be vigilant."

"I see you've been to Kernal Poppy's," Lou said. "You're not afraid of cyanide poisoning?"

"I take this threat very seriously. But it would be a mistake to assume that nothing is safe. As you can see, my wife and I are enjoying an evening stroll and a bag of caramel corn, just like we would any other time. With everyone being vigilant, especially establishments that serve food of any kind, my hope is that the worst is behind us."

"Are you close to making an arrest?" Lou inched closer.

"I'm not going to comment on that. But scores of deputies and police officers are working in shifts around the clock to solve this case—as I will be again in the morning."

Louis pushed the mike in front of Jude's lips. "Can you at least tell us where you had dinner?"

Jude smiled. "Sure. Colette and I had a delicious meal at Zoe B's Cajun Eatery. If you haven't tried it, you really should. Or dozens of other great eating places in town."

Colette squeezed his arm in approval of the free advertising he had just given Zoe and Pierce.

"So you don't think people should avoid eating out?" Lou said.

"I think people should use good sense. Avoid eating foods that have been sitting out where everyone has access. Most restaurants prepare entrees from food delivered by wholesale food suppliers based in other cities. As for bottled water, stay away from Gaudry brand—which has been recalled—and do what we suggested in our briefing: inspect bottles and packaging for tampering. Stay calm, and let my people do their job. We'll get whoever's behind this."

"Sheriff, do you think this is the work of terrorists?"

"I don't," he said, wishing he were as certain as he sounded. "No one has claimed responsibility, which we believe would have happened by now had this been an organized act of terrorism. I can't comment further during an open investigation, other than to say law enforcement isn't going to stop until we find whoever's behind it." Jude looked Lou squarely in the eyes. "Meanwhile, let's not stop living. My wife and I are going on with our lives, and we encourage everyone to do the same." Jude held up his palm, knowing this clip would end up on the eleven o'clock news. He'd said enough. "That's it for now."

Jude took Colette's arm and walked away from the camera, glad that Lou and his camera crew didn't follow.

"You think you eased his mind?" Colette said.

"I doubt it. I gave it my best shot."

Emily Jessup climbed the deck steps at the back of Langley Manor, smiling at a family of raccoons feasting on the Critter Crunch that Vanessa had left out for them.

She unlocked the back door and froze when she saw Vanessa standing there, her arms crossed, her eyebrows furrowed.

"It's late," Vanessa said. "Why didn't you call me? Or return my messages? I've been worried."

"You're such a mother hen." Emily set her purse on the kitchen counter. "My cell battery died. But I told you where I was. I didn't call because I thought you were asleep. I was reluctant to leave Chance by himself. I mean, he just lost both parents. The guy's in shock."

"I can only imagine."

"I wanted to stay overnight and sleep on the couch. But I knew how it might look. So I just stayed with Chance until I felt sure he was going to crash. Okay?"

The tautness left Vanessa's face. "I keep forgetting you're nineteen. To me, you're still my baby sister."

"I like being your younger sister," Emily said, admiring Vanessa's long, dark hair and dainty features, wishing she looked more like her.

"But I'm not a baby. For heaven's sake, I'm going to be delivering them one of these days."

"I told Mom and Dad I would watch out for you."

"You are."

Vanessa picked up a lock of Emily's hair and gave it a gentle tug. "Next time, *call* me. I don't care if you wake me up."

"You even sounded like Mom just then." Emily grinned. "Eerie."

"How about some chocolate chippers?" Vanessa took a Tupperware container out of the cupboard and set it on the table. "So what's your assessment of Chance? Is he okay to be by himself?"

Emily pulled out a chair and sat across from her sister. "I think so. He and his dad weren't close, and I think he's probably got unresolved issues that will catch up with him eventually. But right now, it's his mother's death that's hurting him most. They were close."

Vanessa was quiet for a moment, twisting a lock of hair, seemingly lost in thought. "Emily, you do know that you're not responsible for this guy, right? You've known him all of three weeks."

"But he's my friend. I feel somewhat responsible to be there for him during this crisis."

"I can tell you like him."

"I do." Emily took a bite of cookie. "He's geeky and gorgeous at the same time. I told you he's a med student at Harvard, didn't I—full scholarship?"

"Yes, you told me. Impressive. And he's certainly good looking."

Emily laughed. "Do you think? He's a marathon runner too. If he wasn't so geeky, the gals would flock around him. Actually he's awkward around most women."

"But not around you?"

"No. We speak the same language. I have a lot of geek in me too. That's probably why we hit it off."

"I have a feeling your big blue eyes and long sandy curls had something to do with it."

"I wish I had dark hair like yours. And your drop-dead figure."

Vanessa reached across the table and took Emily's hand. "You're beautiful, just the way you are—inside and out. Don't ever think you have to *settle* for anyone."

"I'm not settling. I like Chance. I just don't know if he'd be as interested in me if other gals were falling all over him."

"I have a feeling he would. You're a real catch, kiddo. And for a guy like that to find a woman who's an intellectual equal is a major plus."

"I don't know that we're intellectual *equals,* but I can hold my own." Emily sighed. "Any hope we had of building a romantic relationship probably went out the window with this tragedy. I just need to be a friend. Chance will spend the rest of the summer grieving and dealing with legal matters. I just hope he can get his head clear enough to keep up his grades so he doesn't lose his scholarship."

"I hope so too. I'm glad he has you to help. But remember, you have another obligation."

Emily nodded. "I want to wait tables at Zoe B's every chance I get. I need the money. I just hope this cyanide scare doesn't wreck the tourist trade. You and Ethan took a big hit two summers ago when that nutcase was on the loose. It's not fair that you should have to go through it again."

CHAPTER 8

Zoe changed Grace and Tucker from church clothes into play clothes and then left both children in Maddie's care and went downstairs to the dining room at Zoe B's. She stopped abruptly in the doorway, shocked to see every table filled and people in the waiting area.

Savannah hurried over to her. "I don't know what's going on, but we need another waitress to keep up with this crowd. It's busier than a normal Sunday, even without the Sunday brunch! One customer said something about Sheriff Prejean giving us the green light. Do you have any idea what he's talking about?"

Zoe moved her gaze across the bustling dining room. "Pierce said Jude was on the eleven o'clock news and mentioned that he and Colette ate here last night. I missed it."

"Any chance you could get another waitress to come in?" Savannah's blue eyes were pleading. "Nanette and I are running our socks off. I thought we'd be twiddling our thumbs."

"I'll call Emily. She said she would come in anytime we needed her. Do you think she's ready to handle *this* kind of busy?"

"Yes, she's great," Savannah said. "It's obvious she's waited tables before."

Zoe walked out to the kitchen and spotted Pierce at the worktable, his chef's hat tall and proud, his smile as wide as the Mississippi.

"Can you believe this?" he said. "It has to be because of Jude's plug on the news last night. Can you get the girls some help waiting tables?"

"I'm on it." Zoe hit the speed dial for Vanessa's cell phone.

"How'd you do at church by yourself?" Pierce said.

"Fine. Grace colored pictures, and Tucker fell asleep."

The phone rang three times, and then Vanessa came on the line. "Hey, Zoe. What's up?"

"My dining room is overflowing with customers, and I need Emily ASAP. I could go down the hall to the office and look up her cell number, but I thought I'd check with you first to see if she's back from church."

"She and Carter went to early church. I think they're playing a video game. Hang on …"

Zoe turned and looked through the window in the kitchen door to the dining room. She saw families dressed in touristy T-shirts. That was a great sign.

"Hello, Zoe? It's Emily. Vanessa said you need me to come in."

"Could you come—like *now*?" Zoe noted all the customers reading menus. "I don't think this crowd is going to clear out for a while."

"Sure. I can be there in fifteen minutes."

"Thanks. You're a doll."

Zoe caught Savannah just as she was coming into the kitchen. "Emily will be here in about fifteen minutes. Meanwhile, I'll take care of seating people. Let me know if you need me to help take orders. Isn't this an exciting twist?"

Savannah laughed. "If it doesn't kill us."

Kill us. An image of the food bar at Marcotte's Market popped into Zoe's mind, and she dismissed it. They couldn't just retreat in fear and let some crazy person or group hold the town hostage. She and Pierce would be diligent to make sure no strangers wandered into their kitchen. But they weren't closing their doors unless they were forced to.

Jude set a cup of coffee on the conference table in his office and then sat at the head of the table and thumbed through the file on the cyanide poisonings. He heard a knock and looked up as Aimee walked in, her uniform pressed, her makeup flawless, and her bleach-blonde hair neatly coiffed.

"Mayor Theroux, Chief Norman, and Dr. Jensen from DHH just arrived," Aimee said. "I've got us set up in interview room one—anytime you're ready."

"I'm ready. I was just about to review the file again, but I could recite it in my sleep."

Jude got up and followed Aimee across the detective bureau and out into the far hallway. He caught up with her and stopped at the first interview room, holding the door and making eye contact with the mayor.

"Good morning, Sheriff." Mayor Oliver Theroux nodded from the oblong table, where he sat between Chief Norman and Dr. Jensen. "You look rested."

Jude smiled politely. Was the mayor being sarcastic? "Looks are deceiving, sir. I rarely get a good night's sleep when I'm up to my ears in a case that isn't moving fast enough to suit me."

Jude came into the room and shook hands with each of the men and then sat at the table next to Aimee, facing them.

"Thanks for giving up part of your Sunday," Jude said. "I promised this meeting would be quick and to the point. So here it is: we have six dead. Ten hospitalized but expected to recover. No suspects yet. Marcotte's Market has been closed. Chief Norman's people and mine are working around the clock to contain this threat and stop whoever's behind it.

"I wanted to bring some new information to your attention. The lab has now confirmed that the chocolate pudding on the food bar at Marcotte's was the only food item poisoned with cyanide. And the poisoned bottles of Gaudry water that claimed five of the six victims were contaminated through a tiny hole made in the bottom of the plastic bottle, where we believe the cyanide was injected, and then the hole patched with a clear, hard adhesive.

"Gaudry bottled water has been removed from the grocery shelves in Les Barbes, and state officials are working to determine which bottles have been tampered with and/or contaminated. There's now a statewide recall on bottles with the same bottling plant code and expiration date as the contaminated bottles." Jude glanced over at Dr. Jensen, who nodded in affirmation.

"What about fingerprints?" Oliver said.

Jude folded his hands on the table. "We were able to identify a few fingerprints on the bottled water but found none that shouldn't be there. We're looking closely at every employee of Marcotte's—and especially the delivery boy, Adam Marcotte, who is the great-nephew of the owner."

"Adam?" Oliver said. "I've known him all his life. My son Stephen is on the swim team with him. There's no way he's involved in this."

Jude pursed his lips. "You're probably right. But Friday afternoon he delivered groceries to three residences, resulting in the five bottled-water fatalities. We can't afford to pass him over just because of his family ties."

"But didn't he take the bottled water off the shelf when he filled the grocery order for those folks?" Ollie said.

"That's what Adam told us, and that's the normal procedure." Jude bounced a pencil eraser on the table. "Judging from the computer records, this water came in Thursday afternoon, was checked in shortly after midnight, and was set out after three p.m. on Friday. We're talking to everyone who would've handled it, starting with the transport driver and his crew and every person who works in the stockroom or has access to it.

"In addition," Jude said, "we've thoroughly reviewed Saturday's security tapes of the food bar at Marcotte's. From 10:33 until 10:56 a.m., three female employees in uniform—all have been confirmed by the manager—were busy setting up the food bar, which opens at 11:00. They finished the job at 10:56 and went back into the kitchen. Sixty-three seconds later, a male, dressed in what appears to be denim shorts and a white collared shirt, walked up to the end of the food bar, his back to the camera. We couldn't tell what he was doing, but twenty-three seconds later, he picked up a big spoon and stirred what we now know is the chocolate pudding that was poisoned. The suspect walked away a few seconds later, his back still to the camera. We enhanced the image of the man from behind, but truthfully, it shows little detail. The man appears to be either

Hispanic or Caucasian, dark hair, medium height and build. Pretty generic."

Oliver sighed. "That's it?"

Jude nodded. "So far. We've questioned the three female workers at Marcotte's food bar. None of them remembers seeing the man in the tape. They seem devastated, especially the older lady who set the pudding out. We can't yet eliminate them as persons of interest, but my gut tells me they weren't involved." Jude looked over at the official from DHH. "Dr. Jensen, would you give us your thoughts?"

The sixtysomething man with gray hair and a beard coughed and then tented his fingers. "Since no cyanide was found in any of the other food-bar selections—or in the covered tub of chocolate pudding in Marcotte's kitchen—we can conclude that cyanide was added either just before or right after the pudding was set out. From what I observed on the security tape, it's very plausible that this man dumped a vial of cyanide into the pudding and stirred it in. Law enforcement searched the trash receptacles inside the store, including the restrooms, and outside the store—but found no empty vial. He could have concealed it as he left the market.

"Another interesting fact—" Dr. Jensen continued, "the bottled water taken into evidence contained ten times the lethal dose of potassium cyanide for an adult male, while the pudding had only about one half the lethal dose. We can only speculate about why the perp did that. Perhaps he decided after he poisoned the water to add the last of the cyanide to the pudding, and there just wasn't enough to do a lot of harm. But I will say that unless he knew the exact size of the stainless steel tubs used on the food bar, he would be guessing how much cyanide to add to make a portion of pudding lethal. Not so with the cyanide injected into the bottled water, since he knew each contained sixteen fluid ounces. He could easily determine what would be a lethal dose after drinking just a few ounces. My opinion is that these were random acts of malice intended to harm or kill as many people as possible—and not directed at a specific victim or victims. But I'll leave that judgment to law enforcement."

Jude nodded. "I'm inclined to agree, but I've got a lot more investigating to do before I come to that conclusion."

"Same here," Chief Norman said. "We need to question every male who handled the bottled water from the warehouse to the stockroom, and every employee who had access to the kitchen. Since we can't identify the man in the security tapes, he could be an employee."

Sax strolled through the flower garden at Langley Manor, his hands in his pockets, and then walked up on the wood bridge that spanned the pond and relaxed for a moment in the shade of a live oak that was probably older than he was.

He leaned on the railing, looking out across the sprawling green lawns dotted with dogwoods, magnolias, and weeping willows, to the manor house standing as tall and elegant as it had been since before the Civil War. It was tranquil out here—serene and natural. So why couldn't he just relax and enjoy it and think positive thoughts? He was already preparing himself for the possibility that Adele Woodmore wouldn't agree to contact Shelby. He had sensed the woman's disgust that he had abandoned his little sister when she needed him most.

What if Mrs. Woodmore simply said *no*? It wasn't as though he could force her to divulge Shelby's whereabouts.

Maybe it was for the best. The closer he got to the potential reunion, the more afraid he was of Shelby's rejection. As determined as he was to earn her trust and forgiveness, he wasn't sure he had the fortitude to push beyond her defenses if she had no interest in building a relationship.

Coward. He had run once. Was he about to do it again? Was he still that spineless teenager at heart? Had guilt taught him nothing?

He sighed. Why did he do this to himself? He had read enough about dysfunctional families to know that his self-recrimination was a black hole. So why did he fall back into it over and over again?

Seven white ibis landed next to the pond and began foraging through the grass for insects and grasshoppers or whatever else suited their fancy. They seemed focused on feeding and oblivious to his presence, which was fine with him. He felt "tucked away" here. Invisible. With space to think, without the distractions of everyday life.

Not that he minded playing gigs seven days a week for months on end. When he had too much time on his hands, his depression got unbearable. But his search for Shelby had come to a head, and it was the only thing that had kept him going for the past three years. If it ended badly, what else was there? He was either going to confront Shelby and work things out—or put an end to all of it.

What purpose did he have for existing? He hadn't made anyone happy. Certainly his ex-wives thought he was a loser.

His playing with the Smooth Blues had been a contribution of sorts. Music helped make others happy. But if he were dead, the band would just replace him. There were plenty of saxophone players out there who could step into his shoes—younger guys with more talent and energy and a more positive outlook. The other musicians tolerated his mood swings, but none understood the desolation he lived with day in and day out. He almost envied the cyanide victims. At least death came quickly for them. He was dying one breath at a time.

CHAPTER 9

Emily came in the service door at Zoe B's, timed in, then hurried out to the dining room, concerned that she hadn't heard from Chance.

Zoe held her hand up and rushed over to her.

"Thanks for dropping everything and coming in." Zoe sounded out of breath. "Can you believe this crowd? I wonder if other restaurants are busy like this or if Jude only convinced them that Zoe B's was safe."

Emily smiled. "I hope they're all this busy. And I hope Vanessa and Ethan don't keep getting cancellations. They really took a hit the last time a killer was on the loose."

"Don't remind me." Zoe swatted at a pesky fly that buzzed around her face. "Let's hope this is short-lived and Jude gets to the bottom of it quickly."

"Maybe he already knows who did it," Emily said. "I doubt he would volunteer anything to the media until they made an arrest. I know my mother wouldn't."

"Oh that's right." Zoe arched her eyebrows. "You and Vanessa grew up around it, so I guess you're pretty familiar with how the authorities do things."

"Kind of. Each case is different, and cops try to use the media to their advantage. They leak information they want the public to know and withhold information the public doesn't need to know."

"So you're saying Jude may have a suspect and not release that information?"

Emily nodded. "Sure. He'll tell the media if and when he thinks it's in the public's best interest to know. But he's not going to jeopardize the investigation. Timing is important."

"Vanessa told me you've seen a lot in your young life."

"When I was nine, a gang member held a neighbor couple and me at gunpoint, hoping he could cut a deal. I really thought he was going to kill us." Emily blinked away the memory. "And my mom was stalked by a man she put in prison. He tried to grab Vanessa, but she got away. The guy almost killed my mom." Emily rubbed her arms. "It still gives me chills."

"Vanessa, too."

"At least we knew who the enemy was. This is almost scarier."

"I hear you," Zoe said. "This killer could be one person or an organized group of people who want to kill as many of us as they can to draw attention to their cause. I'm just so sorry Chance's parents had to be among the victims. How's he doing?"

Emily wrinkled her nose. "Not good. I was with him when the doctor told him his parents were dead. At first he was stunned, but reality started to sink in as the day went on. I stayed with him until he finally crashed last night, but he thinks I'm coming over this morning. If it's okay with you, I'd like to call him as soon as the dining room clears out, and let him know my schedule has changed."

"I'll cover for you," Zoe said. "Go ahead and call him."

"Really?" Emily hated that she sounded so eager. "Thanks. I won't stay on long. I just want to find out what his plans are and how I can help."

Emily hurried out into the alcove and pushed her speed dial for Chance's cell phone.

He picked up on the second ring. "Hey."

"Hey, yourself," Emily said. "Why didn't you respond to my voice or text messages? I was worried."

"Sorry. You said you got called in to work, and I didn't figure you'd be checking your messages. Why'd you get called in? I thought business was slow."

"The sheriff mentioned Zoe B's on the news last night, and this place has been packed out since it opened. You wouldn't believe it."

"When do you get off?" Chance said.

"The second shift comes in at three. I can be available after that. Would you like me to make more phone calls?"

"Thanks, but I made them already," Chance said. "Both sides of my family are equally devastated by this, and several relatives offered to stay with me. I graciously explained I need to be alone, but my aunt Reba won't take no for an answer."

"Maybe you should let her stay there. You have plenty of room."

"It won't be enough. She treats me like I'm still in grade school." Chance sighed. "Seriously, Emily, you're the only person I want to be around right now."

"I want to be there for you as much as I can. But I also have an obligation at Zoe B's." Emily glanced at her watch. "I should be to your house by three fifteen. Will you be okay until then?"

"I'm fine. I'm just staring at the wall, getting up the nerve to go into my parents' bedroom. The mortician asked me to pick out clothes ..." Chance's voice failed.

"Let me help you with that. Just wait for me, okay?"

"All right."

"Did your dad have a dark suit?"

"Yes. He had a nice one he wore to weddings and funerals. Pretty ironic he'll be wearing it to his own."

"Your mother had dresses?"

"A closet full," Chance said. "Maybe you can help me figure out what's appropriate. I always loved her in light blue." There was a long moment of dead air. Finally Chance said, "I don't know what's wrong with me. I just want to go somewhere and scream. I'm so angry that someone stole her from me."

"There's nothing wrong with you. It's totally understandable that you're angry. Who wouldn't be? There's no right or wrong way to feel. It's better to be honest."

Chance sighed into the receiver. "The honest truth is, having my aunt staying here will make things unbearable. Especially since the funeral isn't until Wednesday afternoon."

"When is she planning to come?"

"Tomorrow. She's driving down from Shreveport."

Emily switched the phone to her other ear. "Can you be honest with her about that? Just tell her you handle grief better with some down time to be alone with your thoughts?"

"I tried. It went over her head. I wouldn't hurt her feelings for the world, but I don't have the strength to confront her on this. I feel like I'm going to lose it any second—" Chance seemed to choke on his words.

Emily took a moment and assessed the situation. "Chance, would it take the pressure off if *I* called your aunt? Be honest with me. Maybe I'm being too bold here. But I really think I can get the point across without hurting her feelings."

"You would do that?"

"Sure. If you think it would help."

"It would. Thanks. I just can't deal with anything else."

Emily glanced into the dining room and saw Zoe taking someone's order. "Chance, I'm really sorry, but I really have to go. Zoe's in there taking orders."

"Go. I'll see you when I see you."

"Just wait on the difficult things and let me help you. Promise?"

"I promise."

Sax opened the front door at Langley Manor and went inside, instantly spotting Vanessa watering the plants in the parlor, her long dark hair enhanced by the pale yellow walls.

"There you are." She looked over at him with eyes the color of the summer sky and long, thick lashes perfect enough for a Cover Girl ad. What a knockout. She reminded him of his first wife. For a split second he remembered what it had felt like to be in love.

"Have you been looking for me?" Sax asked.

"I have. I told a couple from Iowa that I would take them on a tour this afternoon and thought maybe you'd like to join us. I'm going to take them through the tunnels used by the slaves when the manor house was a station on the Underground Railroad. Interested?"

"It's nice of you to offer," Sax said, "but I'm really enjoying the opportunity to be alone with my thoughts. Nothing personal."

"But you're enjoying your stay?"

"Well, let's see … I love the room, the chocolate chip cookies, the breakfast, the grounds, the flower garden, and the solitude. So yes, I'm enjoying it very much."

Vanessa smiled with her eyes. "Good. That's what counts."

"Have there been any more cyanide poisonings?" he said.

"No, thank the Lord. But no one has been arrested, and that's almost more unsettling. We're all just waiting for the other shoe to drop."

"I don't think we have anything to fear out here," Sax said.

"Me either. But two people I know have already lost someone they care about. It's scary. I'm trying not to dwell on it." Vanessa moved over to another plant and began watering it. "If you change your mind and want to go on the tour with us, we'll be meeting here in the parlor at two o'clock."

Sax felt the corners of his mouth twitch, despite his mood. Vanessa Langley was a charming young woman. "Fair enough. I'm going to go read for a while, and maybe take a nap. I'm expecting a phone call."

Sax climbed the stately white staircase, the melded smells of old wood, warm bread, and eucalyptus wafting under his nose. He walked down the hall to room four, unlocked the door, and pushed it open wide, glad to see his bed made up and fresh towels on the rack in the bathroom. At least the maid wouldn't interrupt him.

He saw a fresh plate of chocolate chip cookies on the secretary. That should tide him over so he wouldn't need lunch.

Dinner was another matter. Adele had suggested Zoe B's Cajun Eatery and gave him Zoe and Pierce Broussard's business card. It was probably safe to eat there—not that he was worried about dying of cyanide poisoning. At this point, it would be an easy out.

He went over to the window and looked down at the undulating green sea of sugarcane separating the Langley property from the adjacent plantation. He wondered who else might have stood at that same window a hundred and fifty years before and seen essentially the same thing. How had Langley Manor survived the Civil War? According to the brochure, it wasn't even damaged.

Sax sighed. Why was he spending what little energy he had, asking himself questions that no one had answers to? He went over and lay on the bed, his hands clasped behind his head. Adele Woodmore was taking her sweet time getting back to him. He had already psyched himself up for a disappointing next encounter—but the waiting was torture.

Emily parked in the alley behind Chance Durand's house, relieved not to see any media—or yellow crime-scene tape. The authorities must have finished their on-site investigation.

She went up on the back stoop and stood at the kitchen door, aware that she was about to walk into the room where Chance's parents had died. She paused for a moment, and, before she could knock, the back door opened. Chance stood in the doorway, dressed in denim cutoffs and a red T-shirt. He hadn't shaved, but the rugged look was becoming.

He took her hand and pulled her inside, then put his arms around her and held tightly for a moment.

"I'm glad you're here," he said. "I feel so detached from everything. I've never felt like this before."

"I felt that way when my grandparents were killed in a head-on collision." Emily nuzzled closer. "Grief makes you feel a gamut of emotions. Sometimes talking about it helps. Sometimes it doesn't. I'm here either way."

"Thanks. That means a lot."

Emily stepped away from his arms and put her purse on the kitchen table. "Since your aunt's planning to drive here tomorrow, I should call her so she can make arrangements to stay somewhere else. What's her name?"

"Reba Littleton."

"Would staying in a motor inn or B and B pose a financial burden?"

"She's loaded, Emily. Money's not the issue. She just likes to feel in control."

Chance opened an address book to the page with Reba's information and handed it to Emily.

"Are you sure it's such a bad idea for your aunt Reba to take charge? You're not thinking as clearly as you'd like. It might be helpful."

"Not unless she could take charge without treating me like I'm ten. But she can't. Trust me, having her stay here would be downright oppressive."

"Okay. Okay." Emily gently squeezed his hand. "I'll run interference. I'd rather she be mad at me than you." Emily sat at the table and keyed in Reba's phone number, her heart pounding, and put it on speaker.

"Hello." The woman's tone was curt. "Whatever you're selling, I'm not interested."

"I'm not selling anything, ma'am. I'm trying to reach Reba Littleton."

"Speaking."

"Ms. Littleton, my name's Emily Jessup. I'm a close friend of your nephew Chance. Let me say how sorry I am about your sister and brother-in-law. It was a terrible tragedy. I understand you plan to drive to Les Barbes tomorrow and stay at Chance's house."

"My *sister's* house. That's right."

"I'm sure you have Chance's best interests at heart, but the truth is he really prefers to be at the house by himself, where he can let his feelings out and deal with his tragic loss. I'm sure you can understand that."

"I understand no such thing. That boy doesn't know what he needs right now."

"He's quite sure that he prefers solitude."

"My sister would want me there."

"It's really Chance's decision, though, isn't it?"

"That boy's in no condition to decide anything."

Emily glanced over at Chance. "With all due respect, ma'am, he's a twenty-three-year-old genius who has worked his way to Harvard Medical School on a full scholarship and is studying to be a neurosurgeon. He's never been confused about what he wants."

"Well, I never ..." Reba Littleton exhaled into the phone. "If

Chance didn't want me to come and stay, why didn't he just tell me himself?"

"He tried, ma'am. But when you insisted, he didn't have the heart to hurt your feelings. He appreciates how nurturing you are and how natural it is for you to jump in with both feet. But he's been hit with a brutal blow, and he'll do better with some down time to think without anyone else around."

"Well, I'm glad you know the breadth and depth of my nephew's thoughts and feelings. So what about you, missy—are *you* around?"

Emily felt the heat flood her cheeks. "I check in on him when I'm not working. I assure you he's coping as well as can be expected. But he would never have made this phone call and risked hurting your feelings. I probably overstepped, but I thought you should know that he really needs space right now."

"You made your point, Evelyn."

"Emily."

"Tell Chance I will make arrangements to stay elsewhere. But he's going to need help when people start bringing food to the house—assuming they even bother, what with the cyanide scare and all."

"I'm sure he'll welcome your help with that, ma'am. The women at Saint Catherine's will be coordinating the effort. Thanks for understanding his need for privacy."

"I never said I understood. I'll respect his wishes. I suppose I do still think of him as a boy. He's certainly earned the right to be treated as an adult."

"Would you like me to make a reservation for you," Emily said, "at one of the nicer motor inns or a bed-and-breakfast?"

"I'm quite capable of doing it myself, thank you. Good day."

Emily heard the phone go dead and disconnected the call. "I'm not sure that conversation could have gone any better, considering your aunt's feelings were probably hurt."

"Sorry," Chance said. "I doubt she'll warm up to you after this."

"Don't worry. I'll live with it. Do you feel better now?"

"Definitely."

"Now that you don't have to worry about Aunt Reba, what else can I help you with?"

"I need help picking out clothes for the mortician. And also writing the obituaries for the newspaper. They want it before five. We can email it."

Emily glanced at a photo on the refrigerator—Chance was standing arm in arm with his parents in front of the Eiffel Tower. She imagined his mom and dad lying on the kitchen floor, gasping for air, and his poor mother making that desperate 911 call before she died of cyanide poisoning. The only blessing in this nightmare was that Chance's parents died quickly—and he wasn't there to see it.

"Sure," Emily said. "Let's read some of the obits in the newspaper and see what wording was used. We can use that as a model and write something nice. Once that's done, we'll get the clothes laid out. It'll be a load off your mind to have it done."

"I'm so glad you're here." Chance opened the refrigerator. "You want something to drink? I've got Sprite, Diet Coke, Dr. Pepper. And there're a couple bottles of water I found in the pantry—don't worry, it's *not* Gaudry."

"Thanks"—Emily held up her palm—"but for now I'm drinking tap water."

CHAPTER 10

Jude watched the activity in the detective bureau and wondered when he had ever seen it busier. He walked into his office, a cup of coffee in his hand, and sat at his desk. He glanced out the window to where the media had camped out on the sidewalk outside the courthouse. A knock broke his concentration, and he looked up.

Aimee stood in the doorway, a folder in her hand. "Got a minute?"

"Sure. Come in. Make yourself comfortable."

Aimee sat in the vinyl chair next to his desk. She opened the folder and handed him a chart. "This is the lab analysis of the Gaudry water pulled from the shelves in Les Barbes. Only ten bottles contained cyanide—all from Marcotte's Market—and that includes the eight bottles delivered to three households via Adam Marcotte."

"That's good news," Jude said. "Do we have any idea how much Gaudry water was out there in the first place?"

"Sixty thousand cases of water with the June sixth date on them were shipped from Gaudry's Lafayette plant; approximately two thousand of those cases went to outlets in Les Barbes. Each case had twenty-four bottles."

"So we're talking somewhere around ... forty-eight thousand bottles?"

Aimee nodded. "That's right, and the lab's recovered and tested about forty thousand, which leaves approximately eight thousand bottles that might have already been consumed and were perfectly safe, or—"

"They're still out there," Jude said. "I know it's been pulled from the shelves and recalled. But it's imperative that we keep reminding the public that, if they possess Gaudry water, not to open it, but to turn it in to us for analysis. The bottles in question could have been stashed in backpacks, coolers, cars. Tourists could have bought it and taken it with them. It's really critical that we make sure the media gets the word out."

Aimee mused, "Don't you think it's odd that in all that water, there have been so few poisoned bottles and only six deaths?"

"Well, the jury's still out on that," Jude said, "since the remaining bottles are unaccounted for. There could be victims that haven't even been found yet."

"But this guy could have taken out a lot more victims on the food bar," Aimee said. "Why do you suppose he didn't?"

"You heard Dr. Jensen's opinion that he was guessing at the size of the container and didn't know how to measure a lethal dose—or just didn't have enough cyanide left. Why? What are you thinking?"

Aimee shrugged. "Just that it's odd he was so precise in the amount of cyanide injected into the bottles. But not the food bar, where he could've taken out a lot more people. Do you think he's happy with only six dead?"

"We have to assume he isn't." Jude tapped his fingers on the desk. "If he's determined to kill people with cyanide, the only way to stop him is to catch him. Until he's behind bars, no one is safe."

Emily hit the send key on Chance's laptop, sending the combined obituary for Huet and Lydia Durand. "I hope you're happy with it."

"It's fine." Chance's voice was flat, and she noticed tears had welled up in his eyes again.

"Why don't we pick out the clothes later?" Emily said. "This is pretty overwhelming."

"That's why I'd just as soon get it all over with."

Emily glanced at the almost-perfect yellow roses outside the window. It didn't seem right that nature should be so glorious when Chance's world was so dark.

"All right." Emily pushed away from the computer desk and stood. "Let's get it behind you."

She followed him down a hallway to what was obviously the master suite. A king-size bed with an ornate cherry and wrought-iron headboard was centered on the far wall, a family oil portrait hung above it. The three Durands were sitting in the grass, barefoot, a flower garden of some kind in the background. Chance looked like he might have been about four—adorable, but this didn't seem like the right time to say so. Saturday's newspaper was neatly folded on one nightstand, a CPAP machine and mask set on the other.

"One of your parents had sleep apnea," Emily said.

"Yes, Mom did a sleep study recently and was diagnosed. She didn't like wearing the mask, but she was finally sleeping better. I know Dad was." A smile tugged at the corners of his mouth. "I never understood how anyone so delicate and so feminine could snore like a lumberjack. It was something we joked about—with just the three of us. I mean, when we traveled and shared a room, Mom's snoring rocked the walls." He swallowed hard and stared at his hands. "I can't believe she's gone, Emily. This should never have happened."

"I know. The sheriff will find whoever's responsible. Justice will be served."

"So what? She's not coming back! Even if they give the creep the death penalty, it won't make up for what he took from me."

Emily cleared her throat, mentally groping for something profound to say—and drawing a blank. "No. Nothing will ever make up for the loss of your parents."

"Why don't I feel sad about my dad?" Chance looked up at the family portrait. "I should, but I don't. All I can think about is Mom."

"You weren't close to your dad."

"He and I tangled a lot. But he's still my dad."

Emily played with the bottom button on her blouse. "Chance, you told the sheriff's deputies that everyone loved your mom and dad. Was your dad really that well liked? From what you told me, he sounded like a bully."

"He always put on his best face for other people. And he was good to my mom. He just rode me pretty hard, and I never really knew why. It never seemed to make any difference when I succeeded at something. He would always point out where I needed to improve."

"Too bad he didn't realize you needed his approval. Maybe he thought pushing you was the way to make a man out of you."

"Yeah, I suppose. But Mom ..." Chance's voice cracked, and he paused to gather his composure. "She always believed in me. She told me I was smart and encouraged me—even before I got glasses, when I had failing grades. I loved her *so* much. I feel like my heart's been ripped out ..."

Emily fought not to get emotional. Not here. Not now. How could she stay objective and focused if she let herself feel the full weight of what had happened? "Is that their walk-in closet?" she said.

Chance nodded and opened the door wide, the light coming on automatically. "Mom's stuff is on the left. Dad's is on the right."

Emily went inside, stood at the far left of the rack that belonged to Lydia Durand, and moved the hangers to the left as she worked her way down the rack of dresses. She pulled out a light blue silk dress with fluttery cap sleeves and ruffles on the bodice. The iridescent oyster shell buttons reminded Emily of shells she'd collected on the beach in New Orleans.

"This is really feminine and dressy," Emily said. "What do you think?"

Chance seemed lost in thought for a moment. Finally he nodded. "I loved that on her."

Emily handed him the dress and turned around to the other rack, where she spotted a charcoal-gray suit hanging next to several light-colored suits. She stepped over to it and felt the fabric. "This is perfect. Do you have a shirt and tie in mind?"

"A white dress shirt. You pick the tie."

Emily looked through the ties and chose a red, navy, and gray silk tie that looked great.

"You pick out shoes and socks for your dad," Emily said. "And

I'll pick out shoes and hose for your mother. And some jewelry. We'll be done."

Emily got what she needed and followed Chance out to the dining room table.

"That was easier than I thought it would be," Chance said. "Thanks for being here. I'm not sure I could've done it by myself without losing it."

"You're welcome. But you do know that losing it is okay, don't you?" Emily faced him and held his gaze. "It's good to cry. Or scream. Or whatever else you have to do to let go of the pain. Everyone's different. No one else can tell you how to grieve. Just don't hold it in. It'll take a physical toll. And I know your mother would want you healthy and ready to start classes again at the end of August."

Chance actually smiled. "Yeah. She would. I think she knew I was going to be a surgeon way back when I aspired to be an ice cream man."

"An ice cream man?"

"Absolutely. I thought driving that little truck that played music and eating ice cream all day was about as good as it gets."

Emily laughed. "Listen, mister, I wouldn't rule it out."

She relished this lighthearted moment, knowing these would be few, and that the darkness had not even begun to settle in.

Sax followed a cute gal with chestnut hair and intriguing blue-gray eyes to a table across from the window at Zoe B's.

She smiled and handed him a menu. "Your waitress will be right with you. The specials are clipped inside. Is this your first time here?"

"Actually it is," Sax said. "Adele Woodmore suggested I try eating here. She knows the owner and felt comfortable recommending Zoe B's, even with the cyanide scare."

"How do you know Adele?" The woman arched her eyebrows.

"I don't really *know* her," Sax said. "But she seemed pretty sure I would like the food here. I'm here on business. I live in New Orleans."

"I'm a bit partial, since I own the place, but if you like authentic Cajun food, you'll like ours. My husband is the head chef, and his gumbo has won the Copper Ladle award three years running."

"Then you must be Zoe Broussard?" Sax took the business card out of his pocket and held it up. "Mrs. Woodmore gave me your card."

Zoe smiled. "I'm not surprised. Adele's our biggest fan. I assure you we will do everything we can to live up to her recommendation."

"By the way, I'm Sax Henry." He held out his hand, and she shook it, a familiar quizzical look on her face. "Sax is a nickname. I play the saxophone with a jazz band called the Smooth Blues."

"Then it fits perfectly," Zoe said. "I admire people who are musically inclined. I don't have that talent but love listening to it. I'd better let you read the menu. Also, each of the oil paintings you see on the walls was done by a local artist and is for sale."

"Thanks. I'll keep that in mind."

Zoe walked away, and Sax moved his gaze around Zoe B's. What a quaint place—hanging plants, wood-plank flooring, one brick wall to complement the dark gold painted walls and blue-and-gold tablecloths. French country furnishings. Some of the accessories looked as if they might be antiques. Were those genuine D'Arceau Limoges collector plates on the corner cupboard? His second wife had loved them and had the credit card receipts to prove it. At least she'd found a way to fill the emptiness of their failed marriage.

He decided not to let his mind go there. Why wallow in what he couldn't change? Sax opened the menu and saw the house special was crawfish étouffée. Always his favorite. He reviewed the list of what came with it and closed his menu just as a twentysomething woman, her hair pulled back in a ponytail, appeared at the table.

"My name's Savannah. I'll be serving you this evening. What can I get you to drink?"

"Iced tea. I'm ready to order."

Savannah held up her pad and pencil. "What did you decide on?"

"I'll have the crawfish étouffée, extra spicy. Cobb salad, house dressing on the side. Cornbread. And a cup of seafood gumbo."

"Would you like your salad and gumbo at the same time?" Savannah took his menu.

"Sure. That's fine."

"Thank you, sir. I'll be back shortly."

Sax looked around the room, never quite sure what to do with his hands when he was waiting for an order. The three older gentlemen at the table by the window lowered their voices, which piqued his curiosity. He played with the saltshaker and eavesdropped on their conversation.

"I'm telling you, dey aren't going to tell us everyting dey know," said an elderly man with unruly gray curls and a thick Cajun accent.

"Dis could be a terrorist attack. Why *would* dey tell us? People would panic fuh shore, and den we be in a real mess."

A bald man swatted the air. "Hebert, my friend, you're always lookin' at the negative side. That's not helpful. The authorities are gonna tell us what we need to know to stay safe."

"You so sure about dat, Tex?" Hebert leaned forward on his elbows. "Last I heard, dey don't have a clue who's doing dis. Dat means dey can't take terrorism off da table."

"Gentlemen," said a white-haired man in a black-and-white cleric shirt, "we have to trust someone. Right now, that's the authorities—and God."

"Father Sam's got a point," Tex said. "Have a little faith. And let's trust the authorities to fill us in as we go."

"Trust is not my strong suit." Hebert scratched the stubble on his chin. "Don't tink dere's much chance I'm going to change at ninety-nine years old."

"I don't see another choice, do you?" Tex arched his silver eyebrows. "The authorities have been forthcomin' about what we should do and not do. I trust Zoe and Pierce to patrol the kitchen. They're not lettin' anyone back there who shouldn't be there. The food's safe here. But I'm not drinkin' bottled water of any kind until they're sure this crisis is over."

"How you going to know when it's really over?" Hebert said.

Tex sighed. "You're a real downer, you know that?"

A blonde waitress arrived at their table with a big round tray and set it on a stand. "Here you go, guys."

Sax looked at the plates of food, his mouth watering. It looked delicious, and the presentation was beautiful.

Savannah's voice startled him. "Here you go. Iced tea—tea and ice cubes are made from tap water, so no need for concern. Gumbo. Cornbread. And a Cobb salad with house dressing on the side. Our chef's homemade hot sauce is there on the table. It's dynamite—no pun intended."

"Thanks. I'll give it a try." Sax smiled as the aroma of gumbo wafted under his nose.

As Savannah turned and walked away, Sax put the cloth napkin in his lap, his thoughts turning to his sister and the reason for his trip to Les Barbes. If Adele opted not to get involved, how much pressure was he willing to put on her? This was the end of the line. He couldn't go back to New Orleans feeling this lost. Either his life was going to get better—or he would find a way to end it.

CHAPTER 11

Emily walked slowly up the deck steps at Langley Manor, the full moon illuminating the ghostlike haze that hovered above the cane fields.

She stopped at the back door and enjoyed the sight for a moment. Despite the oppressive heat and humidity, there was something unique and amazing about the Louisiana bayou—and the history of the proud Cajuns who made this region famous.

She saw a silhouette in one of the rockers and sucked in a breath.

"I didn't mean to startle you," said a male voice. "I'm a guest. I couldn't sleep and decided to come out here for a while and wait to see what showed up to eat the Critter Crunch Vanessa left out."

Emily walked over to the railing and let her eyes focus on the man's face.

"I'm Sax Henry," he said, "from the Big Easy. I play saxophone with a jazz band called the Smooth Blues."

"I'm Emily—from Sophie Trace, Tennessee. I'll be a sophomore at LSU."

Sax smiled. "Geaux Tigers."

Emily laughed without meaning to. "So are you here on vacation?"

"Business mixed with a lot of down time."

"Vegging is good for the soul," Emily said.

"So they say. So what about you—do you work here?"

Emily shook her head. "My sister and brother-in-law own it. I'm here visiting for the summer until classes start. I wait tables at Zoe B's."

"No kidding. I had dinner there earlier tonight. Fantastic food."

"Pierce is a phenomenal chef," Emily said. "He's won awards. Did you meet Zoe, by any chance?"

"I did. Nice lady. Very cordial. I also amused myself by eavesdropping on three old fellas sitting at the table across the aisle. One of them—a guy named Hebert—seemed concerned that the facts of the cyanide scare are being withheld from the public."

"That would be Hebert Lanoux," Emily said. "He was Zoe's first customer when she opened the place fifteen years ago. The guy is going to be a hundred this year. He's like family to Zoe and Pierce. And pretty set in his ways."

"You think his concern is founded?"

Emily shrugged. "I doubt it. My mom's a police chief, and she never withheld any information the public *needed* to know. But sometimes it's better for us not to know everything. I think that's law enforcement's call."

"Aren't you scared?"

Emily was sobered by his question. "I suppose I should be. I've hardly had time to think about myself. My friend's parents were both cyanide victims. I've been trying to hold him together."

"I'm sorry, Emily. That must be difficult."

"It is. I'm just glad I can be there for him. It was nice meeting you, Mr. Henry."

"Call me Sax. Or I'm going to feel really, really old."

Emily smiled. "I'll try. Easier said than done when you've been raised in the South. I need to go inside. I told my sister I'd be home at eleven."

"Good night," Sax said. "Maybe I'll run into you at breakfast. I may be here a few days."

"Okay, good night." She put her key in the lock and opened the back door, neither surprised nor pleased to see Vanessa sitting at the kitchen table.

"You can't be worried," Emily said. "It's just now eleven. I'm right on time."

Vanessa took a sip of what appeared to be iced tea. "I wanted to talk to you. Why don't you grab a cookie and sit."

Emily opened the cookie jar and took out two chocolate chip cookies, poured herself a glass of milk, and sat at the table. "What's up?"

Vanessa seemed lost in thought. Finally she lifted her gaze and looked into Emily's eyes. "I know you care for Chance and want to help him. But you promised to take Carter miniature golfing. He was so disappointed."

Emily blew her bangs off her forehead. "I can't believe I forgot. Why didn't you call and remind me?"

"I don't know. Maybe I should have. I guess I wanted you to do it because you really wanted to spend time with him and not because you made a promise you were stuck with."

"I adore Carter," Emily said, feeling sick all over. "I never do things with him because I feel obligated. I just got caught up in helping Chance with the obits, picking out clothes to take to the mortician, and listening to him finally open up. Don't worry, I'll make it up to Carter."

Vanessa nodded. "I know you will. There's something else ..." Her eyebrows came together and stayed. "Listen, Shortcake. I'm your big sister, and I love you. So I'm just going to tell you straight out what's on my mind."

Shortcake? Emily thought. *Here comes the lecture.*

"You can't fall in love right now," Vanessa said. "You've got three more years at LSU, then MCATs, medical school, internship, and residency. Romance is a distraction you can't afford."

"I'm not falling in love. Can't I comfort a friend who's been through a tragedy without you making a federal case out of it?" Emily took a bite of cookie, more to look nonchalant as she endured the lecture than to actually taste it.

"Emily ..." Vanessa sighed. "Have you even stopped to consider that you and Chance are unequally yoked? From what you told me, he has no religious beliefs at all. You've walked with God since you were a little girl. Why knowingly encourage a relationship that will surely lead to conflict—and might even cause you to compromise your values?"

"That will *never* happen."

Vanessa shook her head and stared at her hands. "That's what I said. Trust me, Emily, it's much easier to get pulled into darkness than to stand firm in the light. It can happen slowly, even if you have the best of intentions."

Emily rolled her eyes. "I'm not you, and you aren't my mother."

Vanessa reached across the table and took Emily's wrist before she could take another bite of cookie. "But I've loved you since the day you were born, even if I was only ten. I've nurtured you. Calmed your fears. Listened to you. Even taken *your* advice a time or two. I can't let your relationship with Chance go any further without expressing caution. Whether you'll admit it or not, you know I'm right. If Mom and Dad were here, they'd say the same thing."

"I'm nineteen," Emily said. "I'm free to make my own choices, no matter where Mom and Dad are."

Vanessa nodded. "You are. But as long as you're here for the summer, under my and Ethan's roof, it's my responsibility to look out for you."

Emily clamped her eyes shut and counted to ten. "I'm not going to sleep with him, *okay*?"

"I never said you were."

"Isn't that what you're implying?"

"Emily"—Vanessa tightened her grip and looked intently into Emily's eyes—"I'm not implying anything. I'm just concerned that you're so intent on comforting Chance that your compassion could turn to passion before you realize what's happening. That's one of the reasons it's better if women counsel women and men counsel men."

"You sound like Ethan. Stop being a shrink."

"What I'm *being* is a responsible big sister. I made mistakes that I hope you never will."

"I won't."

Vanessa let go of her wrist. "I don't doubt your good intentions. But you're spending a great deal of time with Chance. At least consider what I'm saying and guard your heart. Make sure your choices in this relationship line up with Scripture."

"You're not telling me anything I don't know," Emily said.

"What you may *not* know is that the time to make the moral choice isn't in the heat of passion, but before it ever gets that far." Vanessa held up her palm. "I know it sounds like I'm lecturing you because of my mistakes with Ty."

"Do you think?" Emily sighed.

"Maybe I am," Vanessa said. "But I lived those consequences, and I can tell you it wasn't worth it."

"You have Carter. *And* Ethan."

Vanessa nodded. "Blessings I don't deserve. But I suffered plenty because I chose to be lured into bed by someone who had no regard for my God or my faith."

"Good grief, Vanessa. I've known Chance for three weeks. I'm not being lured anywhere, so don't project your mistakes onto me! Why don't you just admit you don't like him?"

"I didn't say that. I hardly know him. What I *do* know is that you and Chance have vastly different values. Just don't make the same mistakes I did." Vanessa's deep blue eyes seemed to look into Emily's soul. "I love you—almost like you were my own. I'll always be here for you, no matter what you choose. But as someone who knows the pain of having abandoned her values to gain a man's approval and affection, all I can say is *don't.* It will put a wedge between you and God—and when the conviction finally hits, the pain and regret is pretty overwhelming."

Emily popped a piece of cookie into her mouth. "I get it, Vanessa. I appreciate that you want to protect me. But you're worrying for nothing. I don't plan on sleeping with anyone until I get married. And just so you know, Chance is so depressed, it's unlikely our relationship will amount to anything more than my being a good friend."

Vanessa got up, walked over to Emily, and kissed her forehead. "I just needed to get that out. I'm going to bed now. I really do love you."

"I love you, too. But you don't need to worry about me. I can take care of myself." Emily crunched the second cookie and accidentally bit her tongue. Was it going to be like this all summer?

Sax overheard the argument between Vanessa and Emily. He envied the sibling closeness. No matter how indignant Emily was, on some level she had to be grateful for a sister who loved her that much, who wanted to protect her.

Guilt tightened his neck muscles, and he felt another headache coming on. No matter how hard he tried to reason that he was only seventeen when he left home, the ugly truth that he left his kid sister vulnerable to the abuse of their father gnawed through any defenses he put up. What justification could there be? He was a coward. He chose his own safety and comfort over Shelby's. He had to find her and tell her how sorry he was. If Adele chose not to get involved, he would just have to convince her. He had two weeks.

He looked up at the moon, which seemed to have scattered the stars in the summer sky and made him think of the two bronze urns in his closet at home. His parents' ashes needed to be scattered. Why couldn't he bring himself to do it? He told himself it was because Shelby had a right to help him decide where. But the truth was that he couldn't quite let go of his parents and didn't know why.

Sax closed his eyes and breathed in slowly and let it out. Was he supposed to feel something for these people who made his childhood a living hell—his father a mean drunk and his mother a spineless wimp? Did Shelby feel the same way about Sax because he had left her behind?

A raccoon climbed the deck steps and stopped, studying him.

"Don't look at me," he said. "I don't even like Critter Crunch."

A few seconds later, the raccoon scurried down the steps, where Sax spotted three little ones eating the food Vanessa had placed there. How cute!

He sat for a moment, relishing the quiet and the serenity found only in nature. The feeling would be fleeting. It always was. The voice of guilt would once again dispel any semblance of peace. Shelby was his last hope. If she wouldn't forgive him, there was no chance he could forgive himself.

CHAPTER 12

Sax floated somewhere between sleep and wakefulness, vaguely aware of a beeping noise that kept getting louder and louder. He reached over and groped the nightstand and pushed the off button on the clock radio.

He lay quietly for a moment, then opened his eyes. Where was he? He sat up in bed, a little disoriented, and then it all came back to him. Maybe this was the day that Adele Woodmore would decide to help him get in touch with Shelby. Or not.

He threw back the sheets, then sat on the side of the bed, his legs dangling. He glanced out the window at a young boy and yellow lab running through the sprinkler and was transported back to a summer day when he was ten and was chasing his sister with a garden hose....

Shelby darted all over the backyard, squealing at a pitch he was sure only six-year-old girls could reach.

He grabbed her by the arm and pulled her to a stop, his hand held tightly over her mouth. "Shhh! Daddy will hear you."

Shelby's innocent eyes were big and round, her sheer delight turned to dread. She didn't move. Or make a sound.

He waited half a minute, listening intently, then put his index finger to his lips and let her go. "You're lucky Daddy didn't hear you. You know how he is."

Shelby cupped her hands around her mouth and whispered in his ear, "Chase me again, Michael. I promise not to squeal."

A gruff voice bellowed through the screen door and filled the backyard, the words thick and slurred. "What's goin' on out there? I told you two if I heard a peep outta ya, I'd tan yer hides!"

The screen door flew open, and Frank Sieger, unshaven and wearing nothing but his boxer shorts, filled the doorway. He held a pint of whiskey in one hand, the other clenched in a tight fist.

"Both o' ya—in here—now!" Daddy's tone was loud and threatening.

Shelby clung tightly to Michael's arm. He could feel her trembling.

"Are ya deaf? I told ya to git in here. I ain't sayin' it again."

Michael felt Shelby's fingers dig into his arm and couldn't make his feet move until Daddy charged them, rattling off a whole string of obscenities.

Michael gave Shelby a push. "Run, Shelby. I'll meet you on the rock. Go!"

Shelby burst into tears and raced toward the back fence, Michael on her heels. She slipped through the gate just as their father overtook Michael, grabbing him around the throat and pulling him to a stop.

"Didn't I warn ya not to cross me, boy?" Daddy let out a low growl. "You brought this on yerself, ya worthless piece o' garbage! It's all yer fault."

Michael had trouble breathing as his father tightened his grip. He writhed in vain to free himself as Daddy delivered several hard blows to his face, calling Michael vile names, and then pushed him to the ground, kicking him over and over.

As Michael lay curled up on his side, begging his father to stop, he caught a glimpse of Mama standing at the kitchen window, closing the blinds....

The sound of footsteps in the hallway brought Sax back to the present, his heart pounding wildly, his skin clammy, his temples throbbing.

What a beating that was! And could the emergency room visit have been any more of a joke? Mama told the ER doctors that he had gotten beat up on his way home from baseball practice and didn't recognize the assailants, who were about his age. The police made a report and wrote down the phony description Michael gave them of the ringleader, and that was that. What else was a ten-year-old supposed to do? Daddy threatened to kill Mama if he ever told what really happened. Michael believed him. He never told anyone. Not then. Not even after Daddy broke his arm.

Sax wiped the perspiration off his upper lip, staring at the clock on the nightstand. He would never forget the rush of empowerment that coursed through him at the stroke of midnight on his seventeenth birthday, when he stood over his father as the man lay passed out on the floor. Sax spat on his dad—then stepped over him and walked away, suitcase and guitar in hand, and went on a road trip with his rock band.

He went back to Devon Springs after his rock band had completed their first road tour. He called his mother and met her privately at Miller's Deli. It was one of the most disappointing conversations of his life....

"Sorry it took me so long to git here," Mama said. "I walked over. I was hopin' the whole time you didn't just up and take off agin."

"I came back here for a reason, Mama. I want to get you and Shelby out of the house and into a shelter."

"I ain't goin' to no shelter."

"You'll be safe there."

"We been over this already, Michael. It ain't just about bein' safe. Frank needs me."

"All he needs is a fifth of Jack Daniels."

Mama glared at him. "A woman don't just walk away 'cause things ain't goin' the way she hoped. Frank's the way he is for reasons we ain't never gonna understand. I need to help him—not run off like a scared rabbit and leave him to his whiskey."

Michael threw his hands in the air. "You're not going to change him. Stay if you want. But it's wrong to leave Shelby there."

Mama pursed her lips and didn't say anything.

"Shelby's a kid. She has no choice. You need to get her out of the house. You're responsible to protect her."

"Ain't nobody can protect her!" Mama lowered her voice.

"She'll git out when she's of age. Ain't nothin' Frank can do 'bout it then—same as when you left."

Michael shook his head. "You want Shelby there to take the brunt of the abuse. You're using her to protect yourself!"

Mama stood. "I ain't puttin' up with yer lip just because yer all growed up. You don't know half o' what you think you do." Mama's eyes glistened. "It ain't easy for me, knowin' he's hurtin' her. But life ain't always 'bout doin' what's easy. If Shelby leaves right now, Frank'll kill me. You know he will."

"Mama, please. Why don't you just get out. Take Shelby to a shelter where Dad can't find you."

"I told you, he needs me. I ain't goin' to no shelter. You stay away from Shelby. Don't be puttin' no ideas in her head 'bout leavin' right now. She'll git through it just like I did when I was her age...."

Sax called his mother a couple times in the year that followed and implored her to leave. Finally, he gave up trying to change her mind. She seemed comfortable with denial. How could she not see the twisted dynamic that had caused her to stay with a drunk who beat the tar out of her and her children?

Sax never once regretted leaving—only that he had left Shelby behind. But that was the choice that robbed him of joy and peace and had contributed to the failure of three marriages.

It was ironic—perhaps poetic justice—that Shelby was the one who had found peace, and he was the one stashing their parents' ashes in his closet, unable to let go of the past.

Emily waited patiently as Vanessa arranged the sausage, onion, mushroom, Swiss cheese, and spinach crepes on her plate, along with the nice portion of fresh fruit.

"Yum," Emily said. "This looks *so* delicious."

Vanessa handed her the plate. "There you go, Shortcake. Do you still want beignets?"

Emily smiled wryly. "You're kidding, right?"

"They'll be ready in just a second. But you need to let them cool."

"Good morning, ladies." A man breezed into the dining room, dressed in khaki pants and a light blue golf shirt.

Emily recognized his voice from the night before. Sax Henry looked younger than he sounded and decidedly more handsome in the daylight. His moussed hair was cool, and she liked the five o'clock shadow—seemed befitting a musician. He reminded her of someone, but she couldn't quite put her finger on it.

"Hey, Sax," Emily said.

Vanessa glanced up from the deep fryer. "You two have met?"

Emily nodded. "We ran into each other on the deck when I got home last night."

"Emily and I already have two things in common," Sax said. "We're both LSU Tiger fans, and we both like Zoe B's. That's not bad for two strangers passing in the night. I didn't have *that* much in common with my ex-wives."

Vanessa chuckled. "Chatterbox over there can tell her life story without taking a breath."

"She's exaggerating," Emily said, the corners of her mouth twitching.

"So what're you having?" Sax winked and studied her plate.

Emily gave him a rundown of what was in the crepes. "I'm having beignets, too. I can't eat them every day and fit into my jeans, but I *love* them."

"Me, too." Sax's gaze met Vanessa's. "Would you mind fixing me what Emily's having? It really does sound great. Maybe a little heavy on the sausage?"

"Beignets, too?"

"Yes, please, ma'am." Sax poured himself a glass of orange juice and sat at the table. "So, Emily … are you working at Zoe B's *tonight*?"

"As a matter of fact, I am. I'm scheduled from three until eleven."

"I'm planning to have dinner there," Sax said. "Maybe you'll be waiting my table. I hope that won't make you nervous."

Emily shook her head. "Heavens, no. I've waited tables since I was sixteen—first for spending money and now for college money. I have a scholarship, but it only pays the tuition. It doesn't cover housing, books, and other expenses. My parents help a lot."

"So you two gals are sisters?" Sax looked from one to the other. "You're both beautiful, but I don't see the family resemblance."

Vanessa looked up from the beignet machine and smiled. "We favor opposite sides of the family. The family resemblance is there when we're all together."

Emily sat admiring her dark-haired, azure-eyed sister with a figure to die for, who turned heads wherever she went. Emily's hair was the color of sand, her blue eyes boring—not striking like Vanessa's.

No way did Sax think they were both beautiful. But it was nice hearing it anyway.

Emily heard someone whistling and lifted her gaze as Ethan walked into the kitchen and came up behind Vanessa, his arms around her, his cheek next to hers. "I'm leaving for the clinic. Once the day manager gets here, why don't you take it easy and read or something? You've been pushing yourself hard lately."

"I enjoy pushing myself," Vanessa said. "There's always something new I want to try." She sprinkled powdered sugar on the beignets. "Besides, I promised that nice couple from Georgia I'd take them on a tour later."

Ethan kissed her cheek. "Just don't overdo it. See y'all tonight. Sax, you'll still be here?"

"Sure will. I've got business pending."

"Well, sometime before you leave, you really should take the tour through the slave tunnels. It's a sobering experience to walk where they walked when this was part of the Underground Railroad." Ethan popped a mushroom into his mouth. "Gotta run. Have a great day, everyone."

Emily watched Ethan walk out the back door and thought how blessed Vanessa was to find such a thoughtful, caring husband. Her thoughts turned to Chance, and she felt that icky pang of sorrow she knew was part of the package for now.

"The more I think about it," Vanessa said, "I really *would* enjoy an hour in the pool with Carter. He says he wants to show me how he's learned to use the snorkeling getup. What I think he *really* wants is to blast me with a water rifle that a certain somebody brought him from Tennessee."

Emily laughed. "Don't you remember that summer when Ryan brought one home from college and chased us all over the place? Mom said from the time he was little, he never could resist a squirt gun of any kind. It's a guy thing—right, Sax? You had a water rifle when you were a kid, didn't you?"

"I just used the garden hose." He pasted on a smile. "But I think it might be a guy thing."

"Do you have brothers and sisters?" Emily said.

"A younger sister. And yes, I chased her all over the backyard, squirting her unmercifully. She loved it."

"One time," Emily said, "our parents came outside when we were having a water fight, and they got right in the middle of it, laughing their heads off. It was so much fun. Remember that, Vanessa?"

"I sure do. I wondered what the people of Sophie Trace would think of their police chief giggling like a schoolgirl and playing in the sprinkler."

"Your mom sounds fun to be around," Sax said.

Emily nodded. "Definitely. I'll bet yours was too."

"Not so much." Sax's face grew taut. "My mom pretty much ignored us growing up. She was too busy making excuses for my alcoholic father who laid into us if we as much as sneezed the wrong way."

Emily felt the embarrassment scald her face. How did she walk right into that one? "I'm sorry. That must've been painful." She took a bite of crepe and washed it down with a gulp of orange juice.

"Don't be sorry," Sax said. "It's just one of those things you learn to accept. Be grateful your folks weren't like mine."

"All right"—Vanessa's voice went up an octave, and she shot

Emily an empathetic look—"let me prepare the crepes for this hungry man before we girls talk him to death."

Zoe walked over to the table by the window at Zoe B's and handed Father Sam the day's issue of the *Les Barbes Ledger*.

Hebert looked up at her, his gray curls lopsided where he'd slept on his side, his blue shirt missing a button. "Anyting in dere wert reading?"

"According to Pierce, it's mostly old news." Zoe combed Hebert's hair with her fingers. "At least regarding the cyanide scare."

"So da sheriff still not telling us anyting?"

Father Sam took a sip of coffee. "Hebert, my friend, we've been over this a hundred times. The sheriff's telling us whatever we need to know, when we need to know it."

"You don' tink it's strange dat da whole weekend went by and dey still don' know who's responsible for dis? Do we even know if a terrorist group took credit? If dey're planning more attacks?"

"Good heavens"—Father Sam took off his glasses—"this horrible tragedy just happened on Saturday. The authorities have barely had a chance to breathe, let alone figure out the particulars of how all this went down. We need to give them space. A little trust wouldn't hurt either."

Hebert swatted the air. "Dat's all I got: a *little* trust. Dey're not going to tell us anytin' dat could start a panic."

"Well, do *you* want a panic?" Tex hooked his thumbs on his red suspenders. "I sure don't. I opt for bein' told the facts on an as-need-to-know basis. I've lived here twenty years, and I've yet to see law enforcement pull a fast one."

"Dat's true."

"Shoot," Tex said, "the authorities haven't even called in the FBI or Homeland. If they thought it was a terrorist attack, don't you think the feds would jump on it like fleas on a hound dog?"

Hebert scratched his chin. "I suppose dey would."

"I'm just grateful business isn't suffering," Zoe said. "Pierce installed motion detectors at the kitchen doors so they buzz when someone's coming in. He's making sure no one enters the kitchen undetected, including the wholesale delivery guys."

Savannah walked over to the table, her shoulders slumped.

"What's wrong, sweetie?" Zoe said.

Savannah heaved a sigh. "A seventh person has died. Molly Delaney, a thirty-year-old single mother of three."

"Oh no." Zoe felt a pang of sadness but was grateful she didn't recognize the woman's name.

"Savannah, how'd it happen?" Tex asked.

"According to her parents, for her thirtieth birthday, they offered to watch the kids so she could have a weekend by herself in New Orleans. All she wanted to do was lie in the sun and read novels. The maid at the hotel where she was staying found her body this morning. Police discovered a bottle of Gaudry water on the nightstand. It's got the same date and numbers as the bottles here. She must've stopped at Marcotte's and bought it on her way down the bayou."

Father Sam shook his head. "Poor dear probably didn't know anything about the cyanide scare."

Savannah nodded. "You're right. Her parents told police she called when she arrived in New Orleans, all excited about no TV. No news. No stress. They didn't think she was in any danger from cyanide there, so they opted not to tell her about what was going on here until she headed back to Les Barbes. It never occurred to them that she might have stopped at Marcotte's on her way out of town."

"Can you imagine what they must be feelin'?" Tex said.

Hebert shook his head slowly, his hand over his heart. "*J'ai gros coeur.*"

"Makes me want to cry too." Zoe put her hand on Hebert's shoulder. "I'm still hurting over Domi's death. But this is what the authorities have been worried about. They just don't know how many contaminated bottles are still in circulation."

CHAPTER 13

Jude pushed aside Monday's issue of the *Les Barbes Ledger*, his elbows on his desk, his face in his hands. He felt as if his pounding head would fall off his neck at any moment.

A knock at the door interrupted his thoughts, and he sat up straight, glad it was just Aimee and not one of his deputies.

"Molly Delaney's parents just left," Aimee said.

"Sorry I had to bow out. I've got a banger of a headache. How'd it go?"

"They were emotional. Gil and I had difficulty getting them to focus. We asked all the same questions we asked the families of the other victims. We're convinced they don't know anyone who would target their daughter. She's well liked. Taught second grade at Les Barbes Elementary School and has won all sorts of state teaching awards. She was even on good terms with her ex-husband. The Morgan City PD questioned him. He's pretty shaken too. He's squeaky clean, and they don't think he had anything to do with it."

"Did the security tapes at Marcotte's record Ms. Delaney in there on Friday?"

Aimee nodded. "She went through the express checkout at three forty-two. We enhanced the image on the security tape. It appears she had three bottles of water and some snack items. New Orleans police didn't find any other bottles of water in her room. We're assuming she drank them. Guess her luck ran out on the third bottle."

Jude sighed. "How old are her children?"

Aimee sat in the chair next to his desk, her arms folded across her chest, her legs crossed at the ankle. "Two, four, and five. Tell me that doesn't break your heart."

"Where are the kids now?"

"With their father. He has joint custody and has been taking them every other weekend for the past eight months. But I can't imagine a single father taking full responsibility for three small children overnight."

"What does he do for a living?"

"He's an orthodontist."

Jude arched his eyebrows. "Knowing what I paid our orthodontist when Bridgette was in braces, I'm sure he can afford to hire a nanny."

"Thank God. I'm sure the grandparents will help. At least the children won't have to go through the additional trauma of being farmed out to foster homes."

Jude thought about the people in this town whose lives had been wrecked because a loved one was poisoned with cyanide. He slammed his hands on the desk and swore under his breath. "I want whoever's doing this, Aimee! Get out there and find me some evidence. We're missing something. Keep digging." He softened his tone. "And make sure the media reminds the public on the hour to call and report any unopened bottles of Gaudry water. Deputies will pick it up."

"We've got another problem," Aimee said. "Dozens of bloggers are stirring people up, claiming this was the work of Muslim extremists and is designed to slowly wipe out whole communities."

"That's ridiculous!" Jude said. "Homeland won't even get involved in this. They reviewed the facts and decided it's inconsistent with the pattern of Muslim extremists. Don't these people read the paper and listen to the news?"

"Probably. But they don't believe we're telling them the truth."

"Muslim terrorists wouldn't bother doing something this small—just seven victims when they could've taken out hundreds, maybe thousands?"

"So far," Aimee said.

Jude locked gazes with her. "Do *you* have doubts?"

"It's irrelevant. I'm paid to rely on experts to analyze this kind of thing."

"But you think there's a possibility that Muslim extremists did this?"

Aimee shrugged. "I guess until we know for sure who's behind it, I'm keeping an open mind."

"For cryin' out loud, since Gaudry water is bottled and sold only in the state, not even the FBI wants a piece of this. If Muslim extremists were responsible, don't you know they'd be bragging—taunting us? Everything points to this being the work of one twisted individual—or small group."

Aimee's eyes narrowed. "What if it's just a warning shot, Jude? What if they plan to poison the water supply?"

"We've already heightened security at the water treatment plant and added more surveillance cameras. Every employee has been put under a microscope and made aware of the need for vigilance."

"But for how long? Terrorists are patient. They wait months—even years—to pull off some of these attacks."

"Tell me I didn't just hear you say *these* attacks?" Jude didn't bother to hide his annoyance. "Regardless of what's bouncing around inside your head, the experts are telling us this was not done by Muslim extremists. People are scared enough without opening that can of worms."

"With all due respect, Sheriff, the can is open."

Emily poured two glasses of ice-cold lemonade and carried them to Chance's kitchen table, then sat facing him.

Chance put his hand on hers. "I don't know what I'd do without you."

"I'm just glad I can be here for you." Emily glanced at the *Les Barbes Ledger* folded on the table. "I'm glad the newspaper got the times right for the visitation tomorrow night and the funeral on Wednesday."

"I almost forgot," Chance said. "Monsignor Robidoux called back and confirmed that the women at Saint Catherine's are planning to bring food for the family. Imogene somebody will contact us. I wrote her name down. I don't know any of the details, but I'm sure Aunt Reba will gladly take charge."

"Do you know if she's left Shreveport yet?"

"I'm sure she has. She hasn't called. Her feelings are probably hurt."

"She'll come around," Emily said. "It had to be hard for someone who likes to be in control to have a stranger call and tell her that you need space."

"Let's hope she listened."

Emily took a sip of lemonade. "Chance … would it be so hard to make amends and let her help you? I'm scheduled to work the late shift today from three until eleven. And the early shift tomorrow from seven until three. I won't be able to see you in between—and that's a long stretch of time to be by yourself."

Chance squeezed her hand. "You're the only one I want to be with."

"Sorry." Emily's heart sank. "I asked Zoe to give me back-to-back shifts so I could be off for the visitation tomorrow night, have all day Wednesday off, and not go in until Thursday afternoon."

"Whatever." His voice was flat.

"I'm doing my best to be there for you. I'm juggling other responsibilities too."

"I said, whatever."

"Chance, please don't make me feel bad because I have to work. Zoe's counting on me, especially since business has picked up."

"I'll manage."

Emily pulled her hand free and took another sip of lemonade. Chance's self-pity was probably grief talking. The guy had just been orphaned, and he had no siblings. She couldn't even imagine what he must be feeling.

"I'm doing the best I can to help you," she said. "I feel bad I won't see you for twenty-four hours—but then I'll be off for forty-eight."

"Don't worry about it."

"But I do worry about it. I care about you, Chance—a lot. Seeing you hurting isn't easy for me either." Emily blinked the stinging from her eyes.

He looked out the window, his expression stony. "I'm just trying to make it through the day without losing it."

"Maybe you *need* to lose it." Emily put her hand on his forearm. "All that grief needs an outlet, or it'll make you sick. Maybe in your time alone, you'll be able to deal with the severity of what's happened. That's pretty much what I told your aunt Reba."

Chance sighed and stared at his hands.

"It might help to remember that she's hurting too." Emily drew a cross in the condensation on her glass. "She just lost her sister tragically. I can't imagine how I'd feel if I lost Vanessa."

"Try losing your *mother*! Aunt Reba will go back to Shreveport and pick up her life where she left off and not miss a beat. My life will never be the same!"

"Sorry, Chance. I didn't mean to diminish your grief. None of us can know what you're feeling."

Emily sat quietly for a few moments, her gaze fixed on the refrigerator picture of Chance with his parents in front of the Eiffel Tower. The three looked really happy. Was Chance's relationship with his father really so lacking that he felt nothing about his dying—or was it just overshadowed by the deep sadness he felt at losing his mother? Either way, Chance was in for a long, uphill battle of grieving the family unit that no longer existed. And preparing to go back to Harvard Medical School at the end of August, ready to focus on learning.

Sax walked into Zoe B's, the tinkling of the bell on the door causing Zoe to turn in his direction. She picked up a menu and hurried over to him.

"Sax, what a nice surprise to see you again. I wasn't sure whether you were still in town."

"I'm here," he said. "I've got some business pending. I normally don't take time for lunch, but I don't really need to be anywhere at the moment. I enjoyed the crawfish étouffée so much I thought I'd try something else. Zoe B's seems to be the place everyone trusts to be safe right now."

"My husband's watching the kitchen like a mother hen. He even put motion detectors at the kitchen doors so no one can come or go without it beeping. We're getting all our food from a New Orleans wholesaler. And, for the time being, we've stopped getting our fresh produce from the farmer's market."

Sax glanced around the room. "Well, you sure have a lot of customers. I guess everyone trusts you."

"We're not the only ones who are taking serious measures to ensure the safety of what we serve," Zoe said. "But it didn't hurt that the sheriff and his wife ate here the other night and mentioned it on the news."

Zoe led him to the table where he had sat the night before. The same three men were seated at the table by the window and appeared to be playing checkers.

Sax pulled out a chair and sat.

"Mommy!"

Zoe turned just as a little boy and girl broke free from the hands of an attractive young woman wearing a backpack and raced in her direction. Zoe bent down, her arms open, and received them, kissing their cheeks.

"Maddie's taking us to the park," said the little girl with curly blonde pigtails and the face of an angel. "We popped popcorn, and we're allowed to feed the ducks."

"Are those beautiful children yours?" Sax said.

"Yes, this is Grace." Zoe beamed. "She's four going on twenty-one. And Tucker—he just turned one. This is Mr. Henry."

Grace extended her hand. "Nice to meet you, Mr. Henry."

He smiled and shook Grace's hand. She had Zoe's features, but her eyes were the color of topaz. "Well, aren't you the polite one?"

"Grace has been around customers since the day she was born," Zoe said. "She's a real people person. We're not sure about Tucker yet. He's at the age of taking it all in."

"Hey there, Tucker, my man." Sax tickled the boy's ribs, and Tucker giggled with delight, his shiny chestnut hair the exact color of Zoe's. "They look a lot like you. Really cute kids."

"Thanks. They're a blessing." She motioned for the woman wearing the backpack to come. "Sax Henry, this is Maddie Lyons. She watches after the children when I'm working. She's a godsend."

Sax smiled. "Nice to meet you."

"Same here." Maddie turned to Zoe. "I'm going to put them in the red wagon and head for Cypress Park. We shouldn't be gone more than an hour and a half. I need to get Tucker down for his afternoon nap."

"Have fun." Zoe hugged Tucker and then Grace. "Do what Maddie tells you."

"I'll help Maddie make Tucker be good," Grace said. "Bye, Mommy."

"Bye, sweetie." Zoe looked adoringly at her children as Maddie carried Tucker and walked Grace out of the dining room.

Sax was surprised to see Zoe's eyes brimming with tears.

"Sorry." She took a tissue out of her pocket and dabbed her eyes. "I was just thinking about how blessed I am. Dominic Corbin, the little boy who died of cyanide poisoning, was Grace's favorite playmate at preschool. His visitation is tomorrow night, and I'm dreading it."

"I didn't know that. Must be hard on her."

"She's happy Domi's with Jesus. I don't think she really understands that he's not coming back. I suppose it'll have to sink in slowly. This is the first time she's had to deal with death."

"Are you not worried about your kids being out there with the killer still on the loose?"

"If I thought about it, I'd go out of my mind," Zoe said. "Maddie won't let them eat or drink anything she's not brought with her in the backpack. They'll be fine. We can't just hole up and cower in fear."

"I suppose not."

"Do you have children, Sax?"

"No. My third wife and I spent five years and thousands of dollars trying to make it happen. The fertility gods didn't smile on us. Probably just as well. My old man was a mean drunk, and I'm not sure I even know how to be a good dad. I never did the father-son stuff."

"My mother wasn't a good role model either," Zoe said. "But I was surprised at how naturally it all came to me. I never knew I could love anything as much as I love those two little scamps."

"I can tell." Sax smiled. "Good for you. This world needs all the loving moms it can get."

"Well, trust me—it's only by the grace of God that I turned out to be a loving mom."

"I've never quite understood what that expression means. But whatever God's grace is, I missed out."

"You can only miss His grace by choice," Zoe said.

Sax shifted his weight and held up the menu. Was she one of those religious fanatics, just waiting to point a finger at him and say that he had brought all the heartache on himself by the sin in his life? What hideous sin was he guilty of that rendered him deserving of his father's repeated beatings? And what kind of God stood by and did nothing while innocent children were brutalized? The last thing he wanted to talk about was God's *grace.*

"I guess I'd better get out of your hair so you can make your selection," Zoe said.

"I enjoyed meeting your children. You're a lucky woman."

Zoe smiled warmly. "I prefer to think of my good fortune as blessings from God. Savannah will be your waitress. She'll be right with you."

Sax pretended to read the menu for a full minute before he actually began to comprehend what it said. Why was it that anytime he attempted to discuss God with anyone, he got upset? God had never blessed him with anything—and he still didn't know why.

CHAPTER 14

Sax bounded up the steps at Langley Manor, pushed open the elegant door with sheers on the windows, and walked onto the shiny wood floor in the entryway. Soft instrumental music was playing.

The parlor was empty, but he saw Vanessa in the dining room, laying out an array of snacks.

She looked up and smiled. "How was lunch? I was on the phone with Zoe earlier, and she mentioned you were there."

"It was terrific." Sax walked over to her. "I had grilled shrimp, dirty rice, and a vegetable medley. I don't know what the chef did, but it's the best I've ever eaten. The cornbread and gumbo were to die for. I've lived in New Orleans half my life and never tasted anything quite like it."

Vanessa arched her eyebrows. "The food at Zoe B's is addictive. Pierce is an awesome chef. He's won awards for his gumbo."

"I normally don't bother with lunch," Sax said. "I just went there on a whim. Glad I did. But I told Emily I'm having dinner there tonight." He patted his middle. "I may have to order something light this time. I noticed they had a seafood salad on the menu."

"Oh, that's *my* favorite! You should try it."

Sax laughed. "Are you in cahoots with the Broussards? I never go back to the same place three times in a row."

"But if you like it, who cares?"

"This is true. I met Grace and Tucker while I was there. Really cute kids."

"They're adorable." Vanessa set a beautifully arranged plate of chocolate chip cookies and lemon bars on the buffet. "Ethan and I and our son were friends with Zoe and Pierce before they had kids. And while we were renovating this place, we rented an apartment from the Broussards—upstairs from Zoe B's. Their apartment was next door, and I got to know them really well. To tell you the truth, on some level, I think I'll always miss living there. It was magical."

"Even compared to all this elegance?"

Vanessa nodded. "It was the old-world setting, as much as anything. I mean, the apartment was quaint, and we loved it. But it was what we saw from the gallery that was so enchanting. I'd hate to guess how many hours we spent standing at the railing, waving to tourists and listening to Cajun music coming from Breaux's. *Rue Madeline* is closed to traffic after seven p.m. and takes on this festival-like atmosphere. Flashing neon lights. Street entertainers. Horse-drawn carriages. But since you're from New Orleans, you probably see it all the time. It might not seem like a big deal."

"Sure it does," Sax said. "There's no place on earth like south Louisiana. I love it all. I'll have to take a stroll along *rue Madeline* after dark."

He heard the back door slam. A few seconds later, a young boy—the same child he had seen playing in the sprinkler that morning—came out of the kitchen, accompanied by a panting yellow lab.

"Mom, can I have a popsicle?"

Vanessa wiped the boy's hair off his sweaty forehead. "Sure. I think you and Angel should stay inside for a while and cool off. Say hello to Mr. Henry. This is my son, Carter."

The handsome boy, blessed with his mother's deep blue eyes and hair that was neither blond nor red but somewhere in between, smiled politely and shook his hand. "Glad to meet you, Mr. Henry. This is Angel. She knows how to shake hands. Go ahead and try it."

Sax bent down, surprised when the dog lifted her paw and let him shake it.

"Your dog's as polite as you. How old are you, Carter?"

"I'll be nine on July twenty-third. I'm having a swimming party after it gets dark, and we're going to put colored lights on the fence around the pool. Mom's making me a cake that looks like a soccer ball."

Sax remembered that on his ninth birthday, he had hidden under his bed after his father went into one of his drunken rages and threw his cake on the floor and broke his mother's arm. "That sounds fun. So, Vanessa … how do you make a cake in the shape of a ball?"

"I have a mold. You put two halves together. I'll practice first. Getting the icing right will be the hardest part."

"My mom makes the coolest cakes." Carter looked at her adoringly.

"Speaking of *cool,*" Sax said, "I'm ready to enjoy some down time. I found a World War II novel I'd like to read."

"Don't let us keep you." Vanessa glanced at her watch. "The invitation to take the tour at two is still open."

"I'll keep that in mind," Sax said. "I'm sure I'll be seeing Carter and Angel again."

Carter nodded. "We're always around here. If you want to throw the Frisbee, you should come outside sometime and throw it to Angel. She's an amazing catcher."

"I may do that." Sax turned his gaze to Vanessa. "By the way, has anyone called and left a message for me?"

"No one," she said. "I hope that's good news."

So do I. "Just means I'll be here at least another day. See y'all later." Sax winked at Carter and started up the white staircase. Why was Mrs. Woodmore taking her sweet time getting back to him?

Emily stood in front of the mirror above the sink in the staff restroom off the kitchen at Zoe B's. She brushed her hair with her hands.

Savannah came and stood in the open doorway. "Oh good. You're right on time."

"It's in my genes." Emily put on her name tag. "Who came up with the idea to wear black skirts and such pretty white blouses? I've worn uniforms that were really gross. These are nice."

"Zoe found them," Savannah said. "She wants us to think of ourselves as hostesses, not just waitresses. There are three of you tonight. If you have questions or anything comes up you can't handle, pass it on to Nanette. The buck stops with her."

"Thanks," Emily said. "We can handle it."

"How's Chance doing?"

Emily shook her head. "Not good. I feel guilty leaving him right now."

"Doesn't he have family?"

"He does, but he really doesn't want to be around a lot of people. He's comfortable with me. Sometimes we just sit together and don't even talk."

"Still ... it's important for his family to be together right now—even more so, since his parents died tragically. They've all lost someone they love."

"I told him that," Emily said. "Maybe when someone besides his aunt Reba arrives he'll be more receptive. She's the controlling one on his mother's side. She wanted to come stay with him, but he couldn't handle being smothered. So I called and changed her mind."

Savannah arched her eyebrows, her blue eyes wide. "You did?"

"Yes. She seemed insulted, even though I was very nice. But I didn't let her manipulate me. I told her Chance needed to grieve by himself and that her being there wouldn't help him. So she's staying somewhere else."

"Who's helping Chance with the funeral arrangements?"

"I am. His parents had already done most of it. And the women at his church are bringing food after the funeral. Why are you looking at me like that?"

Savannah shrugged.

"What?"

"It's really none of my business," Savannah said. "But it seems like an inordinate role for you to take on when you've only known the guy a few weeks."

Emily bit her lip. "I'm helping a friend through a nightmare. What's wrong with that?"

"Nothing, sweetie. Just be sure you're not setting yourself up to be the one Chance relies on for everything. Let his family help. It's too much for one person."

Emily tried not to show her irritation. Suddenly Savannah was the expert? "It hasn't been too much for me so far."

"I'm sure it hasn't." Savannah's tone reminded her of Vanessa's. "I'm just suggesting you let Chance's family take on some of the responsibility too. Dealing with this tragedy will be ongoing and draining. Girl, you're only nineteen. Soon, you'll be starting another intense college semester—and so will he. Give yourself space to clear your head."

Emily pressed her lips together and counted to ten. Savannah meant well. Just accept her advice and go on. "Thanks. I'll be fine."

Jude took a gulp of Coke, crushed the can, and tossed it into the recycle bin in his office. He heard the bells of Saint Catherine Catholic Church chime eight times and looked outside, the thunderhead in the western sky now rimmed in gold, sun rays shooting out across the expanse. He stood for a moment and admired the beauty, distracted when he heard footsteps coming his way.

Aimee breezed through the door, carrying some papers in her hand. "Why are you still here?"

"Same reason you are. Seven people dead on my watch makes me crazy."

"There's nothing we can do for Molly Delaney's family," she said. "I just wanted to stay and read through the background check that came back on Adam Marcotte." She handed him the papers. "The kid's squeaky clean. There's nothing here to make me think he's capable of murder. The kid is Brad Pitt, Michael Phelps, and Beaver Cleaver rolled into one. He's handsome, athletic, an honor student, the boy-next-door type, and everyone's friend, including Mayor Theroux's son."

"That would make a perfect cover, though, don't you think?" Jude scanned the report.

"Gil and I think it's a dead end. We want to take a closer look at every person who works in Marcotte's stockroom. And every person who had access to the kitchen."

"You said there were no red flags."

Aimee sighed. "There's nothing obvious. At this point, I'm looking for even a *flicker* of a red flag. We have to keep trying to make sense of this."

"Yeah, okay. Good."

"I honestly don't know where it's going, Sheriff. We've got zilch."

"We've got the hind shot of the man on the security tapes. It could be Adam Marcotte."

"Or it could be any guy in Saint Catherine Parish who has dark hair and is medium height and build."

"He walked like he was young," Jude said, "under forty—probably way under."

"Yes, he did. That narrows down the field. But where do we go from here?"

"Review the security tapes from Marcotte's *again.*" Jude held up his palm. "Take a closer look at the outdoor tapes the day of the crime."

Aimee scratched her ear the way she did when she was merely following orders. "With all due respect, we've been over them multiple times. What are we looking for?"

"Someone roaming around outside who seems just a little too interested in the chaos. Let's see if our guy came back to the scene to gloat before Marcotte's shut down."

Sax perused the menu at Zoe B's, aware of someone lighting the candle on his table. He glanced up, glad to see Emily Jessup's smiling face.

"Well, hello there, Miss Emily. I told you I was coming in tonight."

"I'll be your waitress this evening," she said. "What would you like to drink?"

"I'll have iced tea."

"Any appetizers?"

"I'll try the oyster-filled patty shells."

Emily smiled. "Good choice. They melt in your mouth."

"Tell me about the seafood salad. Your sister says it's to die for."

"It's awesome—Gulf shrimp, crawfish, scallops, and crab on a bed of spinach and lettuce, tossed with scallions, green olives, celery, red bell peppers, and artichokes. Topped with your choice of dressing, but I think our cheesy tomato house dressing is the best. It's tangy, slightly sweet, and just a little hot."

"Sounds great," he said. "I'll have the seafood salad with house dressing on the side."

Emily took his menu. "Let me know if you need anything. I'll be back with your iced tea and appetizer in just a minute."

Sax looked over at the table by the window and chuckled to himself that those same three guys were sitting there, playing checkers.

"Sax?"

Sax looked up and saw a tall man with kind brown eyes and a prominent, almost regal nose, peering down at him. He looked to be about forty and was dressed in a double-breasted white coat and chef's hat.

"I'm Pierce Broussard." He offered Sax his hand. "Zoe's husband. I'm the head chef."

Sax shook his hand. Nice grip. "Good to meet you. You have a lot of fans. You should consider using Adele Woodmore and Vanessa Langley in your marketing ads. Thanks to their prodding and your culinary talent, this is my third time here since last night."

"I'm glad you like the food."

"I do. It's superb," Sax said. "And that's saying something since I live in New Orleans and have tried a variety of Cajun restaurants. But I also like the ambiance. It's relaxing. I'm glad your business hasn't suffered due to the current situation."

"We are too. Listen, I just wanted to say hello. Zoe said you met the rest of the family at lunch."

"Beautiful kids."

Pierce flashed a toothy grin. "They take after their mother, thank the Lord. I need to get back to the kitchen. Just wanted to meet you and say thanks for coming in."

"Believe me, the pleasure is mine," Sax said.

Pierce turned and disappeared into the kitchen. How often had a chef come out and said hello to him? Nice gesture. Pierce Broussard was a class act.

He was glad Adele Woodmore had been so insistent that he eat at Zoe B's and stay at Langley Manor while he was waiting on her to get back to him. If nothing else, he had been introduced to fabulous food, a quaint, quiet room, and extraordinarily nice people. He glanced over at the three old guys playing checkers and realized he was smiling. Genuinely smiling.

Shelby crossed his mind. What was he going to do if this trip turned out to be a big waste of time? Could he bear to go back to New Orleans and resume his miserable, empty life? He blinked away the thought. He had twelve more days.

CHAPTER 15

Zoe stood on the gallery outside her apartment, the sky pale blue streaked with pink, and looked down on a sleepy *rue Madeline*, which was starting to come to life. The early morning breeze was thick with humidity and the faint aromas of coffee freshly brewing, bread baking, and bacon frying.

She had lain awake half the night, dreading Dominic Corbin's visitation and funeral. She had offered up so many prayers for Margot and Josh; what else could she possibly say to the Lord about the situation? She couldn't let it drag her down. She needed to be strong for the Corbins. But she had her own family to care for. And a business to run.

Across the street, the Jourdain Dairy truck was parked in front of the Hotel Peltier. On the gallery that jutted out over the Coy Cajun Gift Shop, Madame Duval stood amid a garden of flowers and potted plants, her white poodle in one arm, and waved at Zoe.

Zoe waved back, just as the open sign went on at Breaux's and customers standing at the door were let in. Only a few sat at tables out front, under the awning. Normally the place would be overflowing with tourists eager to have breakfast and get their day started before it got too hot.

A couple with three school-age kids wearing GatorWorld T-shirts walked up on the sidewalk, and she heard the door to Zoe B's open and close.

Thank You, Lord, that my children are safe. And that our business isn't suffering. Help all these vendors. Please don't let this horrible ordeal adversely affect our town's economy.

The sliding glass door opened and closed. A pair of arms went around her, a smooth cheek next to hers, the familiar, woody scent of Tuscany cologne filling her senses.

"Good morning, Mrs. Broussard." Pierce pressed his lips to her cheek. "And what are you thinking about? You've been out here twenty minutes."

"The Corbins are dominating my thoughts. I'm dreading the visitation and funeral. I'm so grateful our children are alive and well. And so sorry their little boy isn't."

"Me, too."

"But I was also thinking how blessed we are to live here in Les Barbes—and especially on *rue Madeline*. You know how I love watching things come to life every morning." She waved at the paperboy. "I keep hoping and praying that business will be good for the other vendors."

"Well, it's certainly good for us right now. Our customer count was up thirty percent over the same day last week. That's a record, babe. You should call Jude and Colette, thank them for the plug, and have them come in for a complimentary dinner."

"Good idea. Are the kids up yet?"

"Not when I peeked in on them a minute ago. I thought we should let them sleep and have Maddie get them dressed and fed."

"I promised Grace she could have her breakfast with Hebert, Father Sam, and Tex. She misses them. Me, too. Long gone are the days when I could sit her at their table to have her snacks. I could leave her with them and go get a few things done. But I can't do that with Tucker. He's a handful."

Pierce chuckled. "You mean just because that skinny wicket can wiggle out of the high chairs at the eatery?"

"It's really not funny. Once he's loose, he runs all over the dining room."

"Just working those little legs," Pierce said. "The kid just learned to walk and he's like a wind-up toy."

"Well, we can't allow him to run all over Zoe B's. I just hate that he won't have the special relationship with the guys that Grace does."

"I know. But by the time Tucker's old enough to understand, I doubt Hebert will still be around. I can't believe he's going to be a hundred."

"I don't want to think about that," Zoe said. "I can't imagine life without him, or Father Sam and Tex. They're such a part of this place—of me. They're my adopted family."

Pierce squeezed her a little tighter. "When the three of them are in heaven, you'll still have the kids and me—and all the Broussards."

"And Adele." *I hope.* "I can hardly believe she's eighty-eight. I know I won't have her forever, but I don't know what I'll do without her."

There was a long pause.

"All the more reason why you should consider contacting your real mother," Pierce said. "Things might be different now."

Zoe slid out of his arms and gripped the railing. "We've been through this enough times that you already know the answer. I've done the counseling. And I've forgiven her. I really have. But that doesn't mean I need to see her."

"People change."

"Not *that* much."

"Our kids will never know their maternal grandmother."

"They're better off. Now let's change the subject."

"Okay," Pierce said. "I've got to get downstairs and help Dempsey fill orders." He stroked her cheek. "I didn't mean to upset you, Zoe. But this is an unresolved issue that, sooner or later, you're going to have to confront."

"Then it'll have to be later." She sighed. "Maybe when Adele is gone, I'll feel a need to contact my mother. But I sincerely doubt it."

"All right. I won't press you about it. But the people you've *adopted* as family are all well up in their years. And you're right—they're very much a part of you and your everyday life. The dynamic you've created will dramatically change when any one of them dies. I think you should start preparing yourself."

"And you really think I could fill that void by reconnecting with my mother?" Zoe turned around and held his gaze. "*Cher*, when my dear friends are gone, the void will be huge—especially when I lose Adele. But my mother could never fill that void with anything but baggage. Besides, you and the kids need me to be the best wife and mother I can be. Once I open that door, it's going to consume my thoughts and energy."

Pierce traced her eyebrow with his thumb. "Conversely, you don't know how long you have. You may regret it someday if you don't try."

Emily sat on the deck at Langley Manor, enjoying a cup of coffee and watching the early morning haze that had hidden the cane fields under a blanket of white.

Vanessa came outside, wearing her floral bathrobe and capturing a yawn with her hand. "You'd better come eat something. You need to leave soon."

"I don't have to time-in until seven. We set the tables last night. And *rush* hour in Les Barbes is a joke. I'm sure the New Orleans traffic will be a culture shock all over again. Between Sophie Trace and Les Barbes, I've almost forgotten how to drive in it."

"I love to sit out here and watch the sunrise," Vanessa said.

"Me, too. It's amazing how the haze turns pink—but just for a couple minutes." Emily glanced at her watch. "I should call Chance. I feel bad I won't see him until after three."

"Is he up this early?" Vanessa said.

"He won't care if I wake him up. I really hate it that I can't be there for him today."

"Aren't his relatives arriving for the visitation and funeral?" Vanessa said.

"Yes, but I know he would like me to be there with him."

Vanessa sat in the rocker next to Emily. "Shortcake …"

"Ah, here it comes," Emily said. "Shortcake is always followed by advice."

"Don't you think it would be good to give Chance a little space—some time to grieve with his family?"

"That's not what he wants."

"But maybe it's what he needs—and what *they* need. Laying his parents to rest is about a lot more people than just Chance."

"Yes, but he's the most affected. Anything I can do to help him through it, I should do."

"Are you the only friend he has?"

Emily felt her face warm. "I guess. I told you he's a geek. Not that many people can relate to him."

"But you can?"

Emily took a sip of coffee. She was not going to have this conversation. "I'm loving my neighbor as myself, Vanessa. If you have a problem with that, take it up with the Lord." She stood and picked up her cup and saucer. "I'm going out on the front steps to call Chance, and then I'm leaving for work at twenty till seven. Just so you know: I get off at three. I'm going to change and go right over to Chance's so I can drive him to the funeral home for the visitation. I doubt I'll be home early. Try to remember your baby sister is nineteen, okay?"

Vanessa held up her hand. Emily took it.

"I just want you to have a lighthearted summer," Vanessa said, "and have space to unwind before you start school."

"I know. But I can't pretend I never met Chance. It's not his fault his parents were murdered. If he were your friend, what would *you* do?"

"Touché." Vanessa squeezed her hand and let go. "Just make sure you're not getting enmeshed in his grief in an unhealthy way."

"You sounded like Ethan just then." Emily smiled wryly. "Look, I appreciate your wanting to watch out for me. I do. But I can't avoid

Chance's grief. That doesn't mean *I'm* getting depressed. Or falling into that dark pit with him. I'm just helping him to think clearly so he can do what he has to do. Between us, we managed to deal with funeral arrangements, pick out clothes for his parents, order flowers, work with Monsignor Robidoux about the details of the service, write the obituaries, and hold off one very controlling relative."

Vanessa looked at her sheepishly. "Sometimes I forget how take-charge you are."

"I'm fine. I'm pumped when I'm helping. You should know that by now."

"I do."

"So lighten up," Emily said. "Nothing is more important to me than becoming a doctor. I'm not going to jeopardize my dream with any relationship. But I happened to be there when Chance found out his parents were murdered. The Lord allowed me to be the one to walk through it with him, so there must be a reason."

"Let's just hope the reason isn't so you can learn a difficult lesson."

Emily sighed. "You just had to say it. I'll see you tonight."

Jude walked into his office, startled when he saw Aimee sitting in the chair next to his desk.

"You couldn't whistle or something so I'd know you were in here?" Jude said.

"Sorry."

"You're waiting for me. Could this mean good news for a change?"

"I wish. We went back and scrutinized Marcotte's outside security tapes from the day of the crime but didn't spot anyone dressed like the guy we saw at the food bar. We enhanced all sorts of images, and he's just not there. We also reviewed the outside images over the next forty-eight hours. No one stood out. I hate to say it, but we're right back where we started."

Jude exhaled. He walked over and sat at his desk.

"Gil has a team looking deeper into each employee at Marcotte's," Aimee said. "Especially those with access to the kitchen and stockroom. Maybe that will yield something."

Or maybe not. "Have you got enough law enforcement to control the crowds at the funerals today and tomorrow?"

"Probably more than enough," Aimee said. "We've got officers from five departments and all the deputies we can spare. The funeral that will probably draw a big crowd is Dominic Corbin's. It's tomorrow. So is the Durands'. The others are this afternoon."

"Make sure you keep the investigation moving. I want every person who has worked at Marcotte's in the past five years put under a microscope."

There was a knock at the door, and Jude turned at the same time as Aimee.

Gil Marcel came in, wearing a somber look. "Bad news. A man and his six-year-old daughter were just admitted to the ER at Hargrave—cyanide poisoning."

"Are they going to make it?" Jude said.

"The father should. Too soon to tell if the little girl will pull through. She's in critical condition."

"Do the doctors know how they were poisoned?" Aimee said.

"The wife said the family was on a camping trip, and her husband and daughter collapsed after drinking from a bottle of water they got out of the cooler. Her ten-year-old son ran to where he could get a cell signal and called 911. Fortunately, the campsite wasn't far from Hargrave, so it didn't take the EMTs long to get there."

"Was it Gaudry water?"

Gil nodded. "Same numbers on the bottle. The family had six more in the cooler, which we're taking to the lab."

"How could this happen?" Jude slammed his hands on the desk. "We've emphasized through every media venue, day and night, for people not to drink Gaudry water!"

Gil sighed. "They were camping, sir. Listening to the news was the last thing on their minds."

Jude took a slow, deep breath and spoke softly. "Aimee, get Chief Norman, and tell him to meet me in front of the courthouse. We need to go on camera and reemphasize that anyone who has a bottle of Gaudry water in his or her possession is at grave risk. We'll appeal specifically to campers, travelers, tourists—and any friend or family member who can contact them and make sure they're informed about this crisis."

"Right away."

"Gil, tell me the victims' names," Jude said.

"The father is Rick Paquet, thirty-nine. His daughter's name is Caissy. They live in Les Barbes. Dad's a supervisor at the sugar refinery. Daughter is going to be in the first grade."

We hope. "Okay. Thanks."

"I'm going over to the hospital," Gil said. "I want to talk to Mrs. Paquet myself."

Jude nodded, aware of Aimee on the phone with Chief Norman's office. He looked out the window at the hungry reporters across the street, just waiting for another tragedy they could spin. On days like this, he felt like the grim reaper.

CHAPTER 16

Zoe walked past the table by the window at the eatery, smiling at Grace, who was chattering nonstop, apparently thrilled to have the undivided attention of Hebert, Father Sam, and Tex.

Zoe took a picture with her phone, and also a video, quietly capturing the adoring look on Hebert's face as Grace sat on his lap, her pink sundress and blonde pigtails tied with matching ribbons—a stark contrast to his hopelessly wrinkled shirt and woolly gray curls. He listened with seeming interest as Grace told him a lot more than he needed to know about her favorite dollies.

Zoe smiled. She wanted Grace to grow up with this memory—or at least the stories they could tell her about it. How much memory could a child retain at four?

She noticed Pierce standing in the kitchen door and went over to him.

"Aren't they adorable?" she said.

"They certainly are." Pierce scratched his chin and seemed lost in thought. "I've been entertaining the idea of having a hundredth birthday celebration for Hebert. When's the big day?"

"November tenth."

Pierce took out his wallet and looked at the pocket calendar he had tucked behind his credit cards. "That's a Saturday this year. You think he would object to us celebrating all day—even with customers? We could tie it in with his being your very first customer—and the fact that he's been coming in every day for fifteen years."

Zoe felt a smile tugging at her cheeks. "You know, he pretends he doesn't want us to make a big deal out of it. But deep down, I think he's hoping we'll do something grandiose."

"Then let's give him the birthday bash of a lifetime."

Zoe pulled up the calendar on her phone. "We don't have anything scheduled for that day."

"Excellent." Pierce flashed a toothy grin. "Let's schedule ourselves off that Saturday so we can enjoy the party. Find out his favorite kind of cake, and I'll make a huge one to share with everyone. Let's not tell him. Let's keep it a surprise."

"Oh, we have to tell him something as we get closer, or he'll *really* be suspicious. He knows I'd never let something that important slip by. Let's invite him to a bogus birthday celebration at our apartment that evening. We'll tell him Tex and Father Sam will be there. But when he comes in for breakfast that morning, the dining room will be decorated, and we'll announce then that he's going to be the guest of honor all day."

Pierce nodded. "We'll get the newspaper, radio, and TV station down here. Let's do it up big."

"We could even put an ad in the *Ledger* that morning. Hebert doesn't read the paper until he gets here anyhow. That way, people in the community would know and could drop by. This is fun. I'm getting excited."

"Do you think we should buy him a new shirt?" Pierce looked over at the table and chuckled.

"No. That's the Hebert I know and love, and that's who I want to celebrate."

"Me, too." Pierce put his arm around her. "It's kind of nice looking forward to a celebration of a long life well lived. Especially right now, after Dominic's life was so tragically cut short."

"Why did you have to bring it up?" Zoe sighed. "I had actually forgotten about it for a few minutes."

"Sorry." He kissed the top of her head. "I've got to get back to the kitchen. When you start feeling sad, think about how you want to do the party."

"I can't wait to tell Adele. I need to call her anyway and see what time she wants us to pick her up for the visitation tonight."

Emily locked the door on the staff restroom at Zoe B's and hit her speed dial for Chance's cell phone.

"Hey," he said. "I thought you were working."

"I am. I'm just taking a quick break. How are you doing?"

"I'm hiding in my room. Aunt Reba got here an hour ago and is busy sizing up the kitchen so she can ramrod the food deliveries."

"Chance, be nice. Someone needs to do it. She's probably really good at that sort of thing."

"Yes, she's like an army sergeant barking out orders."

"Did you eat breakfast?"

"I had a strawberry Pop Tart."

"Are you telling me your aunt didn't offer to make breakfast?"

"She offered. But if I accept her offer, she'll ask me questions ad nauseam—questions I'm not up to answering and some that are none of her business. I really don't want her here. I told you that."

"She just came over to size up the kitchen, though, right?"

"Well, before I realized it, she had started doing my laundry. And she insisted on going through Mom's clothes. She wants to pick out some things for herself and then arrange for the rest to be given to the Saint Vincent de Paul thrift shop. She would be glad to do the same for Dad's stuff."

"It would solve a problem for you, no?"

"I suppose it would—as long as I'm willing to be a prisoner in my own house!"

Emily cringed at his harsh tone.

"Sorry," he said. "I told you the woman makes me crazy. I just don't have the strength to hold my own. If we get sideways, it'll make for an even tougher time tonight and tomorrow. And Mom wouldn't want that."

"Were she and Reba close?"

"Actually, they were. I never understood it. But I don't have siblings and don't understand the bond."

"I'm really close to Vanessa and to my big brother, Ryan. I can't imagine how I'd feel if either of them died."

"Times that by ten, if you lost your mom! Look, I'm sorry for Aunt Reba, but I shouldn't have to put up with her smothering me because she misses my mom—and certainly not in my own home."

"There's nothing I can do about it from here," Emily said. "Just hang on until after I get off at three. Something tells me Aunt Reba will back off when I'm around. If not, we'll have to have a heart-to-heart. I don't have anything to lose. She already resents me."

There was a knock on the restroom door.

"Chance, I've got to go."

"Whatever."

"I'll see you about three fifteen."

Emily put her phone in her skirt pocket, opened the door to the ladies room, and almost ran headlong into Savannah.

"There you are." Savannah locked gazes with her. "Everything all right?"

"Yes, why?"

"I noticed you weren't on the floor. I thought maybe you weren't feeling well."

"Everything's fine," Emily said. "As long as I needed to take a restroom break, I took an extra minute and made a call."

"And how *is* Chance?"

Emily felt the heat flood her cheeks. "He's having to deal with an aunt who's the smothering type. He really doesn't need that today."

"He's a big boy, Emily. He can take care of himself."

"Well, since neither of *us* has lost both parents tragically, I'm not sure it's fair to say that. His mind's in a fog. He needs help, yes. But not smothering."

"I thought you called his aunt so this wouldn't happen."

Emily sighed. "I did, and she agreed not to stay at the house. But once she came over to check on Chance, she just took over. He's holed up in his room, wishing she would leave."

"Then let him say so." Savannah intensified her gaze. "Emily, you're a good friend to want to help this young man through a tough time. But he's a Harvard med student, for heaven's sake. He didn't get there by being helpless. You really don't have to feel responsible to protect him."

"I don't feel *responsible* to do anything. Can't I just be a friend without everyone trying to make something more out of it?" Emily glanced at her watch. Savannah had a lot of nerve lecturing her. "I need to get back. The couple at table four should be ready to order."

Zoe rang the doorbell at Adele Woodmore's house, admiring her manicured green lawn and the bright pink blossoms on the crape myrtle trees that lined the sidewalk along Magnolia Lane.

Isabel Morand, her dark hair in a French roll, opened the door. "Come in where it's cool. Have you listened to the news this morning?"

"No. What now?" Zoe said.

"A father and his six-year-old daughter have been admitted to the hospital with cyanide poisoning."

Zoe's heart sank. "Was it Gaudry water?"

Isabel nodded. "They took it with them on a camping trip and hadn't listened to the news."

"That's awful."

"On a lighter note," Isabel said, "I made a pound cake this morning, and Adele wants me to serve you strawberry shortcake out in the sunroom."

"That sounds good." Why did she say that? How could she even think about enjoying herself when another child had been poisoned?

Adele appeared in the hallway, dressed in an icy pink shift that looked beautiful with her white hair. She took Zoe's face in both hands and kissed her forehead. "I was so excited when you said you were stopping by."

"I'm surprised I didn't hear from you over the weekend," Zoe said. "What have you been up to?"

"I had an unexpected visitor."

"Anyone I know?" Zoe said.

"The brother of a young woman who used to work for me a long time ago. You said on the phone you had something you wanted to tell me."

"I do. We've decided to have a giant birthday bash for Hebert's one hundredth birthday, which will be November tenth, and I wanted you to be the first to know."

"Oh, my. It'll be here before we know it."

Zoe chuckled. "Adele, this is June. We have plenty of time."

"At my age, time whizzes by. Let's sit in the sunroom, and you can tell me all about it."

Zoe followed Adele into the glass room, stopping for a moment to admire the almost perfect lawn and the variety of vividly colored flowers in the beds along the privacy fence. "I think your yard gets prettier every time I see it."

"Noah's a fine landscaper. Vanessa and Ethan are really blessed to have him taking care of the grounds at Langley Manor. It was so good of him to keep me on as a customer when he became their caretaker."

"Noah likes you," Zoe said. "Then again, who doesn't?"

"Enough about me. Tell me about the party. It's hard to believe Hebert is going to be a hundred. He doesn't look a day over eighty."

Zoe sat opposite Adele at the round glass table and told her everything she and Pierce had talked about regarding Hebert's birthday party.

Adele brought her hands together. "Won't that be something? I think a come-and-go party is a marvelous idea. That way, more people can come to congratulate our friend *and* enjoy a piece of whatever scrumptious cake Pierce decides to make."

"Hebert is a chocolate man all the way," Zoe said. "His favorite is Pierce's triple fudge chocolate cake with cherry cream-cheese frosting. We've got a lot of details to nail down. But I wanted you to know now, so you can share the excitement with us."

"I'm so glad you did. It's great fun being in on it."

"Now…" Zoe breathed in deeply and let it out slowly. "I really hate to shift gears, but I need to talk about Domi's visitation for a minute. It's from five until seven. We're thinking of getting there around six. How about Pierce and I pick you and Isabel up at five forty-five?"

"All right, hon. Whatever's convenient for you. We can be flexible. We'll have an early dinner. Would you and Pierce like to join us?"

"Thanks, but we can't," Zoe said. "He's working until five and needs time to clean up. We'll eat late."

"I don't know how you do that. This old stomach of mine would rebel."

"I doubt I'll be hungry after going to the funeral home. I'm dreading it."

"I imagine we all are." Adele reached over and took Zoe's hand. "But I know Domi was special to you—and not just because he was Grace's playmate."

"He was a precious little boy," Zoe said. "I miss him already." She blinked quickly to clear her eyes. "Let's talk about something else. I'll be doing enough of this tonight."

Adele squeezed her hand and let go. "Vanessa told me that your business is booming since the sheriff and his wife had dinner there and announced it on the news."

"It is. We still can't believe it. We're actually up thirty percent over last week."

"Well, that's certainly a blessing in the midst of this horrible tragedy."

Zoe nodded. "I feel a little guilty doing so well when so many people are hurting."

"You're hurting right along with them. We all are. That doesn't mean your business has to."

Zoe smiled. "Come to think of it, you're responsible for part of our increase. You told a guy named Sax Henry about Zoe B's, and he's been there for lunch and dinner ever since."

"Ah, that nice young man from New Orleans—the saxophone player."

"Yes, that's him. How do you know him?"

"I don't really *know* him," Adele said. "But that never stops me from recommending Zoe B's."

"Well, thanks. I think he's our newest best customer. He's also staying out at Langley Manor, which helps Vanessa and Ethan right now when a lot of people are canceling. Sax won't be in town all that long, but maybe he'll go back to New Orleans and tell a few folks that Les Barbes is a great place for a weekend getaway. We could use some positive press for a change."

"Indeed." Adele laced her fingers together. "Every time we turn on the news, it seems another soul has died or is in the hospital."

"Isabel told me about the father and six-year-old daughter. Poor things. All they did was go camping."

"At least, so far, it's just Gaudry water that's been poisoned," Adele said.

Zoe shuddered. "But if someone can inject cyanide into bottled water, they can inject it into almost any container. It scares me to think of what could happen next."

CHAPTER 17

Jude stood at the window in his office and listened to the bells of Saint Catherine's announcing the noon recitation of the *Angelus*. He bowed his head and silently prayed the familiar words he'd known since he was a boy.

The angel of the Lord declared unto Mary, and she conceived by the Holy Ghost. Hail Mary, full of grace, the Lord is with thee. Blessed art thou among women, and blessed is the fruit of thy womb, Jesus....

Jude prayed the prayer, stanza by stanza, glad that no one came into his office to interrupt these precious minutes with the Almighty. Finally, he heard footsteps in the hallway but kept his eyes closed, determined to finish the final prayer:

Pour forth, we beseech Thee, O Lord, Thy grace into our hearts, that we to whom the Incarnation of Christ Thy Son was made known by the message of an angel, may by His Passion and Cross be brought to the glory of His Resurrection. Through the same Christ Our Lord. Amen.

Jude stood for a moment, leaning on the window and aware of someone standing outside his door. "Come in."

Aimee came in and sat in the chair next to his desk, staring at her hands. "Caissy Paquet didn't make it."

Jude refrained from swearing, the *Angelus* still fresh in his mind. "When did she die?"

"The doctor called it five minutes ago. As soon as family members are notified, the doctor at Hargrave will address the media."

"What about the dad?"

"Rick Paquet is expected to make a full recovery."

Jude sighed. "Physically, maybe."

"*And,* as if the poor man didn't have enough to work through, the lab report just came back on the other six bottles of Gaudry water in the Paquets' camping cooler—none contained cyanide."

Jude shook his head. "The guy'll probably be asking himself the rest of his life why they chose that particular bottle of water. And why his daughter died and he didn't."

Aimee pursed her lips. "Haunting questions without answers."

"We need to make sure Chief Norman is informed."

"Gil's doing that now. Also Dr. Jenson from DHH."

Jude paced in front of the window. "There's nothing to be gained by grilling these family members the way we did at the onset of this investigation. It seems pretty obvious now that all eight cyanide deaths were random acts of violence."

"I agree."

"But *this* one was avoidable, Aimee." Jude threw his hands in the air. "That little girl shouldn't have died. We informed the public. We warned them not to drink that brand. We even took it off the shelves. What else were we supposed to do?"

"We did everything we knew to do."

"It wasn't good enough." Jude raked his hands through his hair, then sat at his desk, studying the picture of his three grown kids. "This shouldn't have happened."

"None of it should've happened, Jude. We're not God. We can't know who's listening and who isn't. All we can do is get the word out."

Jude sat back in his chair and let out a sigh of exasperation. "Unfortunately, Caissy Paquet's death will get the word out a lot more effectively than we did."

Zoe walked into the kitchen at Zoe B's and spotted Pierce at the worktable, rolling out a yellow crust, his chef's hat making him look over seven feet tall.

Pierce glanced up at her. "Did you hear about that little girl and her father who got sick from Gaudry water on a camping trip?"

"Yes, Isabel told me when I stopped by Adele's. Any word on their condition?"

"The little girl died. Her father is supposed to recover."

Zoe's heart sank. "I can't think about another child dying. Domi's death is all I can bear right now." She walked over to him and kissed his cheek. "Let's table that conversation for later. Tonight's plan is to leave the kids at home with Maddie, pick up Adele and Isabel at five forty-five, and take them with us to the funeral home. They'll eat dinner before we pick them up. After it's over, we'll take them home. You and I can have a late dinner wherever you want."

Pierce took the tiny fleur-de-lis–shaped cookie cutter and cut the dough into half-dollar–size butter cookies he would bake and then use as a garnish on chocolate mousse, his homemade peach ice cream, and his signature lemonade bread pudding. "If you leave it up to me, I'll pick Louie's for a steak burger every time. Isn't there somewhere *you'd* like to have dinner?"

"Not tonight." Zoe exhaled. "I doubt I'll be hungry after comforting Margot and Josh."

"We don't have to go out. We can come back here, and I'll fix you whatever you like."

"You're off tonight," Zoe said. "I don't want you cooking for me. We can go to Louie's. If I'm hungry, I'll eat. Otherwise, I'll just keep you company."

Pierce set the cookie cutter down and wiped his hands on his chef's apron. He put his arms around Zoe. "I'm upset too, babe. Don't think that, just because I haven't lost my appetite, I'm not sad about Domi. I'm just trying to focus on other things. It was a blessing that Jude and Colette gave us a plug on the news the other night. I want to keep the momentum going. Which reminds me, did you tell Adele that the guy she sent to us has been back three times?"

Zoe nodded.

"Did she say how she knows him?"

"No, but you know how Adele is. She probably met him in line somewhere and gave him one of our cards."

"As long as Sax keeps coming in, I think we should go out of our way to make his experiences here exceed expectation," Pierce said. "It'd be great if he'd go back to New Orleans and pass the word about Zoe B's. And Langley Manor. And what a great weekend getaway Les Barbes is. I mean, he's a musician. He's bound to know a few folks in his sphere of influence."

"What do you think we should do that we're not already doing?"

"Just ramp it up a little." Pierce pushed back and looked into her eyes. "Be your warmest, most charming self. And make sure you personally talk with him each time he's in here. Offer him free beignets. Or the dessert of his choice. Better yet, offer him—on the house—one of the dishes I've been experimenting with and let him give his input. He'd probably enjoy that, and I really could use the feedback."

"You're sure rolling out the red carpet for this one guy," Zoe said.

Pierce arched his eyebrows. "It's good marketing, no? If Sax has a good experience, he's bound to tell others, and Les Barbes is less than a two-hour drive from New Orleans. Why are you looking at me like that?"

"We've had lots of customers from New Orleans. You've never zeroed in on any of them before."

"Because we've never had a food-safety scare before. The negative press has the potential to keep people away for a long time. We need customers—especially those in other cities around the state—to go home with good things to say about Les Barbes. And, specifically, Zoe B's."

"That would be nice." Zoe laid her head on his shoulder. "But I wonder if anyone who's visiting Les Barbes is going to go back home remembering anything other than eight people—two of them children—died of cyanide poisoning."

"Well, let's hope our extra efforts shine through all that. They'll remember they could come here and eat safely. And our Cajun cuisine rivals any in town."

"I can't help but wonder how the Marcottes must feel, knowing the poisonings originated at their market. I don't know how I would've handled it if it had happened here. I'd feel so responsible."

"I doubt it's over, either," Pierce said. "Anyone capable of this can strike almost any place where people let their guard down."

Zoe shuddered. "Don't even think it. I'm scared enough as it is."

Sax held the menu in front of his face, eavesdropping on the old guys playing checkers at Zoe B's, amused to learn that Hebert had won twelve consecutive games, much to the chagrin of Father Sam and Tex.

"Dat all you got?" Hebert flashed a row of stained teeth, his unruly gray curls making him look like the stereotype of a mad scientist.

"That's it for me." Father Sam, his full head of white hair neatly combed, took off his thick glasses and rubbed his eyes. "You know, I wouldn't be offended if you let me win once in a while."

"*My eye*!" Hebert chuckled. "You got to earn it."

"I've lost count how many times you've beat us this year."

"Oh, I stopped dat count at five hundred. But since da New Year, I only lost six games to you and Tex combined. Ha! Not bad for an old duffer who's *going to make a hundred* next birthday."

"You're a legend." Tex arched his thick silver eyebrows, his bald head reflecting the light filtering through the blinds. "I've never seen anything like it."

Sax's cell phone vibrated. He looked at the screen and saw that Adele Woodmore was the caller.

He took a deep breath, put the phone to his ear, and spoke softly. "Hello."

"Hello, Sax. Adele Woodmore here. I apologize for taking so long to get back to you. I've decided to do what I can to put you and Shelby together. I'm working on a strategy, but timing is important. It might take a while."

"What strategy?"

"I really don't want to get into that with you," Adele said. "Can you stay a few more days while I work on it?"

"I don't have much choice. I came here with only one thing in mind: finding my sister."

"I still don't know that she will be open to contacting you."

Sax traced the fleur-de-lis on the tablecloth with his index finger. "Will you tell her that finding her is the only thing that matters to me—and that I want to tell her how sorry I am?"

"I'll tell her," Adele said. "I'm just not sure if she's strong enough to open that door to the past."

"Maybe she would be if she only realized how deeply sorry I am for failing her. Surely there's an emptiness somewhere deep inside her that longs to be reconciled? We were both kids, for heaven's sake. I made a selfish choice that's hurt us both. We're not kids anymore. I really want—*need*—to make things right with Shel—" An unexpected wave of emotion stole his voice.

"I believe you, Sax, or I wouldn't have agreed to help you." Adele sighed. "Will your staying at Langley Manor a while longer pose a financial hardship?"

"That's the least of my worries, ma'am. I'm prepared to do whatever it takes."

"Zoe mentioned that she and Pierce are pleased you've been eating at Zoe B's."

"They've both gone out of their way to make me feel welcome. Actually, their entire staff has. I enjoy eating here. Love the food. But the atmosphere is nice too."

"You're there now?"

"Yes, I'm about to order lunch. And I've been amusing myself watching three elderly guys playing checkers. I've seen them in here before."

"Yes, they're dear friends of Zoe's," Adele said. "All right, then. I'll be in touch soon."

There was a long moment of dead air, but he sensed she hadn't hung up. "Mrs. Woodmore, are you still there?"

"Yes, I'm here. For what it's worth, Sax, I want Shelby to hear you out. But if I find out your intentions are different than what you've presented, you will have me to contend with. And I promise you, you do not want to cross me. I may look like a frail, white-haired old lady, but I can be a she-bear when someone is messing with my cub. Are we clear?"

"Yes, ma'am. Perfectly."

"I will call you when I have something new to say. Otherwise, be patient, and let's see how this plays out."

"Thank you, Mrs. Woodmore."

Sax ended the call and put his phone in his shirt pocket, his heart nearly pounding out of his chest.

Was it finally going to happen? Was he finally going to get the chance to pour out his heart to his sister and try to make up for all the years they missed?

Sax sat there, lost in thought, feeling both excited and a little scared. He was suddenly aware of footsteps and looked up just as Zoe walked up next to his table, wearing a smile that would melt an iceberg.

"How nice to see you, Sax," Zoe said. "Savannah told me you were here. It just so happens that Pierce is experimenting with a new menu item and thought you might be a perfect person to try it—complimentary, of course. It's made with strips of blackened chicken smothered in a wine and cream sauce blended with sautéed celery, pepper, onion, artichokes, ripe olives, and some very special spices. It's served over rice. Interested? Or would you prefer to order from the menu?"

"No need for the menu. I'd love to try it. Thanks."

"Pierce will be excited." There was that warm smile again. "He loves creating new dishes for people who appreciate Cajun cuisine."

"You know I do. But I'm perfectly willing to pay for it."

"Your input will be payment enough."

"Great. I do love the food and the ambiance of the place." Sax nodded toward the table by the window. "The entertainment isn't bad either."

"So you're enjoying my three guys, are you?"

Sax listened as Zoe summed up her longtime relationship with Hebert, Father Sam, and Tex.

"So Hebert was your very first customer?"

Zoe looked over at the three men and smiled. "He was the first to shake my hand and walk into Zoe B's on opening day. Father Sam and Tex began coming shortly after that. The three struck up a conversation, moved to the same table, and have been the best of friends ever since. They're here for breakfast, lunch, and dinner—and much of the day to play checkers or just talk about how to change the world. I've adopted them as family."

"I heard Hebert say he's going to be a hundred on his next birthday. We should all be that sharp at eighty—let alone a hundred."

"Isn't that the truth?" Zoe met his gaze. "I'll go tell Pierce you're eager to try his new dish. I hope whatever business you have in Les Barbes gets resolved the way you want. But as long as you're in town, we hope you'll keep comin' in."

"I'm sure I will." Sax cocked his head. "Is that a Texas accent I just heard in your voice?"

The corners of Zoe's mouth twitched. "I was born in Texas. But I can't believe there's even a hint of the accent left. I've lived in Looziana all of my adult life."

"I guess it takes one to know one. Where in Texas were you born?"

Zoe's face flushed. "Some obscure town no one's ever heard of and that's barely on the map."

"Yeah, me, too. The bayou's in my blood, and I consider Looziana my home. Well, tell Pierce I'm game to try whatever he wants to run by me. He's an awesome chef."

"I'll go tell him." Zoe took his menu.

Sax watched as she walked back into the kitchen and felt that twinge of longing to find his sister. At least Adele Woodmore was willing to get involved. He was *halfway* there.

CHAPTER 18

Zoe went into the kitchen at the eatery and over to the oblong worktable, where Pierce was busy filling orders.

"It's a good thing Savannah told us that Sax was here for lunch," Zoe said. "He's totally game to try your new blackened chicken in wine and cream sauce."

"I'm jazzed. I've only tried it out on a half-dozen people. If he likes it, I'm ready to serve it for a weekend special. Do you think he'd tell me if he didn't like it—or thought it was just so-so?"

"Probably not in those words," Zoe said. "But I'm pretty good at reading people. I think I could tell if he was just being polite. But you've said yourself it's subjective."

"Yes, but Sax loves Cajun food and has eaten at fine restaurants in the Big Easy. I value his opinion."

"You get nervous as a kitten when you introduce a new dish," Zoe said.

Pierce smiled sheepishly. "It's a little like putting my baby out there. I want everyone to think it's perfect."

"Well, I think it's perfect, and not just because you're my husband." Zoe snitched a green olive and popped it into her mouth.

"Sax said something that really surprised me. He asked if it was a Texas accent he detected in my voice. Do I still have that?"

Pierce shrugged. "I don't hear it."

"Sax did. Apparently he's from Texas. He wanted to know where in Texas I was born. I froze for a minute. I was ashamed to tell him."

"Why? What's the big deal?"

"I'm not sure. I just didn't want to admit where I'm from. Isn't that silly after all this time?"

"What *did* you tell him?"

"I said something about it being an obscure town no one's ever heard of and was barely on the map. Which is true. He said his was too. That he has the bayou in his blood and considers himself to be a Looziana boy."

"I still don't know why you didn't just tell him."

"I don't know either. That's what bothers me. I thought I was done with feeling ashamed. Do you think I need to go back to the clinic and do more counseling?"

"I don't know, babe. If you have doubts, maybe you should ask Ethan's advice. But from my perspective, you seem great."

"I feel great." Zoe smiled. "I'm so proud to be your wife and the mother of our two beautiful children. And partners with you in a thriving business we both enjoy. We are so blessed."

"Indeed we are." Pierce took a big pinch of scallions and dropped it into the sauce he was stirring. "I know you balk every time I bring this up, but I wish you'd at least consider going back to Texas and seeing your mother."

"No."

"I'd be willing to go with you."

"No. Why this sudden push to contact her?"

Pierce stopped working and looked up at her. "Zoe, Hebert's turning one hundred. One of these days, he's going to pass away. His absence would dramatically change the dynamic around here on a number of levels. And Adele is getting up there. I'm concerned that if you don't start preparing for the voids that are inevitable, you're going to be depressed."

"You already told me all this. You said you weren't going to push me."

"I'm not pushing you—just nudging a little. I love you and know you better than anyone else. You're going to feel lost when Hebert's gone and the trio is no longer a trio. And when Adele can no longer be the mother you wish you had."

"You don't know that."

"Yes. I do."

"I have you and the kids—and I have your family. And our other friends."

"Just pray about it," Pierce said. "See if you get any insights."

Zoe popped another olive into her mouth and walked toward the door. "I'll let Sax know his lunch will be coming soon."

At exactly three fifteen, Emily knocked on the kitchen door at Chance's house and was met with the stony gaze of a sixtysomething woman with salt-and-pepper hair. The woman wore a black shift, sensible shoes—and an ugly scowl.

"You must be Chance's aunt Reba." Emily tried to smile but

wasn't sure whether her face had cooperated. "I'm Emily Jessup. We spoke on the phone."

"Yes, we did," Reba Littleton said. "You've wasted your time coming here. You're sadly mistaken if you think anything you can do will help matters. Chance is on a toot and isn't about to let anyone help him."

"I just came to keep him company," Emily said. "And then drive him to the funeral home."

"There's plenty of *family* in town that can do that."

Emily bit her lip. "Yes, ma'am. But he asked me to do it. I'm not trying to take the place of family, but Chance and I were together when the deputy called and told him to come to the hospital—and when the doctor told him the terrible news that both his parents had died. We've shared a lot in the past couple days. He knows I can relate to what he's going through. I lost my grandparents in a head-on collision and know what it's like to have someone you cherish taken from you in an instant."

"Hmm … then why don't you go *relate* some sense into him?"

"What do you mean?"

Reba exhaled, her hands on her hips. "He's in his room and won't come out."

"He asked for solitude," Emily said. "He's not feeling social right now."

"How about *civil*? For heaven's sake, Chance swore at me for doing his dirty laundry. I was only trying to help. And he got downright belligerent when I started cleaning out my sister's closet."

"Maybe he's not ready for that to happen just yet." Emily opened the door and stepped into the kitchen.

"He'd better learn to be grateful for whatever help he can get," Reba said. "In a few days, all the relatives will need to return home, and Chance will be left with all of it. Do you really think he's up to *that*?"

"Ma'am, his parents were just murdered. I don't think Chance is up to anything yet. I don't think the full weight of what happened has even hit him. It's pretty sobering to say good-bye to your parents one morning and come back that afternoon—an orphan."

"That's precisely why he needs his aunts and uncles and cousins to rally around him."

"He does—but quietly, and in moderation. He's completely overwhelmed, particularly about losing his mother."

Reba's expression softened. "Yes, Lydia and Chance were close. Huet never appreciated Chance's full potential until the boy got accepted into Harvard Medical School. Even then it was hard for Huet to show how proud he was. The man was such a perfectionist, he could find fault with God Himself. Lydia loved him. I tolerated him—and he made a modest effort to do the same...." Reba's voice cracked, and she waved her hand dismissively. "None of that matters now. I will miss them terribly."

"Have you been to the funeral home yet?"

Reba nodded. "I stopped there first. The undertaker did a surprising job. They both look so natural I half expected them to open their eyes. I still can't believe they're gone. I was pleased to see Lydia dressed in her favorite blue dress." Reba took a wadded-up tissue out of the pocket of her dress and wiped a tear off her cheek. "It seems like only yesterday I was maid of honor at their wedding. You wonder sometimes how the end will come for those you love. But never would I have imagined *this*...."

Emily reached over and squeezed Reba's hand. "Of course not. It's tragic."

Reba seemed receptive for a moment and then yanked her hand back. "I talked with Imogene Fluette at Saint Catherine's. She's coordinating the bringing of food tonight and tomorrow. Chance won't need to burden himself with kitchen matters. It's being handled."

"Thank you."

"But you have to make Chance eat," Reba said. "He ate a Pop Tart for breakfast and refused all my efforts to fix him something substantial."

"I imagine his stomach's upset."

Reba wrinkled her nose. "More like he doesn't want me here."

"In all fairness to Chance, he did ask to be left alone. He's going to resist anyone he feels is pushing him right now."

"He *needs* to be pushed. Lydia understood that about him."

"As only a mother could," Emily said. "Chance is a grown man. And for all practical purposes, he's been on his own since he went away to college five years ago."

"Maybe so, but he just lost his family." Reba dabbed her eyes. "I'd like to think that Lydia is smiling down on me for reaching out to him."

"It's very kind of you to want to look out for your nephew. You strike me as the type of person who needs to show love by doing things for people."

Reba seemed lost in a long pause and then said, "It's about time you figured that out, Emelia."

"It's Emily, ma'am. And I can appreciate how much you long

to help Chance. But perhaps the way to best help him is to trust his judgment and do what he asked."

"Stay away?"

"Not entirely, no. I think he could very much use your help coordinating the food tonight and tomorrow and directing friends and family. But I think beyond that, you might do well to wait until he asks for help."

"When someone dies," Reba said, "there are a number of practical matters that need tending to right away. In this case, there will be twice as many."

"I'm sure you know about these things," Emily said. "But it's hard to say how much of it Chance wants help with. He's a self-reliant person. He's been in contact with the family attorney, and they're supposed to meet day after tomorrow."

"His attorney will direct him each step of the way. But Chance will have to do the footwork. There will be accounts to close, policies to cancel. Names to be switched. He's not in any shape to think that hard." Reba sighed. "I can help him, if only he'll let me. I had to do all this when my husband died. I would really like to save him some of the hassle."

"It's easy to see how sincere you are," Emily said. "Perhaps the more space you give him, the freer he will feel to invite you closer—but when he's ready."

Reba seemed to study Emily's face. "I really didn't want to like you, young lady."

"Should I take that to mean that you do?"

The corners of Reba's mouth twitched. "Go talk to Chance. All I want him to do is come out of his room and not treat me like I have the plague. I promise not to bother him. But I need to be here to receive the food, which should be coming soon."

Emily held out her hand, pleased when Reba took it. "I'm truly sorry you lost your sister. I have one and can't imagine what it would feel like to lose her—and in such a horrible way. If there's anything I can do to help you, I'd be happy to. I know this is so difficult."

Reba's eyes were suddenly dark pools. She squeezed Emily's hand for several seconds, struggling to regain her composure. "Go. Talk to Chance. Make him understand I'm not the enemy, and that he's all I have left of Lydia. That would help me more than anything else."

Emily walked down the hallway and knocked on the last door. "Chance, it's me."

A few seconds later, the door opened, and Chance, unshaven and eyes bloodshot, filled the doorway.

"I'm glad you're here," he said. "It's been a miserable day."

Emily embraced him, then pushed her purse strap higher on her shoulder. "Well, I'm here now and don't have to be back at work until three p.m. day after tomorrow. I want to be here to support you any way I can."

"You can start by telling Aunt Reba to leave."

"I had a lengthy conversation with her just now."

"I'll just bet you did."

"Chance ..." Emily held his gaze. "Maybe you're overreacting to your aunt's being here today. It's not like she's moving in or even staying overnight. She came by to check on you and to make arrangements for the food to be brought in for when the rest of your family arrives."

"Is that what she told you?" He pulled her into the room and shut the door. "She's been barking out orders since she got here."

"Tell me if I'm wrong." Emily set her purse on the desk. "She offered to make you something to eat, did your dirty laundry, and tried to weed out your mother's closet so you wouldn't have to deal with that pain."

"Oh brother! She's gotten to you."

"Is your aunt Reba prone to tears?"

"Absolutely not. I've seen tree bark show more emotion than she does."

"Well," Emily said, "she let her guard down a minute ago with me and got really emotional over her sister's death. And also implored me to convince you that she is not the enemy—and that you're all she has left of Lydia."

"Aunt Reba actually said that?"

Emily nodded. "I think the two of us had a breakthrough. She said she didn't expect to like me. I certainly didn't think I would like her."

"Do you?"

"I sense a real tenderness in her, Chance. Maybe you two have never really understood one another."

Chance shook his head and sighed. "I don't believe this. In five minutes, she's turned you into her puppet."

"I'm nobody's puppet," Emily said emphatically. "But grief has the power to break even people who usually hide their feelings. I expected to see a pushy, obnoxious, overbearing woman. Instead, I saw a vulnerable human being who is genuinely grieving the loss of her sister and wants very much to show her love by watching after her sister's son."

"Who's a grown man, Emily. I don't want or need her help."

"So you say. But you have to admit, having her coordinating the food and directing family and friends is a huge weight off your shoulders."

"But she won't stop there. If I let her help with one thing, she'll start with another—laundry, cooking, cleaning, grocery shopping. The woman pushes and pushes until she gets under my skin, and then she takes over—like a supervirus."

"Or an efficient organizer." Emily took his hand. "There's so much to do, and she's so willing. Would it be that difficult to let her help? She did what you wanted and isn't staying here. She understands you need time alone. I honestly think she would try to stay out of your way."

"But I can't think straight. I don't have the focus or the energy to figure out what needs to be done."

"She does. What if she and I work together to take care of some of the essentials? I'd run it by you first so you'd always know what's going on but wouldn't have to get involved unless you just want to. Or you need to sign something."

Chance let go of her hand and walked over to the bed and flopped onto it. "Do whatever you want. I give up."

Was she going to let him get away with that response? She decided she wasn't. "That's not good enough," Emily said. "I'm trying to help you. We both are. Either you want our help, or you don't. But I'm not accepting 'Do whatever you want.' That's a cop-out."

"I told you what *I want*, Emily. Apparently, it's not what you think I need."

"I don't believe the two are at odds. You can be by yourself all you want. Aunt Reba and I can accomplish a great deal between now and the time I have to go back to work, and then you'll have the house to yourself without the laundry list of to-dos hanging over you."

"Like what? My parents' attorney's taking care of the will and estate issues."

"But you will need to cancel credit cards, policies, car insurance, switch utilities to your name, and things I haven't begun to consider. The man at the funeral home said he would provide you with ten certificates of death, so he must be anticipating you're going to need them. I have never done this before, so I'm learning as I go. But between Aunt Reba and me, we can get it figured out so you won't have to think too hard."

Chance fell back on the bed, lying flat on his back. "I don't even know if I'm going to keep the house. I'm hardly ever here. Why do I want this big expense?"

"You probably don't. But I've always heard that it's good not to make any major decisions for a year after losing someone you love. Selling this house right now would be another loss to deal with."

"That's why I just want some time here—to be by myself and work things out in my head."

"You'll have it. I promise. But there're some practical issues that will require timely attention. I think Aunt Reba can be extremely helpful. She lost her husband and had to go through this herself. She can help you figure out what needs to be done."

Chance clasped his hands behind his head. "You really think she has my best interests at heart?"

Emily nodded. "She wants to do for you what she thinks your mother would want."

"I miss Mom so much." Chance closed his eyes. "This is not the way things were supposed to happen. It's such a nightmare."

"It really is. No one should have to endure the murder of one parent, let alone two. I hope the sheriff locks up whoever's responsible and throws away the key."

"It won't ever get that far. He doesn't have a clue who did this."

"Don't underestimate law enforcement," Emily said. "All criminals make mistakes."

"Not this time."

"Don't be so negative. It just happened Saturday. They need time to fit all the pieces of the puzzle together. I've watched my mother do it time after time."

Chance shot her a patronizing smile. Did she really need this?

"So," Emily said, "are you okay with Aunt Reba and me working together to help get some of the practical matters out of the way?"

"Knock yourselves out."

Emily stiffened at Chance's lackluster response. Did she expect gratitude from a guy who was grieving and just wanted everyone to disappear?

"I'm going to go see what I can do to help in the kitchen. The food will be arriving soon." Emily turned to go.

"Wait." Chance jumped up off the bed, pulled her into his arms, and held her tightly. "Don't go yet."

She rested for a few moments in his arms, surprised and relieved when he began to sob quietly, releasing some of the deep sadness he'd been covering up with rudeness and sarcasm. She didn't move. Or breathe. She held back her own emotion that tightened like a vice around her vocal chords, flattered that Chance trusted her with this moment of frailty.

Lord, help me to be both a light and a comfort to Chance through this terrible season of grief. I can only hope that his sorrow and helplessness will lead him to trust in You. But whatever Your purpose for putting him in my path, help me to do Your will.

CHAPTER 19

Zoe stood outside Blain Funeral Home, under the brick portico, watching people crossing Ascension Boulevard. They were all walking south on Lafayette, some carrying lawn chairs. She remembered the Les Barbes Jazz Orchestra was performing this evening in Cypress Park. She could picture the lively gathering of friends, neighbors, and tourists on the green grassy lawn around the bandstand, some seated in lawn or event chairs, others on blankets, enjoying homemade strawberry ice cream being served up by the Junior League.

Her mind flashed back to one such evening when Dominic and Grace, wearing ice cream mustaches and happy smiles, sat together on a blanket, listening to the concert. They got up, holding hands, and danced to the livelier numbers, uninhibited and giggling as was befitting the innocent children they were.

Were. Zoe felt as if her heart were being ripped from her body. How was it that Margot and Josh managed to greet and talk to all those grieving friends, their son's open casket just feet away, when Zoe could barely keep it together?

She sensed someone tall walk up beside her.

"Zoe? I thought that was you."

"Sax." She quickly dabbed her eyes. "What brings you here?"

"I'm just out taking a walk. I had dinner at your place and heard there was a jazz concert tonight. I thought I'd kill some time and then head toward the park. What about you?"

"I'm here to support my friends who lost their little boy to cyanide poisoning—the one I told you about. And also the friend of one of my employees who lost both parents."

Sax glanced at the sign out front, his cheeks suddenly hot pink. "I'm so sorry. I was just walking by. I … I didn't pay attention to the sign. Talk about insensitive."

"Don't be embarrassed," Zoe said. "I don't read every sign either."

"Is Emily Jessup here?" he asked. "It's her friend who lost his parents, right?"

Zoe nodded. "She's here with Chance's family."

"As long as I'm here, I think I'll go pay my respects," Sax said. "Do you think that would be appropriate?"

"I think it's very sweet. Emily would appreciate it, even if you and Chance haven't met."

"All right. I'll go do that right now. I'm sorry it's such a tough night for you, Zoe. I remember you said the little boy was Grace's favorite playmate. Were you also close to his family?"

"Very. We're all devastated. Domi was the most loving, gentle, adorable child. Too bad he didn't get the chance to grow up and make the world a better place." Zoe brushed a tear from her cheek.

"It's stuff like this that makes me want five minutes with God to tell Him what I think of His will that He keeps imposing on everyone."

"I don't blame God for this, Sax. Some nutcase put cyanide in chocolate pudding."

"Sorry, but I do blame Him. He could've stopped it. I'll never understand why He lets innocent children get hurt, abused, or murdered. I just don't see Him as this loving, protective, wonderful God we're supposed to *praise.* All I want to do is give Him a piece of my mind. Sorry if that offends you."

"I'm not easily offended. But it makes me sad. As long as you have that perception of God, you'll never have the close, personal relationship He wants with you."

"Trust me, God doesn't want me. He turned a deaf ear to my cries decades ago." Sax looked down at his feet. "I'm sorry. This is neither the time nor the place for me to go off on one of my tangents. I'm going to go inside now and find Emily."

Zoe nodded.

Sax turned and left and, seconds later, she heard Pierce's voice.

"Sax, I didn't expect to run into *you* here."

"I was just going to go inside and see if I can spot Emily. I'm sorry about Chance's parents. I'd like to pay my respects."

"She'll appreciate that. It's the last room on the left." Pierce walked over and stood next to Zoe, taking her hand in his. "You've been out here a long time. I thought maybe you could use someone to talk to."

"I couldn't bear another minute of watching Margot and Josh talk about Domi with each person who came to comfort them," she said. "How are they doing it? They're a lot more in control than I am, that's for sure."

"His grace is sufficient, babe. It's pretty obvious they're relying on God to get them through this."

"I'm not sure I could handle it as well as they are."

"His grace would be sufficient for us, too, if we were facing such a tragedy. But we're not, so don't even go there."

Zoe watched a couple cross the street with two little boys, one riding on the man's shoulders. "I can understand Sax's anger."

"So can I, after what you told me of his background. But I know God is good—all the time."

"Right now that seems like a cliché."

"I suppose it does. But God doesn't change just because we're disappointed or sad or even angry. As long as we're in this fallen world, bad things are going to happen to good people."

"And innocent children."

"Yes. But God doesn't change. He's the same yesterday, today, and forever."

Zoe sighed. "Pierce, stop with the clichés."

"Since when is Scripture a cliché? I can't cite chapter and verse, but I know it's in the Bible that God is the same yesterday, today, and forever."

"I believe that God's always the same. But Domi's dead. And the rest of us will *never* be the same."

Pierce tightened his grip on her hand. "I know."

"Sax commented that he couldn't understand why God lets innocent children get hurt, abused, or murdered."

"None of us knows the answer to that," Pierce said. "It's the oldest question in the book. We're never going to understand how these awful things fit into a bigger plan."

"It just brought back a lot of hurtful memories, that's all." Zoe sighed. "There's so much suffering in the world, and little children are the most vulnerable."

"We need to do everything in our power to make sure ours aren't."

"I'm sure Josh and Margot thought the same thing." Zoe blinked the stinging from her eyes. "All they did was stop for lunch when they were grocery shopping. A few minutes later their son collapsed and died right in front of their eyes."

"Some things are out of our hands, babe. We have to trust God. And don't tell me that's another cliché, because I'm not buying it."

Zoe bit her lip. Why was she questioning God all of a sudden? In her heart of hearts, didn't she believe He was sovereign—and that He was good?

"Are you ready to go back inside?" Pierce said.

"I wouldn't say ready. But I suppose we should see how Adele and Isabel are doing and say good-bye to Josh and Margot."

"And Domi. I don't think you should rush off before you've let him go."

"How am I supposed to do that? It's all I could do not to reach down, pick him up, and carry him out of this place. He looks like a sleeping angel."

Pierce slipped his arm around her. "And that's how we should remember him."

"I just can't stand that this is happening, *cher*."

"Who can?" Pierce stroked her hair. "But it's what we have to deal with. Jude will find whoever's responsible. This will all be over soon."

Zoe didn't say what she was thinking. Pierce didn't sound any more convinced than she was.

Emily sat in the quiet, all guests having come and gone from the room where Huet and Lydia Durands' open coffins were laid. The room was swallowed up with flower arrangements. More than once her mind flashed back to that awful night when her parents took her to the funeral home to see her grandparents after the head-on collision that took their lives. The memory still haunted her.

Aunt Reba had herded the family back to Chance's house, where she had the food ready to go. Chance decided to stay behind and asked Emily to wait with him. He said he wanted a few minutes alone. He had been standing at his mother's coffin for thirteen minutes. Emily wondered what was going through his mind—no doubt a heartrending good-bye.

Emily had no idea how many people had come to comfort Chance and his family, but the line had gone down the hallway and out the door. It seemed as if it would never stop. Chance eventually seemed to warm up and receive the love and sympathy that was so graciously extended to him. It was obvious that he recognized many of the people and appreciated their coming.

Emily didn't know anyone and was glad to see Sax Henry's familiar face when he came by to pay his respects.

Chance kissed his fingers and pressed them to his mother's lips, then turned and walked over to Emily and sat next to her.

"Thanks for staying with me."

"You're welcome."

"Why do you suppose everyone always says the deceased look good? They look dead."

"I think it's subjective," Emily said. "Reba thought they looked natural."

"They look dead." Chance's chin quivered. "I can't tell you how desperately I want to take Mom's hand and pull her up out of that coffin. Bring her back to life."

"I know what you're saying. I felt the same way when my grandparents died. I was a little kid, but I loved them dearly. We were close."

"I can't believe this is happening." Chance whisked a tear off his cheek. "This should never have happened."

"Of course it shouldn't."

"You don't understand. My mom never drank bottled water. She said she didn't like the taste. Why did she have to drink it the one time it was poisoned?"

Emily shook her head. "We'll never know the answer to that." She put her hand on Chance's back and rubbed gently, feeling no need to say anything else. How difficult it must be for him, knowing his mother would not be there to celebrate his graduation from medical school. His first surgical procedure. His beginning a private practice. His marriage. The birth of his children. Or any other major event.

"I don't know how I'm going to go on without her," Chance said.

"It'll take time. But from what I observed this evening, you have a very caring family that will be there to support you and celebrate the milestones."

"It's not the same."

"No. But it might be a great comfort down the road. You're certainly not alone. Your aunts and uncles are only in their fifties and sixties. It's likely they'll be alive for a long time. And you have dozens of cousins."

"Why didn't one of *them* die? Why did it have to be my mother?"

"I don't know, Chance. It's just the way it is."

He squeezed her hand. "Sorry. I didn't mean to snap at you. That was a terrible thing to say. I'm just so angry. I don't understand why she drank the water. . . ."

Emily remembered all too well the anger and the questioning stages of grief. Better just to listen to Chance process his pain than to offer empty answers.

She blew the bangs off her forehead. At least this part was over. Now to get through the funeral.

Jude sat at the conference table in his office, the cyanide case files open in front of him. He raked his hands through his hair for the umpteenth time. There was nothing here. Not a shred of evidence that pointed him anywhere. They couldn't even tell if the poisonings had been done by an individual working alone or a terrorist organization. He picked up his pencil and threw it at the window.

Why was he letting Caissy Paquet's death impact him more than the others? Was her life any more valuable—or was it because she reminded him so much of his daughter Bridgette at that age? How tragic it would have been had his beautiful, twenty-four-year-old daughter been ripped from him at six years old and had never lived to bless him beyond measure—not to mention the third-grade class at Saint Catherine Elementary School.

He felt two hands touch his shoulders and jumped, his heart pounding.

"Sorry, Jude," Colette Prejean said. "I didn't mean to scare you."

"I was lost in thought. I didn't hear you come in."

Colette massaged his shoulders as only she knew how, and he relished her relaxing touch.

"Do you have any idea what time it is?" she said.

"No, my watch battery went dead, and I was too lazy to get up and look at the clock on my desk."

"It's nine fifteen. You need to get out of here and clear your head."

Jude winced. "I stood you up, didn't I?"

"That's all right. I went to the concert with Bridgette."

"How was it?"

Colette bent down and kissed his stubbly cheek. "Terrific. It would've been even better if you'd been with us."

He reached up and took her hand. "I'm sorry, sweetheart. Is it too late to go out for dinner? I'm starved."

"I've already eaten, but why don't we go to Zoe B's? You can have dinner, and I'll have a piece of Pierce's lemonade bread pudding. I'm still a little gun-shy of eating anywhere else."

"Don't let anyone else hear you say that." He stood and pulled her into his arms. "Judging by the hordes of people flocking into Zoe B's, the public takes what we say very seriously."

Colette smiled impishly, her round brown eyes animated. "Zoe said business has never been better since you mentioned Zoe B's on the news the other night."

"Kernel Poppy's is thriving too," he said. "But a lot of eating places are really hurting, especially any place with a buffet of any kind—or a salad bar."

"Are you any closer to finding whoever's responsible for this mess?"

Jude sighed. "Not an inch. I don't even know if it's an individual wacko or an organized group of them."

"What about Adam Marcotte?"

"Nah, he's a real altar boy. I thought he was too good to be true, but he's the real deal. There's nothing in his background that leads me to believe he could do something like this. On a scale of one to ten, my interest in pursuing him as a suspect is zero."

Colette locked her arms around his neck. "So, Sheriff Prejean, you haven't got zip?"

"Nada. Zero. Zilch."

"Remind me what you *do* know."

"We know that a dark-haired male, either Hispanic or Caucasian, average height and build, approached the food bar shortly before it opened and lingered in front of the chocolate pudding, then stirred it and hurried off. We believe he's our perp. But we don't know whether he was working alone. No one has claimed responsibility." Jude pursed his lips. "I can't remember whether or not I told you, but the cyanide in the Gaudry water was ten times the lethal dose for an adult male. And the cyanide in the pudding was only one-half the lethal dose."

"Is that significant?"

Jude shrugged. "It's unclear. Dr. Jensen of DHH concluded it would be easy to measure and inject a lethal dose of cyanide into a sixteen-ounce bottle of water. But trying to achieve the same lethal effect in pudding would be dicey, especially since the perp would have had to know the exact capacity of the container and make an educated guess at what constitutes a *usual* serving of pudding. At any rate, DHH concluded that the cyanide was intended to take out as many people as possible and not any individual person."

Colette shuddered. "No matter how many years I've stood by you in law enforcement, I never can get used to the creepy fact that there are people out there who just delight in killing."

"Dr. Jensen thinks we're dealing with a homegrown variety of terrorist, but no group has come forward."

"Jude, the people I run into are starting to think it could be the work of Muslim extremists. I know Dr. Jensen thinks they're homegrown. What do *you* think?"

"I don't know yet. It's someone wicked enough to target the community at large. And with this many victims and all this media hype, I'm guessing it's far from over."

CHAPTER 20

Emily sat on the back deck at Langley Manor, enjoying a bagel and a glass of orange juice, amused at a bobcat that popped up in the groundcover on the forest's edge, pouncing on some unwary prey.

Vanessa came outside, dressed in her pink terry bathrobe and carrying a cup of coffee. "You're up early for a young lady who doesn't have to work today."

"Did you forget the funeral for Chance's parents is today?"

"I didn't forget." Vanessa set her coffee on the table and sat in a rocker. "How's he doing?"

"Not great. Plus his aunt Reba is driving him a little crazy, but I think they've found a middle ground. Frankly, she's been invaluable at keeping track of family and making sure there's food there for all those people. I'm going to be working with her to knock out a long list of things that have to be done."

"I thought you said there was a family attorney handling matters."

Emily nodded. "He's handling the will. Chance's parents left everything to him. They had a healthy investment portfolio and were almost totally debt-free. We don't know if inheriting money will change his eligibility for a full scholarship. But there are practical details to do while all that's pending, like canceling his parents' credit cards. Getting utilities switched to his name. Closing out their bank accounts and opening one in his name. Plus cleaning out his parents' closets—and the garage. Aunt Reba knows what needs to be done. I'm following her lead."

Vanessa didn't say anything.

Emily sighed. "What now?"

"I don't have any new advice," Vanessa said. "Are you sure you're not jumping the gun on some of the details? Does Chance even plan to keep the house?"

"He doesn't know what he wants to do yet. The house and the cars are paid for, so once they're titled in his name, he'll probably keep them until he knows what he wants to do. I think it'd be good if he decided to wait and deal with it next summer—after he's had time to grieve. He might even decide to move to Boston."

"Was he raised in Les Barbes?"

Emily nodded. "But without his parents, I don't know how strong his roots are. I don't think moving to the East Coast would be a culture shock, since he's already gone to school there for five years."

"This is a lot for you to get involved in."

"Not really."

"What's your work schedule this week?"

"I'm not going to shirk my duties, Vanessa." Emily softened her tone. "I don't go in again until tomorrow at three. I'm hoping to get a lot done between now and then. I'm pretty sure his aunt Reba won't stay much beyond that, so we have a lot to accomplish."

Vanessa took a sip of coffee. "What then?"

"What do you mean?"

"Are you single-handedly going to take responsibility for Chance?"

"I'm planning to keep him company and be there if he wants to talk. Not a whole lot else unless he asks for my help."

"Do you think that's going to make for a relaxing summer?" Vanessa said. "Because you need to wind down so you can gear up for this next school year."

"Unfortunately, big sister, tragedy is no respecter of persons or agendas. I think my first responsibility as a Christian and as a friend is to be there for Chance. Everything else will take care of itself."

"What about your nephew, Emily? Carter's dying to spend time with you."

"I'm not going to neglect Carter. I've got all sorts of fun things planned. But he's going to have to share my time. We'll work it out."

"Not if you're at Chance's every minute you're not working."

Emily counted to ten and sat quietly for a few more seconds and then looked squarely at Vanessa. "That was unfair. His parents were murdered over the weekend. That pretty much trumps everything else. It's been all of a few days that I've been distracted with Chance's situation. You make it sound like I'm obsessed or something."

"I already told you how I feel. I can't tell you what to do. I doubt if you'd listen anyway. But Carter adores you and wants your attention. He's getting older, and that may not always be the case. Once he's in middle school, he'll probably choose to pal around with his friends over family. Your best days with him are going to be now."

"I get it," Emily said. "I love Carter and don't need to be told to spend time with him. Truthfully, you're the one being insensitive.

What happened to Chance was devastating. If it had happened to me, I'd like to think my friends would be there for me."

"The operative word, Emily, is *friends*—plural. You seem to be the *only* friend Chance has. You can't do it all."

"What is your problem? I told you I was working with his aunt Reba on the practical matters, and his attorney is doing all the legal stuff. Chance needs help as much as Carter needs to play miniature golf. So get off my case, Vanessa!"

Emily clamped her eyes shut in the silence that followed, in an effort not to say something she would be sorry for. *Lord, I'm not going to let Vanessa lay a guilt trip on me. Help me find time to do all the right things.*

Zoe unlocked the front door at Zoe B's and waited as the paperboy ran over to her with two copies of Wednesday's *Les Barbes Ledger*. She went back inside and turned on the open sign, the aroma of freshly brewed coffee and brown-sugar cinnamon buns filling her senses.

A few seconds later, Father Sam came inside, wearing his cleric shirt and black pants, a handsome contrast to his snow-white hair.

"Good morning, Zoe, dear. And how are you holding up?"

"Not great. I'm trying to gear up for Domi's funeral this morning. I can't think of anywhere I would rather not go."

"I hear you," Father Sam said. "I'm not looking forward to it either. How are the boy's parents doing?"

"Better than they should be. Their faith is holding them together. Well, that and lots of friends, family, and prayer."

"Monsignor Robidoux is doing the funeral Mass." Father Sam arched his eyebrows. "He's excellent with eulogies."

Zoe nodded.

The front door opened again, and Hebert came in wearing the brown polyester double-knit suit he had bought at a secondhand store and saved for weddings and funerals.

"*Bonjour, mes amis.*" Hebert went over to the table by the window and sat across from Father Sam. "*Comment ça va*?"

"Not that great." Father Sam nodded toward Zoe. "We're feeling somber about Dominic's funeral."

"Everybody sad about dat *p'tit boug*," Hebert said.

Zoe blinked the stinging from her eyes. "Domi was a special little boy. He was remarkably compassionate and unselfish for a four-year-old. I will always wonder what he would have grown up to be, had he lived."

Hebert patted her hand. "He so sweet dat God Almighty want him now."

"But why?" Zoe said. "Wouldn't the world have been a better place with Domi in it? And why did he have to die of cyanide poisoning?"

Father Sam looked up at her, the empathy in his hazel eyes magnified in his thick lenses. "His thoughts are not our thoughts."

"At least da poison took him real quick," Hebert said. "Da boy didn't suffer."

Zoe sighed. "But his parents are suffering terribly."

"Dis is true. His parents are *mal pris.*"

"Stuck in a bad place is right," Father Sam said. "And they'll be there for a long time. Grieving is especially difficult for parents who've lost a child."

The bell on the front door jingled, and Zoe glanced over just as Tex came in the eatery. He was dressed in dark khaki trousers, a navy sport coat, and a pale blue shirt.

"Hey, everybody." He raised his hand. "Y'all beat me this mornin'."

Tex came over and hugged Zoe, the scent of his Old Spice wafting under her nose. "How're you holdin' up, Missy?"

"So-so," Zoe said. "It's going to be a hard day. I'm eager to get it behind us."

"Well, one thing's for sure." Tex rested his hand on Zoe's shoulder. "We're gonna help you through it."

Savannah came over to the table with the coffeepot, all the expression gone from her face. "You're not going to believe this. Rick Paquet, the father of the little girl who died after the camping trip, had a heart attack."

"From the cyanide?" Tex said.

Savannah shrugged. "It must've been a factor. The man's only thirty-nine."

"Is he alive?" Zoe said.

"He is. According to the news, he's stable. His wife collapsed and had to be sedated. Poor thing."

Zoe sighed. "Do you suppose she'll have to go through her daughter's funeral without her husband there? Wouldn't that be the ultimate slap in the face?"

"I heard that Caissy Paquet's kindergarten class is going to sing at her funeral," Savannah said. "That should be a tearjerker."

Zoe pulled out the chair next to Father Sam and sat. "I can't handle this today. I only have room in my heart for one dead child and one set of grieving parents. I can't take on anything else."

Jude sat at the conference table in his office with Deputy Chief Aimee Rivette, Chief Detective Gil Marcel, and Police Chief Casey Norman, discussing the details for the two funerals today at Saint Catherine's.

"Sounds like y'all have got your people lined up about right," Jude said. "Shouldn't be difficult to manage the traffic flow at Saint Catherine's, especially since the Corbin funeral's at ten thirty, and the Durand funeral isn't until two."

Aimee nodded. "The Durands are having a private burial at the mausoleum before the service, so we won't have to deal with escorting the congregation there after the funeral. Dominic Corbin's service will involve the traditional funeral procession to the cemetery, and we're thinking there will be hundreds lined up along the route to pay their respects."

Jude took a sip of coffee. "What's being done to manage the crowd of mourners at the church?"

"Monsignor Robidoux has arranged for the funerals to be broadcast in the high school gym," Aimee said, "and in the chapel. But we think there will be an overflow of people milling about outside with the media. We'll have officers in place for crowd control. We're not really looking for any problems. The mood should be somber. But we'll be prepared for anything."

Jude looked across the table at Chief Norman. "Casey, I can't thank you enough for all the help you've given us—and without much recognition. You've let me take the lead and have been an invaluable partner. I really appreciate it."

Casey flashed a crooked grin. "Glad to oblige, Sheriff. Want to guess which of us is sleeping better at night?"

Jude chuckled. "You sly devil. There *is* a method to your madness. Listen, before we disperse, I should mention Rick Paquet, father of the little girl who died after the camping trip. I'm sure y'all heard he had a heart attack this morning."

The three nodded.

"Thankfully, he's expected to recover. The death toll stands at eight. Five still in the hospital. We've done everything we know to get the word out to the public that Gaudry water is potentially deadly and not to drink it."

Casey tented his fingers. "I think every smorgasbord and food bar in town has closed its doors or switched to menu service only. That certainly cuts down on the potential risk of someone pulling this stunt again."

"It does," Jude said. "But we need to keep stressing that the general population has to stay vigilant. Since no group has come forward to claim responsibility for this, it's possible that the man on the security tape is working alone or with a partner. And if he's looking for attention, all the media hype might just egg him on to strike again."

"That's a terrifying thought," Aimee said.

Jude nodded. "But isn't that the whole point—keeping people terrified? I hate giving the creep air time, but it's important for the public not to get complacent."

CHAPTER 21

Sax sat on a wrought-iron bench near the duck pond at Cypress Park, watching a pair of roseate spoonbills and a half-dozen black-necked stilts sifting through the shallow bottom along the bank. A lone white ibis scoured the wet grass for insects and grasshoppers, and a tricolored heron stood motionless in the center of the pond as if his only purpose for existence was to draw admirers.

The morning sun had cleared the tops of the Spanish-moss–draped cypress trees that marked the eastern boundary of the park.

Under the arched bridge that spanned the pond, a wood duck caught a glimmer of sun, its color pattern resplendent with rich chestnut, splashes of black and white, and golden flanks. If there was a more beautiful duck, he had yet to see one.

On the high point of the bridge stood a boy about nine or ten and a much smaller girl with long brown hair, each blowing bubbles out over the pond. That could have been him—and Shelby—at that age. Had their lives really been as bad as he remembered? Or had the good memories been snuffed out by the pain?

The bells of Saint Catherine gonged nine times, and he glanced over at the parking lot just as a white Toyota Camry pulled in. He recognized the car as Isabel's.

He waited until Mrs. Woodmore got out, and then rose to his feet and walked toward her across the wet green lawn.

The elderly woman's white hair caught the morning rays and contrasted with the black dress she was wearing. She looked rather elegant, even with the cane she used to steady herself—or perhaps because of it.

"Hello, Sax." She extended her hand, and he shook it. "I appreciate your meeting me here. I didn't want to talk about this over the phone. I have a funeral to attend this morning, and there will be people coming and going at my home all day. I didn't want to take a chance on anyone seeing us together and asking questions. I'd like this matter to remain private."

"Not a problem, Mrs. Woodmore. I saved us that bench over there in the shade. There's a nice breeze."

He walked with Adele to the wrought-iron bench, waited until she was seated, and then sat beside her.

"Isn't the park lovely?" Adele said.

Sax nodded. "Especially nice for a town this size."

"I come here when I miss my home in Alexandria. Were you able to see the grounds at Woodmore when you were there?"

"Just as I drove up the circle drive," Sax said. "What I saw of it was gorgeous."

"Did you know my Alfred bought the land and had that big, beautiful house built for me as a wedding gift? Before it was even finished, friends and neighbors referred to it as Woodmore

House—and it just stuck. Eventually, we just referred to the entire estate as Woodmore. It seemed fitting."

Sax looked over at her; her faded blue eyes were suddenly animated.

"I lived there sixty years," she said. "In many ways, Woodmore was its own little world. Everything I loved was there—Alfred, our lovely home, the rolling grounds. We didn't have children and traveled a great deal when Alfred was alive. But after he passed away, the people who worked for me became my family."

Sax listened patiently, wondering why the woman was going on and on about nothing.

"But it wasn't always perfect," Adele said. "I lost a child before she was born. It changed me—and not for the better. I never conceived again, and I blamed God and took my anger out on my staff. I was cruel and verbally abusive—so much so that Alfred had to pay ridiculously high salaries in order to get them to stay and put up with my ill treatment of them."

"I would never have guessed that about you," Sax said. "You seem like a gentle person."

"I'm a different person now. But only since Alfred died, and I let the Lord have my heart. God changed me. But I had belittled and deeply wounded a number of people in the wake of my grief. I regret it, of course. I've gone to those people and asked forgiveness. Some gave it. Others asked me to leave and never come back."

Sax just listened. He couldn't imagine Adele Woodmore as abusive.

"I tell you this so you'll realize that I understand the guilt you're carrying and your need to reconcile with Shelby. She came to work for me after I had worked through my anger and bitterness. She was a trusted member of my household staff for six years. Did you know that?"

Sax shook his head. "Honestly, I don't know much about what Shelby did after she finally left home. Mom said Shelby worked several jobs and saved until she could afford a car, then moved in with a girlfriend. My dad showed up at their doorstep, drunk and holding a ball bat, threatening Shelby if she didn't come home. The police came before it got violent, but the friend was freaked out and told Shelby she would have to move out. Shelby disappeared after that and didn't contact Mom for a couple of years. I found you listed in Mom's address book as Shelby's employer. That's really all I know. Shelby obviously told Mom where she was, but she never went back."

"But you did?" Adele said.

Sax shrugged. "I didn't really have much choice. When my dad died, Mom needed me. I dropped out of the rock band and went home for the funeral. And stayed while the will was probated. My parents didn't have much, but it all went to Mom. She had more than enough to live on. Her grief was surprising to me, since she was finally free. I guess she didn't know how to be free. Didn't matter. A short time later, she was diagnosed with lung cancer. She went through six months of agonizing pain, chemo, and adverse side effects before she finally died. I was with her through it all."

"I'm sorry to hear that, Sax. How did your father die?"

"He stopped at a bar on his way home from work and got smashed out of his mind. He stepped in front of a delivery truck and was killed instantly. Never knew what hit him. Mom, on the other hand, suffered for six long months. Go figure."

"You think your father should have suffered instead?"

"Let's just say I hope there's a hell." He folded his hands in his lap. "Mrs. Woodmore, I don't think you asked me to meet you here so we could discuss my dysfunctional family."

"No. But I'm very interested in every aspect of Shelby's life. And since you're her closest flesh-and-blood relative, I'm also very interested in you."

"I already told you about myself. I'm a jazz musician, a three-time divorcé with no kids, no significant history, and no peace in my future unless I make things right. If it's the last thing I ever do, I need to clear things up with Shelby."

"And you think admitting you left her behind and asking her forgiveness will make things right?"

Sax breathed in and exhaled loudly. "I don't know exactly *what* it will take to make things right. I just know I have to try. I don't see how it can do anything but make things better for Shelby to know I'm sorry for abandoning her—whether she can forgive me or not."

"And what if she can't? What will you do then?"

"I'll keep asking—and keep trying to earn her trust so she *can* forgive me. It might take a long time."

"Two of the people I hurt have never forgiven me—even after going to them several times. It's very painful. But I've finally accepted it."

Sax studied her profile. "Did you ask me here to tell me that Shelby isn't going to forgive me?"

Adele lifted her gaze and turned to him. "Sax, I'm not sure I can even get Shelby to contact you—let alone forgive you."

"Have you asked her?"

"I dropped a pretty strong hint. I'd prefer to be direct, but I think that would be overstepping. I'm trying a different angle."

"What's that?"

"I've talked with her husband. I know he wants her to reconcile her past. He's been working on her for years to go home and make peace with your mother. I'm afraid if she's told both parents are dead, she won't even try to dig up the past."

"But isn't that a good reason why she *should* do it?" Sax said. "The ashes of our parents have been stored in my closet for three years. I've held off doing anything with them until I could find Shelby. She may hate Mom and Dad, but there's a flicker of attachment. I know there is. They're our parents, for heaven's sake. Why do you think I stayed and helped my mom? My relationship with my parents has always been complicated. Still is. I can't seem to let them go."

Adele looked out toward the duck pond. "Sax, tell me what Shelby has to gain in exchange for opening the door to a nightmarish past that she's already put behind her—because I need to know."

"All I can offer her is my deepest apology and a relationship with her brother, if she wants it. Why did you ask me to meet you, if you haven't got anything new to tell me?"

Adele patted his hand. "Two reasons. I want to get to know you because you're a part of Shelby. And I thought you should know a little about my past so that you'll see I do understand why you need to tell Shelby how sorry you are."

Sax sat back and sighed. "I'm relieved. I thought you were going to tell me you'd changed your mind."

"Of course not. But I do think Shelby's husband may be the one who can convince her that it's in *her* best interest to hear you out. It may take time. You indicated you could stay a few days. I know your jazz band is going on tour. But if you could stay here a while longer, her husband might be able to convince her to see you."

"Are you saying she's here, in Les Barbes?"

"Don't read into what I said, Sax. People have cars."

"All right. Sure. I came here with one goal: to find Shelby and make things right. I'll stay."

Zoe, holding tightly to Pierce's hand, sat several rows behind the Corbin family at Saint Catherine Catholic Church. The remainder of the pew was taken up by Adele and Isabel, Hebert, Father Sam, Tex, and Savannah. A heaviness hung over the congregation, even though Monsignor Robidoux wore white vestments and the altar was practically swallowed up by a plethora of brightly colored flower arrangements.

Zoe's mind drifted during the Requiem Mass, and she thought back on one of her favorite memories of Domi. She had volunteered as a teacher's helper at Grace's preschool and noticed Grace having a confrontation at recess with Patty Muise, who pulled the ribbons off Grace's pigtails and called her ugly. It was all Zoe could do not to rush in and handle it for Grace. A few minutes later the kids came in from recess, and she overheard Domi and Grace talking....

Domi reached over and stroked Grace's curls. "Don't cwy. You don't need pink wibbons to look pwetty."

"Patty thinks I'm ugly." Grace stuck out her bottom lip.

Domi shook his head. "Patty's ugly. She never smiles. I think she took your wibbons because everyone likes you and no one likes her."

"That's because she's mean."

Domi was quiet for a moment. "I think Patty needs a hug."

Grace pursed her lips and folded her arms tightly across her chest. "I'm not hugging Patty."

"I will." Domi stood. "She's going to be mean until someone likes her."

"She's going to hit you," Grace said.

"I'm not hitting her back. I'm going to pwetend I like her. Then if she stops being mean, maybe I weally will like her...."

Zoe was jolted back to the present when Monsignor stepped up to the lectern to deliver his sermon. What would he say—could he say—to make the family feel better?

A hush fell over the congregation, and then Monsignor looked out at the people and spoke in his deep, resonant voice.

"I baptized Dominic Nicholas Corbin four years ago last week. I remember it for a number of reasons, not the least of which is because he seemed totally relaxed in my arms, even when I poured the water on his forehead. He looked into my eyes and seemed to hang on every word. I honestly wondered if the child understood exactly what was happening."

Zoe smiled in spite of herself, aware of Pierce squeezing her hand.

"Dominic had a teachable, cooperative spirit. He was a true peacemaker. He didn't hit. He didn't lie. He didn't steal. He wasn't disruptive. He shared what he had. He obeyed without arguing—well, most of the time. I understand he wouldn't wear red."

Margot and Josh and other family members laughed among themselves, and Monsignor paused to let others enjoy the moment.

"Dominic just didn't like red." Monsignor chuckled. "But when we stop to think about this little boy's life, it's exemplary. He was only four. But his example is something we should think about. What kind of world would it be if we all shared freely of whatever we had? If we didn't lie? Or steal? If we were never disruptive or rude? If we obeyed the people God has put in authority over us? The apostle Paul wrote about it in the thirteenth chapter of First Corinthians. This is what he said: 'If I speak in human and angelic tongues but do not have love, I am a resounding gong or a clashing cymbal. And if I have the gift of prophecy and comprehend all mysteries and all knowledge; if I have all faith so as to move mountains but do not have love, I am nothing. If I give away everything I own, and if I hand my body over so that I may boast but do not have love, I gain nothing.

"'Love is patient, love is kind. It is not jealous, is not pompous, it is not inflated, it is not rude, it does not seek its own interests, it is not quick-tempered, it does not brood over injury, it does not rejoice over wrongdoing but rejoices with the truth. It bears all things, believes all things, hopes all things, endures all things.

"'Love never fails.'"

Monsignor paused and then looked out across the congregation. "Love is quite simple, really, though we make it complex. Dominic didn't. In his childlike way, he taught us what love looks like. 'Don't hit. Don't lie. Don't steal. Talk nice to each other. Don't get even. Don't be jealous. Share with everyone. Obey the rules. Don't talk back. Give lots of hugs.'"

Monsignor seemed to have lost his voice for several agonizing seconds, and then continued. "Dominic's life was an example for us all. I challenge us to remember this child's innocent, cooperative spirit and apply those same simple principles to our everyday lives.

"As we mourn today, let us not forget that Dominic is not sad. No! He is enjoying his eternal reward in the presence of the God who made Him and who was not surprised by what we see as this child's shocking and untimely death. God had a plan for Dominic Nicholas Corbin. That plan *was* fulfilled. The lost soul that put cyanide in chocolate pudding did not have the power of life and death. Our God reached down at that moment and lifted Domi into His arms and into the *forever and ever* that still awaits each of us who believe. Jesus Christ conquered sin and death. And because of Him, Dominic never tasted death—and now lives forever in glory.

"This knowledge does not eliminate our need to mourn Dominic's passing. But hopefully it changes the way in which we mourn. For we do not mourn as those who have no hope. Though we don't know when our individual chapter will end, we do know the ending of the bigger Story. And when the last page is turned, and the end comes, there will be no more weeping, no more pain, no more death. And we, who love and serve the Lord, will be reunited with Dominic and all those who have gone before us—never to be separated. Praise be to God.

"Let us pray. Father above, who knows firsthand the pain of losing a beloved Son, be with Josh and Margot and their entire family and all of us gathered here as we, in our human frailty, grieve the loss of this precious child. Help us not to forget for a moment that, because of Jesus Christ, death has no sting, and that Dominic is rejoicing with the angels. We leave him in Your tender care, in the name of the Father, and of the Son, and of the Holy Spirit. Amen."

"Amen," Zoe whispered.

She took a fresh tissue out of her purse and wiped the tears off her cheeks and then blew her nose. What a beautiful thought to remember Domi as an example for adults. She'd never thought of him that way before.

Zoe couldn't focus on the Mass, Monsignor Robidoux's eulogy resounding over and over in her mind. For the first time, she could truly sense that God was in control and Domi's life had a purpose. As long as she lived, she would never forget Domi's example—so sweet and simple and pure. The way love was supposed to be.

Pierce took one of her tissues and dabbed his eyes. All Zoe wanted to do was to go home and hug her children.

CHAPTER 22

Zoe sat on the couch in her apartment, holding Grace in her arms, rocking her gently, thinking about Monsignor Robidoux's eulogy.

"Are you sad, Mommy?" Grace reached up and touched her face.

"A little. I'm trying not to be. After all, Domi is with Jesus. What better place could he possibly be?"

"I'm sad he died." Grace wrinkled her little nose. "Now Patty will be mean again."

"Maybe it's time *you* hugged Patty. She's going to be sad that Domi's gone. This would be a good time to make Patty your friend by being kind to her. I know Domi would be happy if you did."

"*And* Jesus," Grace added.

"Yes, especially Jesus." Zoe tightened her embrace. "I'm glad you're my little girl, Grace. You're such a blessing, and I love you more than you can possibly imagine."

"More than ice cream? And Tootsie Pops? And tea parties?"

"Oh, much more."

"More than *Tucker*?" Grace's voice was playful.

Zoe smiled and looked into Grace's topaz eyes, her daughter's elfin grin telling Zoe she already knew the answer. "As much as Tucker."

"If I died, you would be *very* sad."

"Of course I would be very sad." *More like devastated.* "I have an idea. Why don't we go downstairs and let Maddie stay with Tucker while he's napping. You can sit with your uncles and watch them play checkers, and I'll have Daddy make you an orchard smoothie."

"Yay!" Grace clapped her hands.

Zoe told Maddie what she and Grace were doing, then took Grace by the hand and walked her downstairs to the dining room, which was only about half full—normal for three forty-five on a weekday afternoon.

Zoe turned loose of Grace's hand, and Grace ran over to the table by the window and stood next to Hebert.

"Dere's my *petite fille.*" Hebert put his arm around her. "Watch dis." Hebert picked up his king and made three jumps, a fake look of surprise making his faded gray eyes wide and animated. "Well, looky dere, I win." He threw his head back and laughed. "Tell us, Grace. Who da king of checkers?"

"Hebert!" Grace clapped her hands.

Tex, his navy sport coat hung on the back of his chair and his sleeves rolled up, took out his handkerchief and wiped his bald head. "I'm not quittin' until I win one. Put the checkers on the board and prepare to be humbled."

Zoe started to go into the kitchen and spotted Sax sitting at a table by himself, sipping an orchard smoothie. She took out her cell phone and dialed Pierce's number.

"Yeah, babe. What's up?"

"Would you make Grace an orchard smoothie?" Zoe said. "She's sitting with the guys. Sax is here, and I'm going to go talk to him for a minute."

"Sure. I'll bring it out to her."

Zoe went over to Sax's table. "Nice to see you again. What do you think of the smoothie? It's something Pierce recently added to the menu. Grace can't get enough of them."

Sax smiled, the light casting a yellow shade in his brown eyes. "I can see why. This is delicious. I've never tasted anything quite like it."

"Glad you approve. So how much longer do you think you'll be in town?"

"Not sure. A few days at least." Sax stirred the smoothie with his straw. "Look, I apologize again for being insensitive last night. That was neither the time nor the place to get into my personal disappointment with God."

"Don't worry about it. I think everyone's struggling on some level. It's not easy coming to grips with the death of a child—and the fact that it was murder makes it a double whammy. Monsignor Robidoux, God bless him, gave a powerful eulogy."

"What more could he say than the child's 'in a better place'?"

"That's a given. This had to do with what an amazing example Domi was for the rest of us."

"Now that's a different slant," Sax said. "How did he say a four-year-old victim of cyanide poisoning could be an example?"

"Do you mind if I sit with you a minute?" Zoe said. "I'd love to tell you what Monsignor said. It certainly changed the way I look at Domi's death."

Sax pulled out a chair. "Not at all."

Zoe told Sax everything she could recall of Monsignor Robidoux's eulogy, feeling energized as she repeated it. "Isn't that a perfect way for us to remember Domi?"

"Yes, it is." Sax glanced over at the table where the three old guys were doting on Grace. "He sounds like the perfect little boy from the perfect intact family."

"I can't help but hear the cynicism in your voice."

Sax's face turned bright pink. "I think it's great that this child left such a positive impression on everyone. But I came from an abusive, dysfunctional family. And I honestly can't relate to all that sweetness and light."

"Neither can I," Zoe said. "Not from my childhood, anyway. Maybe that's why I'm determined to keep my children safe and happy and innocent as long as possible."

"But then something like this comes along and forces your hand. So what did you say to Grace? You either had to lie—or tell her the brutal truth that would surely strip away some of that innocence."

"I told Grace the truth. I didn't dwell on how Domi died, but on the fact that he's going to live with Jesus forever. And I told her all about Monsignor's eulogy. She totally *got it.* Grace knew Domi was special."

"It's neat that he had loving parents. I honestly wonder if mine would have been more relieved than grieved, if I had died as a kid."

"How can you say that?" She knew how. Hadn't she felt that way too? "Were you a problem child?"

Sax shrugged. "I always thought I must be bad, and that's why my dad hit me. But as I got older, I realized it was the whiskey that made him mean."

"He was an alcoholic?"

"For as long as I can remember. I saw him drunk a lot more than I saw him sober. He wasn't likeable in either state."

"Well, my father was a drunk too," Zoe said. "And he didn't need a reason to abuse me or my brother—or my mom, for that matter."

Sax arched his thick, bushy eyebrows. "Now that I *can* relate to. I guess the cynicism you heard is coming from childhood issues that are still unresolved. I didn't mean for it to come out that way. Domi sounds like a great kid who had a life filled with happiness, however short it turned out to be. He was luckier than a lot of us."

"I don't really believe in luck. God is in control of my life. I see the good as blessings from Him."

"Really?" Sax pursed his lips. "Then how do you see the bad?"

Emily sat with Chance on the white leather couch in his living room, sampling the finger food on her plate and watching Chance's two extended families interacting.

Chance picked at what she had put on his plate and then set it aside.

"You have such nice relatives," Emily said. "You're really blessed."

"I'd rather have my mom back."

Emily looked at her plate. "I know you would. I'm so sorry. At least your parents' siblings are really nice. Your cousins, too."

"They're all right. I don't really know them that well. Truthfully, I wish they'd all leave. The whole day's been overwhelming."

"Now that the funeral and mausoleum services are behind you,"

Emily said, "your family will go back home, and you'll have space to grieve."

"Not until Aunt Reba leaves. And that's not going to happen until you two get through the list of things I'm supposed to deal with."

"We'll do as much as we can without bothering you," Emily said. "We're supposed to pick up the death certificates tomorrow. We'll need them to close accounts and cancel credit cards."

"I can't deal with any of that." Chance squeezed her hand. "But I'm glad you're willing to help. I know it's important. I just don't have the presence of mind to think that hard."

"Of course you don't. That's why you have us."

"How long do you think Aunt Reba's going to stay?"

Emily shrugged. "As long as it takes. But I'm thinking we can accomplish an awful lot in a short period of time. In fact, I called Zoe and asked her to change my schedule. I don't go in until Saturday at three. That'll give me almost three full days to help Reba."

Chance turned to her. "Really? That was awfully nice of you."

"I felt it was necessary."

"That's a chunk out of your college money."

"A small chunk." Emily smiled. "Helping you is more important right now." *Though Vanessa will be all over me.*

Chance kissed her cheek. "You're an amazing friend, Emily. I would never have made it through today without you."

"Sure you would've. Your family was holding you up."

He lowered his voice and whispered in her ear. "But it's you who gave me the strength to stand."

Emily felt tingly all over, as much from his breath brushing her ear as his words. "You serious?"

"Absolutely. I've never felt this way about anyone before."

Emily heard footsteps moving in their direction and sat up straight.

"Chance, we've got to head back," said his uncle Frank. "I have a meeting in the morning."

Chance stood and bear-hugged his uncle. "Thanks for being here."

"Look, I know you've got a rough road ahead. Promise me you'll call if there's anything your aunt Marie and I can do for you."

"I will," Chance said.

Aunt Marie hugged him and seemed too emotional to say anything.

"It was nice to have met you, Emily," Uncle Frank said.

One by one, family members and friends of his parents came up to Chance, expressed their deepest sympathy and support, acknowledged Emily—and then left. A few minutes later, only Aunt Reba remained in the house with them. She was out in the kitchen.

"I should go see if I can help her," Emily said. "There's a lot of food left over, and we need to store it properly so you can have it again when you're hungry."

She started to get up, and Chance held her hand. "Don't go. Aunt Reba wanted to control the kitchen. Let her."

"I feel like I'm being rude."

"She's in hog heaven out there. It's her private domain."

"Aren't you being a little hard on her?" Emily said. "The woman just lost her sister, and yet she's doing everything she can to help *you.*"

"I told you I don't want her here. It's just a matter of time before she gets overbearing."

"I'm sure that's not her intent."

Chance arched his eyebrows. "Believe me, she can't help herself."

Emily stayed with Chance, feeling guilty about leaving Aunt Reba to clean up the kitchen, and wondering how this young man who had won her heart could be so unsympathetic and selfish. Then again, he was an only child with no concept of sibling ties. How could he understand that his aunt Reba was suffering too?

Zoe sat for a moment, staring at Sax, wondering how to answer such a poignant question.

"I'm not being facetious." Sax folded his arms on the table and leaned forward on his elbows. "I'd really like to know how you look at all the bad things that happen. I get it that Christians thank God for all the blessings. But what do you say to Him about all the heartache?"

"First of all," Zoe said, "it's a privilege that He's even invited us to approach Him and talk about the heartache. Being a Christian is all about a relationship with Him. But that doesn't mean we're on the same page. Or that I'm ever going to understand the mind of God. I heard someone say that our trying to understand God's thinking is like an ant trying to understand the Internet. There's just no way we can comprehend the big picture of how it all fits together. We mourn our losses, but there really is a reason for them. God's in control. We just need to trust Him."

"You haven't answered my question," Sax said. "If you give God the credit for the blessings, don't you give Him the blame for the bad things?"

"Blame is the wrong word," Zoe said. "He allows everything that happens in my life—for reasons I may never know. But I thank Him and love Him and praise Him in the midst of hard times, knowing that He's right there with me and will use it for my good."

"What basis do you have for that?" Sax's eyebrows came together.

Did she really want to try to explain something this deep to an unbeliever? How could she not when he had asked outright?

"Sax, I believe the Bible's the Word of God. It's what we believers have to go by. And in the book of Romans, chapter eight, verse twenty-eight, we're told that in all things God works for the good of those who love Him, who have been called according to His purpose. In other words, He uses everything for our good, one way or another. That doesn't mean it's always easy. But there's always a takeaway that serves to bring us closer to Him, if we let it. You look surprised."

"I am. Most Christians back off the discussion about now. You actually had an answer." He took a sip of the smoothie. "So you believe good will come out of this boy's death?"

"It already has," Zoe said. "God used Monsignor Robidoux to give Domi's parents—and all of us who loved him—a positive way to remember him that will far outlive the pain. Ultimately, the pure and simple love that this child showed was a reflection of Jesus, who is our perfect example."

"And you think God needed to let a little kid get murdered to make you see that?"

Zoe sighed. It had gone right over his head. "No. I'm saying the Lord didn't let this tragedy be all about the bad guys. He used it to show us, through Domi's example, what living a simple, pure life looks like."

"Why didn't God just stop it from happening in the first place?"

"Only He can answer that. He gave us all free will. And sometimes one person uses his free will to hurt or kill someone else. I don't think God is *ever* happy about that. Vengeance belongs to Him, and there will be a day of judgment. But isn't it significant that God speaks to us, even in our pain—and the things that hurt us He will use for good in a believer's life?"

Sax was quiet for a moment. "Can I ask you a personal question?"

Zoe nodded.

"As a Christian, how do you deal with the way your father treated you?"

"I've forgiven my dad."

"From what you've said, he didn't deserve it."

"You're right," Zoe said. "But neither did I. I've made a lot of mistakes that have hurt a lot of people. God forgave me anyway and commands me to do the same. It's all about grace. In fact, that's why Pierce and I named our daughter Grace. But that's another story."

"So did forgiving your father bring you peace?"

"Forgiving him was an act of obedience. I didn't really feel anything. It wasn't until after I let go of the anger and bitterness that I began to experience peace like I had never known."

Sax wrapped his hands around his orchard smoothie and seemed far away for a moment. "Thanks for giving me straight answers. I don't get that much. Usually when someone finds out I'm ticked off with God, they run the other way, as if they think the lightning is going to hit me and they don't want to get too close."

"I'm not worried about the lightning," Zoe said. "But my past is intensely personal. I really don't want to rehash it."

"Don't worry. I'm not going to ask you any more personal questions. I just wanted to understand how Christians handle disappointments with God. I'm in the pursuit of peace at the moment and really believe the key lies in reconciling my past mistakes. God's not really in the equation. I don't trust Him or want His help."

"I'm going to pray your perspective changes. I don't think you can find true peace and be at odds with the Prince of Peace." Zoe rose to her feet. "I should get busy. I have orders to place this afternoon before my babysitter leaves. Will you be coming in for dinner?"

"I'll be here around six. And should Pierce want to pass another fine dish under my nose, I'm totally open. He's an amazing chef."

Zoe smiled. "I'll tell him."

She turned and walked toward the kitchen, relieved to stop talking about issues that were difficult enough for believers to understand.

Lord, why does he make me so uncomfortable? Is it because I haven't completely dealt with my own past? Is it time for me to go home and see my mother?

CHAPTER 23

Just before bedtime, Zoe stood on the gallery that jutted out above Zoe B's and looked at the swarm of tourists that covered *rue Madeline*. Closing the street to traffic after 7:00 p.m. was one of the wisest moves the city council had ever made.

She never grew tired of watching people from all over the world enjoying her city. All up and down *rue Madeline*, colorful neon lights flashed outside quaint shops and eateries that offered every imaginable food, gift, or souvenir. A Cajun band played at Breaux's and filled the street with lively music. Three white-faced mimes did a skit in front of Beads-a-Plenty, and Madame Duval, poodle in arms, looked down from the gallery above the Coy Cajun Gift Shop.

The first of two horse-drawn carriages, filled to the brim with tourists, pulled up in front of the Hotel Peltier to let passengers off and make room for the next group. Zoe glanced at her watch. It was ten forty-five. The carriages would be on the move until eleven.

She could smell the faint aroma of mesquite wood coming from the Texas Cajun Grill, where a young man, his bare chest and arms covered in tattoos, was standing on the sidewalk outside, juggling bowling pins.

Directly below, in front of Zoe B's, Andre-the-street-vendor was selling *andouille* corn dogs to a long line of people. She wondered if the man ever slept.

How she loved this community. And how grateful she was that the cyanide scare hadn't kept tourists away for long.

She heard the sliding door open and close and then felt warm hands kneading her shoulders.

"The kids are out like a light," Pierce said. "I'm glad I got off a little early and could help. I had to rock Tucker forever to get him to sleep. I think he senses something's wrong."

"Hopefully, our sadness won't be apparent for long. Monsignor's eulogy was something, wasn't it?"

"It was. I didn't know what he could possibly say that would've made a difference. But he definitely hit a home run."

Zoe nodded. "I shared it with Sax when he was in this afternoon, having a smoothie."

"I'm surprised you brought it up, after your awkward exchange at the funeral home last night."

"He apologized for being insensitive, and I said it was okay, that everyone is struggling on some level. One thing led to another." Zoe told Pierce about the entire conversation and how good it felt to share Monsignor's words but how uncomfortable she was with the conversation that followed.

"Sounds like Sax is searching."

"Maybe." Zoe relished Pierce's fingers massaging the tightness in her shoulders. "But he's furious with God, and I didn't sense he was open to anything Christian. He's trying to find peace in his life and thinks that reconciling his violent childhood is the ticket."

"That's a good start, no? You, of all people, understand how important that is."

"But I didn't even start the process until I had given my life to Christ. Where is he going to draw the strength? It's sad. I don't think he can do it alone. But he'll never find true peace as long as he's at odds with God."

"You told him that."

"He wasn't open. I could tell."

"Maybe you planted a seed. He's going to be here for a few days—maybe we should invite him to come back to the kitchen and eat with us. He might get a kick out of it. And it might open up some good dialogue."

Zoe turned around and looked in Pierce's eyes. "I can't remember a time when you've shown this much interest in a customer."

"We had this conversation already, babe. You can't deny it's good marketing to befriend a customer with connections in New Orleans. And I admit it's great hearing his raves about my cooking. But someone with his pain and his questions … well, I don't think the Lord would have us ignore him, do you?"

"I suppose not. I just don't like talking about my past." Zoe sighed. "I *have* forgiven my parents, Pierce. Why does it still hurt? Why am I still ashamed?"

"You've overlooked a very important detail, babe."

"I don't want to talk about it."

"You never do. But you still haven't forgiven your brother."

Zoe felt her shoulders tighten again. "For what—being smarter than the rest of us?" The tears in her eyes belied her words.

Pierce cupped her face in his hands and wiped her tears with his thumbs. "You're so angry with him, you've blocked it from your mind."

"Good. Then let's leave it there."

"It's your call. But as someone who loves you with all my heart, believe me when I tell you it's going to catch up with you at some point. Why not deal with it? I'll help you."

Zoe laid her head on his chest and rested in his arms. "I know you will. I'm just not ready."

Emily approached the back steps at Langley Manor and smiled at the family of raccoons devouring whatever goodies Vanessa had left for them. She went up the steps and, in the dim light of the back porch, spotted a silhouette sitting in a rocker.

"Sax, is that you?"

"It's me."

Emily laughed. "Don't you ever sleep?"

"I could ask you the same thing."

She went over and sat in the rocker next to him. "It's been a *long* day."

"How was the funeral?"

"Beautiful, but so sad. The church was packed. Chance's parents had a lot of friends and family. I suppose tragedies pull people together."

"How is Chance?"

"Depressed. He and his mother were especially close."

"I'm really sorry for what he's going through."

"Me, too. I'd better get inside. I'm sure my big sister is waiting for me with her hands on her hips."

Sax chuckled. "I overheard her mothering you the other night. I thought it was sweet. You're really fortunate to have someone who cares that much about you."

"I guess." Emily sighed. "But is she ever going to realize I'm nineteen? At some point she has to trust me to make decisions for myself."

"Can I ask you a personal question—regarding something Vanessa said?"

"Sure."

"What exactly is unequally yoked? That's a Christian term, isn't it?"

Emily nodded. "It means having a different set of values. I guess you heard her say Chance and I were unequally yoked."

"That's considered a bad thing?"

Emily started to say something flippant and then realized Sax was serious and she should give him an honest answer. "The Bible teaches believers not to be yoked with unbelievers because when they're not on the same page, there's usually conflict, and it's much harder for a believer not to compromise. Unequally yoked can involve more than just a marriage relationship though. Any kind of serious partnership."

"I take it Chance isn't a believer?"

"Right. Vanessa is getting way ahead of herself, though. I'm not planning to marry the guy. We're both working toward medical degrees, and that just opened up a unique kind of camaraderie. But now that his parents have been killed, I'm just being a friend."

"Thanks for explaining the term to me."

"You're welcome." Emily nodded toward the door. "Here goes."

"Remember, she loves you," Sax said.

Emily unlocked the back door and went inside, surprised to see the stove light on and the kitchen table empty. She unlocked the door to the living quarters and went inside.

The lights were on, and Vanessa was asleep on the couch.

Emily tiptoed across the creaky wood floor—but not quietly enough.

"Hey there," said a sleepy voice.

"Hey. Sorry I woke you.'

"I thought about you off and on all day." Vanessa sat up. "Tell me about the funeral. You want some tea?"

"Not really."

"I do. Would you mind sitting with me?"

Emily followed Vanessa out to the kitchen just as Sax was passing through on his way upstairs.

"Good night, ladies." He winked at Emily.

Emily went over to the cookie jar and peeked inside. "You want cookies?"

"No, thanks."

Emily took three and sat at the table. She told Vanessa everything that had happened from the time she arrived at Chance's house that morning until she left him just a few minutes ago—except for the part about his telling Emily she gave him the strength to stand. That was private.

"You're a wonderful friend," Vanessa said. "I hope he appreciates you."

"I'm sure he does. Aunt Reba and I have a ton of details to tend to over the next few days."

"How are you going to help her, when you have such a busy schedule at work?"

Emily paused and took a bite of cookie. "I don't have to be at work until Saturday at three."

"You told me this morning you had to be at work at three tomorrow."

"I called Zoe and changed it—so I can help Aunt Reba. I expected to dislike the woman. But frankly, she's really sweet. I think she just needs to do something for Chance to feel useful and honor her sister's memory. Chance thinks she wants to ramrod things. I told him I think he's wrong—and that I would be there to make sure things didn't get out of hand."

"You what?" Vanessa exhaled loudly. "Did you not hear a word I said this morning?"

"I heard you. I just don't agree with you."

"Emily, I understand your wanting to help Chance. I do. But you're getting enmeshed in his life in a way that's going to interfere with every other commitment you have."

"We both know that's not your real beef. You're afraid I'm going to get romantically involved and pulled into a sexual relationship."

"I won't pretend it hasn't occurred to me. But I really am concerned that you're taking on too much responsibility for Chance. He's a big boy. He doesn't need you to babysit him every waking moment."

"That was so cheap." Emily pushed her chair away from the table and stood. "I'm going to bed. If you want me to be open and honest with you, Vanessa, this isn't the way to do it."

Vanessa grabbed her wrist and held her gently. "I do want you to talk to me. The last thing I want is for you to shut down."

"Then trust me a little, will you? You act like I'm not capable of making a rational decision."

"It's not that I don't trust you." Vanessa let go of her wrist. "I was your age when I got pregnant. And I had convictions every bit as strong as yours."

"I'm not you. Stop trying to project your weakness onto me!"

"I don't mean to do that. But you're so trusting, Emily. I just don't want you to get hurt. There is no future for you and Chance. You have to know that."

"Of course I know that." Emily sat again and held her sister's gaze. "How many times do I have to tell you I'm not romantically involved with him? His parents were murdered, and he could use a friend. Do you think you could cut me some slack?"

Vanessa paused and seemed to study her face. "Of course I can. I'm sorry. You have a good head on your shoulders. I should trust you to use it."

"Thank you." Emily sighed. "Stop worrying about me, and give me a little support. It's been difficult trying to hold things together during such a traumatic situation. But I think my being there is making a positive difference."

"I'm sure it is."

Emily popped the last of the cookie into her mouth. "I'm going to go crash. I am wasted."

"All right. 'Night, Shortcake. Sleep tight."

Emily smiled without meaning to. How many times had Vanessa put her to bed as a little girl and said those words?

Emily walked through the living area and down the hall to her room, wondering if she was being honest herself. She was feeling increasingly close to Chance, and the idea of their relationship turning romantic didn't seem far-fetched anymore. Whether it did or didn't, it was none of Vanessa's business. Whatever relationship she built with Chance could only last until they went back to separate colleges in August. She had no intention of getting involved in anything permanent. How risky could it be?

CHAPTER 24

Jude sat at the conference table in his office, Thursday's issue of the *Les Barbes Ledger* set off to the side, as he mulled over the facts they had on the cyanide case. Whoever had done this terrible deed knew exactly what he or she was doing. No suspicious DNA or fingerprints were found on any of the bottles. So far, none of the employees at Marcotte's or Gaudry's warehouse or the transport company looked good for this. All law enforcement had was the security tape showing the back of the man they believed poisoned the food bar. Dark hair. Medium build. Caucasian or Hispanic. Might be young. Or not. About as generic as it gets.

He picked up the report from the Department of Health and Hospitals and reread it. Why did he keep coming back to the fact that the cyanide concentration in the bottled water was consistently ten times the lethal dose, and the concentration in the pudding on the food bar was only one-half the lethal dose? Was that significant? Or was it just easier to measure what was injected into the bottles, as Dr. Jensen had suggested?

Even though the bloggers were having a heyday stirring up the public to suspect Muslim extremists were behind this, the MO didn't fit. Not even for domestic terrorism. Anyone wanting to make a statement would have claimed responsibility long before now—and would have taken out more people. If they could inject cyanide into pudding, why not the entire food bar? And why not more bottled water? Were they waiting until the dust settled to strike again?

A knock startled him. He turned and saw Aimee standing in the doorway.

"Come in," he said. "I was just going over the files on the cyanide case."

"You've been going over the files for more than two hours, Sheriff." Aimee glanced down at the conference table. "Did you find anything?"

"Not really. I keep coming back to what you said, that whoever did this could've taken out a lot more people. We're missing something, but I can't put my finger on it. What's up?"

"I cleaned out my inbox and was just coming to see what you wanted me to concentrate on."

"Have we finished questioning everyone who handled the Gaudry bottled water from its origin to Marcotte's?"

"I think so," Aimee said. "We've had scores of police officers helping us. I have to say that nothing I've seen so far has given me pause. No one we've questioned has come across as smug or condescending. Everyone seemed genuinely outraged by what happened and eager to cooperate. I know the perp could be faking it. But the investigating officers just haven't found anyone to be suspicious."

Jude brushed the hair off his forehead. "Maybe it's time to take an even closer look at the victims."

"We've pretty well established that the victims weren't targeted. There doesn't seem to be any connection."

"It's that pesky word, *seem,* that bothers me."

Aimee smiled. "How would you like me to proceed?"

"I want a spreadsheet listing each victim's name, personal stats, where and how they ingested cyanide, and if any of the victims knew each other or frequented the same establishments. Hired any of the same people. Ever worked for the same company. Anything that might link any of them together. You'll have to go back to the families. I know they're grieving, but we need their help for this."

Aimee started to say something and then didn't.

"You think this is the wrong play?" Jude arched his eyebrows.

"Sheriff, it's your call, and I'll support you. But my gut feeling is that it's a time-intensive, desperate measure that isn't going anywhere. Our victims are old, young, black, white, brown, middle class, upper class. It doesn't seem like there's any pattern there."

"There's that pesky word, *seem,* again," Jude said. "We really haven't dug very deeply into the victims' lives."

"Why would we? Everything points to their being random victims."

Jude held her gaze. "I've been sitting here for two solid hours trying to find anything that points us to whoever's responsible. It's not in the information we've gathered so far. If you have a better idea, I'm listening."

Aimee shook her head. "I don't."

"I want you to get Gil focused on gathering this information. We're missing something. Let's find it."

Sax sat at the dining room table at Langley Manor, eating the breakfast crepes Vanessa had served him.

"These are delicious. I can taste every ingredient." Sax closed his eyes. "Andouille sausage, Swiss cheese, onion, mushroom, black olives. Oh, and red bell pepper. The sauce you use is out of this world. What's in it?"

"Cream, butter, ricotta, fresh-grated parmesan, a touch of Chardonnay, a little of Pierce's signature hot sauce, and spices. There's not enough of it in there to clog your arteries." Vanessa laughed. "I'm glad you like it."

"I'm getting really spoiled. It's going to be boring going home to microwave sausage biscuits for breakfast. Where did you learn to cook like this?"

Vanessa smiled. "I've always loved trying new recipes. But I learned most of what I know from Pierce Broussard."

"He's an incredible chef."

Vanessa nodded. "Did you know he was a high school history teacher when he and Zoe met? He hasn't been to fine cooking schools or gotten all the enviable degrees. Zoe recognized his talent and hired him. He's mostly self-taught."

"Good for him," Sax said. "Same for me with the saxophone. I played electric guitar with a rock band way back when. As I got older, I got interested in jazz and picked up the saxophone. I haven't put it down since."

"That's so neat. Pierce loves jazz and has been sharing some of his CDs with Ethan and me."

"It's in my blood now," Sax said. "I don't think I could give it up if I tried. Not that I want to. I love playing professionally."

"You said you've been with the same group for ten years. I imagine y'all are close."

"There's a lot of loyalty there. They're the only family I have. I'm the moody one in the band, and the guys have cut me a lot of slack over the years."

"You don't strike me as moody," Vanessa said.

Sax lifted an eyebrow. "I'm in relaxation mode. I should do it more often. It's kind of hard to be anything but mellow in a gorgeous place like Langley Manor, with a beautiful and gracious hostess cooking me breakfasts like this. Plus I've truly enjoyed getting to know the Broussards and savoring Pierce's cooking for lunch and dinner. I may go back to New Orleans with an extra ten pounds on me."

"Good morning, everyone." Emily breezed into the dining room.

"Well, don't you look pretty," Sax said. "That blue sundress brings out the color of your eyes."

Emily's face turned as pink as her lip gloss. "Thanks. I'm going over to Chance's this morning to work with his aunt Reba on getting some accounts canceled. We need to get his parents' closet cleared out too."

"Then I guess it's good you wore your work clothes." Vanessa's sarcasm didn't seem lost on Emily either.

"Chance seems like a very nice guy," Sax quickly added. "I wish we had met under better circumstances. Didn't I hear someone say he was a student at Harvard Medical School?"

Emily popped a mushroom into her mouth. "Yes, he's studying to be a neurosurgeon."

"Impressive. And what about you? Have you narrowed down your specialty?"

"Absolutely. I'm going to be an ob-gyn. I've wanted to deliver babies almost as long as I can remember." Emily sat at the table and glanced over at Vanessa. "I was in the delivery room when Carter was born. I thought it was about the most miraculous thing I'd ever witnessed."

"Speaking of Carter," Vanessa said, "he's still gung ho about you taking him to the water park."

"I will—soon." Emily poured herself a glass of orange juice. "I just need to get this week of helping Chance's aunt Reba behind me."

Sax sensed the tension between the two sisters and felt awkward that he had eavesdropped on their private disagreement of a few nights ago and knew more than he should. As an objective observer, he could clearly see both sides of this argument.

How he envied their relationship. He wondered how many times Shelby had needed advice, whether she knew it or not, and there was no older sibling there to look out for her.

He took the last bite of crepes and wiped his mouth on the napkin, then stood. "That was superb, Vanessa. Now if you ladies will excuse me, I think I'll take a stroll on the grounds before it gets too hot."

"I'll be serving breakfast until eleven," Vanessa said, "if you decide you want seconds."

Sax winked. "Don't tempt me. I think I overdid it as it is."

He walked into the kitchen and out the back door onto the deck, standing for a moment to admire the cane fields that swayed in the breeze. Maybe this would be the day that Shelby agreed to see him. The thought both energized and terrified him. He kept telling himself he was prepared for her anger and even her rejection. He had already decided that, no matter how Shelby reacted, he wasn't giving up. He had to prove to her that he was serious about wanting back into her life. But if it got ugly and she ripped him apart, did he have enough resolve to withstand her fury?

Zoe left Grace and Tucker in Maddie's capable hands and walked downstairs and into the dining room at Zoe B's, thrilled to see it bustling with customers. The hum of happy chatter was better than music to her soul and just might help her forget the sadness that was just under the surface.

She walked over to the table by the window, where Hebert, Father Sam, and Tex were eating breakfast, and Savannah was pouring coffee.

"Good morning, everyone," Zoe said.

Hebert, his curls unruly as ever, flashed a warm grin and took her hand. "How you feel dis morning?"

"Better," she said. "Monsignor's eulogy is still playing in my head. It gave me such a positive way to think of Domi's life."

Father Sam nodded. "I can't imagine what he could have said that would have been any more suited."

"Yeah," Tex said, "Monsignor carried the ball to the goal with that one."

"At the risk of sounding insensitive"—Savannah filled Tex's cup with coffee—"I'm glad I don't know any of the other victims. I don't want to go through this again."

"Maybe the crisis is over now." Tex sat back in his chair, his thumbs hooked on his red suspenders. "Won't fix the pain, but it'd sure be nice if we didn't get news of any more deaths."

"Jude has certainly seen to it that the public is informed about the threat," Zoe said. "I can't imagine there's anyone left on the planet that doesn't know better than to drink Gaudry water."

Hebert let go of her hand and seemed far away for a few moments. Finally he said, "But Domi didn't die from da water. I don't tink we can let down our guard."

"I agree," Savannah said. "Is anybody else paying attention to what the bloggers are saying?"

"They're just stirring up trouble," Father Sam said. "The authorities have as much as said they don't think this was done by terrorists—Muslim or otherwise."

"You expect dem to admit it outright?" Hebert shook his head. "Dey not going to scare everyone."

"But Jude wouldn't lie to this community either," Zoe said. "If he suspected terrorists, he'd say so."

"We've been over this ad nauseam." Tex waved his hand. "We've got to *trust* the folks in place to deal with it. They'll tell us what we need to know."

"Dey might." Hebert pursed his lips. "And dey might not."

"All right, moving right along"—Father Sam raised his voice slightly—"since Domi's funeral is behind us, and Monsignor did an extraordinary job of leaving us with positive thoughts, perhaps we could choose to dwell on that for a while."

"Amen." Zoe lowered her voice. "Guys, let's not get into these discussions when customers are in the eatery. The last thing we need is to stir things up with tourists."

Tex wiped his forehead with his kerchief. "I'll change the subject. That fella that's been comin' in every day—Sax Henry—sure is nice.

I got to talkin' with him and found out he's from Texas too. Small world."

"Did he tell you he's a saxophone player?" Zoe said.

"Sure did. Said he plays in a jazz band in the Big Easy."

"And," Zoe said, "he's enamored with Pierce's cooking, so we're going out of our way to make him feel welcome and hope he'll go home to New Orleans and tell a few folks about Zoe B's—and our fair city."

"I sure hope he's able to hook up with the gal he's lookin' for," Tex said.

"He said he was here on business." Zoe looked over at Tex. "I didn't realize he was looking for someone. Did he say who?"

"Nah, just a gal from Texas he's lost touch with over the years—someone he knew from Devon Springs."

Devon Springs? Zoe breathed in and didn't exhale, her mind racing in reverse. Adele's visit from the brother of a woman who worked for her. Adele's insistence that Sax eat at Zoe B's. Pierce's peculiar interest in keeping Sax coming back. Pierce's sudden push for her to go back to Devon Springs and see her mom. Sax's violent background. His Texas roots. His bitterness.

"Zoe, you look mighty pale," Tex said. "You feelin' okay?"

"I'm not, actually. I'll see y'all later." Zoe turned and marched toward the kitchen. Could Adele and Pierce and Sax have been any more obvious? How could she not have seen it coming? This was all a setup!

CHAPTER 25

Zoe pushed open the kitchen door and spotted Pierce standing at the worktable with Dempsey Tanner.

"Can I talk to you privately?" she said to Pierce.

"Babe, I can't lose my train of thought just now. I've got crusts in the oven and my lunch special half made. Can it wait for a bit?"

"No, it can't," Zoe said.

Dempsey put his hand on Pierce's shoulder. "I know what to do. Go ahead. I can handle it."

"Sure?"

Dempsey nodded.

"Thanks." Pierce picked up a towel and wiped his hands.

"Not here," Zoe said. "In the office."

Zoe turned and hurried out of the kitchen, across the dining room, and out into the alcove. She heard footsteps behind her as she put the key in the knob and opened the office door.

She let Pierce in and closed the door behind her.

"What's this about?" he said.

"Oh, I think you know *exactly* what this is about!"

"I don't."

Zoe held his gaze and steadied her voice. "Do you really think I'm so weak and incapable that you had to team up with Adele and trick me into meeting my brother?" She threw her hands in the air. "Good grief, Pierce! This is *huge*!"

"I know." Pierce scratched his ear and shifted his weight from one foot to the other. "I wasn't trying to trick you. I was going to tell you who Sax really is, but I was waiting for the right time. How did you find out?"

"Sax said something to Tex about being in town to find a gal he used to know from *Devon Springs*. It took me about thirty seconds to put it all together. When did he first contact Adele? How long have you known? Why didn't you just—"

Pierce held up his palm. "On Saturday evening, Sax showed up on Adele's doorstep, claiming to be Shelby Sieger's brother, Michael. He had an old driver's license with his picture. He's since changed his name. He wanted to know if she could tell him where you were. Apparently he'd been looking for you for a long time."

Zoe listened as Pierce told her everything he knew about the encounter, including Adele's questioning why Michael had left Shelby in an abusive situation.

"Adele knows how I've struggled with this." Zoe took the back of her hand and dabbed the perspiration from her cheeks. "Why would she tell Michael how to find me?"

"She didn't," Pierce said. "In fact, she pretty much gave him the third degree and told him that *if* she was convinced he had your best interests at heart—and not just his own—she would consider contacting you and letting you make the first move, if you wanted. She made it clear it would be your choice."

Zoe flopped into the desk chair and tried to comprehend what was happening. "You call this a choice? Why didn't Adele come to *me*?"

"Because every time she's broached the subject, you've brushed her off. She's well aware of how potentially life-changing this encounter could be. But she also knows how hard you've worked to put the past behind you. So she came to me and asked what I thought."

"That's just great." Zoe shook her head. "So what did you tell her?"

"I told her what I told you, that I'm concerned it's going to be devastating to you when you lose the people you've adopted as family—especially Adele and Hebert. And I think it's important that you settle things with your blood family. She's talked with Sax at length and is convinced what he has to say is worth your hearing."

"I'm glad everyone thinks they know what's best for me!" Zoe folded her arms across her chest and rocked nervously. "So Sax doesn't know who I really am?"

Pierce reached over and gently grasped her arm. "He hasn't got a clue. Adele didn't tell him anything about you, other than you're married and have kids and have a good life. He's hanging around Les Barbes, waiting for Adele to see if Shelby's *husband* can convince her to see him."

"And he hasn't figured it out?"

Pierce shook his head. "And he won't hear it from me or Adele. It's your call."

"Good." Zoe moved his hand. "Because I'm not talking to him anymore. I told you I wasn't ready."

"Babe, we didn't go looking for this. Your brother came here, looking for you. God put him back in your path for a reason."

"You don't know that!"

Pierce held her gaze, and she looked away.

"You've already broken the ice with him on a number of levels," Pierce said. "He's not a total stranger. You've already had a couple of poignant conversations."

Zoe picked up a pencil and bounced the eraser. "I'm not going to be manipulated into doing something I'm not ready to do!"

"No one means to manipulate. But this is a window that may not be open indefinitely. If you refuse to talk to Sax, you don't know that the opportunity will ever present itself again." Pierce bent down next to her chair, his dark eyes filled with compassion. "I can only imagine how you've pictured what it would be like to see your brother face-to-face. No one is telling you how to act or what to say. But even an explosive encounter is better than a lost opportunity."

"Easy for you to say. You're not the one he left trapped in a nightmare with a sweaty drunk pawing me … forcing me …" Zoe swallowed the emotion that balled up in her throat. "I'm not doing this. Nothing you say is going to change that! I loathe Michael! Why shouldn't I? If he wants forgiveness, he came to the wrong place. He's the one who left me. Now it's my turn to walk away."

Pierce was quiet for half a minute. Finally he exhaled loudly and rose to his feet. "All right."

"That's it—all right?" Zoe studied his face. "You're not going to try strong-arming me into meeting with him?"

"Not if your heart's not in it."

She was quiet for a moment, caught off guard that Pierce didn't push her. Was she willing to let Michael go away without telling him exactly what she thought?

"Maybe you're right," she said. "Maybe I *should* confront him. Let him have it with both barrels and get it off my chest. Then send him packing."

"I know the type of Christian you are," Pierce said. "You won't feel better unless you're willing to forgive him."

"I'm not ready."

"That's what you said."

"Stop trying to make me feel guilty. I don't want to feel this way!"

"I'm not trying to make you feel anything," Pierce said. "Feel whatever you feel. I just think you're stronger than you realize."

Zoe cocked her head and shot him a crusty look. "I'm glad you have me all figured out."

"Can you honestly tell me that it wouldn't be a relief to make peace with Michael? You've been forgiven so much, Zoe. You know what that is, what it feels like. Forgiving him doesn't mean that his abandoning you was right or that you weren't deeply wounded. It just means you clean the slate and start over. It's grace."

Zoe fingered the gold cross around her neck, remembering the meeting in this very office five years before, when an extraordinary act of grace on Adele's part had changed their lives forever.

Pierce kissed her forehead. "You'll do the right thing. When you're ready."

"I need time to think."

"Take all the time you need. If you want to leave town and spend a few days by yourself, I'll keep the kids. I'm sure Dempsey would jump at the chance to take on more responsibility."

"I don't know what I want." Zoe brushed a tear off her cheek. "I'm scared. I never expected Michael to show up out of the blue."

"Or to be so likeable?"

Zoe sighed. "I envisioned him to be a hippie-looking, pot-smoking, whiskey-guzzling guitar player in some wacko rock band. I didn't expect him to be so nice and refined—and normal looking." Zoe turned her gaze on the framed family portrait on the desk. "Grace has his topaz eyes. I see it now."

"Adele thinks you should hear what he has to say. I get the feeling that he's stuck in a nightmare too."

Emily straightened another shelf in the garage at Chance's house, wishing she had on shorts and a tank top instead of a sundress.

"How's it coming out here?" Reba stood in the doorway.

"I'm making good headway." Emily wiped away the perspiration dripping down her temples. "I've just about got these shelves straightened and the junk thrown out. I can see that Mr. Durand was a very different temperament than Chance."

Reba put her hands on her hips. "Huet was a proverbial pack rat. Lydia was constantly throwing things out, trying to reduce the piles of magazines and such. She and Chance always preferred that things be neat and tidy."

"I've made a significant dent out here," Emily said, "but it's getting too hot to work outside. Maybe there's something I can do indoors to help you. I can come back to this in the morning."

"Yes. Yes. By all means, come in where it's cool and have some lunch. I laid out the leftovers for us. Chance fixed himself a plate and went back in his room. I wish he didn't resent me so. I'd like to think it's the grief talking. But the truth is, I don't think he's ever been fond of me."

Emily followed her inside to the kitchen, where Reba had laid out quite a lunch spread.

"Seems a shame for this fine food to be shared by only three people," Reba said.

"Well, there was quite a crowd here yesterday." Emily popped a green olive into her mouth. "The family seemed to appreciate being together. It was so kind of the women at Saint Catherine's to take care of providing all this food."

"It certainly was. So tell me … are you and Chance going steady—or whatever it is young people call it today?"

Emily shook her head. "We're not exactly *together,* but we've been through a lot together, which does make us feel close. Plus we both want to be doctors, and that's a major thing we have in common."

Emily filled her plate and told Reba about her longtime desire to be an ob-gyn.

"It's really nice that you know what you want," Reba said.

"I do. I'm not sure where the idea came from, but after I was present for my nephew's birth, I just *knew*. I've never considered anything else."

"Few people decide at age ten what they want to do with their lives."

"I know." Emily set her plate on the table and sat. "It's a real blessing to know where I'm headed."

"So you'll be at LSU for another three years. And Chance will be at Harvard. Not exactly ideal for romance."

Emily smiled. "There's always email and texting and Skype. People don't have to be cut off anymore. Chance and I can continue building our friendship from wherever we are."

"Doesn't sound terribly romantic."

Emily stared at the food on her plate. "Truthfully, romance would complicate things. We have a lot of schooling in front of us. We're better off to stay just friends."

Reba smiled wryly. "Pity. I like you. I think you're good for Chance. I'm sure Lydia would've liked you."

"I met Chance's parents once. They seemed happy."

"They had their bumps, like every other couple. But they worked through them. If you ask me, Lydia was a saint. I would never have put up with Huet's cruel humor or his carrying on with that woman." Reba put her hand to her mouth, her eyes welling with tears. "I didn't mean to say that. Lydia swore me to secrecy. Huet had been having an affair for some time with a woman they knew from the country club. Needless to say, Lydia was devastated and didn't want Chance to find out."

"He won't hear it from me," Emily said. "But are you sure he doesn't know? He has a big chip on his shoulder where his dad's concerned."

"That's because Huet rode him all the time." Reba stared at her hands. "Lydia confided in me and no one else. She made sure Chance knew nothing about the affair. She felt their father-son relationship was too fragile to handle more disappointment."

"I can't argue with that," Emily said.

"So you'll keep this between us?"

Emily nodded.

"All right, then," Reba said. "I'm finished with canceling accounts. How about, after lunch, we clean out closets? Whatever we decide to give away, pending Chance's approval, of course, we can take down to the Saint Vincent de Paul Thrift Shop."

"Sure. I'll do whatever helps."

Emily took a bite of potato salad, wishing Reba hadn't told her about Mr. Durand's indiscretion. How was she supposed to build an open, honest relationship with Chance while protecting a secret like that?

CHAPTER 26

Sax sat at a corner table at Zoe B's, finishing a lunch portion of chicken and andouille sausage jambalaya, surprised that neither Zoe nor Pierce seemed to be around. He watched with amusement as Hebert, Father Sam, and Tex talked out the problems of the world over a game of checkers they all knew Hebert would win.

He looked out the window and saw a horse-drawn carriage pull up in front of the Hotel Peltier and let off passengers, many of them smiling children. He could count on one hand the times he remembered smiling and laughing as a child. There must have been good times. Why couldn't he remember them?

Savannah appeared at the table, her ponytail tied with a flowered scarf. "Here, let me take those dishes out of your way."

He noticed a redheaded man in chef's attire walking in his direction, carrying a plate of something.

"Mr. Henry, I'm Dempsey Tanner, the sous chef. Chef Broussard isn't here this afternoon, but left instructions for me to bring you a complimentary dessert he would like you to try."

"That was nice of him." Sax smiled. "It looks delicious."

"It's strawberry banana nut cream cake." Dempsey set the dessert on the table. "Four layers of Chef Broussard's signature buttermilk cake filled with a special blend of whipping cream, cream cheese, ricotta, as well as vanilla, amaretto, and almond extract. We add to the layers fresh-sliced strawberries, bananas, and pecans—and *voilà*. We're still tweaking and would appreciate your input. You'll be the first to try it, except for Chef Broussard and myself. *Bon appetite*!"

"Thanks. I'm sure it's going to be wonderful."

As Dempsey disappeared into the kitchen, Sax eyed the culinary delight, flattered that Pierce thought to instruct his sous chef ahead of time to serve it. He picked up his fork and took a bite, letting the icing melt in his mouth, able to taste every flavor Chef Tanner had named, surprised at how nicely the rich buttermilk taste held its own. Another culinary masterpiece by Chef Broussard.

"Hi."

The little voice startled him, and he turned, surprised to see Zoe's daughter looking him squarely in the eyes.

"I'm Grace. Remember me?"

"I certainly do. My name is Sax, in case you forgot. I know you meet lots of people. It's hard to remember all those names."

"My daddy's the chef. But he has a helper chef."

"Your daddy's a very good chef," Sax said.

Grace bobbed her head, soft blonde curls framing her face. "He makes the bestest grilled cheese samwiches in the whooole world! I like mine with pickles. Yum."

"Me, too. What color cheese do you like—white or yellow?"

"The yellow kind."

Sax smiled. "Me, too. Sounds like we have a lot in common."

"Grace, let the man enjoy his lunch." Maddie arrived at the table, holding Tucker in her arms. "I'm so sorry. I apologize for the interruption. Grace's extroversion gets the best of her."

"She's not bothering me," Sax said. "She's delightful."

Grace's face beamed as if she understood the compliment. "Did you know I live here?"

"You do?"

"Yes, up the very big stairs. Mommy and Daddy and Tucker and *me*." She pointed to herself with her thumb.

"That's perfect, isn't it?" Sax said. "You can come visit your parents while they work."

Grace put her index finger to her rosebud lips. "But I have to use my indoor voice when I come here."

"That's right," Maddie said softly. "Can you tell this nice man good-bye now? I need to get Tucker down for a nap."

Grace's eyebrows came together. "I want to go swimming."

"We'll go later this afternoon, after Tucker wakes up. Your mom said you could sit with your uncles and watch them play checkers, if you like."

"Yay! Bye, Mister Sax."

"Bye, Grace. It was nice seeing you again. You can come talk to me any time." He smiled at Maddie. "Really. She's no bother."

"Okay, lacy Gracie," Maddie said. "Let's go see who's winning."

Maddie took Grace by the hand and walked over to the table by the window, where Grace's booster seat was waiting for her in the chair next to Father Sam.

Grace opted instead to crawl up into Hebert's lap. It was so obvious the three men adored her. Sax felt a pang of disappointment that he had never been able to father a child.

Sax took another bite of the scrumptious dessert and stole a few well-spaced glances at the old guys doting on Grace Broussard. What a lucky kid. He remembered when Shelby was as innocent and adorable as Grace. It was unconscionable that their father had violated her. But almost as unthinkable that he and his mother had let it happen by choosing to remain ignorant.

Sax put his fork down. What was he doing here? Did he really think Shelby could ever forgive him when he couldn't even forgive himself?

Emily knocked on Chance's door. "It's me."

"Come in," he said.

Emily went in and shut the door. Chance was lying in bed with his hands behind his head.

"I was hoping you'd have lunch with us," Emily said.

"I don't feel much like talking. All I can think about is how I'm going to go on without my mom."

"You will. It'll take time. My family went through it when my grandparents died in the car wreck. My dad seemed lost for a while. Even as a little kid, I knew some of what he was feeling. I missed them dearly too."

"I don't think grandparents are the same as a mother."

"No, but I do know what grief and sorrow feels like. It's a deep aching that never goes away. It's there when you close your eyes and hope you can fall asleep. And it's there when you open them and remember what's happened. It's like a giant weight that sits on your heart. It's awful."

"That's about it." Chance sat up and moved to the side of the bed. "Come sit with me."

She walked over and nestled beside him.

"I'm glad you're here." He slid his arm around her. "Thanks for helping Aunt Reba."

"You're welcome. We're thinking of cleaning out your parents' closet and dresser this afternoon, if that's okay with you. What Reba can't use, we'll give to Saint Vincent de Paul."

"That's fine. I really don't want to be involved in it."

"I wanted to check first."

He pulled her closer. "You've been such a great friend, Emily. Thanks for everything. When we started hanging out I never dreamed what a nightmare I was pulling you into."

"You didn't pull me into it; I came willingly. Did you really think I would leave you to deal with this by yourself? What kind of friend does that?"

"I haven't had many friends—and none I would call close. I guess I really don't know much about friendship."

"You're doing just fine. We'll take it one day at a time."

"*Un jour à la fois,* as Mom used to say."

Emily patted his knee. "I should finish having lunch with Aunt Reba and keep the momentum going. I want to get as much done as we can before I have to go back to work on Saturday."

She started to get up. And before she realized what was happening, Chance cupped her face in his hands, his warm lips melting into hers. Emily went limp, her heart fluttering, and let herself enjoy the moment.

Chance slowly, seemingly reluctantly, ended the kiss and looked into her eyes. Finally he said, "Wow. I didn't plan that. You're not mad, are you?"

"Did I act mad?" Emily poked him with her elbow. "Some of the nicest moments in life are unplanned."

Chance's face turned bright pink. "Spontaneity's good?"

"It certainly was just then."

"You're a great kisser."

Emily felt her own cheeks warm. "I haven't had all that much practice."

"Apparently, you don't need it."

There was a comfortable pause.

"Emily, I need someone like you in my life," Chance said. "You're a sensitive person in every way. And yet you're strong, decisive, and persuasive. Don't ever change. The only other person I know with those qualities was my mother."

"Thank you. What an incredibly nice thing to say."

"I wish you'd had time to really get to know her."

"Me, too." *I hate that I know something about her life you don't.* "I'd better go find Aunt Reba. I'm sure she's wondering what's keeping me."

"We wouldn't want her to think there was any hanky-panky going on in my parents' house, now, would we?" Chance winked.

"Don't spoil what happened by saying that. I made it clear to her what our relationship is."

He took her hand. "I'm kidding. But we're a little more involved than we were when you last talked to her about it."

"An innocent kiss in no way could be classified as hanky-panky." Emily laughed. "The only time I've heard that term used is in old-timey movies."

"Well, maybe I have an old-timey crush on you."

"A crush, huh?"

"Absolutely." He kissed her cheek. "I can't think of anyone I would rather be with. I just wish it were under better circumstances."

"It is what it is. That doesn't change our relationship."

"Good."

"I should go." Emily rose to her feet.

"If it's okay with you, I'm going to turn on my iPod and let the music put me to sleep while you two clear out my parents' room. I'd just as soon not see or hear anything until it's over."

Zoe sat on a bench in Cypress Park, staring at the duck pond and feeling like a stranger in her own skin. She couldn't relate to Shelby Sieger anymore. She was no longer that vulnerable, pathetic, angry girl whose brother left her in that living hell on his seventeenth birthday and never came back. Never called. Never even sent a letter or a birthday card. She was Zoe Broussard, an adopted child of the most high God. Happily married to Pierce, and the proud mother of two precious children for whom she would die before ever allowing them to be abused the way she had been.

What did Michael want from her? It had been hard enough coming to a place of forgiveness for their parents. In some ways, forgiving her brother would be even more difficult. How could he have just abandoned her when he knew firsthand the helplessness and hopelessness of being at home with Raleigh and Frank Sieger?

Zoe's mind flashed back to the last encounter she'd had with Sax....

"You haven't answered my question," he said. "If you give God the credit for the blessings, don't you give Him the blame for the bad things?"

"Blame is the wrong word," Zoe said. "He allows everything that happens in my life—for reasons I may never know. But I thank Him and love Him and praise Him in the midst of hard times, knowing that He's right there with me and will use it for my good."

She sighed. If that was true for Zoe Broussard, it was true for Shelby Sieger. Any conversation with Michael would require her either to live up to her faith or to let her brother reduce it to the meaningless crutch he had suspected it was all along. If only she hadn't had that conversation with him!

Lord, I'm not ready to be an example. This is too hard.

She heard children laughing. She glanced up at the bridge that spanned the pond and saw two little girls leaning over the railing, dropping popcorn into the water. Her mind flashed back to a vivid memory....

"Shelby, you don't have to be afraid of the geese," Michael said. "I won't let them hurt you."

"They might bite me."

"They just want the popcorn." Michael took her hand. "Let me show you how to give it to them. Do you trust me?"

She nodded.

Michael led her to the water's edge and opened the bag of

popcorn. The geese came swimming toward the shore, honking incessantly.

"I'm scared." Shelby froze. "They're going to get me!"

"Watch." Michael reached into the bag and flung a handful of popcorn into the water.

The geese all went for it and then came out of the water and surrounded them. Michael threw a couple handfuls of popcorn on the ground and let the geese fight over it, and then held out a piece to one goose that seemed to have gotten pushed out.

The goose came up to Michael and gently took a single piece of popcorn from his hand. He held out another, and a different goose snatched it in the same way.

"They won't hurt you, Shelby. You have to hold the popcorn so they can grab the end of it. Sometimes it tickles, but they're not biting you."

She clung tightly to Michael's arm with both hands, giggling and thoroughly entertained, but content to let him do the feeding. She trusted him to protect her from scary things....

Zoe heard a car door slam and looked over at the parking lot. She spotted a white Camry, and her heart sank. Pierce must have told Adele about their confrontation.

Isabel walked around the car and helped Adele out of the passenger side. Adele took her cane and steadied herself, and then hobbled across the grass toward Zoe.

Lord, I don't want to have this conversation.

CHAPTER 27

It was all Zoe could do not to get up and assist Adele as she took those last tedious steps across Cypress Park to the bench where Zoe sat. But why act as if she welcomed Adele's involvement in something so shameful and embarrassing? Still, this precious woman loved her with a maternal love that Raleigh Ruth Sieger never had.

Adele arrived at the park bench and paused a few moments, trying to catch her breath.

Zoe had no idea what to say to her, so she said nothing.

Finally, Adele sat next to her on the bench. "This is awkward for both of us. Pierce told me the details of your confrontation earlier. So you're aware your brother came to me, not the other way around."

"You could have turned him away," Zoe said.

"Not without lying. He asked me point-blank."

"Adele, you could have found a way to dismiss him without lying, if you'd wanted to. I haven't worked for you in fifteen years. I left no forwarding address. That's the truth, and it would have been enough."

"I suppose it would have." Adele took a hanky out of her pocket and dabbed the perspiration from her face. "But an important opportunity would have been lost. I didn't feel I had the right to make that choice for you."

Zoe sighed, her hand gripping the left arm of the wrought-iron bench.

"Do you want me to refer to your brother as Michael or Sax?" Adele said.

"I don't know. They seem like two entirely different people."

"Is it so hard to believe Michael could've changed that much after all this time? You did."

"This is not about *me*."

Adele raised an eyebrow. "Isn't it?"

"No, it's about Shelby Sieger, who no longer exists. I don't want to resurrect her or anything from the past."

"You changed your name, Zoe. You very effectively ended the paper trail. You didn't change your DNA or your history. That reality must be dealt with."

"I did deal with it. I forgave my parents and put the past behind me. I've moved on."

"Michael's a significant part of your past. And he's anything but behind you."

"That's his problem." Zoe linked her fingers together. "I shouldn't have to make it mine. I haven't seen him in almost three decades. What's the point in stirring up all those bad memories?"

"He's been looking for you for a long time. He has a lot to tell you."

"Maybe I don't want to hear it."

Adele gently rubbed Zoe's shoulder. "From what he told me, hon, I think you do. He didn't come here to hurt you. He came here because he knows he already has. He's trying to reconcile the past. I think you both want the same thing."

Zoe listened as Adele told her every detail of her first conversation with the man legally known as Sax Michael Henry.

"Believe me, I didn't make it easy for him." Adele took her hand. "He owned up to his responsibility for leaving you in that dreadful environment. He's deeply sorry. I think it would help you to hear him out."

"Am I supposed to jump because he's *finally* accepted responsibility? It doesn't change anything."

"Zoe, when a broken person comes to a Christian, seeking forgiveness, it most certainly does change things."

Zoe pulled her hand away from Adele. "I am *not* forgiving him just because his guilty conscience got to him! Why should I let him off that easily? He doesn't deserve it."

"No. Perhaps not." Adele looked out at the pond, fingering the gold cross around her neck that was identical to the one around Zoe's. "Do any of us?"

Zoe's eyes stung with tears as she remembered all too well Adele's act of grace that had changed the course of her life—and Pierce's. Why was it so difficult to find that same absolution for her brother?

"Adele, I can't. I'm sorry. Tell him to go home. I don't want to see him."

"God is with you, child. There's nothing to fear."

"Maybe someday. Not now."

Adele was quiet for half a minute, then she stood, both hands resting on her cane. "I know you, Zoe—to the depths of your heart and soul. I want you to sleep on this. Do it for me. All I ask is that you don't make a hasty decision that you'll regret. Get alone with God and think seriously about this and pray. If you still feel the same tomorrow at this time, I'll tell your brother you don't want to see him."

"I'm not changing my mind."

"Twenty-four hours," Adele said. "And I suggest you get down on your knees and try to remember what it feels like to be broken."

Emily and Reba pulled all the clothes out of the Durands' closet, put them in boxes, and stacked the boxes in the back of Reba's minivan.

Emily followed Reba back into the house, and Reba dropped into a chair at the kitchen table.

"That's about all the energy I have for today," Reba said. "I think I'll sit here a minute and cool off, then run these clothes to the thrift shop before it closes."

"Why don't you let me help you with that?" Emily said.

Reba waved her hand. "The folks at the loading dock will unload the boxes. Why don't you stay here and keep Chance company? You can tell him how much headway we made today. Mercy, we got a lot accomplished."

"We did, didn't we?" Emily opened the fridge, and a few of the leftover containers nearly fell out. "Would you like something cold to drink before you leave?"

"Thank you, dear. A green tea sounds wonderful."

Emily took a can of Coke for herself and handed Reba a green tea, then sat at the table, facing her. "What's your plan for tomorrow?"

"I'd like to help you finish cleaning out the garage in the morning," Reba said. "With two of us, we ought to be done in a few hours. After that, we can come inside and start on Lydia and Huet's dresser drawers. Once that's done, I think I'll drive back to Shreveport. The attorney will guide Chance through everything else. Probate should be easy since he's the only heir. I assume you'll be there to support him through that process. That's probably all he'll need."

"You know I will," Emily said. "It's sweet of you to give so generously of yourself, especially when Chance doesn't seem to appreciate your presence here."

"I'm doing what needs to be done—not so much for Chance as for Lydia. She would want me to look out for him, no matter how much he protests. She loved that boy, and always believed in him. . . ." Reba coughed as if to cover her emotion. "I do miss my sister so very much."

Emily put her hand on Reba's. "I know you do. All the more reason why I admire you for choosing to stay and work at a time when you're hurting too."

Reba's cheeks turned pink. "I didn't expect you to say that. I thought you were tolerating me because you had to."

"Not at all. I admit we got off on the wrong foot. But you've been invaluable. I'm sure Chance sees that, even if he doesn't feel like talking right now."

"It's easy to see he's devastated," Reba said. "I just hope he's able to pull himself together before he starts classes again in August."

"I hope so too. Maybe with enough time by himself, he'll be able to sort out his feelings."

"Emily"—Reba looked into her eyes—"it's bothered me all day that I let it slip about Huet's indiscretion. Please assure me I can count on you to help me honor Lydia's memory by not telling anyone, especially Chance."

"I won't say anything. I promise."

"Thank you. That means a lot to me." Reba stood and picked up the bottle of green tea. "I should get down to the thrift shop before it closes. There's still plenty of food in the fridge for dinner."

"We'll be fine."

Emily walked her to the kitchen door. "Until Chance wakes up, I think I'll work on his dad's dresser. I'll leave your sister's for you to sort through. There might be something personal you'd like to keep."

"Sounds good."

In the next second, Reba's arms went around Emily.

"I'm glad you're here, young lady—and I didn't think I would be. I guess we each prejudged the other."

Emily smiled. "We make a pretty good team. I'm thinking of coming back in the morning around seven. I'd like to get started before it gets too hot."

"I'll come with my sleeves rolled up." Reba winked. "Bye, now."

Emily took socks and handkerchiefs out of the smaller drawers in the dresser that belonged to Chance's dad and put them in boxes, stealing a glance every now and then at the huge family oil painting that hung on the wall above the bed. Chance was blond as a little boy, but his smile was unmistakable. So cute, dressed in pale blue shorts and a matching shirt with a sailor collar. The adoring look on his mother's face said it all. His father's expression, though pleasant enough, looked shifty. Was he cheating back then, too? Were there other affairs?

Her mind flashed back to that dark time in her own childhood when she realized her father had had an affair. She would gladly have gone the rest of her life without knowing that about him. She applauded Chance's mother for wanting to keep her husband's affair from their son. Emily certainly wasn't going to tell him.

She opened the bottom drawer and removed some beautiful cotton sweaters that had probably gotten little wear in this warm climate. No point in keeping them. Huet was at least two sizes larger than Chance. She pulled out the last sweater, which still had a price tag on it, and spotted an envelope on the bottom of the drawer.

She picked it up and noticed it wasn't sealed. She peeked inside and saw only photographs. Probably something Chance would want to take a look at. She pulled out the photos and started looking through them. All the pictures were of one woman—fiftyish—shapely and attractive. Emily didn't remember seeing this person at the funeral home. Was it someone they failed to inform of his parents' death?

Emily looked through the entire stack of pictures. The last photo was a close-up of this same woman with Huet Durand. They were cheek to cheek, and it was obvious that he was holding the camera. Was this the woman he'd had the affair with? She turned over the photo and saw a name written in pencil. *Joanna Arceneau*. Where had she heard that name recently?

Emily studied the woman's face. She looked familiar, though Emily couldn't place her. Perhaps she was a customer at Zoe B's. That had to be it. Emily had likely seen her name on a credit card.

Emily put the pictures back in the envelope and set it aside. She closed the empty drawer and opened the one above it. She began removing golf shirts and shorts and putting them in the box.

"Where's Aunt Reba?"

Emily turned and saw Chance standing in the doorway, looking disheveled.

"She left," Emily said. "She took the clothes from the closet and some boxes from the garage down to the Saint Vincent de Paul Thrift Shop."

"Is she coming back?"

"Not today." Emily stood. "I'm emptying your dad's dresser now. I thought Reba should do your mom's. Are you hungry?"

"Not really. But it would be nice to come out of my room. When's Aunt Reba going back to Shreveport?"

Emily shrugged. "Maybe tomorrow afternoon. We're going to finish cleaning out the shelves in the garage in the morning and then empty your mom's dresser. I doubt it will take long. After that, we're pretty much done with everything we can do. Your attorney will take it from here."

"What's in the envelope?"

"Photos of a woman. I thought she might be a relative."

Emily handed the envelope to him and studied his expression as he quickly sifted through the pictures. He didn't flinch and either missed or pretended not to see the picture of his dad and the woman on the bottom of the stack.

"I have no idea who this woman is. I might as well trash these."

"Okay," Emily said, folding down the flaps on the box with the sweaters, pretending not to notice that his tone belied his words.

Chance must have known about the affair. She wasn't going to add to his shame and pain by telling him that she had seen the picture of his father with the woman or that Reba had blurted out the ugly truth. Some secrets were not meant to be shared.

CHAPTER 28

Sax went for an evening stroll on the grounds at Langley Manor, feeling a little sad that he hadn't seen any of the Broussards when he was at Zoe B's for dinner. He hadn't realized how much he enjoyed what little of their time and attention they had shared. Not only had it helped pass the time, but it helped him not feel so lonely while he waited for Shelby's husband to talk her into meeting with him.

"Hi, Mr. Henry!"

Carter Langley waved from about thirty yards away and ran toward him, Angel barking and romping playfully.

Carter came to an abrupt stop and immediately started talking. "Would you like to throw the Frisbee for Angel? She's really, *really* good at this. I'm not just saying that because she's mine."

Sax nodded. "Sure. Let's see what she's got."

"Angel, sit," Carter said. "On your mark … get set … *go*!"

The yellow lab ran full throttle across the grounds. Sax took the Frisbee and gave it a good spin in her direction. Angel lunged and caught it in midair, then brought it back and laid it at his feet.

"Good girl." Carter bent down and rubbed her neck. "See? Isn't she awesome?"

"She sure is. Did you train her?"

"All by myself." Carter looked up at him, a mop of strawberry-blond hair covering the boy's eyebrows, a grin stretching his cheeks as Angel licked his face. "She was a rescue dog. We don't know if she got lost or if someone just couldn't take care of her. But she's part of our family now. I'm never ever letting her go."

"I don't blame you."

"Do *you* have a pet?"

Sax shook his head. "They don't allow pets where I live."

"Too bad," Carter said. "Do you like to swim?"

"Sometimes."

"Well, I'm going to be in the pool later." Carter stood, his bright blue eyes looking remarkably like his mother's. "If you feel like it, I could play volleyball with you."

"I might take you up on that. I don't have swimming trunks with me. Would cutoffs be okay?"

"Oh, sure."

A loud whistle came from the direction of the manor house.

"That's my dad," Carter said. "I'm supposed to do my chores. Maybe I'll see you in the pool, Mr. Henry."

"Call me Sax."

"My parents might not like that."

"I'll tell them it's okay, that I like it better."

Carter cocked his head and flashed a lopsided grin. "Good-bye, Sax." He laughed. "I think I'll have to practice. It's weird calling a grown-up by their first name."

"You'd better answer your dad's whistle. I'll come to the pool around eight."

"Okay, bye." Carter ran off toward the manor house, Angel alongside.

Sax's cell phone rang. He looked at the screen and saw that it was Adele Woodmore. Was this it—the moment he had been waiting for? He took a slow, deep breath and put the phone to his ear.

"Hello, Mrs. Woodmore."

"Hello, Sax. I wanted to keep you apprised. I have contacted Shelby and talked with her personally. At the moment, she refuses to see you. But as a favor to me, I've asked her to take twenty-four hours to think and to pray. Her husband also approached her. I can't say it went any better. But I know what Shelby's made of. She'll make the right choice."

"And you believe the right choice is for her to contact me?"

"Truthfully, I'm unsure about the timing. But when the time *is* right, I do believe her contacting you is the right choice."

Sax's heart sank. Could he endure weeks, months, maybe even years of waiting for Shelby to act? "Sounds like you have real doubts that it's going to happen anytime soon."

Adele sighed. "I wish I could tell you something definite, hon. But the truth is I just don't know. I'm not sure you realize the full extent of that girl's suffering and how hard she worked to forgive your parents and put the whole nightmare behind her. Asking her to open that door again, especially when you've been out of the picture for almost three decades, is asking a lot."

"I just want to tell her how sorry I am. That's all. She deserves to hear it from me."

"I agree with you. That's why I chose to get involved. But Shelby has to want this for it to have the desired effect. Otherwise, you're going to be sorely disappointed and end up with a worse situation."

"I doubt that's possible," Sax said.

"It certainly is for Shelby. And she's the one I'm most concerned with at the moment."

"I'm not asking her to talk about the details of what she suffered," Sax said. "I just want to apologize for leaving her there and explain some things."

"I hope you're not thinking about offering excuses, young man, because she—"

"I'm not. I made a choice, and I'm responsible for it. But Shelby also deserves to know that I did go back several times and tried to convince Mom to take Shelby and go to a shelter, and she never would. I think if I hadn't been in denial about the extent of Shelby's abuse, I would have taken her myself and let the shelter deal with getting her into foster care. But I believed my dad would kill my mother if I did. It was a terrible choice for a teenager to make."

"Yes, it was." Adele's tone was tender. "I'm very sorry the two of you had such dreadful experiences."

"You told me that Shelby was happy and had found peace. If that's true, how hard can it be for her to share with me how she got there? Because I really need to know. I'm hanging by a thread here...." His voice cracked. "Look, you didn't ask for this. I don't want to create a problem for Shelby. But she's all I've got left. I've pretty much staked my future on this reunion."

"It'll never be enough, Sax. You're just asking to be disappointed."

"How can you say that?"

Adele sighed into the receiver. "Because even if Shelby welcomes you with open arms, it can't give you the peace you're looking for."

"You don't know that."

"Actually, I do. You'll never find true peace while you're at odds with the Prince of Peace."

Sax paused for a moment, his mind racing in reverse.

"I hope I didn't offend you," Adele said. "I tend to get right to the point."

"I was just trying to remember where I'd heard that before. It was in a conversation I had with Zoe. She said the same thing."

"Maybe God wants you to listen."

"Please don't take this personally, Mrs. Woodmore, but I really don't care what He wants. He's never been there for me. I've never understood why. But I've ceased to care. I'm not giving Him my heart, my life, or my attention. About the only thing I *am* willing to give Him is a piece of my mind."

"And you keep falling deeper and deeper into self-pity," Adele said. "I've been there, Sax. You will never find peace without Jesus. You wonder how Shelby did it. That's how."

"Shelby's a Christian?"

"She doesn't wear it on her sleeve. But yes. She's given her heart to Christ, and those terrible memories have become a distant shadow. I think she's afraid that seeing you will bring them back. I have faith it won't. But only God knows the perfect timing for the two of you to connect."

Sax moved the phone to his other ear. "Okay, let me make sure we're clear on something. Y'all can involve God all you want. Just leave me out of it."

"I respect that. But there's something you need to understand. If you're expecting Shelby to give you a how-to lesson on finding peace, she's going to tell you it begins and ends with God."

Sax looked up as three ibis flew overhead, pure white in the evening sun. "If that works for her, I'm glad. Just don't try to push it on me."

There was a long moment of dead air.

Finally Adele said, "I know you feel as if the Lord has turned a deaf ear to your suffering. That's a difficult place to be. I've been there myself. But things may not be what they seem."

"Meaning what?" Sax sat on a wrought-iron bench near the flower garden.

"Have you ever considered that it might not be God who's turned a deaf ear? That He's tried to speak to you and you've turned Him off?"

"Speak to me how? I've never heard anything."

"He speaks mostly through the Scriptures. But He also speaks through music, books, people. A still, small voice. A strong nudge."

"Not to me, He doesn't."

"You're here, aren't you? Perhaps it was God prompting you to pursue Shelby."

"It took me three years," Sax said. "It wasn't easy. Trust me, I didn't get any divine intervention."

"Are you so sure? God works in mysterious ways, Sax. And He's in relentless pursuit of souls who need His love and grace."

"Well, *I'm* not one of them." Sax lowered his voice. "Look, I truly appreciate your trying to help, but we're never going to see eye to eye on religion. Let's just wait and see what Shelby decides and go from there."

Zoe stood on the gallery above Zoe B's and watched the nightlife on *rue Madeline*—neon lights flashing, people going in all directions, horses pulling carriages, street entertainers, folks waving from neighboring galleries. How she loved this unique little corner of America, a place where families and friends came to make memories and celebrate the Cajun culture. It was here she had found her heart's desire. Here she had nearly lost it all, but for Adele's willingness to forgive Shelby Sieger for stealing her valuable ring and selling it to get money to start Zoe B's under a whole new identity. If it hadn't been for Adele's example of grace, Zoe's marriage to Pierce might not have survived. And she might never have known what it was to give herself—heart and soul—to the God who wanted a relationship with her. Who had already paid the price for her trail of deceit.

Adele told her to remember how it felt to be broken. But Zoe had never forgotten the violent past that had taken away her voice and her hope. Or the dishonesty that began when she stole Adele's ring and continued until she got caught in a web of her own lies. In God's plan, none of it was wasted. Not a single tear. Not one gut-wrenching moment. He had known from the beginning of time that, when she finally came to the end of herself, He would be there with open arms to cleanse the memory of her father's despicable acts and give her a new identity in Christ. That He would wipe the tears from her eyes and the sin from her own heart.

Zoe sighed. God had forgiven her for being a thief and a liar. So had Adele and Pierce. Was her brother's sin any worse than hers?

Lord, I know I need to forgive Michael. Help me. Make me willing.

She heard the door slide open and close again.

"Would you rather be alone?" Pierce said.

"Not really. I've been standing out here since the sun went down, and I'm no closer to knowing what to do."

He came up behind her and put his arms around her, his cheek next to hers. "Adele told you to take twenty-four hours before making your decision."

"I'm not sure it will matter. I know I need to forgive Michael. I'm not ready."

"Maybe it would help to hear what he has to say. It couldn't have been easy for him to come here, looking for you. Adele thinks he's sincere about wanting to make amends."

"Good for him," Zoe said. "But I'm not prepared for his showing up out of the blue. I had accepted that he abandoned me and haven't thought about it in a long time. I don't want to talk about the past and dig up all that pain."

"Maybe what still hurts is just the unfinished business you have with Michael."

"I'm really scared to deal with it, Pierce. It's terrifying, feeling this vulnerable again. But I'm also scared that, if I don't meet with Michael, he might disappear again, and someday I'll be sorry I passed up the opportunity."

Pierce kissed her cheek. "That's an awful lot of scared. Would it make any difference if I went with you?"

Zoe reached up and touched his cheek. "Thanks. But whatever I decide, I have to stand on my own two feet as the adult I am now, not as the frightened, helpless victim he left behind. I'm Zoe Broussard, not Shelby Sieger."

"And he's Sax Henry—not Michael Sieger. You were both terrified teenagers the last time you saw each other."

Zoe shuddered. "Well, one of us had a lot more to be terrified of than the other."

CHAPTER 29

Emily pulled into the guest parking lot at Langley Manor and spotted Sax and Carter in the pool. She got out and walked over to them, the smell of mock orange permeating the night air.

"Hey, guys. How's it going?"

"Sax and me are the champs!" Carter declared. "We beat Mr. and Mrs. Adams in every game of volleyball."

"The couple from North Carolina?" Emily said.

Carter nodded. "We beat them three times."

"They were no match for this guy." Sax splashed Carter and made him squeal. "I was just here to complete the team."

"I'm glad you two *boys* had fun." Emily stepped a little closer, her gaze on Carter. "I'm sorry I've had to be gone the past few days. There's been a lot going on with Chance's parents' funeral. And now his aunt Reba and I are cleaning out his parents' closet and personal things. But soon I'll be able to spend some time with you."

"It's okay," Carter said. "Sax and me are having fun."

Emily glanced at her watch. "It's after ten. How come you're still up?"

"Mom said I could. I can sleep late."

Sax splashed Carter again and got him in a headlock and started tickling him.

Emily smiled despite feeling jealous that she wasn't in the pool with Carter instead of Sax. "Have fun, guys. I'm beat."

"Good night, Auntie Em!" Carter let out a husky laugh.

Sax shot her an amused and quizzical look.

"We can all thank *The Wizard of Oz* for that one." Emily chuckled. "I started referring to myself as Auntie Em when Vanessa was pregnant with Carter, and it stuck."

"I think it's sweet," Sax said.

"Well, Auntie Em is off to bed. Good night, guys."

Emily walked down the sidewalk and up the back steps to the deck. She went in the back door, a blast of air-conditioned air cooling her face, and saw Vanessa and Ethan sitting at the kitchen table.

"Wow, do you look tired," Vanessa said.

"I am. Reba and I worked hard and got a lot accomplished."

"Want a cookie?" Ethan held up a plate, neatly arranged with peanut butter, oatmeal raisin, and chocolate chip cookies.

"No, thanks. I'm too tired to chew."

"What did you accomplish?" Ethan said.

"I cleaned out shelves in the garage and helped Reba empty out the closets in Chance's parents' room. Then we filled Reba's minivan, and she took everything to the thrift shop. It was a lot of work, but it feels good to have it behind us."

"What's left now?" Vanessa said, in that nosy tone Emily resented.

"We have to finish emptying the shelves in the garage and the dresser drawers, and then we're done. I doubt Chance is going to do anything about selling the house for a long time. He just needs time to grieve and get his thoughts together over the summer so he can get back to Harvard."

"Do you think he can do that?" Ethan said. "His whole world just shattered."

"I don't know. I hope so."

"Maybe he should take a semester off." Ethan took a bite of cookie. "Just to clear his head."

Emily shrugged. "I doubt that's even occurred to him. He's too dazed at the moment to think that far ahead. I'm going to bed. I promised Reba I'd meet her in the morning so we could finish up. Good night."

Emily walked down the hall and into the guest room. She closed the door and flopped onto the bed, her hands behind her head, watching the ceiling fan go round and round. It felt so good to get off her feet, cool off, and just let her thoughts wander. She had grown fond of Reba and was actually sad that she would be going back to Shreveport so soon.

Emily lay in the quiet, thinking about Chance's unexpected kiss that had left her wanting more. She replayed the moment over and over in her mind. An innocent kiss certainly didn't mean she was falling in love with him. But being that close to him affected her in a way that was new and exciting. She certainly wouldn't resist if he kissed her again.

Emily yawned, her body sinking into the mattress, her muscles relaxing, her thoughts slowing down. She imagined herself drifting on a sea of calm, floating weightlessly, her mind emptied of tomorrow's to-do list…

Joanna Arceneau! Emily opened her eyes, suddenly remembering where she had heard that name. She got up, went over to the dresser, picked up Monday's *Les Barbes Ledger*, and turned to the obituaries.

There she was: Joanna Arceneau, the woman she had seen in the photograph with Chance's father. She was one of the cyanide victims who was discovered dead on Saturday morning—the same morning Chance's parents died. It might have been coincidence that Huet Durand and his lover were both victims. But what if it wasn't? What if there was a common thread that could point to the killer?

Emily sighed, bemoaning for a moment the inconvenience of being the daughter of a police chief. There was no way she could ignore this information. She would have to confront Reba with it in the morning and find out if Lydia ever told her the name of the woman who was having an affair with Huet.

If Reba confirmed it was Joanna Arceneau, they would have to inform the sheriff. So much for protecting the secret.

Sax sat out on the deck at Langley Manor, too stimulated to sleep after spending the evening trying to keep up with an active almost nine-year-old. Carter was a fun-loving, happy kid, enjoyable to be around, especially at a time when Sax's own haunting childhood memories were being replayed in his mind with stark realism.

It occurred to him that he'd had more quality time in the pool with Carter in three hours than he'd spent with his own father the entire time he was growing up. Why did he still feel as if it must have been his fault that his father hit him? Common sense now told him that a child is not responsible for the actions of his parents. But his dad had blamed him, and Sax always wondered if it really was his fault—if he was sorely lacking as a son. That made no sense since his dad was cruel to his mom and Shelby, too. But he couldn't seem to shake the feeling that if he'd been the kind of son they'd wanted, Frank and Raleigh Sieger might have been different parents.

He wondered if Shelby was as happy as Adele Woodmore seemed to think she was. Didn't battered children often grow up to be abusers—or marry them? Perhaps it was a blessing that he'd never had children—not that he could imagine ever doing to a child what his father had done to him. Or to Shelby. He cringed at the thought and blinked away the image that popped up in his mind.

He wiped the perspiration off his forehead. Would Shelby feel compelled to unload the details of her abuse that he had no desire to know—details that would sicken him and add to his already overwhelming guilt? Was he prepared for her fury? For her hatred? For her rejection?

Rejection. He'd lived with it for a lifetime. Both parents. Three wives. Even God. But he needed to get this right. Shelby was his ticket to finally finding peace. He could not allow himself to be defeated simply because this was hard. Leaving her without some sort of resolution was not an option.

The last time he'd left Shelby, he had been the one in control....

Michael picked up his suitcase and guitar and walked softly toward the front door, startled by a voice that seemed to come from nowhere.

"Where are you going?"

Michael cringed at the sound of Shelby's voice. Why wasn't she asleep?

"My band's got a gig," he told her.

"In the middle of the night?" Shelby's tone told him she wasn't buying it.

Michael stopped and turned his gaze on his father's passed-out body, the smell of whiskey permeating the living room and making him feel sick to his stomach.

"Look, Shelby, three minutes from now, I'll be seventeen. I don't have to put up with this anymore. I can do what I want now."

"*I* can't."

Michael turned to her. "Don't even think it. You're not coming with me."

"Why not?"

"Because you're a minor. It's kidnapping. I have no legal right to take you."

"Even if I want to go?"

"No. The cops will find us and drag you back here. Whatever you tell them, Mom and Dad will deny it and make them believe you're just a rebellious teenager who's making it all up. Then Dad will be furious, and things will be worse than they already are."

"Then we'll hide from the police," Shelby said.

"Playing gigs makes it a little hard to do that. But being on the road with a rock band is no life for a young girl."

"And this *is*?"

"Look, I'll find a way to get you out of here. But you can't go on tour with me and the band."

"When are you coming back?"

"I'm not sure. But when I do, I'll have a plan to get you away from here."

"Promise?"

He nodded. "I'll figure out something."

Shelby ran over to him and clung to his arm, tears streaming down her cheeks. "I don't want you to go, Michael. I love you."

"I love you, too. Don't be scared. This won't be forever."

The grandfather clock began to strike midnight. With every gong that resounded, Michael felt an adrenaline rush of freedom and empowerment. "Time to go, Sis. I'll talk to you soon."

Shelby clung to him a few seconds longer and then let go.

Michael stepped over his dad and stood straddling his passed-out body, gripping a guitar in one hand and suitcase in the other.

"Good riddance, old man. And just for the record: *you're* the miserable, good-for-nothing piece of garbage." Michael spit on him and then left by the front door....

He never did contact Shelby. When his efforts to get his mother to leave failed, he decided it would only make things worse. How could he look into Shelby's eyes and see the fear and despair he remembered all too well but was powerless to change? The longer he went without contacting her, the easier it was to let her go....

Sax looked out into the darkness and then felt enveloped by it. *I was a coward, Shelby. I should have fought for you. I'm sorry. I'm so sorry.*

Unwanted tears trailed down his cheeks, and he was no longer able to keep his thumb in the bulging dike of emotion that had been building for a lifetime. Anger. Guilt. Shame. Sorrow. Regret. All breaking through his defenses, forming a flood of tears and sobs he hadn't heard since he was a boy. Sax stopped trying to control it. He just buried his face in his hands—and wept.

CHAPTER 30

Emily glanced at her watch, then downed a lukewarm cup of coffee and picked up her purse.

"Are you leaving already?" Vanessa said.

"I told Reba I would meet her at Chance's at seven."

"You're going to get sick if you keep up this pace and don't start sleeping more."

"I slept for over seven hours, Vanessa. That's more sleep than I get at college."

"I just don't want you to be wiped out on Saturday when you're supposed to go back to work."

Emily counted to ten and then turned to her older sister. "I have *never ever* missed a day's work because I wore myself out. I've always been a responsible employee. For heaven's sake, I got through a year of college with a 4.0 without anyone babysitting me. I think I can handle helping a friend clean out closets and drawers without you making a federal case out of it. So will you please just back off?"

Vanessa bit her lip. "You're right. I'm doing it again. Sorry."

Emily lowered her voice and spoke calmly. "I talked to Carter last night. I told him we would start doing some fun things soon. He seemed like he was having a ball playing in the pool with Sax."

"He really likes Sax. Ethan and I are always watchful of any male who wants to spend time with him. But Sax seems really nice."

"Just know I haven't forgotten Carter. I need a few days to help Reba sort through things and to help Chance get on his feet."

"Go," Vanessa said. "You're a good friend, Emily. I hope Chance and Reba appreciate you."

"They do. Talk to you tonight."

Emily went out the back door, down the deck steps, and out to the guest parking lot. She got in her blue Honda CR-V and headed for Les Barbes.

Zoe closed the door to her apartment and went downstairs and through the alcove, the melded aromas of brewed coffee, sausage cheese bread, and spicy bacon wafting from the dining room.

She walked through the doorway and spotted Savannah at the table by the window, pouring coffee for Hebert, Father Sam, and Tex, who were eating breakfast.

"Good morning, everyone." Zoe came alongside Savannah. "Y'all doing all right?"

Three heads bobbed in the affirmative.

"Did you hear that a Hispanic roofer was hospitalized with cyanide poisoning?" Tex said.

Zoe sighed. "No. When?"

"Last night. He worked until dark and then drank the bottle of

Gaudry water he had stashed in his truck." Tex shook his head. "So help me, I can't figure out how anyone could not know by this time that the stuff's been recalled—even if they don't speak much English."

Hebert looked up at her, his face unshaven, his woolly gray curls tamer than usual. "At least it's not someting new. We know not to drink da water."

Savannah poured Hebert a cup of coffee. "Hebert's right. Maybe whoever did this is done with Les Barbes and has skipped town."

"Or is regrouping," Zoe said. "Who knows what could be poisoned next. I don't think we should take anything for granted."

Father Sam's eyebrows came together. "You seem bothered by something, Zoe. Is it just sadness over Dominic?"

Zoe shook her head. "I have to make a decision about something, and I'm a little distracted. I'll be fine."

"Want to talk 'bout it?" Tex said.

"It's not that kind of thing. It would take too long to explain it. But thanks."

Zoe felt four pairs of eyes staring at her. She pasted on a smile. "I've got work to do. I'll see y'all later."

She walked to the kitchen and saw Pierce at the worktable, filling orders. He glanced up and smiled. "Hey, babe."

"Hey yourself."

"I was glad to see you finally fell asleep."

Zoe sighed. "Finally. I'm not operating on all cylinders, though."

"You had lots of time to think. Have you decided what you're going to tell Adele?"

"I still have six hours."

Pierce's eyebrows came together. "You really haven't decided yet?"

"What choice do I really have? If I refuse to see Sax, I negate everything I told him about God using the bad things for good. He already thinks faith in God is a crock."

"What do *you* think?"

"You know what I think."

"I know what you *said*." Pierce wiped his hands and came over to her, looking into her eyes. "I don't pretend to know what you're feeling or what it was like to come from an abusive home. But if you believe Romans 8:28 is true, and that God uses all things for good in a believer's life, then you should be able to face your brother with some confidence, right?"

"I should. So why am I so scared?"

Pierce put his arms around her and held her close. "It has to be scary opening a door to a violent past. But remember, it's history. It's not your reality anymore. You're safe now. And you're a healthy, well-adjusted, amazing wife and mother." He kissed her forehead. "I love you with all my heart and soul. I know you can do this."

A tear trickled down her cheek. "I really don't want to."

"I know. But this is the last chapter, Zoe. This is it. Once you face Michael, there are no more secrets. Nothing left undone. That has to be worth whatever pain is involved. I know you think you have to do this by yourself, but my offer to go with you stands."

She nestled closer. "Thanks. But I have to face him alone."

"So you're definitely going to meet with him?"

"I guess. But I'm not admitting it to myself for another six hours."

"If you've made the decision, babe, why wait? Why not go out to Langley Manor and face him? Get it over with before you have time to talk yourself out of it."

"What if I get angry and tell him off?"

"Ask the Lord to help you let go of your anger appropriately. He brought Michael to you for a reason. Michael may not know that, but we do."

"I'd give anything for another way. But I'm never going to be completely free until I resolve this issue with Michael."

"Agreed." Pierce looked into her eyes and seemed to touch her soul.

"I need to tell Vanessa first. She'll be glad this is finally happening after all the years she's been praying for me. She and Carter are taken with Sax. She's going to be shocked to find out he's my brother."

Emily unlocked the kitchen door at Chance's house and let herself in. She listened for any indication that Chance was up.

"Hello? Chance, it's Emily. Are you awake?"

She walked through the living room to the hallway and saw that his door was closed. Let him sleep. She needed to talk to Reba first thing.

She went back into the kitchen, just as Reba was coming in the door.

"Good morning, Emily." Reba wore white crop pants and a royal-blue tunic, a nice contrast with the white highlights in her hair. "Are you ready to get started?"

"Almost." Emily motioned toward the table. "Sit with me for a minute. I need to talk with you about something before Chance gets up."

The two women sat at the table.

"I was going through Mr. Durand's dresser after you left yesterday," Emily said, "and found a stack of pictures—almost all of them were of one woman, salt-and-pepper hair, blue eyes, fiftyish, attractive. Mr. Durand was in one of the photos with her. A woman's name was written on the back. Chance came in and saw the photos and thumbed through them. I'm not sure if he saw the one of her and his dad together. He said he didn't recognize the woman and that he would trash the pictures."

"Well, good," Reba said.

"The thing is, after I got home, I remembered where I'd heard the name that was written on the back of the photo: Joanna Arceneau was a victim of the cyanide poisonings. She was brought to the emergency room DOA on Saturday morning, same as Chance's parents. Did you know that?"

"No, I didn't. But I don't see what that has to do with anything," Reba said.

"It might if Joanna Arceneau is the woman Mr. Durand was having an affair with."

Reba folded her hands on the table. "Why?"

"Because if two victims—who died in the same way on the same morning—were having an affair, there could be a connection that might lead to the killer. The sheriff needs to know that."

"I … I can't tell the sheriff about the affair. He'll want to talk to Chance. I promised Lydia that Chance would never find out."

"So it was Joanna Arceneau?"

"I don't think it's any of your business who it was."

"Reba, if I don't tell the sheriff what I've discovered, I would be withholding evidence in a murder investigation—evidence that might help the authorities find out who killed your sister. You want that, don't you?"

"Well, of course I do. But just because two people were having an affair and each drank a certain brand of bottled water doesn't mean there was a connection."

"I realize that. But the sheriff needs to know everything because he's the one putting pieces of the puzzle together. My mom's a cop. I grew up around this kind of thing. You never know. It might be important."

Reba tapped nervously on the table. "What do you suggest?"

"We have to give this information to the sheriff."

"Poor Lydia would turn over in her grave, if she knew what was going on."

"She'd want you to do the right thing." Emily sighed. "We should tell Chance first and give him the option to go with us when we give our statements."

"I can't tell him," Reba said. "I just can't."

"Then I will."

Reba put her fist to her mouth and seemed to choke back the emotion. "It's all for naught. What are the chances that Huet and Joanna's affair will shed any light on this case?"

"I don't know. But any connection between victims is something the sheriff needs to know about."

Emily sat on the side of Chance's bed, holding his hand, waiting for him to react to the news that his father had been having an affair.

"So you're saying the woman he cheated with was the one in the photographs I threw out?" Chance finally said.

"Yes. Reba confirmed that Joanna Arceneau was the woman your mother said he was having an affair with."

Chance sighed and shook his head. "I had a bad feeling yesterday, when I thumbed through the photos and saw my dad and her together in one of the pictures. Dad was such a fake. People thought he was a wonderful husband and father. I always knew he flunked the father category. But this? I don't even know what to say. I never thought he'd betray Mom."

"I'm so sorry to be the one to tell you."

"Don't worry about it, Emily. It would be hard to make me think less of my dad than I already did."

"We really have to tell the sheriff."

"No. We really don't. It's nobody's business. I don't want Mom's memory tarnished with this."

Emily squeezed his hand. "I understand. But the sheriff isn't going to make it public knowledge. He just needs to know, that's all. It might not be important at all. But it's information he doesn't have."

"Can it wait a couple days—just until I have a chance to assimilate what you're telling me?"

"The sooner we tell the sheriff, the sooner he can see if the information can help move the investigation forward. I'm sure the sheriff would send deputies here to the house, if we call him. All we have to do is tell him what we know. That's it."

Chance looked over at her. "You really think this piece of embarrassing information is going to help solve the case?"

Emily shrugged. "If I learned anything growing up around law enforcement, it's that every piece of the puzzle is important. If there's even a slim chance this could help the sheriff find out who killed your parents, I think it's worth reporting it."

CHAPTER 31

Zoe sat at the kitchen table at Langley Manor and finished telling Vanessa about the chain of events that had begun when Sax Henry appeared on Adele's doorstep, claiming to be Shelby Sieger's brother, Michael.

Vanessa stared at her, seemingly struggling to find words. Finally she said, "Adele called and told me Sax's sister was coming to see him at ten o'clock in the flower garden. I never expected it to be you."

"Sorry for shocking you like this, but I wanted to tell you myself. You're the only person besides Pierce and Adele who knows my life's story. I never expected to see my brother again. And now that he's here, I'm terrified of dealing with the memories—and almost angry enough *not* to see him. But Pierce and Adele have convinced me I'd be sorry if I let this opportunity go by."

"I can't say that I disagree." Vanessa put her hand on Zoe's. "What are you going to call him—Sax or Michael?"

"His legal name is Sax, just like mine is Zoe. For all practical purposes Michael and Shelby Sieger no longer exist."

"But it's Michael who left you," Vanessa said. "And it's Shelby he's trying to find. I think it's important that you deal with who you were and what really happened."

"I'm not sure I can, without letting him have it with both barrels."

Vanessa squeezed her hand. "I have to believe he's expecting you to be angry. Who wouldn't be? But at least you got to know a little of Sax Henry—and that's who your brother has turned out to be. He seems like a really nice guy."

"This would probably be easier if he weren't so nice." Zoe sighed. "It's Michael I'm angry with. It's hard to realize they are one and the same."

"So face him as Michael the teenager and say whatever needs to be said. Then forgive him as Sax, the adult brother who has been searching for you for three years."

Zoe ran her thumb across her diamond wedding band. "I wonder how he'll react when he realizes *I'm* Shelby. Adele didn't tell him. All he knows is that his sister agreed to meet him in the flower garden at ten."

"I have a feeling he'll be pleased." Vanessa glanced into the dining room and then at her watch. "I've got to go serve my guests. And you need to go meet your brother. Let me pray with you first." Vanessa paused for a moment, holding tightly to Zoe's hand. "Lord, there's not a lot left to ask of You, since we've laid this at Your feet many times over the years. We believe that You brought Michael here and that You want this brother and sister to have an honest exchange that will bring healing and peace. Let Zoe be a peacemaker, whatever that needs to be in this situation. Let her sense Your presence every moment. And most of all, we pray that it will be honoring to You. We pray this in the Name of Your Son, our Lord and Savior, Jesus Christ. Amen."

"Amen." Zoe rose to her feet, feeling a little light-headed.

"This is exciting on one level," Vanessa said. "It has to change your life for the better."

"If I live through it."

Vanessa hugged her. "I'll call Pierce and Adele and let them know you're on your way. Just be honest with him. We'll be praying."

Emily sat on the white leather couch between Chance and Reba and across from Deputies Stone Castille and Mike Doucet.

"Let me make sure I'm hearing this correctly," Stone said to Reba. "Your sister, Lydia Durand, informed you that her husband, Huet Durand, was having an affair with Joanna Arceneau, is that correct?"

Reba nodded. "It is."

"When did Lydia first inform you of this affair?"

"On Valentine's Day last year," Reba said. "She had gotten roses and chocolates and a beautiful card from Huet. But she was crushed by his deceit because she had stumbled onto a monthly statement, hidden in his closet, for a Visa card she knew nothing about that had been sent to a PO box she knew nothing about. There were multiple charges for flowers, perfume, lingerie, theater tickets. Restaurants." Reba sighed. "Lydia confronted Huet with it, and he admitted he was seeing a woman they knew from the country club—Joanna Arceneau. She was ten years younger than Huet, and was Lydia's Facebook friend, for heaven's sake."

"Did Huet end the affair?" Stone said.

"Said he did." Reba pursed her lips. "But things between them were strained, and Lydia got suspicious as time went on. One morning last fall, Huet said he was going to play golf, and she followed him—to a garden home across town. She saw the name Arceneau on the mailbox." Reba sighed. "Lydia waited two hours for Huet to come out. It was all she could do *not* to pound on that door and embarrass him. But instead she drove home and decided she was done trying to win his affection. She didn't believe in divorce, you know. She decided to settle for a platonic relationship—to live her own life and let Huet live his. Her life revolved around Chance anyway. She was so very proud of his being in medical school and all. That's what she lived for."

Chance quickly whisked a tear off his cheek. Emily squeezed his hand.

"Do you know if Joanna Arceneau had ever been married?" Stone said.

"Yes." Reba's eyes narrowed. "She was divorced."

"Any idea what her ex-husband's name was?"

"Alan." Reba fingered the hem on her tunic. "He lives in New Iberia."

Mike wrote something on the clipboard.

"Any chance Alan Arceneau is the jealous type?" Stone said.

Reba shrugged. "I wouldn't know about that."

"Do you think the ex-husband might have had something to do with the poisonings?" Chance leaned forward, his hands clasped between his knees.

"I'm not going to speculate. As of now, everything points to someone who wanted to kill as many people as possible and no one in particular. But we'll definitely talk to him."

Zoe walked slowly down the brick walkway toward the flower garden at Langley Manor, feeling weak-kneed and energized at the same time. An hour from now, this would all be over. More bad history she could write off.

Lord, don't let me go off on him. Help me to do this right.

She scanned the grounds as she walked, relishing the blossoms on the crape myrtle trees, her thoughts wandering back to a happy childhood memory she hadn't thought about in years....

Michael ran up to her, hiding something behind his back. "I have a surprise for you. Close your eyes."

"What is it?" Shelby clamped her eyes shut, giggling with delight.

"No peeking ... okaaay, you can look now."

Shelby opened her eyes and saw Michael holding a large bouquet of gorgeous pink blossoms.

"They're *princess* flowers!" he said proudly.

Shelby brought her hands to her mouth. "You found them!"

Michael put the bouquet in her arms, his smile as wide as the Rio Grande.

"They're beaut-i-ful!" Shelby studied the blossoms. "Are they *real* princess flowers?"

"Absolutely," Michael said. "And they're pink—just like the ones in my story."

"I love them!"

"I'll go find something big enough to put them in. But you have to keep them outside. If Daddy finds out where I got them, I'll be in big trouble."

"Okay."

Michael ran into the house, and Shelby searched the back of the property for the perfect place to hide the flowers.

Real princess flowers, she thought. Had she ever loved Michael more than at that moment ...?

Zoe blinked the stinging from her eyes. A neighbor had come to the door shortly after that and complained to Mama that Michael had broken some branches off their crape myrtle tree. When Daddy got home from work, he gave Michael a whipping with a belt, but Michael never told him that he'd done it for Shelby—or why. It remained their secret. Poor Michael had welts on his legs and bottom. But he told Shelby he wasn't sorry. She cherished those blossoms and tended them carefully until they finally turned brown.

Why did she have to remember Michael's tenderness now—when she needed to get the anger out of her system? The sweet things he did could never make up for his having abandoned her.

Zoe walked toward the flower garden. There he was. Sitting on the wrought-iron bench. Everything in her wanted to turn around and run. But something seemed to nudge her forward. This was it. This was the moment she had always wondered about. And she still didn't know how she was going to handle it.

Emily sat with Chance in the glider on the patio at his parents' house.

"I wish you'd talk to me," Emily said. "I get that you're mad at me for involving the sheriff. But try to understand that I grew up around this stuff. If I hadn't made sure the sheriff knew that two victims in a criminal case were having an affair, I would have been withholding evidence."

"I'm sick of hearing about how you grew up with a mom who was a cop, Emily. This information was private. There was no reason to air my mother's dirty laundry, just so you could feel like Miss Ideal Citizen."

"I'm sorry you see it that way."

"So am I."

"Would you prefer I leave?" she said.

Chance took her hand and held it. "No. I'll get past it. It's just a huge shock to find out all those disgusting details about my dad. And all that my mom went through because of it. I can't believe I was so blind. But they slept in the same bed—at least when I was home. Dad was nice to her and vice versa. I never thought to look for anything, you know?"

Emily nodded. "The sheriff isn't going to make the information public. The way people remember your parents won't change."

"But mine did."

Emily kept silent. What could she say?

"Really, what are the odds my dad's affair had anything to do with the cyanide poisonings?"

"I have no idea," Emily said. "I just know better than to withhold information. Sometimes it fits the puzzle. Sometimes it doesn't. But you never know when it could be important, especially when we don't know everything the sheriff knows."

"I want to know more about Alan Arceneau. If I find out my mom was killed because this guy was ticked off about his ex-wife's sleazy affair with my dad …"

"Don't think about that now," Emily said. "Let the sheriff's deputies talk to him. Believe me, if they suspect anything, they'll push him to the edge of the cliff to get answers."

"They'd better."

Emily linked her arm in his. "They will. Let it go. You have enough to deal with."

Chance sat quietly for half a minute. "I'm really glad Aunt Reba is leaving this afternoon."

"She's been invaluable. I hope you realize that. And she could hardly stand the idea of breaking your mother's confidence about the affair. She only did it because I convinced her it was the right thing to do."

"I don't doubt that." Chance brushed the hair out of his eyes. "I could see how torn up she was. I'm just uncomfortable having her here. We've never been close. I don't want to feel obligated to share my private feelings with her."

"I understand. But you really should thank her, Chance. She saved you a lot more hassle than you realize right now."

"Don't worry. I'll thank her. I'm just glad she's leaving. I like my privacy."

"So you'll be honest when you want *me* out of your hair, right?"

Chance put his arm around her. "It's totally different with you. I don't ever mind your being here. You're the only person I know, besides my mom, who knows when to talk and when to just be there."

"Thanks. I try to be sensitive."

"You are."

Chance tilted her chin and kissed her ever so softly. Emily was lost in the moment until she heard Aunt Reba calling from the house.

"Chance, Uncle George is on the phone!"

The kiss ended abruptly, Emily's cheeks burning, both of them smiling.

"Don't go away," he whispered. "This shouldn't take long."

Emily watched him walk up on the back stoop, her lips still tingling, her heart pounding. At least she hadn't lost him by insisting Aunt Reba tell the sheriff about his father's affair.

CHAPTER 32

Zoe reluctantly approached the flower garden at Langley Manor, feeling as if her breakfast might come back up at any moment. Could she go through with this? Did she really want to have the confrontation with her brother that she had imagined a thousand times in her mind? Why did he have to be so nice? Why couldn't he be the long-haired, unkempt, crackhead guitarist she had envisioned all these years?

Michael spotted her. He got up from the wrought-iron bench and turned, locking gazes with her, his expression going from surprise to realization in a matter of seconds. "You …?"

Zoe studied his face with new eyes and instantly saw the resemblance until tears clouded her vision. "I never expected to see you again, Michael."

"I … I wasn't trying to trick you. I had no idea you were Shelby … until this very moment."

"I know. Adele told me everything. I didn't recognize you either. I put two and two together after you told Tex you were looking for someone from Devon Springs."

"I'm a little shell-shocked," Michael said. "Would you sit here with me and let it sink in?"

Zoe sat, her hands clasped in her lap, her heart pounding so loudly she was sure it must be audible to him, too.

"I … I don't know where to begin, Shelby." Michael's voice was shaking. "I can hardly believe I found you. I've been looking for three years."

"I'm Zoe Broussard now. I walked away from Shelby a long time ago."

"So did I," Michael said. "That's why I'm here."

"I don't know what you want from me."

"I want to earn your forgiveness—and your trust. That's all."

"That's *all*? That's everything!" Zoe wiped a tear off her check. "You think you can walk out of my life and leave me in hell—then just show up on my doorstep almost three decades later and pick up where you left off?"

Michael shook his head. "Of course not. I have a lot of explaining and apologizing to do first."

"Do you think?" Zoe got up and moved over to the ivy-covered arbor that marked the entrance to the flower garden. She turned and faced Michael, her knees feeling as if they would give out at any moment. "Why didn't you come back like you promised?"

"I did come back—several times. I met with Mom privately so Dad wouldn't know. I tried to get her to leave him and take you to a shelter. She insisted she couldn't leave him."

"Why not?"

"She said Dad needed her."

"Needed *her*?" Zoe felt an anger rise up in her that she had never felt before. "For what—to pop a TV dinner into the microwave? I'm the one whose bed he crawled into!"

Michael winced and began cracking his knuckles. "I never knew for sure. I suspected it, but you never said anything. And neither did Mom. I didn't know for sure until Mrs. Woodmore told me."

"Tell yourself whatever you want, Michael. But you weren't that blind."

He sighed. "I suppose I didn't ask because I didn't want to know. If no one talked about it, I could pretend it wasn't true."

"But it was true." Zoe looked him squarely in the eyes. "And the only thing *I* could pretend was to be somewhere else—until Daddy staggered out of my room and I could run to the bathroom and throw up."

Michael put his face in his hands. "Why didn't you tell me he was abusing you?"

"It started when I was in second grade. I had no frame of reference for what was happening to me. I was confused and ashamed. Daddy told me it was our secret, and if I told anyone, I'd have to go live with strangers—that I'd never see *you* again. That scared me more than anything. So I never told anyone. You know what the big irony was? Once you left, I never saw you again anyway."

"I was a scared teenager who wanted out as badly as you did. When Mom refused to take you and leave, it was useless for me to try going up against Dad, knowing she would back up his lies. I was afraid he'd kill her if you weren't there." Michael lifted his gaze. "What was I supposed to do?"

Zoe marched over to him and stood nose to nose. "Were you afraid he'd kill her if you sent a Christmas card? Or a birthday card? Or called once in a while? You *abandoned* me! You walked away and left me trapped in an unspeakable nightmare, and"—Zoe choked on the words—"you wrote me off. You were the one person in my life who loved me. You ... broke my ... heart." She flopped onto the bench next to him, hot tears streaming down her cheeks. "You were the only one who *could.* You were my hero ..."

"I'm so sorry, Shelby. As long as I couldn't get you out of there, it was easier to let you go if I cut off all communication. And I've regretted that decision every day since. The guilt has eaten me up. It's contributed to the failure of three marriages and any chance of finding peace."

"Am I supposed to feel sorry for you?"

"No. I chose what I chose. My hope is that, over time, you will be able to understand what was going on in my head—and forgive me."

"All I understand is that you were a coward."

Michael nodded. "Fair enough. Let's forget the fact that Dad would probably have killed Mom if I took you out of the house—was I supposed to take you on the road with me? Let you drop out of middle school? Run from the law? Live on the bus with the losers in the band—who were drugging and drinking and bringing in women to spend the night? It's not like there's any privacy in a bus, if you know what I'm saying. It was no place for a young girl."

"But our home *was*?" Zoe threw her hands in the air. "Tell me how it could have been any worse for me than it was in my own bedroom!"

"I was in denial about what was going on in your bedroom. But Mom told me you'd make it through, just like she did when she was your age. And that you would be free to leave at seventeen. I didn't see any alternative."

"Or you weren't looking for one."

Michael turned to her. "You had other options. If things were intolerable, why didn't you go to a shelter yourself? They would've put you in foster care, where you'd be safe."

Zoe sighed. "Safe? I was afraid that, if I admitted Daddy was abusing me, I would be forced to go to court and describe every detail—in front of a whole lot of people, including Mama. And I would have to be examined and probed by doctors so they could prove what he'd been doing to me. Frankly, that was more terrifying than the abuse."

Michael rocked, his hands folded across his chest, his eyes glistening. "I'm so sorry, Shelby. I can't even tell you how sorry. I know I let you down. But neither of us had the coping skills to deal with the horror of our childhood. Surely you understand that?"

"Don't tell me what I should or shouldn't understand, Michael. I've forgiven Mom and Dad. You're the one who broke my heart. It's you I need to forgive. I know that. I'm just struggling with it."

Michael exhaled. "There's more—about Mom and Dad."

"I don't need to know anything."

"Actually, you do." Michael held her gaze, his eyes the color and shape of Grace's. "There's no easy way to tell you this. Mom and Dad have both passed away."

"How'd they die?" she asked, surprisingly devoid of feeling.

"Dad died first—about five years ago. He was drunk and walked out in front of a delivery truck. He never knew what hit him. Mom was diagnosed with lung cancer the next year. She battled it for six months, enduring rounds of chemo that made her deathly sick. I was with her when she died. She welcomed it."

"Are they buried in Devon Springs?"

Michael shook his head. "They were both cremated. That's what they wanted. I still have their ashes. I haven't been able to scatter them. I thought you had the right to know they passed, and the right to give your input on how their ashes should be dispersed."

"Me?" Zoe said. "Didn't they tell you what they wanted?"

"Actually, they didn't. Mom kept Dad's ashes, so I have both their ashes in separate urns in my closet. I thought you might have some idea of how to disperse them. Truthfully, I couldn't decide whether to scatter them in the Gulf—or the landfill. I'm extremely conflicted in my feelings about both of them, so I haven't done anything."

Zoe held up her palm. "This is just too much for me to take in all at once."

"I'm sorry if I've upset you. I've waited a long time to tell you. I wanted to be sure I got the chance, just in case you told me to get lost."

"I'm not upset," she said. "I'm not anything. I don't have any feeling about it, one way or the other."

"I've done most of the talking," Michael said. "I'm ready to listen to anything you have to say for as long as it takes to say it."

Zoe stared at her hands, her mind racing back through her conversation with Michael. Finally she said, "You were right to come here. We've needed to deal with this issue for a long, long time. But forgiveness is too important to rush, and right now, I don't know how I feel about anything. In the past forty-five minutes, I've lost both parents and rediscovered a brother that I've tried to hate for twenty-eight years. I need time to process."

"I understand."

Zoe rose to her feet, avoiding eye contact. "I'm going to leave now. Please don't follow me. Or call me. Let me decide when I'm ready to see you again."

"All right. Shelby"—Michael took her hand—"I *never* stopped loving you. I just want you to know that."

Her brother's words lanced a wound deep in her soul. Even if she'd known how to respond, she couldn't have formed the words.

Zoe hurried up the brick path toward the manor house, walking faster and faster, barely able to see through the tears that soaked her face. She didn't want to talk to Vanessa yet. Or even Pierce or Adele. She just needed to be alone with God.

CHAPTER 33

Sheriff Jude Prejean sat at a small table in the manager's office at Rousseau Sporting Goods, next to Deputy Chief Aimee Rivette. Alan Arceneau came in and shut the door and sat across from them.

"We appreciate your store manager lending us his office," Jude said. "We're just following up on some information that could be relevant in your ex-wife's death."

Alan, a man in his midfifties with a receding hairline, stroked his salt-and-pepper mustache, his dark eyes wide. "What information are we talking about?"

"Sir, were you aware that your ex was having an affair with a married man who was also a victim in the cyanide poisonings?"

Alan laced his fingers together. "I don't keep up with Joanna's sex life."

"How long have you been divorced?"

"Just over three years."

"Did you end things amicably?"

Alan smirked. "Ever been divorced, Sheriff? No, I wouldn't say it ended amicably."

"How would you describe it?"

"Strained. Joanna was cheating on me."

"Did she file for divorce—or did you?"

"She did. We didn't have a covenant marriage, so we did the six-month separation first. Then she filed. Why?"

Jude studied Alan's expression. "You could've filed immediately—on grounds that she committed adultery. It would've sped things up."

"I wasn't interested in speeding things up. I wasn't going to make it easy for her. She said she wanted her freedom. I made her wait for it."

"Why'd you do that?"

Alan leaned forward on the table, his eyebrows arched. "Why are you asking me personal questions that have nothing to do with Joanna's death?"

"I'd appreciate it if you'd just answer the questions," Jude said. "I can't discuss the details of the case. But this could be relevant."

Alan sat back in his chair and seemed far away for a moment. "She said she didn't love me anymore. That I was a *boring cheapskate* and she'd found someone more exciting—and willing to spend money on her."

"Did she say who?"

"No, sir. She didn't."

"Did you ask her?"

"Sure, I asked, but she wouldn't tell me. Said he was married and she wanted to keep his name out of it." Alan rolled his eyes. "I thought I deserved to know who stole my wife. Joanna said it was none of my business."

"That must've made you mad."

"You have no idea."

Aimee wrote some notes on her pad.

"Did you press the issue?" Jude said.

"Kind of hard to do when you're separated."

"So you just let her go without a fight?"

Alan's face was suddenly flushed. "Not exactly. I hounded her with phone calls at her apartment and office, but she refused to talk to me. So I followed her one night after she got off work—to a dinner theater in Lafayette. I figured she was meeting lover boy, so I waited until he showed, then got up in his face. Things got a little heated, and someone called 911. I left before the police showed up. I decided she wasn't worth fighting for."

"Just like that? Come on, man. First your wife tells you it's none of your business she's cheating on you, then you finally eyeball the guy and still don't know his name—and you expect me to believe you just let it go?"

Alan cracked his knuckles. "Joanna got a restraining order. There wasn't much I could do."

"Did you still love her?"

Alan's expression softened. "We were high school sweethearts. Joanna was my first and last love, and my feelings hadn't changed, in spite of what she'd done. But actually *seeing* her with another man jolted me into reality."

"Can you describe him?"

"He was taller than me—maybe six two or three—and a few years older. Nice looking. Fit. A full head of graying hair. Well dressed. He grabbed me by the collar and told me to stay away from Joanna. She stood next to him, in front of God and everyone, and said she had no idea what a real man was until she got rid of me."

"That must've cut deep. I imagine you wanted to get back at them."

The corners of Alan's mouth curled up. "Oh, yeah. I amused myself by imagining all the ways I could make them die. Some of them pretty creative."

Jude didn't say anything.

Alan lifted his gaze. "Wait just a minute … you don't think I had something to do with poisoning Joanna?"

"You tell me."

"So that's why you asked me here—to accuse me of poisoning my ex-wife? And what about all those other people?"

"It's not an accusation," Jude said. "I'm merely asking questions. But you just said yourself that you'd thought about it. Did you act on it?"

"Absolutely not! I was just fantasizing. If I had actually done it, do you think I would've been stupid enough to admit I'd entertained myself with the idea?"

"You'd be surprised what guilty people reveal when they're questioned."

"Do I need a lawyer?"

"Not unless you're afraid of incriminating yourself."

"I'm not. I haven't done anything wrong. I didn't even know Joanna was dead until I heard her name on the news. … " Alan's voice cracked. "I couldn't believe it. No one in her family thought to call me. Why would they? I'll bet lover boy got a call."

"Actually, he didn't. Lover boy's name is Huet Durand. He was one of the cyanide victims—so was his wife, Lydia." Jude maintained eye contact. "Am I telling you something you already know, Alan?"

"What are you talking about?"

Jude slid a photograph across the table. "Is this the man you had the altercation with?"

"That could be him."

"Is it, or isn't it?"

"Yes, that's him." Alan stared at the picture, his neck muscles taut.

"His name is Huet Durand," Jude said. "Now you know."

"Okay." Alan handed the picture back to Jude. "So what?"

"I expected a stronger reaction."

"Sorry to disappoint you, Sheriff. It's been a long time."

"Then why are you so tense?"

"Seeing his face took me back to the one and only time I saw Joanna with another man. It was humiliating. But I've let it go."

"Have you?"

"What's that supposed to mean?"

"It's not a trick question, Alan."

"Look, I've done the best I can to let it go." Alan combed his hands through his hair. "I'm not a part of Joanna's life anymore. What do you want from me?"

Jude held his gaze. "The truth."

"I've told you the truth."

"Don't you find it just a little too tidy that your ex and her lover both died of cyanide poisoning on the same day—by drinking the same brand of water—and they weren't even together at the time?"

Alan shrugged. "Other people died that day in the same way. You told the media you didn't believe the victims were targeted—that they were random."

Jude pasted on what he hoped was an irritating grin. "We don't tell the media everything we know." He touched Aimee with his elbow. "Isn't that true, Deputy Chief Rivette?"

Aimee nodded. "You see, Alan, we know that it's possible in this type of case that the killer was willing to take out a few innocent victims to make sure he got the ones he wanted—and to throw law enforcement off his trail."

Alan stared at them blankly, his jaw dropped. "I don't believe this. You're trying to pin the cyanide poisonings on me."

Aimee held up her palm, shaking her head. "We're just exploring every possible avenue."

"Well, this avenue is a dead-end street!" Alan said. "I couldn't care less who Joanna was involved with. I've moved on."

Jude bounced his pencil eraser on the table. "So if we obtained your phone records, we wouldn't find Huet Durand's phone number listed?"

Alan wrung his hands, then wiped the perspiration off his upper lip. "All right, look … right after Christmas, Joanna and Huet came here to the store. They were exchanging a warm-up suit for a different one. It involved a cash refund, so the cashier called for the department manager to approve the transaction. When I walked up to the checkout, they were as shocked to see me as I was to see them. I recognized the guy as the one I'd had the altercation with. I initialed the transaction and read Huet Durand's name."

"Why didn't you say so?"

"That's not what you asked me."

"Did you call him?"

Alan bit his lip. "Not him. His wife. I thought she deserved to know about the affair."

"How did she react?"

Alan shrugged. "She already knew her husband was cheating with Joanna. I felt pretty stupid. Before I could hang up, her son grabbed the phone, hollering and swearing. He told me, in no uncertain terms, not to call again. I never did."

"You're sure it was her son?"

"Said he was. I'll tell you one thing, he was a lot more upset than she was."

Jude walked across the customer parking lot at Rousseau Sporting Goods and got in his squad car. He shut the door just as Aimee got in the passenger side.

"I can feel your wheels turning," Aimee said. "What are you thinking?"

"I'm thinking a lot of things." Jude backed out and pulled onto Ascension Boulevard. "I'm thinking that if Alan Arceneau lied once, he would lie again to protect himself. I can't trust what he says. But *if* Chance Durand knew about his father's affair, he went to a great deal of trouble to pretend he didn't. I'd like to know why. Was he protecting his mother's good name? Lydia Durand certainly had the motive to kill her husband and herself and Joanna. But was she crazy enough to do it—and to take out innocents with her?"

"I can't imagine the woman we heard about being capable of such a thing. Not only is it cold and criminal, it would be extremely difficult to pull off."

"We both know that guilty people often appear innocent. This case is going nowhere, Aimee. We can't afford to blow off anything, even if it's far-fetched."

"What do you want to do?"

Jude tapped his fingers on the steering wheel. "We've questioned Alan. We've questioned Chance. We've gotten a glimpse into Lydia's mind through her sister, Reba. Let's question Emily Jessup."

"Chance's friend? Why?"

"For one thing, she was forthcoming with the knowledge about the affair. That gives me a reason to trust her. She's also had personal conversations with Chance and with Reba that we weren't privy to."

"She seems too honest to withhold important information."

"Intentionally, yes," Jude said. "But she may know something she doesn't even realize is important. I'd like to talk to her without Chance present and get her perspective on Lydia Durand."

Zoe sat in a side pew at Saint Catherine Catholic Church, aware that those who had come at noon to say the *Angelus* had all left now and the church was quiet again.

She gazed up at the statue of the Sacred Heart and the red roses someone had set in front of it. In light of all He had suffered for her, after all He had forgiven her, how could she hold on to her anger at Michael?

Lord, I know I need to forgive him. Why am I holding back? Why is it so difficult?

Her mind raced back through a childhood scarred with horrific images that she had dealt with years ago—images that no longer gave her nightmares. The memories she had saved, the ones that made her smile, were of Michael. He had been her refuge when everything else was unbearable. And then he was gone. His abandoning her was devastating on so many levels and had left her empty and aching.

Zoe was aware of the main door opening and closing, and then footsteps coming up the side aisle. She just wanted everyone to go away and leave her in solitude.

The footsteps slowed, and she looked up just as Adele slid into the pew next to her.

That's all it took. Zoe broke down and sobbed.

Adele put her arms around her and just held her while she wept.

Minutes passed. Finally Zoe's tears stopped. She took a tissue from the pocket in her sundress and blew her nose. "How did you know where I was?"

"I know you pretty well by now." Adele brushed the hair off Zoe's wet face. "How was your meeting with Michael?"

"Difficult."

"I'm sure it was painful, dredging up the memories he wanted forgiveness for."

"Excruciating." Zoe settled into the pew next to Adele. "I told him about the sexual abuse. I didn't think I'd be able to talk about it, but I did."

Zoe told Adele everything she remembered about the conversation.

"Actually, the most difficult part," Zoe said, "was telling Michael that he broke my heart. I realized when I got so emotional about it that part of my heart is still broken."

"Perhaps that will heal now that you and Michael have talked openly."

"I haven't forgiven him, Adele. I'm struggling. Why is it I was able to work through the memories of my father's unspeakable abuse and forgive him—and my mother for turning a blind eye—but I can't forgive the one person I actually loved?"

"Perhaps it's because you learned not to expect much from your parents. You expected Michael to always be there for you. You never thought he'd walk away."

"He didn't just walk away. He abandoned me. He cut me off."

Adele nodded. "Yes. He explained what was going on in his mind at the time. If you'd been faced with his impossible decision, what would you have done to survive? I know how you looked up to him. But Michael was a teenager too. He didn't have the life experience or coping skills to save you."

Zoe sighed. "I know that in my head. My heart doesn't want to accept it."

"Did you do what I suggested, hon? Did you think back and remember what it feels like to be broken?"

"I tried. But my heart seemed hardened."

Adele sat quietly for a moment and then took her hand. "Remember the day you drove up to Woodmore and confessed to me that you were the one who'd stolen my precious fiftieth anniversary ring—and that you'd *sold* it, changed your name, and used the money to start Zoe B's?"

"Of course I remember it. I'd never been so scared in my life. I thought I was going to lose everything. Having to admit that I—your trusted employee of six years— had deceived you and lied to the police was humiliating."

"Yet you weren't broken at that point." Adele looked over at her. "You were trying to fix all the lies you'd told so whoever was blackmailing you wouldn't have anything to hold over your head.

I knew that. I was willing to let you pay back the thirty thousand dollars over the next thirty months. That would have squared things with us."

"What's your point?"

"Do you remember what happened when I came to you and Pierce, bringing that repayment agreement for you to sign?"

"How could I ever forget? It was the most generous gesture I've ever witnessed. You canceled my entire debt, paid off our mortgage on the building, and forgave me for stealing the ring and betraying your trust. It was far above and beyond anything I deserved or expected. I was speechless."

Adele brushed the hair out of her eyes. "And what did I say to you, Zoe?"

"You said there would come a day when someone I know was in desperate need of grace, to remember how … I felt at that very moment … and to"—Zoe's voice cracked—"to pass it on." She held the gold cross hanging around her neck, her vision clouded with tears. "You're saying that day is now? That I should just write off the past and start fresh with my brother?"

"Why not?" Adele said. "Healing comes as much in the giving as in the receiving. What earthly good can come from hanging on to the anger that divides you? It will make you both miserable. And don't you both really want the same thing?"

Zoe sat quietly, tears trickling down her cheeks, as she considered all the events that had brought her to the present. She was wholly in touch with the desperate, deceitful Shelby Sieger who had changed her identity and made selfish choices that broke Adele's heart and nearly cost Zoe Broussard her marriage and her business. Was she any better than her brother? They had both made choices that had wounded others, choices they deeply regretted.

"What are you thinking, hon?"

"That I haven't forgotten what it feels like to be broken." She turned and put her arms around Adele. "I love you so much. Your generosity to me in my most desperate moment was a perfect picture of God's grace. It dramatically changed my life."

Adele pushed back and held her gaze. "It wasn't meant just for *your* life, Zoe. What you do with it now will tell Michael who you really are."

CHAPTER 34

Emily finished cleaning out what remained of the leftovers in the refrigerator in Chance's kitchen and sat at the table, adding a few items to the grocery list.

The phone rang, and she grabbed it on the second ring, hoping it didn't wake up Chance from his nap. "Durand residence, this is Emily Jessup speaking."

"Emily, it's Deputy Chief Rivette. I got your cell number from your sister and left two messages, but you haven't returned them, so I thought I'd try to reach you at Chance's. Can you speak without Chance hearing you?"

"Yes, he's napping in his room. Why?"

"Sheriff Prejean and I would like to ask you a few more questions. We'd like to do it without Chance present this time."

"Is something wrong?" Emily said.

"Nothing to be alarmed about. We'll explain when we see you. But we'd like to meet as soon as possible. Obviously, we can't do that at Chance's house."

"I was just headed up to Lafayette to buy groceries."

"Perhaps we could talk to you before you get on the road. The sheriff's department is practically on your way. Could you meet us there?"

"All right. It'll probably be twenty minutes."

"Sounds good. Emily, we'd appreciate it if you didn't tell Chance we want to talk to you."

"I'm uncomfortable keeping secrets from him."

"We wouldn't ask if it wasn't necessary."

Emily sighed. "Okay. I'll see you soon, and you can explain this to me."

"Thanks."

Emily hung up the phone and stared at the list, trying to remember the item she was about to add before the phone rang. *Mayonnaise.* She wrote it down.

"So who was on the phone?" Chance's voice startled her, and she dropped the pencil.

Was she supposed to lie to him? She hated this. "It was for me."

"Who knows to call you here?" Chance said.

Emily smiled and tried to look as natural as possible. "It's no secret I'm over here helping out."

"Why didn't they just call your cell?"

"Not everyone is privy to my cell number. Listen, I need to change the subject. I've compiled a grocery list and think I'll run up to Lafayette and get what we need."

"You don't have to leave town to get groceries."

"I do, if we want to be safe. I'm not comfortable buying food in Les Barbes right now."

"I'm not afraid of getting poisoned," Chance said. "It's kind of obvious it's Gaudry water we need to stay away from."

"I don't see how you can say that. Until they catch whoever's behind the cyanide poisonings, I'm playing it safe."

Emily rose to her feet, and in the next second Chance was beside her, pulling her into his arms.

"You going anywhere else?" he asked.

"I have a few errands to run."

"Maybe I should go with you."

Emily shook her head. "Your attorney is supposed to call at two."

"I'm not too excited about having you gone." He brought her face closer and gently pressed his lips to hers.

Emily relaxed in his arms, yielding herself completely. Finally she ever so slowly pulled away, her pulse racing. "You are a major distraction!"

"I hope so. I'm glad Aunt Reba is finally gone and we can spend some time together. I'm starting to really care for you. You're the person I trust the most in the entire world. I really like the openness and honesty between us."

"Me, too." Emily slipped out of his arms. "I'd better get going. I want to get back in time to put things away and cook dinner."

"You're going to cook for me too?"

Emily smiled. "I thought it might be nice, since I have to go back to work tomorrow afternoon." She folded the list and put it in her purse.

"How do you plan to pay for the groceries?" Chance grinned knowingly.

"Uh … I guess I do need some money. Aunt Reba put a lot of cash in that cookie jar and said to use it until you go down to the bank and open your account."

Chance opened it, took out a roll of bills, and peeled off two hundreds. "It's more than you'll need for groceries. But go ahead and gas your car, too."

She kissed his cheek. "Thanks. I'll see you in a few hours."

Emily left by the kitchen door, hoping the sheriff had a good reason for her to keep this meeting from Chance.

Sax stood looking out the window in his room at Langley Manor. Why didn't he feel any better after talking with Shelby? He had waited more than half his life for that confrontation. He didn't expect her to forgive him right away. But he had expected to feel some semblance of peace. Some flicker of joy or hope. All he felt was raw shame. Shame that he had left his kid sister in a volatile environment. Shame that he'd deliberately chosen not to ask her the one question to which he feared the answer. Shame that being a part of the rock band was more important to him than staying home and fighting for Shelby. Shame that he hadn't even started looking for her until she was all he had left.

Sax stared at the sea of cane fields undulating in the breeze. What it boiled down to was that his living in a bus with the drinking, drugging, womanizing guys in the band had been less oppressive than living in a violent home. With the band, it was always party time. And playing electric guitar was energizing. Rock music made him feel alive, especially when he was high on pot. It became a great escape—as long as he didn't have contact with Shelby. As long as he didn't have to be reminded that he had gotten out and she hadn't.

Sax sighed. Today's encounter with Shelby was supposed to be the answer for his depression. Admitting his mistakes was supposed to bring him the peace he so desperately wanted.

I don't think you can find true peace and be at odds with the Prince of Peace.

Zoe's words rang in his head. Adele had said something similar. But why should he turn to God when God had turned away from him?

Sax figured his eternal judgment would come soon enough. But as long as he had both feet in this life, he refused to take one step toward the all-seeing, all-knowing God who had turned a deaf ear when he was a helpless and defenseless child.

Emily followed a male deputy into an interview room at the Saint Catherine Parish Sheriff's Department and seated herself at the oblong table.

"Would you like something to drink?" the deputy asked.

"No, thanks. I'm good."

"The sheriff's just finishing up a phone call. He'll be with you shortly." The deputy smiled and left.

Emily folded her hands on the table, feeling surprisingly at home. She looked around the room and wondered if interrogation rooms everywhere looked about the same—pastel walls, a solid table and chairs, a two-way mirror, and no pictures or windows. The two interview rooms her mother used at the Sophie Trace Police Department were slightly smaller but very similar in appearance.

She heard footsteps coming her way and looked up just as Deputy Chief Aimee Rivette walked in, followed by Sheriff Jude Prejean.

"Thanks for coming in to talk to us." Jude sat on the other side of the table with Aimee.

"I'm glad to cooperate," Emily said. "Though I'm puzzled why you're being secretive."

"Not secretive—discreet."

"What's this about?" Emily moved her gaze from Jude to Aimee and back to Jude.

"After the deputies talked with you and Chance and his aunt Reba this morning," Jude said, "we spent some time talking with Alan Arceneau."

Emily arched her eyebrows. "Is he a suspect?"

"Merely a person of interest. But something he said raised a question in my mind as to whether Chance might have known about his father's affair."

"You wouldn't have any doubt," Emily said, "if you'd seen Chance's face when I told him about it. He was shocked and devastated. According to his aunt Reba, his mother did everything in her power to keep it from him."

"I don't doubt that. But is it possible he had found out and just didn't tell you or Reba? Could he have been faking his reaction?"

Emily was taken aback by the question. It had never occurred to her that Chance might have known and just pretended not to. "I don't think he would deceive me. If he knew, why wouldn't he just say so when I came to him with it?"

"I don't know," Jude said. "But what Arceneau told us and what Chance told us is inconsistent."

"What did Arceneau tell you?"

"I'm not at liberty to say. But I have good reason to believe that Chance wasn't ignorant of his father's affair."

"Even if he wasn't," Emily said, "what difference does it make?"

"Maybe none. But I'd like to ask you a few more questions."

"All right."

"Does Chance talk much about his mother?"

Emily nodded. "A lot. They were really close. Her death impacted him in a way his dad's didn't."

"What do you mean?"

"Chance and his dad weren't close. His dad rode him pretty hard and found it difficult to affirm him, even after he got a scholarship to Harvard Medical School."

"You're speaking from Chance's perspective, I assume?"

"Yes, but also Reba's. She wasn't all that crazy about Huet either. She told me how hard he was on Chance. But I think they were both surprised that he cheated on Lydia."

"Why?"

"Apparently, Huet was good to Lydia—at least when other people were around. I only met him once. He seemed very nice."

"What can you tell me about Lydia?"

"She was gracious and hospitable, and I never sensed any tension between her and Huet that one time I met them. According to Chance and Reba, she was the self-sacrificing type. Attentive. Relational. A wonderful mother—a real cheerleader for Chance."

"Intelligent?"

"That, too. She had a degree in pharmacology. She was a pharmacist for a few years until she got pregnant with Chance and decided to be a stay-at-home mom."

Jude shot Aimee a knowing look, and Emily wondered what that was all about.

"Did Chance or Reba ever give you an indication that Lydia had a temper? Could be vindictive? Hold a grudge?"

"No. They both thought she was a saint. Sheriff, what's going on?"

"We're just gathering information. You, of all people, understand how that works."

"Are you looking this hard into the background of the other victims?"

"All seven."

Emily ran her thumb across her silver pinky ring. "I'm just surprised you're talking to me personally, rather than having your deputies questioning me. Should I read something into that?"

"It would be unwise of you to read into anything we're doing."

Emily leaned forward on her elbows. "Can you at least tell me if bringing the affair to your attention was helpful?"

"It's always helpful to have all the information. We have to do more digging to know if that information's relevant."

Emily sighed. "I get it. You can't tell me anything during an ongoing investigation."

Jude and Aimee both smiled at her.

Emily glanced at her watch. "What other questions do you have for me?"

"That's really all for now."

"That's it?"

Jude nodded. "We just wanted to get your assessment of Huet and Lydia Durand without Chance present, just in case there was a negative you'd be reluctant to mention in front of him. And we were curious whether you sensed that he had known about his dad's affair."

"I told you what I know. I don't think Chance knew anything about the affair."

"We appreciate your coming in." Jude stood and shook her hand.

Aimee followed his lead. "Thanks, Emily."

"Can I tell Chance I came and talked to you about his parents? I don't feel right about keeping secrets."

"I can't tell you not to," Jude said. "But I'd appreciate it very much if you didn't."

"Can I ask why?"

"I really can't get into it. We're exploring a possible connection between victims."

"So you're asking me not to say anything?"

"That's correct."

Emily studied the sheriff's face. What in the world was he not telling her?

CHAPTER 35

Emily put the last of the canned goods in the pantry in Chance's kitchen and heard footsteps moving in her direction. She turned just as Chance came through the doorway.

"Hey, you," he said. "Why didn't you wake me so I could help put the groceries away?"

"You needed the rest. And I didn't mind. I'm finished." Emily brushed her hands together and closed the pantry door.

"So did you get your errands done?"

Emily's pulse quickened. "I did. And I filled the car. I had forty-three dollars and change left, and I put it in the cookie jar with the receipts."

"I don't need receipts, Emily. I trust you." Chance pulled her into his arms and held her gaze. "I *can* trust you, right?"

She felt heat scald her cheeks and hoped she hadn't turned red. "Of course you can trust me. I'm your friend."

He moved his face slowly toward hers. "I'd say you're becoming more than just a friend."

Their lips met softly, and Chance drew her in—this time eagerly, longingly, expectantly. Emily didn't resist, her heart hammering, her unexpected surge of passion quickly squelched by Vanessa's voice replaying in her mind.

You can't fall in love right now. You've got three more years at LSU, then MCATs, medical school, internship, residency. Romance is a distraction you can't afford.

"I should probably cook dinner," Emily said.

Chance left her standing there and went over to the table and sat. Was he angry?

"Emily, what are we doing here? I feel something happening. I thought you did too."

"I do. But I think we need to take a step back."

"That's not what it felt like to me just then," he said.

Emily walked over to the table and sat across from him. "We're both leaving for college in August. No good can come from our getting romantically involved."

"Feels pretty good to me."

Emily sighed. "Chance, you're grieving. I don't think you can trust your feelings right now. For you, romance might seem like an escape. But for me, it would be all-encompassing. I don't do things halfway, and education has to be my focus for a very long time. Allowing myself to get romantically involved right now would be foolish. I'm just being honest with you. I wouldn't be much of a friend if I wasn't honest with you."

"Really?" His eyebrows came together. "When were you going to tell me you went to talk to the sheriff?"

Emily felt as if she had a wad of peanut butter stuck to the roof of her mouth.

"I picked up the phone at the same time you answered it," he said. "I heard the entire conversation."

"Then you know the sheriff asked me not to say anything."

"Why was he in such a hurry to talk to you? What did he want?"

"To get my assessment of what your parents were like. I guess he thought that having you go with me might prejudice what I said. Of course, it wouldn't. I don't have anything to hide from you."

"What did you tell him?"

"Just what you and Reba have told me about your parents. And what I observed."

"Specifically what?"

Emily told him everything she could remember telling the sheriff concerning Chance's father and mother.

Chance looked agitated. "Why would you tell him Mom had a degree in pharmacology?"

Emily shrugged. "Because she did. Is that a problem? Her diploma is framed and hanging in the study."

"I just don't get why he's going around me to ask you to reveal personal information about her."

"The sheriff said they were digging deeper into the backgrounds of all the victims, exploring a possible connection."

Chance tapped his fingers on the table. "Did the sheriff say whether he's talked to Alan Arceneau yet?"

Emily met Chance's gaze. Why had the sheriff put her in such an impossible situation?

"I know you're hiding something," Chance said.

"I was asked not to talk about it, but I don't see that I have a choice now. Yes, the sheriff talked with Alan Arceneau."

"And?"

Emily sighed. "Something Alan told them is inconsistent with something you told them."

The expression left Chance's face, but he didn't flinch. "What was it?"

"The sheriff wouldn't say, other than"—Emily bit her lip—"it leads him to think you knew about your dad's affair and might have been faking your reaction when I told you. I made it clear I thought he was wrong. Besides, I don't see what that has to do with anything."

Chance raked his hands through his hair. "That's because you're not looking for anything."

"What are you talking about? Why are you upset?"

"They know about the phone call!" Chance swore under his breath.

"What phone call?"

"Nothing. Forget it. Emily, you really need to leave."

"I'm not going anywhere until you tell me what's going on."

"Please, just go home. I need to be alone for a while."

"Chance, I—"

"Go!" His gruff tone told her he wasn't in the mood to argue about it. "I'll call you."

Emily sat in her car in the parking lot at Cypress Park, her mind reeling. What phone call was Chance so upset about? What wasn't he telling her?

Emily thought back on the questions the sheriff had asked her about Lydia Durand. The questions were basic enough. Why was

Chance irritated that Emily had told the sheriff his mother had a degree in pharmacology?

Unless … Emily's heart sank. Lydia would have known chemistry. She would have known exactly how cyanide worked. Did the sheriff suspect that Lydia and Alan had staged Huet and Joanna's murders by poisoning the bottled water? If that were true, then who poisoned the pudding? And who killed Lydia … *Alan*?

Emily sucked in a breath. But what if Lydia wasn't a victim? What if she knowingly drank the poisoned water when her husband did? What if she had conspired with Alan to kill Huet and Joanna … then, rather than face the consequences—and her son—decided to take her own life?

Emily blinked the stinging from her eyes, her mind racing in reverse to a conversation she'd had with Chance right after his parents died.…

"I miss Mom so much." Chance closed his eyes, his chin quivering. "This is not the way things were supposed to happen. It's such a nightmare."

Emily nodded. "It really is. No one should have to endure the murder of one parent, let alone two. I hope the sheriff locks up whoever's responsible and throws away the key."

"It won't ever get that far. He doesn't have a clue who did this."

"Don't underestimate law enforcement," Emily said. "All criminals make mistakes."

"Not this time."

Emily felt a wave of nausea and waited until it passed. Had his mother left him a suicide note? Had she explained everything to him? Was he covering up her involvement in the cyanide poisonings—and her suicide?

Emily blew the bangs off her forehead and started her car.

Lord, I have to go back. If Chance is covering for his mother, I have to convince him to go to the sheriff before he gets charged with being an accessory after the fact. Help me know what to say.

Emily saw Chance's car backing out of the driveway. She started to pull in and wait for him to return, but something prodded her to follow him instead.

He stayed on Bayou Parkway across town and out of the city limits. She kept a reasonable distance so he wouldn't spot her and wondered why he was turning off onto a side road. She pulled over on the shoulder and waited a full minute before following him on the road marked B-2.

She drove over a small steel bridge that crossed the bayou and continued on a narrow road that wound through acres of undeveloped land thick with live oaks and cypress trees draped with Spanish moss. Finally she spotted Chance's black Jeep Cherokee parked in front of a house partially hidden in the trees.

An ominous feeling came over her. Should she just turn around and mind her own business? Pretend she didn't know anything, even if she knew just enough to be suspicious? Chance was hiding something. She needed answers. And she needed them now.

She turned her car into the long, gravel driveway and pulled up behind Chance's Jeep. She got out and high stepped through the weeds toward the tan house with a badly stained roof. It looked as if it might have been very nice in its day. A wood deck went all the way around the house to the back, where it extended out over a small yard that sloped down to a pier. She spotted several houses on the other side of the bayou and someone in a motorboat moving away from her.

Emily walked around to the front of the house and spotted a Keep Out sign nailed to a tree. She paused to consider how Chance would react to her showing up uninvited. How could she worry about that now? If she didn't talk some sense into him, sheriff's deputies might show up at his house—ready to charge him with covering for his mother.

Emily started to go up the front steps when someone grabbed her from behind and clamped a hand over her mouth.

"Emily?" Chance sounded surprised and angry. "What do you think you're doing? If I'd wanted you here, I'd have driven you myself." Chance took his hand off her mouth and gave her a gentle shove.

"You scared me half to death!" Emily said.

"Sorry. I heard someone out here snooping around. I didn't realize it was you until I grabbed you."

She saw what appeared to be a can of pepper spray in his waistband. "What's going on? Why did you come here?"

"It's not something you need to be concerned with. Get back in your car and go home."

"I'm not leaving until you give me some answers."

"Answers about what?"

"Your mother and Alan Arceneau."

"I have no idea what you're talking about."

"You can trust me. Just tell me what's going on."

Chance took her arm and started walking her briskly toward her car. "I'm not kidding, Emily. You need to leave. And you need to do it now."

"What are you hiding?"

"Just because I don't want to discuss it doesn't mean I'm hiding anything. I told you, it's not your concern."

"It pretty much *is* my concern. I'm in this whether I should be or not." Emily stopped and yanked her arm free.

"You're *not* in it. It's a private matter that I really don't want to talk about."

Emily locked gazes with Chance. If he wasn't going to volunteer anything, what choice did she have but to ask him outright? "Chance … did your mother and Alan conspire to kill your dad and Joanna?"

Chance's eyes grew wide and animated. "*What*? Is that what the sheriff told you?"

"He didn't tell me anything. But am I right?"

Chance gripped her wrist again and started pulling her toward the car. "You're not going to manipulate me into having this conversation, Emily. Just get in your car and go."

"If you're covering for your mother, the sheriff's going to figure it out, if he hasn't already. And you could be charged with being an accessory after the fact."

"You don't know what you're talking about," Chance said.

"Then set me straight."

"You won't like it."

"That's beside the point. How can I support you if I don't know what's going on?"

"I don't need you to support me, Emily. I need you to leave."

"You said you trusted me."

"It's not a matter of trust." Chance held her chin and looked her squarely in the face. "If I told you, I'd have to kill you."

Emily slapped his hand away. "I'm glad you think this is funny. Stop joking around. Because I'm dead serious."

"So am I." Chance turned around and started up the steps. "Go home. I'll call you."

"Am I supposed to just ignore that your mother conspired with Alan Arceneau to kill your father and Joanna? Innocent people died—two of them little kids. This is a major murder investigation. You can't protect your mother. It's going to come out."

Chance spun around. "I'm warning you: leave it alone. Whatever you think you know, you *don't.*"

"It doesn't matter. Sheriff Prejean must suspect something. Why else would he ask me not to mention that I talked to him? It's just a matter of time before he figures out whatever it is you're not telling me."

Chance stared blankly for a moment, seemingly lost in thought.

"I care about you," Emily said. "And I can only imagine how much you want to protect your mother's good name. I know how much she meant to you. But being charged as an accessory after the fact is serious—probably a felony. If either of us is convicted of that, we can kiss medical school good-bye. I'm not willing to let this go that far."

Chance let out a sigh of resignation. He turned and started up the stairs. "Come inside. I'll tell you everything."

CHAPTER 36

Jude sat at the conference table in his office, comparing case files on the cyanide victims, when he heard a knock at the door.

"Come in," he said.

Aimee walked over and stood next to the table. "Gil took a team back to Marcotte's Market, and they went over every inch of the interior, the parking lot, and the grounds a second time. We found something we'd missed. It just might make your day." She set some photographs on the table in front of Jude.

His pulse quickened, and he leaned forward. "Is this the syringe used to poison the pudding?"

Aimee nodded. "It had been thrown under a hedge at the back parking lot and was wedged in the bottom branches. Deputy Castille found it. It tested positive for potassium cyanide. And a trace of chocolate pudding. *And* ... we've found a partial thumbprint. It doesn't match anyone in the system. But it's a clear print, and no doubt matches the guy in the security tape. We know his body type and hair color, and we know he's young. We're getting closer to nailing him."

"Good work." Jude realized he was smiling. "Are you also testing the syringe for DNA?"

"Yes, we'll know something before the day's over," Aimee said. "That's the good news. There's also bad news."

Jude sat back in his chair and looked up at her. "Let's hear it."

"Rick Paquet had another heart attack. He didn't make it."

"I thought he was being monitored. How can that happen?"

Aimee shrugged. "He's been under so much stress with his little girl's death and not being there to help his wife plan the funeral. The doctor said his heart just gave out—weakened by the stress the cyanide put on his organs. I can't imagine what kind of shape his poor wife is in. She lost her only daughter and her husband within a few days of each other."

"Is little Caissy's funeral going to be held as planned?" Jude handed the photos back to Aimee.

"We haven't been advised otherwise. I know the Paquets have family coming in town for tomorrow's two o'clock funeral. I'm thinking Mrs. Paquet may decide to have a combined service for her daughter and husband—assuming the funeral home could get her husband's body ready in time. If not, she might decide to postpone it a day or two. They'll keep us posted."

"Nine dead." Jude brought his fist down on the table. "I want the guy who emptied that syringe into the pudding, Aimee. Find him!"

"We know it's not Alan Arceneau. The man in the security tape is a lot younger and doesn't have a bald spot on the top of his head."

"Maybe he and Lydia hired someone," Jude said. "With her pharmaceutical background, we can assume she'd be able to obtain cyanide. But getting it is one thing. Actually using it to kill is another. They would have needed a professional—someone to plan out and execute every detail. Her suicide may have been a decision she made without telling Alan or whoever else was involved."

Aimee arched her eyebrows. "She could have done all that without taking out innocent people."

"It had to look like a random attack in order to protect Chance from ever suspecting she was involved." Jude laced his fingers together. "Thing is, I think Chance suspects his mother conspired with Alan to do it."

"He's clearly grieving her death. And just because he played dumb about the affair doesn't mean he's hiding anything else."

Jude traced the rim around his coffee mug. "No. But I have to ask myself why he felt compelled to lie to Emily, to his aunt Reba, and to us. Why didn't he just tell us he learned of the affair when Alan Arceneau called his mother?"

"Maybe Chance was embarrassed about blowing up at Alan."

"Or maybe he suspects his mother and Alan. It's those pesky *maybes* that keep me up at night." Jude pushed back his chair and stood. "Let's get Alan Arceneau in here and push him. Let's see what we can scare out of him before he decides to lawyer up."

Jude looked through the two-way mirror, watching as Gil and Aimee finished up their questioning of Alan Arceneau.

"How many times do I have to tell you," Alan said, "you're absolutely wasting your time with me? I've already told you everything I know—at least twice."

"So you would really have us believe"—Gil leaned forward on his elbows—"that the only contact you ever had with Lydia Durand was the one phone call you made to her on December twenty-eighth?"

Alan nodded. "That's right. Her son got on the line and chewed me out but good. He called me a few colorful names that disrespected my dearly departed mother, and told me never to call again."

"And that was enough to stop you?"

"I had no reason to talk to Lydia Durand again. I only called her because I thought she deserved to know her husband was cheating with my ex-wife. End of report."

"So it's your contention that you didn't know anything about her background?"

"That's exactly right."

"Or that she had a degree in pharmacology?"

Alan cocked his head. "I didn't even know there *was* such a thing. But she didn't strike me as the agricultural type."

Gil stared at Alan for several seconds, probably trying to determine whether he was playing games with his answer.

"Pharmacology," Gil said, "as in pharmacist."

Alan's face turned crimson. He looked genuinely embarrassed. "Oh."

"So did you know Lydia had been a pharmacist at one time?"

"How would I know that?"

"Please answer the question."

"No. I told you I didn't know anything about her. I don't even know what the woman looks like."

"You never went to her home?"

"No."

"Are you telling me that you finally found out who your ex was sleeping with—who she left you for—and curiosity wasn't eating you up?"

There was a long pause, and Alan shifted his weight. "I didn't exactly *go* there. I drove by, the day after I called. I wanted to see what the house looked like. I don't know why, really. I just did."

"You didn't get out?"

Alan shook his head. "I slowed down and looked it over. I'll say one thing for Joanna: she doesn't waste her time on men with no money. That's a really nice place he's got."

"It had to be hard on your ego, knowing Joanna left you for Huet—a nice-looking, physically fit, classy dresser who lived in an upscale neighborhood. I'll bet you paid attention to what kind of car he drove too."

"You mean that red Cadillac CTS with chrome wheels that he left parked out front so the neighbors could drool?" Alan rolled his eyes. "Yeah, I paid attention to what kind of car he drove. So what? I got the curiosity out of my system—and that was that."

Gil smirked. "I take it you drove by more than once, since you indicated Huet left the car parked out so the neighbors could drool?"

"I did drive by more than once, but I never got out. And I never laid eyes on Lydia Durand."

"Then explain why she didn't strike you as the agricultural type."

Alan shrugged. "She had a soft, delicate voice, that's all."

"Did you ever run into either Huet or Lydia any place else?"

Alan shook his head. "Nope."

"Did you ever, under any circumstances, communicate with Lydia Durand again?"

"Never."

"No texting? No email?"

"I do know what *communication* means, detective. The answer's no. The only thing I'm guilty of is curiosity. And thinking Lydia Durand deserved to know her husband was a louse. That's it. You can question me until doomsday, and you're going to get the same answer. Now are we done? If you keep hassling me like this, I'm going to demand a lawyer."

Jude talked into his shoulder mike. "Gil, wrap it up. Let him go."

Jude turned around and leaned against the glass, his arms folded across his chest. If Alan had conspired with Lydia Durand to kill Huet and Joanna, he was a very convincing liar. Yet what were the odds it was purely coincidence that Durand, his lover, and his wife were victims of cyanide poisoning within hours of each other?

The only person left to push was Chance Durand. The poor kid was really grieving, and it seemed almost cruel to question him about his mother. But what choice did they have? They were merely fishing at this point and didn't begin to have enough for a warrant.

Emily followed Chance up the front steps to the run-down house that backed up to the bayou. He opened the screen door, and she stepped inside, hit with a damp, musty odor and thick, warm air being stirred only by a ceiling fan.

"Whose place is this?" Emily said.

"It belonged to my dad's parents." Chance's voice sounded flat. "Dad should've sold it after my grandmother passed, but he never could bring himself to put it on the market. He rented it one summer. But it's been sitting vacant five years, and I don't think he'd been out here in all that time. Mom either."

Emily took the back of her hand and dabbed the perspiration from her face. "So why did you come out here?"

"To think."

"You have a beautiful, air-conditioned house to yourself—and you came out here to think? It must be a hundred degrees in this place." She glanced around the living room. Wicker furniture. Worn tan carpet. A framed picture of a flock of white ibis flying above the bayou.

"I didn't know how else to get away from you."

"*Me*?" Emily didn't bother to hide her annoyance. How many times had he told her how much he needed her and enjoyed having her around?

"The situation took an unexpected turn, and I really didn't want to involve you in this. But you've left me no choice."

"Would you please just tell me what *this* is?"

Chance motioned for her to sit in the cane rocker. He sat on the wicker couch, facing her.

"Emily, when I was home on Christmas break, Alan Arceneau called the house. He told Mom that his ex-wife and my dad were having an affair."

"Reba said your mother knew about the affair last year."

"She did." Chance held her gaze. "*I* didn't. I was sitting at the kitchen table and overheard every word Alan said. I couldn't have been more shocked—or devastated. I grabbed the phone and went off on him. Finally, I told him never to call the house again and hung up. Mom calmed me down and admitted she'd known about the affair since February of last year but never wanted me to find out such a horrible thing about my dad. Mom pretty much fell apart. I'd never seen her cry like that before. It broke my heart...." Chance's voice failed.

"So," Emily said, "it was after you went back to school that your mother and Alan got together to plan the murders?"

"Mom was crushed, but she didn't have a vindictive bone in her body. She didn't kill my dad or Joanna Arceneau." Chance lifted his gaze. "I did."

CHAPTER 37

Emily stared at Chance, her pulse racing, his words bouncing off her brain.

"You heard me correctly," Chance said. "I killed my dad and Joanna Arceneau. I know this is a shock. But it's true."

"I … I don't believe you could poison all those people," Emily finally managed to say. "You're protecting your mother's reputation."

"Go look on the dining table behind you."

Emily got up and walked into the dining room. The oblong table was cluttered with syringes, a cylinder marked KCN, mixing bowls, measuring spoons, a flask, surgical gloves, and unopened bottles of Gaudry water.

She stood motionless, stunned, the truth beating her heart like a punching bag, her mind racing in reverse, searching for clues she must have missed.

Chance came and stood next to her. "Now you know."

Emily's eyes pooled with tears, and she couldn't seem to form any words—not that she knew what to say. Chance was not the person she had come to care about. She'd been deceived. Used.

"I know this is difficult to accept," he said. "That's why I tried to get you out of here. I never wanted to involve you in this. But you just wouldn't leave it alone."

"Why did you poison your mother?"

"That wasn't supposed to happen." Chance's voice was deep and solemn. "I never once saw my mother drink bottled water. She didn't like the taste of it. I have no idea why, on that particular morning, she drank it. It was Dad I wanted to poison. When the deputy called and said both my parents were unconscious, I was in shock. I realized something had gone wrong." A tear trickled down his cheek. "I never intended to hurt my mother. I loved her so much."

"It's not just your mother, Chance! Or your dad and Joanna! How could you kill all those other people?"

"I'm sorry about them. I needed to be sure the suspicion was deflected away from me. Making everyone think there was a nutcase poisoning the food and water seemed like a perfect cover. It would've worked, too, if you hadn't discovered those photographs of Joanna Arceneau and started nosing around. Then insisted we had to tell the sheriff about the affair."

"But I was right."

"Yes, you were. Not only was the affair relevant—it was my motivation. I killed Dad and Joanna Arceneau for cheating on my mother. I'm not sorry. I'd do it again."

Emily felt as if she were someone else, watching this taking place. "Where did you get the cyanide, Chance? Isn't it a controlled substance?"

"You just have to know who to ask. When I went back to Harvard after Christmas break, I was at Starbucks, doing research for a physiology paper, and met Kurt, a freshman at Boston University who was struggling to pass calculus. He worked part-time for a local jeweler who specialized in gilding. I remembered from my chemistry class that KCN—potassium cyanide—is often used in that process. Long story short, I agreed to do Kurt's calculus term paper in exchange for his getting me some KCN from the jeweler's stockroom. I told him I was going to use it for an experiment that I hoped would advance the cure for breast cancer. I kept it locked up and shipped it back here the day I flew out of Boston for summer break. When the package arrived, I told my folks I had forgotten my camera and the school had shipped it to me."

"Did you know how you were going to use it?"

"I started planning every detail after I got the cyanide from Kurt. Mom was willing to live her own life and let Dad do what he wanted. I wasn't."

"Was it worth going to jail for the rest of your life?" Emily said. "Or living on death row?"

"Don't worry. I'm not going to jail."

"The sheriff will figure it out. He already suspects you're covering for your mother."

"He can't prove she was involved because she wasn't."

"When that doesn't pan out, he'll keep digging."

"Let him. I made sure there's nothing on any of the bottles to connect me. And I'm about to destroy all this evidence."

Emily wiped the sweat off her forehead, trying to accept that the Chance Durand she knew and had grown fond of no longer existed—if he ever did.

"Chance, just out of curiosity, what had you planned to tell your mother? Did you really think she would chalk it up to coincidence that your dad and Joanna were both found dead of cyanide poisoning on the same day?"

"As long as there were other victims, yes."

"This is insane. You'll never get away with it."

"We'll see. The important thing is that Dad and that woman got what they deserved."

"What about your sweet, precious mother?"

Chance grabbed her arm and squeezed. "Don't you think I'll regret her dying the rest of my life? At least she's not hurting anymore."

"No, you are. So what happens now that you've confessed everything to me? Are you going to kill me, too?" Emily shuddered.

Chance let go of her arm, his voice softer, almost mournful. "I don't know yet. Give me your cell phone."

Emily handed it to him.

"Go sit on the couch, where I can see your face," Chance said. "And don't even think about trying to bolt. I can run a lot faster than you can, and I'll use the pepper spray to subdue you if I have to. I really don't want to hurt you. Just leave me alone for a few minutes. I need to think this through."

Emily felt the sweat dripping down her temples. She walked back into the living room, where the fan was blowing on her, and sat on the couch.

Lord, I need help. There's no way he can let me go now. I've got to escape—and I've got to do it quickly.

Zoe sat on a shady bench in Cypress Park, watching children playing around the duck pond and missing Grace and Tucker. After the cyanide scare, Dominic Corbin's death, and her brother's showing up, she'd had little emotional energy left for anyone else. As soon as her nerves settled down, she planned to take a couple days off and give her children her undivided attention.

She heard footsteps and looked up, surprised to see Pierce standing there.

"I hope you don't mind my intruding on your space," he said. "Dempsey's covering for me."

"Actually, I'm glad you're here." She patted the bench.

Pierce sat next to her and took her hand. "Adele told me about her conversation with you at Saint Catherine's."

Zoe nodded. "I remembered what it feels like to hit bottom—and then to have grace lavished on me when I least deserve it. There's nothing else like it."

Pierce slid his arm around her. "Have you decided what you're going to do about your brother?"

"There's really only one thing I can do—I'm going to tell Michael I forgive him. I'm going to put the past behind us. And then I'm going to welcome Sax Henry into our lives and start building a relationship."

"That's a huge step all at once, especially since, for all practical purposes, you just lost your parents."

Zoe wiped a tear off her cheek. "I should've gone back to Devon Springs while I had the chance—and made peace with them. I should've told them I had forgiven them and moved on with my life. I guess I always thought there would be time. They really weren't that old."

"I'm sorry, babe. It's one more thing to work through."

"It's my own fault. I'll have to deal with the regret. But at least I had already worked through my anger at them."

"Have you worked through your anger at Michael?"

"I've been sitting here for two hours, talking to the Lord about it. I don't suppose it's going to go away overnight. But I must admit I feel a tenderness for Michael that wasn't there before I met with him. It's hard not to be touched by the fact that he's been searching for me for three years. And that the only thing he wants from me is forgiveness—and a relationship, if I'm willing." Zoe sighed. "I actually like the man he's become. I'm trying to imagine what it'll be like for our kids to have a blood relative on *my* side of the family. I never even considered that possibility."

"You know I like Sax a lot," Pierce said. "I'm very willing to welcome him into the family. As far as I'm concerned, he gets free meals from here on out."

Zoe smiled. "It feels strange to think of him as *family.*"

"Yes, but we've gone through a similar experience of welcoming brothers- and sisters-in-law to the Broussard family. It really doesn't take long to get the hang of it."

Zoe sat quietly for a moment. "You know, Pierce, my brother spent three years looking for me, but God knew before we were ever born the exact time and place we would meet again. God never took His eyes off us. Not when we were children. Not even when I was living a life of deception, and Michael was losing wives and losing hope."

"True." Pierce kissed her hand. "The Lord just waited for the right moment to touch your heart. And He did it through Adele."

"Wouldn't it be something," Zoe said, "if this was the right moment to touch Michael's heart—and He did it through me?"

Emily felt weak and light-headed as she sat trapped on the couch in the bayou house that had once belonged to Chance's grandparents. Every time Chance looked away, she glanced over her shoulder at the screen door, trying to decide if she was fast enough to get to the door, undo the latch, and push it open before Chance was on to her. If she could get a head start running, she might be able to disappear into the woods without being caught. She shuddered to imagine the soggy ground and alligator dens. Not to mention the hungry mosquitoes. But if she could hide from Chance until dark, she could run back to town and call the sheriff.

If she tried to escape and failed, and Chance used the pepper spray to subdue her, she would be in no condition to try a second time. Whatever she decided to do, she was only going to get one window of opportunity.

Chance paced in the dining room, sweating profusely, his hair soaked as if he had just come out of the shower. He looked and seemed like an entirely different person. Whatever feelings she'd had for him died the moment she knew what he was capable of—what he had done. All she could think of now was surviving this nightmare.

There was no way she could outrun a marathon runner. But could she outsmart him? He was the genius, but she was a cop's daughter and a lot more street-smart than he realized. She would have to catch him off guard. Disable him, if possible. Her mind raced with the techniques her mother had taught her for self-defense. Would any of them work in this situation? Whatever she chose to do, she had to be quick and decisive and get it right.

What if she didn't make it out? What if Chance decided to kill her right there and leave her body down in the bayou? She would likely be devoured by an alligator, and no one would ever find her or figure out what had happened.

Emily was aware that Chance had stopped pacing and was standing at the table, facing her, and mixing something in a bowl. Next to him was a bottle of water, three-quarters full, the cap removed, and a small funnel set in the opening. Her heart sank. Was he going to try and force her to drink cyanide water? Was she strong enough to fight him if he tried?

Father, is this it? Am I going to die? Is this my appointed time?

Emily held her gaze on Chance, her heart nearly pounding out of her chest, her mind a slide show of all the dreams that would die right here with her in the blink of an eye. Medical school. Delivering her first baby. Getting married. Having a child of her own.

Why hadn't she called her parents and told them she loved them? Why had she argued with Vanessa? Why hadn't she spent more time with Carter? More time studying her Bible? More time alone with God?

Lord, I'm not ready to die. I haven't lived my life. Unless this is Your will for me, help me get out of here!

Emily readied herself. If she sprang to her feet and made it to the door, Chance would probably stop her cold. If he grabbed her from behind, could she remember how her mother taught her to bring him to his knees and then run like the wind?

Chance glanced up at her. "Don't even think about it, Emily. The solution to this dilemma is right here."

Emily sucked in a breath. She was not going to drink the poison. If he tried to force her, she would go down fighting with every ounce of strength she had.

"I'm sorry it has to end this way," Chance said. "At least I didn't fail."

"You think your life being reduced to *this* isn't failing? For a genius, you're talking like a moron."

"Well, thanks for the vote of confidence, Emily. You sound like my dad."

"Your dad demeaned you to be cruel. I'm just trying to get you to be rational for a moment."

"I've never been more rational in my life."

Emily pointed to the oblong mirror on the wall. "Take a good look at yourself. Does that sweaty, unkempt fiend frantically mixing another batch of cyanide look rational to you? Is that the Chance Durand your mother would be proud of?"

"You're not going to talk me out of it, so don't bother trying. I have nothing to live for now. I'm going to die the same way as the others."

You …? Emily shuddered as the realization hit. "Chance, it doesn't have to be this way. God made you for more than this."

"I don't want to hear your misguided opinion about God."

"It's not an opinion," Emily said. "Do you think that once you're dead, it'll be over? Because it won't. You might escape judgment in this life, but I promise you, you won't escape it in the next. God will hold you accountable for what you've done. The time to face Him is now. He wants a relationship with You. There's nothing He won't forgive if you're truly sorry."

Chance smiled wryly. "Therein lies the rub. I'm not sorry for poisoning my dad and his lover. I'd do it again. I just feel bad about Mom—and those other people."

"Feel bad? You should be ashamed."

"Shut up, Emily! I don't need to hear this."

"It's exactly what you need to hear. Someone has to say it. You took innocent lives. You *are* going to be held accountable. You can choose whether you want to face the consequences now or later. But once you drink that poison, there's no turning back from judgment—or hell."

"I said, shut up!"

"What kind of friend would I be if I didn't tell you the truth?" she said. "You're deceiving yourself. Taking your own life won't make all this go away."

"Emily, get out. *Now*! Your keys and cell phone are on the end table. Go!"

"Please, Chance. I know, in your heart of hearts, that you believe all this is too complex to have just evolved. God is real. Shouldn't you be sure of what He says is going to happen when we die? Eternity is a long time to get it wrong."

"You've got ten seconds to get out," Chance shouted, "or, so help me, I'm taking you down with me!"

Emily jumped to her feet, her palms held up. "Okay. Okay. I'm going. Just remember, it's not too late to be the man your mother knew you were—that I know you still *are*—and face up to what you've done. Taking the coward's way out won't end it. You can't escape judgment."

"Five … six … seven …"

Emily turned and grabbed her keys and cell phone, then darted to the door, unlatched it, and raced toward her car.

Lord, help him. He's worth so much more than this.

Emily ran as fast as her legs would move, relieved when she reached the car. She fumbled to open the door, slid in behind the wheel, made a U-turn, then pushed the accelerator, kicking up gravel and leaving a trail of dust behind her.

She drove back to the highway, her temples throbbing, thoughts bouncing off her brain. Had she said the right thing? Had she been too blunt? Had she pushed him too hard? Was there any part of his Catholic upbringing that made him think twice about killing himself?

Emily felt her stomach drop as if she were on a roller coaster. If Chance had drunk the cyanide water, he was already dead.

She picked up her phone and keyed in three numbers.

"911 operator, what is your emergency?"

"I know the man … behind the cyanide poisonings!" She struggled to catch her breath. "But I'm afraid he … might have just … killed himself!"

CHAPTER 38

Jude started to walk out of his office, a cup of lukewarm coffee in his hand, and ran headlong into Aimee, coffee spilling down the front of her uniform shirt.

"Sorry, Aimee. I don't know where my head is. I didn't see you."

She took a tissue out of her pocket and dabbed her wet shirt. "You're not going to believe this: a 911 call just came in from Emily Jessup! The details are sketchy, but she told the operator that Chance Durand confessed to being the cyanide killer, but that he may have just committed suicide."

"She doesn't know?"

Aimee shook her head. "Emily made the call while driving back to town from bayou road B-2. She had followed Chance to a house that used to belong to his grandparents. That's where he poisoned the bottled water. All the paraphernālia is still there. They had some kind of confrontation, and he admitted he poisoned the water to kill his dad and Joanna Arceneau, and that his mother's death was an accident. Gil's en route."

"Where's Emily now?"

"On her way here. Poor thing." Aimee glanced at her watch. "Now we know why we haven't been able to reach Chance this afternoon."

"I want you to stay and get Emily's statement," Jude said. "Sounds like she's going to need some TLC. I'll go meet Gil. One of us will call you when we know the details."

Jude hurried down the hall, his shoes squeaking on the polished floor. He stopped at the elevator and pushed G.

He rode the elevator down to the ground level, walked out to his squad car, and sat for a moment, trying to comprehend that this ugly nightmare might actually be over.

He pulled out onto Courthouse, turned on his siren, and headed for Bayou Parkway, not sure if it would better serve the victims' families if Chance Durand were dead—or he were alive to stand trial.

Zoe walked into the eatery, the aroma of warm buttermilk cake permeating the dining room. She spotted her three friends playing checkers and walked over to their table.

Hebert looked up, his leathery face suddenly animated. "Dere you are."

"When Savannah said you and Pierce were both out," Tex said, "we got nervous that somethin' might be wrong."

Father Sam nodded. "Especially since you never mentioned taking the day off."

"I'm fine. I have something to tell you—something I never dreamed in a million years I would be telling you. Don't worry, it's a good thing." Zoe pulled out a chair and sat next to Father Sam and across from Hebert and Tex.

Father Sam turned to her, his hazel eyes a bright contrast to his black cleric shirt. "Tell us this good news."

Zoe coughed to clear her throat. "The three of you have gotten to know Sax Henry, since he's been coming in every day for a while."

"He's a great guy," Tex said. "We connected right off 'cause he's a fellow Texan."

Zoe smiled. "Well … here's something you don't know: I'm the gal from Devon Springs, Texas, that he's been looking for."

Three pairs of eyes were fixed on her, but no one said anything.

Zoe tented her fingers and moved her gaze around the table. "Sax is my brother. I didn't recognize him because it's been twenty-eight years since I've seen him, and he changed his name. Plus, the two years before he left home, his hair was long, and he had a beard. I hadn't really seen his face since I was eleven."

A row of lines formed on Hebert's forehead. "You said your brudder run off and you hope he stay gone."

"I know. I don't feel that way now. It's complicated. But what's important is that he came back to make peace and wants to be a part of my life. Actually, he's been searching for me for three years. He finally found me through Adele."

Zoe gave the guys a brief overview of the events, starting with her brother's showing up on Adele's doorstep and ending with Zoe's meeting with him in the flower garden at Langley Manor.

"Most of what we said to each other is private," she said, "and I know you fellas respect that. But I wanted y'all to know that Sax

Henry is my brother, since, for all practical purposes, you're family too."

"Dis is a miracle, Zoe." Hebert took her hand. "Now your two angels got anudder uncle."

"And Pierce has a new brother-in-law," Tex added. "How's he feelin' about all this?"

"He's great with it," Zoe said. "After all, he teamed up with Adele to get us together. Pierce has always known this area of my life needed to be dealt with. Guys, Sax brought bad news too." Zoe paused and swallowed hard. "Both my parents have passed away. I will always regret that I didn't go back home and tell them in person that I had forgiven them and moved on with my life. They died thinking I hated them."

Father Sam gave her arm a gentle squeeze. "Don't be too hard on yourself, Zoe. They may not have even realized how angry you were. They were absorbed in their own troubles."

"But I'll never know," Zoe said. "It's something I'll have to live with."

Hebert sat back in his chair. "So are dey buried in Devon Springs?"

Zoe shook her head. "They were cremated. Sax has their ashes in two urns he keeps in his closet. He's as conflicted as I am in his feelings about them. He hasn't been able to release their ashes yet. He seems to think I should have a say in how it's done."

"Maybe you should," Father Sam said. "When the time is right, you'll know what to do."

Savannah came rushing to the table. "Y'all are not going to believe this: they're about to arrest someone in the cyanide poisonings!"

"Get outta town," Tex said. "When?"

"It just happened. Authorities are following a solid lead to a house down on the bayou. Wouldn't it be great if this was the end of it?"

Jude got out of his squad car and walked toward the front steps of the tan house on bayou road B-2, Gil waiting for him on the deck.

"Is the kid alive or dead?" Jude said.

"Come see for yourself."

Jude walked into the hot, stuffy living room, a ceiling fan swirling overhead, and saw Chance Durand sitting on the couch, cuffs around his wrists.

"He didn't resist arrest," Gil said. "He confessed to injecting cyanide into the pudding and the bottled water. He was working alone. I read him his rights. He doesn't want a lawyer."

Jude surveyed the dining table, where Castille and Doucet were already taking pictures and gathering evidence, and then went over to the couch and bent down in front of Chance and made eye contact. This sweaty, anxious young man bore little resemblance to the handsome, Ivy League med student he had questioned earlier in the day. "Son, what were you thinking?"

"What do you want me to say?" Chance said.

"Why don't we stick with the truth?" Jude rose to his feet and then sat opposite Chance in a wicker chair.

Gil sat in the rocker with a pad and pencil.

"Chief Detective Marcel will make some notes." Jude leaned forward on his elbows, his hands clasped between his knees. "We'll get your written statement when we take you in. But right now, I want you to tell us what happened."

"I poisoned the bottled water and the pudding. What else do you need to know?"

"Why you did it, for starters."

"My dad badgered me all my life," Chance said. "I put up with it because I kept hoping I could earn his respect. Even my getting a scholarship to Harvard Medical School wasn't impressive enough to suit him. But when Alan Arceneau called the house, and I found out my dad was cheating on my mom—the one person who was always there for me—something snapped. I just wanted him dead. I started planning how to kill him when I went back to school after Christmas break."

"Where'd you get the cyanide?"

Jude listened as Chance told him about meeting a freshman from Boston University, whom he knew only by the name Kurt. And how Kurt had gotten him the KCN from the jeweler he worked for in exchange for Chance doing his calculus term paper.

"How did you get the cyanide here?" Jude said.

"The day I flew home for summer break, I shipped the KCN to myself at the house. I told my parents the box contained my camera, that I had accidentally left it in the dorm room and asked the school to ship it. They had no idea."

"Tell me how you executed your plan. Obviously, a lot of things had to go right for it to work."

"I planned every move ahead of time," Chance said. "I began by going into the stockroom at Marcotte's and picking up a case of Gaudry bottled water that had been checked in and was ready to be put on the floor. I slipped out the delivery entrance and brought it here. I drilled a tiny hole in the bottoms of twelve of the twenty-four bottles. I used a syringe and injected them with ten times the lethal dose of potassium cyanide, then sealed the holes with a clear adhesive I bought at Home Depot. I snuck six bottles back in the store and put them in the refrigerator case with the tamperproof seal still in place."

"What day was that?"

"Last Friday."

Jude scratched his head. "The bottled water that poisoned your parents was delivered by Adam Marcotte and came in a case with the plastic netting still on it. When and how did you slip the poison bottles into the case?"

"I didn't. I waited until my parents were in bed, and then I swapped three of their bottles for poisoned ones." Chance stared at his hands. "My mom never drank bottled water. She didn't even like it. I have no idea why she drank it this time. I never meant to kill her. I was trying to rid her of the heartache of having her husband openly cheating with that woman."

"You still had three bottles of cyanide water left. How did you manage to get the poisoned water to Joanna Arceneau?"

Chance stared at his hands. "That's another story."

"I'm listening."

Chance sat there a long time and then let out a sigh. "I went to her house on Friday evening, the night before she was found dead. I told her who I was and asked if I could come in and talk. I told her I knew she'd been carrying on with my dad." Chance looked out the window and seemed far away.

"So you two talked?"

"It was a one-way conversation. I told her exactly how I felt. I didn't hold anything back. I was really angry, and I'm sure she was intimidated."

"How did you get the poisoned water into her refrigerator without her seeing you?" Jude said.

"I put the last two bottles in there—after she was dead."

"After?"

"I made her drink the first bottle."

"By force?" Jude said.

A tear trailed down Chance's cheek. "I brought a Buck knife with me and threatened her. I wouldn't have used it," he quickly added. "I just needed her to think I would. I persuaded her that having her throat cut would be a lot worse than dying of cyanide poisoning."

"So she drank it, and you watched her die?"

Chance nodded. "More or less. It was more dramatic than that. But after I told her my dad was going to die too, she drank it down and collapsed in a matter of seconds on the living room carpet. I put two poisoned bottles of water in the refrigerator so you'd think it was part of the case that came from Marcotte's. Then I left by the back door. My car was parked on the next block."

Jude paused, trying to imagine this brilliant young scholar as a cold-blooded killer. "Did you also inject cyanide into the pudding on the food bar?"

"I did—but as a diversion. I didn't think it was potent enough to kill anyone. I just wanted to make a few people sick. I met Emily at Zoe B's a few minutes later. That was my cover. I was expecting to get a call any time on Saturday that my dad had died. But not my mom. Everything backfired."

"How'd you justify killing the other victims, Chance?"

"I wouldn't let myself think about it. I did what I had to do to make this look random. I thought it was the perfect crime. I never expected to get caught. And never dreamed my mother would drink the water."

Jude glanced up at a bottle of water with a funnel set in the opening. "Emily called 911. She thought you had downed the cyanide water. Why didn't you? You know you'll get the death penalty—or, at best, life without parole."

"That's between me and Emily. She didn't know about any of this until a couple hours ago. And just so you know, she tried to get me to turn myself in."

"Well, she did it *for* you. Come on. Chief Detective Marcel will take you to the sheriff's department. We'll need your statement in writing." Jude rose to his feet. "Inhale deeply. It's the last whiff of freedom you'll ever get."

Gil took Chance by the arm and started to lead him away.

Chance looked over his shoulder. "Sheriff, when you talk to Emily, would you tell her I agree with her—that eternity is a long time to get it wrong? She'll know what I mean."

CHAPTER 39

Emily sat at an oblong table in the interview room where she had just given Aimee Rivette her statement and where she had spoken with Aimee and Sheriff Prejean earlier in the day. Tears streamed down her cheeks, and she didn't even try to stop them. How could her life have changed so dramatically in just a few hours?

The thought that Chance had killed himself was all-consuming. She had grown more fond of him than she dared to admit. Regardless of what he had done, his soul was worth saving. He mattered to God.

Aimee came through the door, a box of tissues in hand, and sat opposite Emily at the table.

"There you go." Aimee put the box on the table.

"Thanks." Emily plucked a tissue and blew her nose. "I'm sorry I'm such a mess."

Aimee pointed to what appeared to be coffee stains on her uniform shirt. "As you can see, I'm not so perfect either at the moment. Emily"—Aimee's eyes grew wide—"I have good news. Chance didn't kill himself."

Emily's heart raced. "What? Are you sure? How do you know that?"

"I just spoke with Sheriff Prejean. He's bringing him in now."

Emily laughed and cried at the same time. "That's the last thing I expected you to tell me. I just can't believe this! He's alive?"

"The sheriff wanted me to give you a message. Chance said to tell you he agreed with you that eternity was a long time to get it wrong. That you would know what he meant."

Emily put her hand over her mouth and muffled her sobs. *Thank You, Lord. You got through to him.*

"Whatever you told him," Aimee said, "it must have made an impression. However, the bad news for Chance is that he will likely get the death penalty—or at best, spend the rest of his life in prison."

"You probably think I'm crazy, but even that's good news. There's hope that he'll get right with God—that's the only way he'll find peace in this life or the next." Emily wiped the tears off her cheeks. "I still can't believe he killed all those people with cyanide. I never suspected him. How could I have been so blind?"

"Don't feel bad. We hadn't gotten to the place where we suspected him either. We were taking a hard look at his mother and Alan Arceneau, but we hadn't made the connection."

"Everything backfired when his mother drank the water." Emily dabbed her eyes. "Chance really is devastated about her dying."

Aimee pursed her lips. "Actually, I think it was his genuine grief over his mother's death that threw us off. He behaved totally in character for someone whose parents were murdered. And since the poisonings didn't seem to target anyone in particular, we had no reason to suspect Chance."

"I sure didn't," Emily said.

"His mother's death may have been an accident, but the other eight were murder."

Emily twisted the pinkie ring on her little finger, Aimee's words bringing her back to the harsh reality she had to accept. There was a side to Chance she didn't know or understand.

"You did great," Aimee said. "I don't know how you got Chance to confess. But we all owe you a debt of gratitude."

"Thanks. But I really can't take credit. It was a God thing."

"You were the one who talked him down. You're the one who'll get a commendation from the mayor."

Aimee made some notes and avoided pursuing any further discussion about God. It seemed obvious Aimee wasn't comfortable with the truth. But Chance was. That was all that mattered.

Zoe walked down the stone pathway toward the flower garden at Langley Manor, assuming Michael was already there waiting. When she called and asked him to meet there, he had sounded surprised to hear from her again so soon.

It seemed odd, starting over after all this time. He was a very different man at forty-five than he had been at seventeen. Would she still feel like his little sister? Her mind flashed back to a conversation she'd had with Michael while he walked her to school, the day she started the first grade....

Shelby kept stride with Michael on the sidewalk, both of them toting backpacks.

"First grade is a big deal," Michael said. "You'll hear some kids say words as bad as Daddy's. And a few of the bigger kids will try to scare you. But as long as we're in the same school, no one is going to bully you. If they do"—Michael pointed to himself with his thumb—"they'll answer to me."

"I hope my teacher won't get mad at me like Daddy does."

"You don't have to be scared, Shelby. The principal is the boss of him, and she won't let him."

"Is he allowed to give us a whipping?"

"Unh-unh. He's not allowed to hit you *or* yell at you. You're safe here." Michael stopped and turned to her, his hands on her shoulders. "I will always be your big brother, and I promise to stick up for you. Someday I'll even be big enough to stop Daddy from hurting us."

Shelby put her arms around him and squeezed. "You're my bestest friend and brother. I love you most of all...."

Zoe blinked the stinging from her eyes and kept walking.

Lord, I really do forgive Michael. Don't let me dwell on what he didn't do but on the good things I remember. He's here now. And we have a chance to start over. Help us do that.

As she neared the arched trellis that formed the entrance to the flower garden, she saw Michael standing next to the bench, his hands in the pockets of his cargo pants. He turned when he saw her, his demeanor nervous, like that of a kid on his first date.

"Thanks for coming," she said.

"Same here. Would you mind if I sat? My knees feel like jelly."

"So do mine." Zoe sat on the bench next to Michael.

A long moment of silence passed, and she felt no compulsion to fill it with words.

Finally she said, "I know you've waited a long time for this, Michael. And frankly, I never dreamed I would ever see you again. I wasn't sure I even wanted to. I'm surprised and overwhelmed. You're nothing like the long-haired, bearded guitar player that left home at seventeen. Actually, you're pretty cool looking with the moussed hair and five o'clock shadow. The George Clooney look suits you."

"Thanks." The corners of Michael's mouth turned up. "When I first learned who you were, I was instantly reminded of that wedding picture of Grandma Adams when she was young. She was radiant. You have the same features. Her hair was even cropped like yours."

Zoe smiled. "I remember that picture."

"I saved it when Mom and Dad's house sold. I also have the photo albums of us when we were kids."

"Did we ever smile?"

Michael nodded. "I was surprised at the good memories that came rushing back when I looked through them. Our childhood wasn't all bad."

Zoe sighed. "I have one picture of you with long hair and a beard and one of Mom and Dad, when they got married. I kept them in the bottom of a shoe box. I didn't want anyone to know anything about my family. I was ashamed."

"Is that why you changed your name?"

"Partly. But I did something awful, too, that I had to cover up." Zoe fiddled with the pocket on her sundress. "When I worked for Adele, I took advantage of her trust and stole a valuable ring from her that had great sentimental value. She didn't know I was the thief until I went back ten years later and confessed everything. It's a long story about why I went back, and I don't have time here to get into it. Suffice it to say, I spent a lot of years deceiving people and trying to be someone I wasn't. My point is that you're not the only one who's let people down. I have no right to throw stones."

"Adele seems crazy about you," Michael said. "How is that possible?"

"That's another long story I'll whittle down for now. I had agreed to repay the value of the ring to the tune of thirty thousand dollars—a thousand a month for thirty months. Adele's attorney drew up the papers. But when Adele came to Pierce and me to get our signatures, she informed us that she had changed her mind. About the time my heart sank, she told us that she had forgiven me for stealing the ring and had canceled the entire debt—*and* paid off the mortgage on our building. I couldn't believe it. I had stolen her most prized possession. I had lied to her. Betrayed her trust. Her gracious generosity was beyond anything I could have hoped for. I certainly didn't deserve it. Adele said she didn't expect me to deserve it. It was a gift. It was grace. And giving it to me would help her move forward too."

"Amazing," Michael said. "But there must have been more to it than that."

"I thought so too, so I asked her about it. She told me she hadn't always been the person I knew. That she used to be verbally abusive and had hurt a lot of people."

Michael nodded. "She mentioned that. Hard to believe."

"I asked if *she* had received grace from someone. She said yes, a King. But that was a story for another day."

Michael's eyebrows came together. "A king?"

"It took me a while to figure it out. Adele was referring to the King of Kings—to God Himself."

Michael's face turned pink. "Please tell me this conversation isn't going to turn to religion. You know I don't see God the way you do."

"You came here to find peace, and I already told you that you'll never find true peace while you are at odds with God." Zoe took his hand. "Michael, I'm more than willing to put the past behind us. But in order to find true peace in your heart, you'll need more than just *my* forgiveness."

"Maybe. Maybe not. But it's a good start."

"Definitely. I just hope someday you'll want to know more about what Jesus has done for Adele and Pierce and me. He's our peace and the central figure in our family, of which you're now a part. I'm looking forward to getting to know my brother *Sax*. Pierce is excited to have a new brother-in-law who appreciates his cuisine. Grace is going to flip when I tell her she's got another uncle, and Tucker won't remember you any other way. You will always be their uncle Sax."

"I love the sound of that."

Zoe cupped his cheeks in her hands, the way she'd often done when she was little, and gazed into his topaz eyes that looked so much like Grace's. "But what I came here to say, and I want to make sure you hear from my lips, is that I forgive you for everything. And I love you for all the reasons I always did. I want you in my life."

Tears filled her brother's eyes, and he struggled to find his voice. "I … I don't know what to say. I thought you'd be angry and bitter and throw it in my face for a long, long time."

"So did I. But this is so much better." Zoe felt the heaviness push off from her heart like a bird taking flight. "Sax, I'll tell you what Adele told me when she gave me this same gift: a day will come when someone you know is in desperate need of grace. Remember how this moment feels, and pass it on."

CHAPTER 40

Three weeks later, Emily sat nervously on the visitor side of the glass at the Saint Catherine Parish Jail and watched as a burly deputy escorted Chance to a seat on the prisoner's side. It was all Emily could do not to cry at the drastically different look of this handsome, Ivy League scholar, now dressed in an orange jumpsuit, his hair in a buzz cut.

Chance put the phone to his ear, and Emily did the same, not knowing if she could remember any of what she had planned to say.

"I'm surprised you're here," Chance said flatly.

"Why? Regardless of what you've done, I care about you."

"Does anyone know you're here?"

Emily nodded. "Vanessa and Ethan. But I'm not trying to hide it."

"You should be. I'm about the least-liked man in town."

"I didn't come here to judge you."

Chance held her gaze and seemed to study her. "So why *are* you here—to tell me I need to get saved?"

"Your heart already knows that, or you would have drunk the cyanide."

"It's not that clear-cut, Emily. You're right: eternity *is* a long time to get it wrong. But the reason I didn't kill myself is because I have doubts, not because I have answers. I'm not even sure what questions to ask. So if you came here to preach, don't. I'm in a very dark place, but I've never seen things more clearly."

"What things?"

Chance sighed. "How wrong it was for me to kill my dad and Joanna—and all the other people I treated as if they were nothing more than collateral damage. In the end it cost me the most precious thing in my life—my mother. But it also cost me my dignity, my freedom, my peace of mind, my future as a surgeon, and any chance of a relationship with you. I let my anger rob me of everything. I'm sorry. I really am. . . ." Chance's voice trailed off, and he paused, seemingly to gather his composure. "The truth is, after I ran you off and started to drink the cyanide, I got scared. Really scared. My life flashed in front of me, and I realize that I've been totally self-absorbed. It was always about what I could get, not what I could give. I thought everyone owed me because I'm a genius. In my arrogance, I thought I was smarter than the cops. I even thought I was smarter than God." Chance twisted the phone cord around his finger. "I've had a lot of time to think. Telling myself the truth really hurts, but it's a good hurt. I don't know what this dark place is, but I'm more honest with myself than I've ever been in my life. And I don't want you or anyone else messing it up with religion."

Emily forced herself not to smile. "Okay."

"Just okay?" Chance's eyebrows came together, a row of lines forming on his forehead. "You're not going to try and pull me out of it?"

"Chance, if you were really in the dark, you'd be blinded to the truth. It sounds to me like the Lord is so close, you're standing in His shadow. You're right where you need to be."

Chance's face went blank. He stared at her for a moment and then blinked. "Whatever."

"Listen, my brother-in-law, Ethan, belongs to a group of guys that make prison visits. He'd like to come by and see you and keep up with you after you're sentenced."

"Why?"

"Because we care about you. And when you figure out what questions to ask, he can make sure you get answers."

"I ask hard questions."

"Then you two should hit it off."

Chance was quiet for a moment and seemed far away. "So … it won't be long before you're back at LSU."

"Just a few weeks."

"I know you're going to make a wonderful ob-gyn, Emily." Chance hung his head, but he sounded sincere. "I'm happy for you. I really am. It's your dream, and you deserve it."

"It'll take years of hard work. But it's all I've ever wanted."

"I'll miss you," Chance said. "You're really the only person I know who cares about me now."

"That's not true. There *is* someone else."

Chance lifted his gaze. "Who?"

"Aunt Reba. She's … waiting outside."

"I don't know why. She must hate me too."

Emily shook her head. "She doesn't. She's heartbroken for you. I think if you'd let her love you, you'd find a little part of your mother. She wants to support you through this. I hope you let her."

Chance's eyes glistened. He took off his glasses, and a runaway tear trickled down his cheek. "You've helped me to see her differently. I'm grateful for that—and much more than you'll ever know."

In the long moment of silence that followed, Emily could almost feel an emotional wall go up between them.

Chance wiped his face with his sleeve and put his glasses back on. "I'm glad you came, Emily. But it's time to say good-bye. You need to forget about me now and go live out your dream."

"I'll write to you."

"No. Please don't. It'll just make things harder for both of us. I'll keep up with you through Ethan—when he comes to visit."

"Then you're open to his coming?"

"I'm open. Just don't expect miracles."

Emily's gaze collided with his, and for a split second, she saw his heart. "I always expect miracles, Chance. Always."

CHAPTER 41

Five months later …

Zoe cut another piece of triple fudge chocolate cake with cherry cream-cheese frosting and brought it to the head of the long table where Hebert sat with Father Sam, Tex, Adele, Sax, Pierce, Tucker in his high chair, and Grace.

"There you go. A third piece for the birthday boy." Zoe set the slice of cake in front of Hebert, who was wearing the blue sweatshirt they had gotten him for his birthday party. Across the front and back were white letters: *Kiss me. I'm 100!*

Zoe kissed his cheek. "*Joyeux anniversaire, mon ami.*"

Hebert reached up and gave her hair a gentle tug. "*Je t'aime, Zoe.*"

"*I love you, too,*" she whispered.

Zoe stood for a moment, admiring the colorful streamers hanging down from the one hundred helium balloons on the ceiling. And the huge banner above the cake table that read, *Happy 100th Birthday, Hebert!*

"So, you ol' polecat," Tex said, "how does it feel to be a hundred years old?"

Hebert was uncharacteristically quiet for a moment. Finally he said, "It's a privilege dat I'd better not waste. I know dis: I gonna beat you at checkers as long as I got a pulse." Hebert winked at Grace, and she giggled.

Zoe heard the bell tinkle on the front door and glanced up. "Well, look who's here!"

She walked out to where Vanessa, Ethan, and Carter Langley were standing and hugged each of them. "Welcome!"

"Wow!" Carter reached up and touched the streamers on one of the balloons. "Cool!"

"Come join us," Zoe said. "We've pushed tables together so we can all sit together."

"We left the B and B in the hands of our day manager," Ethan said. "I didn't even wear my watch. We're here to help celebrate Hebert's big day."

Zoe showed them to the table, and each of them wished Hebert a happy birthday and then sat, Carter and Sax already chatting about the Saints game tomorrow.

"I'll get you some cake and punch," Zoe said.

"Let me help you." Vanessa walked with Zoe to the cake table, her gaze dancing around the room. "This is wonderfully festive. Hebert must be so pleased."

"And a little embarrassed. It's a lot of attention. I think half the people in town have already been by. Putting that ad in the paper was a great idea. He doesn't know it yet"—Zoe glanced at her watch—"but the crew from Channel Five is coming to film a clip for the evening news."

"Hebert deserves his 'fifteen minutes of fame,'" Vanessa said.

"It's quite a milestone to hit one hundred." She filled three cups with punch. "Oh, I almost forgot to tell you, Emily sends her regrets. She planned to drive up for this but has a biology paper due Monday and is spending the entire weekend at the library."

"Does she still love LSU?"

"Are you kidding? Geaux Tigers!" Vanessa laughed. "Plus she's started hanging out with a great group of kids in the premed program. She sounds really happy."

"I'm glad. Does she ever hear from Chance?"

Vanessa shook her head. "Ethan keeps up with him through the prison ministry. Chance is doing okay for a guy who'll never get out of prison. He thought Jesus was all hype until he read *The Case for Christ.* Now he's not so sure. He's reading every Christian apologetics book he can get his hands on, and a Parallel Bible with four translations. I'd say he's in good hands."

Zoe saw Jude and Colette Prejean being seated at the table. "Looks like we'll need two more of those." She finished cutting five pieces of cake and set them on the tray with the punch.

"Hey, boss, I'll get that." Savannah smiled with her eyes. "Go sit with your friends. I'll bring it to the table."

Zoe went back to the table and greeted the newcomers, then sat between Pierce and Adele.

"Isn't this splendid?" Adele said. "What a wonderful thing to live to be a hundred."

Zoe held her gaze. "Promise me you'll live that long, Adele."

"That's up to the Lord, hon. But I'm certainly open to it. I love living here, close to you and Pierce and the children. These past couple years have brought such joy."

"For us, too."

Pierce took his fork, tapped it on his punch glass, and stood, looking very official in his double-breasted white coat and chef's hat.

"I don't want to get too syrupy here," he said, "but while we have a full table of folks who came to honor our friend Hebert on this special birthday, I'd like to say something. We each have our own memories of Hebert. As I'm sure you know, he was the first customer to walk into Zoe B's fifteen years ago. And he's been in at least once a day almost every day since." Pierce picked up his punch glass and turned to Hebert. "My friend, it's an honor to know you. You have become an icon at Zoe B's and are, indisputably, the best checkers player in Saint Catherine Parish. But most of all, you've brought us love and laughter, compassion and camaraderie, wisdom and warmth. You're much more than a customer. Much more than a friend. You're *family*. Happy hundredth birthday!"

"Hear, hear." Everyone around the table spoke in unison as they raised the glasses.

"And may God bless us with your presence for many more years." Father Sam patted him on the back.

Hebert's leathery cheeks were flushed as he looked around the table and nodded at each of those present. "Tank you, *mes amis*. Tank you. You're da best dere is."

"Can I get anyone another piece of cake or refills on punch?" Zoe said.

Carter raised his hand. "Cake, please."

Tex nodded. "That's the best cake I ever sunk my teeth into. I could handle another piece."

"Anyone else?" Zoe said. "Okay, I'll be right back."

She got up and walked to the cake table, the colorful balloon streamers dangling about a foot above her head, and realized Sax had followed her.

"I really hate to leave," he said, "but I've got to head back to New Orleans. My jazz band has a gig tonight. This was really something. You and Pierce did a great job planning this open house for Hebert. I'm glad I came."

"I can't believe you drove up just for this." Zoe took his hand. "It was great seeing you. You're coming for Thanksgiving, right?"

"Are you kidding? I hear Pierce makes the best fried turkey in Looziana."

Zoe smiled. "That he does."

"Listen, I don't have a gig *next* weekend. Have you thought any more about what we talked about?"

"Actually, I've thought about it a lot. Pierce said he would take off and watch the kids, whenever I felt ready to go through with it."

"I've got the whole weekend free. I'm ready to get this behind us. Are you?"

Zoe nodded. "As ready as I'll ever be, I guess. Devon Springs is less than a day's drive."

Sax put his arms around her and kissed the top of her head. "I love you, Sis. I'll call you tomorrow, and we can work out the details."

CHAPTER 42

The following Saturday, Zoe trudged behind Sax along a narrow earthen path that led upward through the piney woods toward a ridge that overlooked the Devon River. How many times had she come this way to hide from her father? This time, she clutched a bronze urn that held his ashes.

Sax stopped and turned to her, sounding as if he'd been running. "I don't remember … this climb being … so steep."

"Me either."

"You okay?" Sax seemed to study her face.

"A little out of shape … but I'm fine."

"That's not what I meant."

Zoe looked up at the glints of sunlight peeking through the canopy, the scent of pine wafting under her nose. "I admit it feels strange. Who would ever have guessed that one day we would be taking our parents' remains to the very place we ran to hide from them?"

"Come on"—Sax turned and continued along the path—"we're almost there."

Two minutes later they reached the base of a giant rock that jutted out from the rocky ridge. *Story Rock*! It looked exactly as she remembered.

"Here, give me the urn," Sax said. "Go ahead and climb up, and I'll hand both of them to you."

Zoe climbed up on the smooth, flat rock and took the urns from Sax, one at a time, set them carefully on the rock, and then stood, not too close to the edge, a chilly breeze nipping at the back of her neck.

The Devon River glistened in the noonday sun and snaked through a magnificent tapestry of crimson, orange, gold, and purple, intermingled with pines. Billowy white clouds hung in the crisp November sky, a red-tailed hawk soaring like the notes of a song.

"It takes my breath away," Zoe said, suddenly aware of her brother standing next to her. "It's even more beautiful than I remember. The fall colors are exquisite."

"Brings back a lot of memories."

Zoe nodded. "I wonder how many stories you made up while we hid here, trying to take our minds off the situation at home."

"I don't know—a bunch. And you"—Sax nudged her with his elbow—"never forgot a single detail."

Zoe linked her arm in his. "Most of the happy memories of my childhood happened right here. Story Rock was our safe zone. It seems like the perfect place to let go of the past."

"I thought so."

"I'm really glad you waited to release the ashes," Zoe said. "This is too important for you to have done it alone."

"I always knew that. I just wasn't sure if I would ever find you.

But truthfully, until now, I wouldn't have been able to do it with respect."

Zoe looked out at the raw beauty she hadn't fully appreciated as a little girl. "I wish I'd had a chance to tell Mom and Dad I forgave them."

"So do I."

Zoe looked up at him. "Really?"

"Don't look so shocked. I've been doing a lot of soul-searching myself. I even started going to a Bible church."

"When did *this* happen?"

"A couple months ago. I didn't want to tell you about it over the phone. I'm learning a lot. I'm not at the place you are with God, but I don't blame Him for the abuse anymore, and I know He's forgiven me for failing you. *And* I'm building a relationship with Him." Sax smiled. "Don't say anything. I know you're pleased."

Zoe closed her eyes and filled her lungs with the crisp autumn air. "You know what amazes me? How unfailing God's love is. He wasn't about to let go of us. He was with us through all the nightmares—even the ones we created for ourselves. We just needed to trust Him."

"Took me long enough to realize it," Sax said. "Adele knew. She told me that God is in relentless pursuit of souls who need His love and grace. If only I'd known He was the Father I so desperately needed, I would've stopped running from Him a long time ago."

"It seems so strange, standing here on this rock where we once ran to hide from our painful reality, and realizing how blessed we are now."

"It really is." Sax was quiet for half a minute and then squeezed her hand. "I'm ready to do this whenever you are. Would you like to say something first?"

"I deliberately didn't plan this moment," Zoe said. "I wanted us to do whatever felt right when we got here."

"That's okay, take your time…."

Zoe clung to her big brother, her mind racing with memories—some good, most not so good. But none of them overwhelming.

"Father," she finally said, "we thank You for taking even our parents' mistakes and using them to bring about good in our lives. I never dreamed I would see my brother again—let alone love him the way I used to. Or that I would be capable of enjoying a healthy marriage relationship. Or possess the skills to raise children in a family completely devoid of violence and abuse. And never did I imagine that You—the God of all creation—would want a personal, up-close relationship with me. Out of those locust years, You've given me the desire of my heart…." Her voice cracked, but she pushed on. "I love You, Father. Thank You for being my Abba. Be with us as we turn loose of the past and embrace the *now,* knowing that You're holding us in the palm of Your hand and that it's Your desire, not to harm us, but to give us hope and a future."

Zoe rested in the silence a few moments.

Sax pulled her closer. "Father, Zoe said it better than I could. I don't know why it took me all these years to realize You've been there all along. I'm one of the new kids in the kingdom. Thank You that I'm Yours now. Thank You for helping me to find Zoe and her wonderful family. I'm ready to let go of the past. I forgive Mom and Dad for hurting us. I only wish they would've known You. That would've made all the difference." Sax exhaled and turned to her. "You ready?"

Zoe nodded. She had tried to envision this moment a hundred times but still didn't know what she would do.

Sax wet his finger and held it up. "The breeze is steady and blowing at our backs. I think if we move to the edge of the rock and face each other, and give the urns a gentle shake, the wind will take the ashes out over the river. Let's do this."

Zoe picked up the urn holding her father's ashes and knelt sideways at the edge of the rock that jutted out from the ridge, high above the Devon River Valley. Sax knelt facing her, holding the other urn.

"Okay," Sax said. "Let them go."

Zoe and Sax removed the lids and shook the urns gently, the ashes of their mother and father forming a pewter cloud that seemed to vanish in the chilly breeze in a matter of seconds.

Zoe was strangely exhilarated and somber as she turned the urn upside down and gave it a final shake, and nothing came out.

She groped for her brother's hand, her vision clouded with tears, the sanctity of the moment rendering her mute.

Minutes passed before Sax broke the silence.

"Do you see the parallel here?" he said. "Our parents are gone, but this rock is still here. Steadfast. Unchanging. God is our Rock now. He is and will always be our place of refuge and strength."

"Amen," Zoe whispered.

She set the empty urn on the rock and lay flat on her back, her knees bent, relishing the warmth of the sun bathing her face.

"This was the perfect place to do this," she said. "I'm glad you thought of it. You must be so relieved to finally have it behind you."

"I am." Sax lay beside her on his back, his hands clasped behind his head, the posture he always had assumed when they were kids and he was telling his stories. "You know what else I'm feeling?"

"Tell me."

"Peace. From the top of my head to the tips of my toes and deep down in my heart. And there's nothing make-believe about it."

Zoe smiled knowingly, her heart overflowing. "Did someone give you peace, big brother?"

"Not just someone, Zoe—a *real* Prince. Well, actually a King. But that's a story for another day."

after
words

... a little more ...

When a delightful concert comes to an end,

the orchestra might offer an encore.

When a fine meal comes to an end,

it's always nice to savor a bit of dessert.

When a great story comes to an end,

we think you may want to linger.

And so, we offer ...

AfterWords—just a little something more after you

have finished a David C Cook novel.

We invite you to stay awhile in the story.

Thanks for reading!

Turn the page for ...

- **A Note from the Author**
- **Discussion Guide**

A NOTE FROM THE AUTHOR

Blessed are the peacemakers, for they will be called sons of God.
Matthew 5:9

Dear reader,

Nothing gave me more satisfaction in this final story than seeing Sax come to peace with the God who had never left him, who was in relentless pursuit of him throughout his life of failure, sadness, and regret. The kind of peace Sax desired could only come as a result of reconciliation with his heavenly Father and being adopted into the family of God, where shame is washed away and sins are removed as far as the east is from the west.

The secrets uncovered in the Roux River Bayou series presented a few challenges, and it was especially satisfying for me to reunite Zoe and Sax and create a way for them to say good-bye to their parents, their shame, and their violent past.

But it was also fun seeing Langley Manor take shape as a bed-and-breakfast, and watching Vanessa, Ethan, and Carter grow as a family. I loved bringing back Vanessa's sister, Emily Jessup (from the Sophie Trace Trilogy), as a young college student. She is indeed her mother's daughter, pointing the way for Chance to find freedom, even though he will remain behind bars for the rest of his life.

Jude and Aimee represented the kind of caring law enforcement people that keep our communities safe. I liked making us privy to their thought process as they solved the crimes and showed us the more human side of themselves.

I relished eavesdropping on the conversations between Hebert, Father Sam, and Tex—especially when they involved little Grace. In many ways, Zoe B's was a character too. How fitting that our last glimpse of it was during Hebert's hundredth birthday celebration!

I admired Pierce as a self-taught chef and never loved him more than when he stuck by Zoe after her secrets came out. But my favorite character was Adele, and I'll miss her more than all the others. Her unwavering faith caused me to reevaluate my own, and I want to be like her when I grow up.

It's bittersweet saying good-bye to this colorful cast from the Roux River Bayou, but they will always be a part of me. I hope you've enjoyed reading these stories as much as I enjoyed writing them.

Though we must bid farewell to Cajun country, I'm already working on another trilogy, Tales of Foggy Ridge, which will be set in the Ozark Mountains of Arkansas. And to help the transition, I'm bringing two characters from this series with me. The new series promises more intrigue, fast-paced suspense, and characters you'll want to take home with you!

I would love to hear from you. Join me on Facebook at www.facebook.com/kathyherman, or drop by my website at www.kathyherman.com and leave your comments on my guest book. I read and respond to every email and greatly value your input.

In Him,

Kathy Herman

DISCUSSION GUIDE

1. Would you describe peace as a feeling—or is it something more? Do you believe that true peace comes only after a person is reconciled with God? Why or why not?

2. Is the peace the world offers different from God's peace? Is the pursuit of worldly peace a bad thing? If Sax had only reconciled with Zoe and not dealt with his hostility toward his parents, could he have found peace? Have you experienced God's peace and the world's peace? If so, how would you compare them?

3. Is it possible to experience God's peace even when your life is not going the way you want? Have you experienced the "peace that passes understanding"? If so, can you describe when—and how—it felt?

4. Matthew 5:9: "Blessed are the peacemakers, for they will be called sons of God." How would you define peacemaker? Is that role necessarily devoid of conflict? What distinguishes a peacemaker from a peacekeeper? Which do you think is superior? Have you been in the role of peacemaker? Peacekeeper? Which of the two ultimately leads to peace? Explain your answer.

5. Assume for a moment that world peace was within your grasp. Which would you need to be in order to bring it about: a peacemaker or a peacekeeper? Can you name the people in this story

you would consider to be peacemakers? Which one impressed you the most, and why?

6. Psalm 34:14 admonishes us, "Turn from evil and do good; seek peace and pursue it." What does it mean to you to turn from evil and do good? What does it mean to seek peace and pursue it? Do you think it's possible to find peace while harboring bitterness? By hiding our shame or guilt? By denying our sin?

7. Romans 8:28 tells us, "And we know that in all things God works for the good of those who love him, who have been called according to his purpose." Do you ever struggle with some of the difficult, even awful, things God uses for our good? Be honest. How important is trusting God in our pursuit of peace? Will we ever understand the mind of God and how events are part of a bigger picture?

8. Zoe and Sax were both emotionally scarred from the terrible abuse they suffered as children. In their effort to find peace, how important was forgiveness? Based on the line from the Lord's Prayer in Luke 11:4—"Forgive us our sins, for we also forgive everyone who sins against us"—is forgiveness an option? Must forgiveness be earned or deserved? Does forgiveness often benefit the giver as much or more than the recipient?

9. Sax was angry at God and blamed Him for his violent upbringing and for turning a deaf ear to his cries. Is it sometimes necessary

to forgive God before we can move beyond our pain? Is trust in God a choice or a feeling?

10. Do you agree with Adele, that God is in relentless pursuit of souls in need of His love and grace? Were you ever aware of God's pursuing you? If so, how did it make you feel? Did it frighten you? Anger you? Humble you? Or was it something you realized only in hindsight?

11. Do you think it's possible for someone like Chance to find peace in prison? If so, what do you think would need to happen first? If Emily had chosen to think only of her safety and surviving the moment, how might this story have ended for Chance? Would you consider Emily to be a peacemaker or peacekeeper? Explain your answer.

12. Was there a special takeaway for you in this story? In this series? Which was your favorite book in the trilogy? Which of the three stories could you see made into a movie? Who was your favorite character, and which actor or actress would you like to see play the part?